# BOSTON BOLTS HOCKEY:
# PLAYBOY

## BRITTANÉE NICOLE

# BOSTON BOLTS HOCKEY: PLAYBOY

## BRITTANÉE NICOLE

# CONTENTS

Missing Piece - Vance Joy

Seeds - Yoke Lore

Adore You - Harry Styles

Blessings - Hollow Coves

Highs & Lows - Chance Peña

You and I - SYML

Simply The Best - Billianne

Coastline - Hollow Coves, Vancouver Sleep Clinic

Out of My League - Fitz and the Tantrums

Dermot - Fred again..., Dermot Kennedy

Ordinary - Alex Warren

Carry You Home - Alex Warren

Perfect to Me - Michale Sanzone

When I Get My Hands On You - The New Basement Tapes

# DEDICATION

*To believing we can have it all.*

*And as Demi Moore said: in those moments when we don't think we're smart enough or pretty enough or skinny enough or successful enough or basically just not enough, remember you will never be enough, but you can know the value of your worth if you just put down the measuring stick.*

# CALLIOPE'S COLUMN

*ISSUE 10*                                     *MARCH*

## The Real Heroes: Men Who Get Pierced for Their Woman's Pleasure

I'm going to be *real* real this week, ladies. I'm riding the struggle bus lately. While all my friends are riding their significant others. Being single has never bothered me. I've done the marriage thing; it's not for me. Until recently, I truly believed monogamy was a fable. How could one person truly commit to spending their life with another when I can't commit to wearing the same denim style for more than a season? In high school, it was the widest bell that dragged on the ground, tearing at the seams. Then there was the low-rise style, the pants that barely covered my pubic bone. A year later we were wearing jeggings. I'm sure I'm not the only person who packed on a few pounds because I didn't have to worry about a button or a zipper. Then jeans were gone completely, replaced by black leggings. The jeans have returned, and currently, not only do we need one button, but apparently, we need an entire row to do up the high-waisted style that comes up to our boobs.

My point being, if my taste in denim is continuously changing, how am I expected to commit to one man who may not change with me?

Until recently, I stood fully behind that sentiment. Then my best friends met men who are pierced, and I've completely changed my mind. Let's be clear, ladies: if a man gets himself pierced, he's proven that not only will he be good in bed, but he's willing to do the hard work. Because a pierced penis is for our pleasure, not theirs.

And there is nothing hotter than a man who is willing to do the work, am I right? Now let me tell you about each piercing, and what they tell us about the man adorned with them…

# CHAPTER 1
# DANIEL

"Calliope, guys." I shake my head as I close out of Calliope's article. I pulled it up on my phone ten minutes ago, and already I've read the entire thing. If not for practice, I'd read it again and take notes.

Calliope is a genius. Her articles changed my dating game and my sex life. The woman is honest and direct, and though her column is catered to an audience of women, I find that, time and again, it gives me direct insight into how to please the opposite sex. As a man who's determined to give 110 percent to every task, I take her word as gospel.

So far, she hasn't steered me wrong.

Our captain, Tyler Warren—War to his teammates and Bolts fans—groans. "Could you at least try to make it one day without mentioning her name?"

Brooks, our goalie, chuckles as he laces up his skates. "Leave him be. What was the article about today?"

Here's the tricky part. Calliope is absolutely a genius, but if I tell them about what she's pushing, they'll be on my case again.

War, Brooks, and our center, Aiden—who's one of Brooks's brothers—all have blinged-out dicks. It's been a bit of a sore subject for me—no pun intended—because though I really want one, I chicken out every time we walk into the tattoo shop to get it done.

The three guys got their piercings before I was drafted to the team. It sounds ridiculous, but it's like the event bonded them, and I feel left out. But I can't quite get past the idea of a man sticking a needle through my precious jewels.

Before I can decide whether to tell them about the article or make something up, our coach walks in, all business.

All chatter dies at the expression on his face. Gavin Langfield isn't a hard-ass coach. He's a genuinely nice guy and we respect the shit out of him. He and my dad have been best friends for years, and since he married my twin sister last year, we're exceptionally close. So the formal expression on his face throws every one of us. Especially knowing that the trade deadline hits at midnight. Is he coming in here to break some bad news?

He and my dad have been best friends for years, and since he married my twin sister last year, we're exceptionally close. So the formal expression on his face throws every one of us. Especially knowing that the trade deadline hits at midnight. Is he coming in here to break some bad news?

I scan the locker room, studying my teammates. Our team is good, though there's always room to be better. This season especially. Something has been off, and I can't quite put my finger on it.

Normally, I wouldn't be concerned. I've played on the first line since I was drafted during college. While War is known for protecting the guys on the ice, taking the hits when a fight breaks out and instigating them when necessary, I have a different set of skills. As the other winger, I have to anticipate War's moves, as well as those of our center, Aiden. I've got to be ready to make the play or put Aiden or War in position to make it. It's why the guys started calling me Playboy—despite the other obvious connotation. I always find a way to make a play work. Essentially, my goal has been to be good at everything. In turn, though, that means I'm not particularly fantastic at one specific skill.

War, Aiden, and I are one hell of a line, but I've heard the rumors about Noah Harrison, and if they're true, they won't lead to anything good for me.

Harrison is one of the best snipers in the league. He's a winger like

I am, but he's just as adept at scoring as his center. The whole league knows it. If he gets the biscuit, the man somehow finds the back of the net, even from the most improbable angle.

He's a coach's dream and is well-liked by everyone he's ever played with. His college team called him Beauty, and that name stuck when he was drafted to the NHL.

In hockey, that's the gold standard. A player who is talented and well-liked.

His nickname is the kind a player should be proud of. The kind that commentators can't make jokes about. He's hall-of-fame worthy.

If I wasn't already playing with two of the best guys in hockey, I'd be pumped about the possibility that the guy has been traded to the Bolts. Passing the puck to a player like Noah Harrison would be a dream.

But I am playing with two of the greats. *I* am the weakest link.

And if I were Gavin Langfield and I had the opportunity to trade for Noah Harrison, I wouldn't hesitate.

"I've got some exciting news," Gavin says. He glances in my direction, a quick acknowledgment. He doesn't look ashamed or guilty. And he shouldn't, whether he's done what I'm pretty sure he did or not. I may be his wife's twin and his best friend's son, but he's never shown favoritism to anyone in this locker room, including his own brothers. Outside this arena, the dynamics between all of us are different, but here, we are his players and he's our coach. And he's a damn fair one. He decides who plays and how hard we practice. And we listen. Every one of us wants to please him, since it's up to him whether we do the one thing we love the most—play hockey.

"Noah Harrison—"

I don't hear the rest of his sentence, but from the cheers going up around me, it's easy to guess what he's just announced. We've secured Noah Harrison in a trade.

And whoever Gavin traded for him isn't in this locker room. Our coach-slash-owner is far too respectful to make an announcement like this before notifying the player affected by the negotiation. He would have thanked them for their dedication to the team and wished them luck ahead of time.

I take in the faces around the room, and once I've accounted for all the guys I'm close with, I breathe a sigh of relief.

"This is fucking awesome." Aiden rubs his hands together, nudging War in the ribs with his elbow. "Don't you and Harry have matching tattoos?"

War glances at me, his eyes full of concern. He knows I'm secretly freaking the fuck out. "They're not matching tattoos. It's our college team's logo."

Oh, did I forget to mention that Brooks, War, and Harrison played together in college? That they've been friends for years? Yeah, this just keeps getting worse.

War tips his chin at Brooks. "This guy was too chickenshit to get one."

Without shame, Brooks says, "Always knew I was going to be a Bolt. No need to put some other logo on my body."

"Spoken like a Langfield." In the next breath, War's eyes light up. "But you don't have a Bolts tattoo."

Brooks rolls his eyes. "What is it with you trying to get everyone tatted?"

"Your fiancée would think it's hot." War raises a brow.

"Does Harry have a dick piercing?" The second the question is out, I want to punch myself in the face. What the fuck is wrong with me?

The guys' faces scrunch up in various *what the fuck?* expressions.

I double down. "Well, does he?"

"No, that's a Bolts thing," Brooks says, eyeing War. "That's *our* Bolts thing." His voice is stronger now, like he just found his way out of getting inked. "No need for a fucking tattoo when I have Bolts blue bars through my dick."

I wince. Fuck, that sounds painful. But it's a Bolts thing. Their thing. *Our thing.*

"After practice," I say, forcing the words to sound resolute.

"After practice, what?" War watches me, his lips twitching like he knows where I'm going with this. So what if I'm insecure about Harrison's impending trade? So what if I'm acting like a fucking toddler having a temper tantrum and trying to hold on tight to my friends? They're *my* friends. Anyone would be a little territorial.

I meet War's eyes, determination setting in. "After practice, we're going to the tattoo shop."

"You really think you'll go through with it today?" War sounds all sorts of skeptical.

"Yeah, Calliope says that real heroes pierce their dicks for their women's pleasure."

"Fuck yeah, they do," Aiden says, wearing a too-big smile. "Can't wait to use that line on Lex later." He holds up his fist for Brooks to bump, but his brother just glares at the outstretched arm. He shrugs and holds it out to me instead.

"Fuck yeah, they do." I bump him back. "And real friends have matching dicks."

My stomach bottoms out. *What the fuck, Playboy?*

I have two choices here: punch myself in the face or own the comment and hold a fist out to War to complete the assholery.

I go with the latter, leaning into this moment, a moment that, with any luck, will bind these guys to me for life.

War chokes on air. "You need help, Playboy. So much fucking help." He shakes his head, but with a laugh, he bumps my fist.

# CHAPTER 2
# DANIEL



"Are you going to hold my hand when he does it?"

War blinks at me, his expression one of disbelief. "You're going to need to start over, and do not repeat that question."

My stomach twists. "I really hate blood. I'm a lover, not a fighter."

Chuckling, Brooks slaps me on the back. "Come on, Playboy. I'll hold your hand."

Behind us, Aiden lets out a *humph*. "You wouldn't hold my hand when I did it."

"Because I was too busy holding my own damn dick." Brooks grabs himself as if he's experiencing phantom pain. "You sure you want to do this?"

"Oh my god, stop babying him. If I have to hear him cry about not having a blinged-out dick one more time, I'm going to personally stab a bar through it for him." War glares at me as if he's imagining doing just that.

Suddenly, it's all I can picture. The instigator coming at me with a needle, holding me down and—

With a shudder, I cup myself and will away the mental images before they get more graphic.

"I have no idea how you got Ava to marry you."

His wife is the sweetest woman. The exact opposite of War. She's the head of charitable relations for Langfield Corp, the parent company of the Boston Bolts. I bet she knits sweaters for the homeless in her downtime.

"It was the glitter dick." Aiden laughs. "It's how I got Lex and how Brooks got Sara."

Sara, Brooks's fiancée, is the head of PR for our hockey team, and Lennox works with Ava, handling the party planning for the charity events. The three of them, along with my sister and Hannah, are close friends. Hannah is quite literally the hottest woman I've ever met. She's gorgeous, sure, but her beauty and sex appeal come from so much more than just her looks. It's her attitude that really does it for me. The way she talks down to me. Maybe it's sick, but I fucking love it.

"Speaking of Sar," Aiden says as he lifts his phone.

"Why is my fiancée calling you?" his brother grumbles, pulling out his phone. "I don't even have a missed call."

"It's 'cause I'm the fun one," Aiden says as he taps the screen. "Hi, Sar."

Brooks snatches the device from Aiden's hand and taps the speaker button. "Why are you calling my brother and not me, crazy girl?"

"Brookie, are you getting jealous?"

His response is an unintelligible mumble.

Sara's voice softens. "I only called him because he's not replying to my texts."

"Why aren't you replying to Sara?" I swear Brooks looks like he'll fight his brother for ignoring his fiancée. He is the definition of *touch her and die*, only it's more *make her sad and die*. He'll do just about anything to keep a smile on that woman's face.

"Because I'm sitting here being a good friend to Hall so he can finally get the glitter dick."

"Oh my god!" Sara screeches, her tinny voice piercing my eardrums. "He's finally going to do it?"

Head dropped back, I groan. "Seriously."

Aiden shrugs. "They'd all find out anyway. You know we don't keep secrets from the girls, and they don't keep secrets from one another."

"Oh, Hannah and I planned to get our nips pierced when you finally did this. Should I call her? We can be there within the hour."

"Nipples pierced?" My mood lifts instantly at the idea of Hannah's nipples.

"Yeah, your sister suggested them."

And there goes any and all excitement surrounding nipple piercings.

"Ya know what? I think we're going to keep this activity for the boys only," Aiden replies, giving me a knowing look. He holds out his hand for his phone.

Sara huffs. "Fine. But could you please send me the link to the house Lennox booked? She can't find the email, and I want to show it to the girls."

"Okay," Aiden says, tapping at the screen of his device, "it's sent. I'll talk to you later." After they disconnect the call, he holds the phone out. "House is sick, right? Just think, if you get pierced tonight, you might just be ready to test it out the weekend we're in Arizona."

Alarmed, I straighten. "That's almost two months away."

"Have you not done any research since you started whining about not having your own?" War says with a laugh. "You can't have sex for six to eight weeks."

I frown at Brooks, who just shrugs. "Didn't matter to me. I wasn't going near anyone back then."

Aiden shakes his head. "I'd rather not think about when I was with Jill, but I can promise that if I'd been with Lex then, I couldn't have done it."

I swallow slowly. Do I really want to do this?

Calliope's words replay in my mind. *If a man gets himself pierced, he's proven that not only will he be good in bed, but he's willing to do the hard work.*

"Ya know," Aiden says, leaning against the brick wall outside the tattoo shop. "We ended up here because of a game of truth or dare."

War nods. "Yeah, and?"

"Maybe we need a little truth or dare to get him motivated."

Brooks nods. "Yeah, I only went through with it because I didn't want to admit that I was a twenty-nine-year-old virgin saving myself for Sara."

I can't help but laugh. Thankfully, the tension in my shoulders dissipates a little as I do. "Worked out well for you, I guess. You ended up fake dating her not too long after that, right?"

Brooks nods. "And I asked War about why he wasn't honest with Ava about missing the charity event at the YMCA when we all knew he had a perfectly good reason."

"Oh yeah?"

Our captain just shrugs. "Brayden called that day. His mom didn't show up to get him after school. But at the time, Ava hated me, and I was tired of wasting my breath trying to explain to her that I wasn't a bad guy. My vicious wife never would have believed me." Brayden is fourteen now, and War and Ava are raising him, along with their two daughters.

"You're leaving out the part where you refused to admit you were obsessed with her at the time," Brooks adds.

"And then you ended up in a fake marriage with the woman," I point out.

"My marriage isn't fake," War grumbles.

Brooks arches a brow.

"Fine. It started out *kind of* fake. For her. I was always all-the-fuck-in."

"What was the truth you refused to give them?" I ask Aiden.

Jaw tight, Aiden nods at War. "He asked me why I hated shamrocks."

"Back then, none of us knew that Lennox used the word when she broke your heart back in high school."

"And after getting pierced, you ended up fake engaged to her." I'm beginning to sense a pattern. *Fuck.*

War laughs. "That's about right. After getting our piercings, Brooks fake dated Sar, Aiden ended up fake engaged to Lennox, and I ended up"—his voice dips, and he grits out the words—"*fake* married to Ava."

I swallow and nod. "Yeah."

"What's the worst that could happen, Playboy? You take it one step farther and get a girl fake pregnant?" He laughs.

My balls have officially ascended into my body. "None of you are faking anything."

Brooks rubs at his face, trying to hide a smile. "Yeah, Sara likes to say it's the glitter dicks that got us all together."

"Except I'm different. I'm not getting this for anyone." *Except them,* but we won't tell them that.

War smirks. "Calliope."

Rolling my eyes, I laugh dryly. "Yeah, as if I'll ever get to meet her."

"If you do, you better be prepared to knock her up, Playboy."

"I don't remember a truth being lobbed my way."

"Fine." War fixes me with a hard look. "Truth or dare?"

I stare right back, refusing to back down. "Truth."

He folds his arms across his chest. "Why do you really want to get pierced? Why today? What changed?"

I think of the article. I think of Noah. Both are part of my why. But I refuse to admit either fact out loud.

Because what kind of man gets their dick pierced with the hope that one day he'll impress a faceless woman hiding behind a pseudonym who writes articles about improving a person's sex life?

And who gets pierced so they can prove they're closer than some other guy is to a group of friends?

Not the kind of man who admits to it, that's for damn sure.

"Let's go inside."

"Yes!" Aiden hollers. "This deserves a song."

"No singing," War growls.

"Can't stop it," Aiden says as he pushes off the wall and holds a hand up in front of him like he's got an invisible mic. Before we can stop him, he dives into his own version of Taylor Swift's "Don't Blame Me."

> *"Don't blame me, the bling made Lex crazy*
> *Playboy wants it and he's doing it tonight.*
> *Oh, Brooks baby, the bling made Sara crazy*
> *Playboy wants it, he's giving up the fight.*

*Playboy's—"*

War clamps a hand over his mouth. "If you use my wife's name in your song about Playboy's glitter dick, I'm going to put my fist through your face."

Aiden blinks.

"So you're going to stop singing, right?"

Aiden nods, his dark eyes wide.

War angles in closer, and I'm pretty sure he's growling. Finally, he releases Aiden. "If we're all ready to act like big boys now, can we get this over with?" He motions toward the door.

I give myself one final pep talk before heading in.

When I walk out of here, I'll finally have the glitter. And considering I can't have sex for months, no one is getting fucking pregnant. Fake or otherwise.

# Chapter 3
# Hannah



"Are you sure you don't mind?"

"Mind? Are you crazy? I would be offended if you didn't stay here. I'll be gone for the next six weeks, and my place has two bedrooms. You can take mine and Oliver can have his own bed. At least while I'm gone. At your dad's, you'd have to bunk up, wouldn't you?"

Noah's deep chuckle fills my bedroom. "Yeah. I still can't believe we're moving to Boston."

I smile at the phone in the middle of the bed as I stuff a pair of shoes into my suitcase. "I can't believe you're going to be a Bolt and that I get to see Oliver all the time. It's still wild to me that you have a kid, and he's already four. It's going to be incredible to have you here. It feels like forever since we got to spend this much time together."

"You were still in high school—"

I frown down at my suitcase. I'm an excellent packer. It's a skill I mastered after my mother's third divorce. More than once, I was given a half hour to fit the stuff I wanted into one suitcase before it was time to leave and start our next life. That's how she phrased it. She'd dump her current husband and instantly move on to the next. Every time, she was certain this new life would be better than the last.

The hardest departure was when she left Noah's dad. The boy a couple of years older than me was everything to me back then. He was a true big brother, blood or not. He loved me for who I was, and even when he left for college, he made sure to call and text regularly. And if he wasn't coming home to visit me, I was traveling there to spend time with him.

For the first time in my life, I felt like I was enough for someone.

I'd never been enough for my mother. It took a long time to understand that she was the problem, not me. Not a single one of her husbands was ever enough. She's currently on her fifth. He wasn't around for Christmas, so I can't help but think that's already over. Though if it was, she would have shown up on my doorstep, needing a place to stay. Since I settled in Boston—after she left stepdad number three—she comes to me between divorces.

It's serendipitous, I suppose, that Noah will be staying here. That means mom will have to find somewhere else to go.

A smile curves my lips. "Yeah, high school. Anyway, how did Oliver take the news?"

"He's thrilled. With Jen's husband starting work in Boston, it couldn't have worked out better. I'll miss my team and building bonds with new teammates will take work, but you know Oliver comes first for me."

He does. Every time we're together and I witness the way Noah parents his son, my scars heal a little more. He's the exact opposite of my mother. That four-year-old has always come first, despite the unplanned pregnancy. Jen was a one-night stand, but from the beginning, the two of them have been dedicated to putting Oliver first. They're exceptional co-parents. Jen recently got married, and her new husband received a job offer he couldn't refuse. A job that happened to be in Boston. So without hesitation, Noah and his agent worked a deal with the local hockey team.

And since I work for the Bolts' sister organization, the Boston Revs —a baseball team owned by the same family—it means I get to spend lots of time with him.

Not only that, but Noah's dad lives in Boston as well. It's like it was meant to be.

Lips pursed, I eye my closet. I've already packed shorts, T-shirts, three skirts, and seven blouses.

The blue bodycon dress I bought last week from Lulu's grabs my attention. Will I even have time to go out? As head of PR for the Boston Revs, almost every minute of my time during spring training will be accounted for. Maybe with a more mature team, I could catch some downtime at the beach or at least hang by the pool, but with so many young guys on the roster, they're keeping me busy and driving me absolutely batty, and the season hasn't even begun.

Jasper Quinn is at the top of that list. That boy can't keep himself out of trouble. Though at least some of the shit he gets into is entertaining, like the time he ended up sexting with a nun. If Channel Seven hadn't been working on an exposé of that specific parish, he might never have gotten caught.

But he did, which meant I had to do damage control.

Spinning sexting is never easy, even if it's between two consenting adults—why the world gets so butt hurt about sex, I'll never understand. Sex is amazing if both people know what they're doing, but I digress. Sexting with a nun? Yeah, that took some work.

I roll the bodycon dress neatly and put it in the suitcase. I miss sex. It's been way too long since a man has turned me into a pretzel and fucked me sideways. While I would never touch a baseball player, there are plenty of men in Florida to keep me entertained.

And the hockey team will be in the state for at least one of those weekends.

Though I haven't touched any of them in the four years I've worked for the Revs, there's no rule against it.

"Do you know which weekend the Bolts are playing Florida?"

Noah hums. "I haven't looked at the schedule, but I'll text you as soon as I do."

"Perfect." I zip up my suitcase and yank it off the bed. "I better go. I'm meeting the girls for drinks to say goodbye." I pout at the mere thought of being without them for so long. Before working for Langfield Corp, I never really had girlfriends. It's always been easier to relate to men.

I like sex. Men like sex. I like sports. Men like sports. Instead of searching for other women like me, I disappeared into books. I looked for characters with similar interests there, but after I'd read more books than I can count about meek women who'd never had an orgasm until they met a billionaire who saved them from their boring existence, I decided I'd write my own. I'd create stories that featured the kind of women I wanted to be friends with.

Fierce women who had careers, aspirations, dreams…and knew their way around a vibrator. Because let's be honest, sometimes we're our own best orgasm.

Working in the sports industry, luckily, has led me to finally making female friends who share some of the same interests and are more like the heroines in my books.

When I met Sara, I knew instantly we were two sides of the same coin. Like me, Sara had a difficult upbringing. And she struggled to trust men. That changed, though, when she started dating Brooks Langfield, goalie for the Bolts and brother to the bigwigs at Langfield Corp, my employer. She's loud, like me, and loves talking about sex. We're a match made in heaven.

Then there's Lennox, Sara's best friend from college, who married Aiden Langfield—also of the Langfield Corp Langfields and the youngest of four brothers. She's ridiculous in all the best ways, so we clicked instantly.

Rounding out the trio of women dating or married to a Langfield— the owners of both the local hockey team and baseball team—is Millie. While she's the youngest of all of us, she's a mom to a one-and-a-half-year-old and married to Gavin Langfield, her dad's best friend and not only the Bolts' owner but also their coach.

But my actual best friend would be Ava. Though she's the quietest, most demure of the group—and my total opposite—the two of us just work. She's also in a relationship with a hockey player, Tyler Warren, a reformed playboy who's now a father of three non-biological children.

I'm going to miss all four of them while I'm gone.

"Can't wait to meet your friends," Noah says.

"They're all dating or married to men on your team, so you'll definitely get to know them soon enough."

"And yet you're still single," he teases.

"You know me—anti-commitment right here."

Noah laughs, the sound reminiscent of the boy I was so close to during my high school days. "So you always say. All right, I'll let you go. I have to call War anyway. He's been blowing up my phone since the news dropped."

I smile. War likes to hide behind the tattoos and the bad-boy exterior, but he's a complete softie for Ava and their kids. "I'm sure he's ready to get the gang back together."

"Yeah, we'll see how I fit in with the team."

My chest pinches. "You'll fit in perfectly. The guys are all great. Seriously. I spend more time with them than the baseball guys, which means you'll get to spend even more time with me." I fall onto my bed and stare up at the ceiling.

"We both know you're my favorite part of this move, so that works for me."

His words leave me feeling warm. Not many people have made it past my defenses, but Noah Harrison wormed his way into my heart years ago and never left. And now I get him and Oliver. It'll be a change, living with them, but it's one I'm excited about.

"I CAN'T BELIEVE YOU'RE HEADED TO FLORIDA WHILE THE REST OF US ARE stuck in this miserable weather." Lennox holds up her rosé, which is almost the exact shade of her pink shoulder-length hair, and tips it toward me. "But cheers to you anyway. I hope you meet a sexy pool boy who services all your needs."

It's been too long since anyone has serviced anything, but I tip my glass in her direction to the laughter of all my friends. We're seated in a booth in the corner of my favorite restaurant—one perk of being besties with the Langfield girls? They can get a reservation anywhere at any time because of who they're married to. Though it's nice, I'd prefer it if my own name garnered that kind of service.

*One day.* It's what I tell myself constantly. One day I won't spend all my time cleaning up the messes of others. I'll be a well-known author, and people will bend over backward to please me.

"Eh, you know how the guys are. Especially Jasper freaking Quinn. I'll probably be on babysitting duty the entire time."

"After the nun thing, he'll surely be on his best behavior," Ava says.

Oh my sweet, innocent Ava. She only ever sees the best in people.

"You should all come when the guys play Tampa. We can make it a girls' weekend."

Millie nods. "I'm in. Gavin will take any excuse he can get to bring Viv and me along with him when he travels with the team."

"Obviously I'll be there," Sara adds.

I glance toward my redheaded bestie. "What about you?"

Ava winces. "I'm not ready to leave Josie, Scarlett, and Bray yet. Arizona will be hard enough."

As disappointed as I am that I won't get to see her, I don't give her shit. She's still adjusting to being the mother of three. "That's okay. Arizona is going to be a blast. Three days, a hot tub overlooking the mountains, and time with all my favorite people? I couldn't ask for more."

"Speaking of your favorite people," Sara says with a wiggle of her shoulders. "Guess what Daniel Hall did today?"

Millie groans. "Oh god, do I even want to know?"

Poor Millie. While I have quite a few stepbrothers from my mother's many marriages, details about their sex lives don't bother me. Probably because I only ever spent a couple of years living under the same roof. We aren't nearly as close as she is to her brothers.

Millie, along with the rest of America, had to watch her older brother cheat on the woman who is now her stepmom. When Lake— yes, Lake Paige, international pop star and my idol—found out Paul was cheating on her, rather than fall apart, she slept with his dad. And then became Paul's stepmom. That's boss-bitch level shit.

Daniel, Millie's twin, is literally the biggest player on the Bolts' roster. That's saying something, because those guys get around.

Not that I'm bothered by his player status. I like a man who knows what he's doing, and like they say, practice makes perfect.

Not that I'd ever go near him. There was a time when I had the tiniest crush on the guy.

But sex with the brother of one of my besties would be complicated, and one thing I don't do is complicated.

"He finally got bedazzled!" Sara does jazz hands to celebrate.

The table erupts in laughter.

Everyone except Millie, whose face is twisted in disgust. "Ew. Why?"

"Why does he want to get pierced?" I lean forward, brows raised, and hold up a finger so I can count off the many reasons he may have chosen this path for himself. "For one, it's hot. Two, it's hot. Three, have I mentioned before, it's fucking hot?"

Lennox and Sara both nod obnoxiously in agreement. When Millie sees Ava biting back a smile, she points at her. "You too?"

Our sweet, reserved friend holds up her hand. "What can I say? It feels fantastic."

Millie's head falls back. "Gah, even she gets to ride a piercing."

A bark of a laugh escapes me. "She married Tyler Warren. Was there ever any real question that he was pierced?"

Arms folded, Millie huffs. "I guess not."

Sara presses her tongue to the inside of her cheek. "You're just jealous because yours is the only Langfield who didn't get pierced."

"Please, there is no way that Beckett Langfield is pierced."

"I have a rule!" Ava yells in a voice louder than I thought she was capable.

We all spin in her direction.

"We don't talk about Beckett's dick. He's just...I like him as a person and I don't want to think of him sexually."

Millie throws up her hands. "That's what I'm saying!"

"Bet you he has a really dirty mouth," Lennox mutters.

"He's a Langfield. Of course he does," Sara muses.

Ava glares at them both, and they hold up their drinks in defeat.

"Fine," Sara says. "No talking about Beckett's dick. But Daniel's?"

Millie scowls. "You are dead to me."

"No, I'm your favorite sister-in-law."

"Hey!" Lennox whines.

I roll my eyes. They're always like this. "Who's getting Danny Boy on the phone? I'm curious about what kind he got."

"Don't look at me." Millie holds up her hands.

She's taking this way too seriously. What's a little dick piercing? Well, okay, hopefully there's nothing little about it. I'd like to imagine that Hall is well endowed. Not that it matters. Like I said, not going near that complication.

"I'll call him," Sara offers, no shame in her game.

When the sound of the FaceTime request ricochets off the walls of the restaurant, a couple from one table over glares in our direction. Sara doesn't bat an eye. She just lowers the sound and smiles.

"He probably won't pick up since he's—"

Millie's words are cut off when Daniel's pretty face fills the frame. God, I forgot how boyishly good-looking he is. Dark brown hair that's always a bit messy, high cheekbones that belong on a model, and scruff that exists purely to fuel fantasies of what it would feel like between a woman's legs. And my biggest weakness: wide brown eyes that hold more depth than he lets the world believe he's capable of. Though right now, they're glazed over.

"*Sara*!" he drawls.

Yup. The boy is either high or drunk. Maybe both.

"Awe are you in pain?" Sara uses the voice she typically reserves for talking to Beckett's twin babies or Vivi.

"Yes. So much pain. But I got the glitter, Sar. I got the mother-fuck-ing-glitter."

The snort I hold in is so violent it hurts. The rest of the girls are either full-on laughing or covering their mouths.

All but Millie, who stands and angles over the table, then snatches the phone from Sara. "You're an idiot."

"Awe, Mills. I got my pee-pee pierced."

Tears stream down my face. This is gold.

She shakes her head. "Why?"

He sighs, but he's wearing a dopey smile. "Because I wanted to be matchy-matchy with my boys. And now I am."

"Oh my god," Lennox says between giggles.

"And it's the one for pleasure. I'm a hero," he says nonsensically.

"Real hero," Millie mutters. "You put a pin through your penis and you want a prize."

Behind us, chairs screech along the floor. Oops. Looks like the couple at the next table isn't interested in our conversation.

Millie holds up her hand. "Sorry."

"Nope. My prize is my penis. My penis is my prize." Squinting, he looks away from the phone. "Aiden, I have words for a song. Penis song. Penis prizes."

"Oh, someone better be recording this," I say.

"*Hannah*? Is that Hannah?" Daniel drawls.

I take the phone from Millie and wave at him. "Hi, Baby Hall. How you doing?"

"If I tell you it hurts, will you kiss it better?" He puffs his lip out in an exaggerated pout.

Beside me, Millie tries to steal the device out of my hand. "Oh, for the love of god."

I pull it back before she can get to it. "You couldn't handle me, Baby Hall."

"I'm willing to try." He scrunches up one side of his face in what I think is supposed to be a wink.

His image shakes, and War says, "Your dick is officially off the market. Talk to Hannah in two months." Then the Bolts' instigator appears on the screen. "Sorry, girls. I gotta put this one to bed."

"*Hannah!*" Daniel screams from off screen. "Please, I got the pleasure one!"

I laugh as I shake my head. "I'm leaving for spring training anyway, Baby Hall. Now be a good boy and listen to Daddy War."

When War rolls his eyes, I just blow him a kiss and wink.

"I'll miss you, dream girl," Hall yells in the background.

"Sorry," War says, walking out of the room. "He had a few shots to numb the pain. Can you put my wife on? I think I'm going to be late getting home."

I hand the phone over to my bestie, a big smile on my face. God, I love these people.

# CALLIOPE'S COLUMN



## Oral: The Lost Art

It's about time we sit down and have an honest conversation, because the number of women who have written in saying they've never experienced this is criminal. Married women. Older women. Women in their twenties. What do you all have in common? Your man doesn't go down on you.

In any spicy book, you can point out the ex-boyfriend almost immediately. He's the guy who says he doesn't do *that*.

Like *that* is a dirty word.

Let's be clear, ladies: oral has become the lost art. Because make no mistake about it, there is an art to the female orgasm when it comes to a little tongue action. And if a man doesn't tell me to sit on his face, then he's not the man for me.

Now do me a favor: forward this article to your boyfriend, because I'm about to give him a step-by-step guide to pleasuring you.

And if he tells you he doesn't do *that*, then it's safe to say this is the last chapter of your book you'll allow him to be part of.

# CHAPTER 4
# DANIEL

Noah pulls back his stick, and with barely a flick of his wrist, the biscuit is flying past Brooks's shoulder and into the net.

Gavin closes his eyes and breaks into a smile. Then, with a clap, he yells to the guys on the ice to switch out. To me, he silently nods, telling me I'm up.

With that look, I know what he's going to say at the end of practice. It's been coming for the last six weeks. Since Noah showed up and Gavin announced that we'd test out different lines.

We've done it before: Brought Camden up to first line with me or War. Put our second-line center in for Aiden. But for the majority of the last two years, War and Aiden and I have made up the first line. We have a chemistry that hasn't been replicated.

Then Noah walked in, and from day one, he's fit perfectly. No matter where Gavin puts him. I'm pretty sure he could hang with the defensive guys and still score. He's just that sly.

Even on second line, he's incredible. But there's no denying that he and War communicate better together than he and Camden. I'm close to both guys. I've practiced with them for two years. I know that's at the heart of this decision. Noah and War played together in college and in Minnesota. He doesn't know the rest of the team. After the hefty chunk of change Bolts' management surely paid to get him here, putting him anywhere else makes little sense.

This is what's right for the team.

But that doesn't mean I have to be happy about it.

Aiden and I run the same drills. I pass to him, and he sinks it into the net.

The result may be the same, but if I have any chance of staying on the first line with my boys, this doesn't help one bit.

I try not to be too hard on myself. Whether I scored that last goal or not, Gavin says exactly what I expect when he's speaking to the whole team at the end of practice.

"Warren, Harrison, and Langfield are on line one this weekend. Hall, Snow, and Keegan on line two—"

He continues, firing off line assignments. Assignments that haven't changed at all. The only person who has been moved is me, and the glances from the guys tell me I'm not the only one who's realized this.

"Now go get some rest. The flight for Arizona leaves early."

I'd been looking forward to this weekend for months. Now, though? I can't get out of this arena fast enough.

As I step onto the plane in my travel day suit, duffel in hand, and find Noah already settled beside Aiden—the seat I normally occupy— a surge of pain overtakes me.

As soon as War sees me, he slides from his aisle seat to the window and nods at me. War never sits in the window seat. Fuck, am I pathetic. My ass has barely touched the cushion when he leans forward. "How are you doing?"

"I'm fine." I adjust my seat belt so I'm comfortable. "You all don't have to keep checking on me like I'm going to lose it any minute."

With a grin, War glances down at my groin and back up. "I was asking about your dick. It's the big weekend. You're finally off probation."

At the mention of it, phantom pain tingles inside my pants. Dammit. I'm not sure I'll ever get used to the feel of the bar or the ring. "Since when do you care about my dick?"

His smirk grows. "Since I'm trying to get you to smile."

I roll my eyes, but his comments have the desired effect. "I'm fine. Seriously."

I glance at Aiden. His head is bouncing, which means he's singing the songs he's made up for each play as he and Noah run through them two rows in front of us. It's what he and I would normally do before a game. Aiden communicates by singing. It throws off the other team. Every game is different. He changes up lyrics and song choices in order to keep our opponents from figuring out our plays. It's not easy to keep up with his brain, but it is fun. And it's like using flash-cards to study. It's not the physical flashcards that cement the informa-tion in a person's brain. It's going over the plays consistently that makes our game strong. Putting lyrics to plays creates little ear worms, and they get stuck in our heads. It's kind of genius, really.

I glance back at Keegan. Wonder if we should come up with our own thing?

"You know he's not replacing you, right?" War says.

Without my permission, my attention darts to Noah. "No, he actu-ally literally replaced me," I say evenly. There's no sugarcoating it.

"I mean as our friend." War's voice is low. Like he knows I wouldn't want this conversation to be broadcast to the entire team. "Regardless of what line you're playing on, our friendship hasn't changed."

I survey Aiden. It certainly feels like it's changed. Though I keep that to myself. War isn't an emotional person when it comes to most things, but he makes an effort when it matters. When the people who matter to him need it.

I'm touched that he's gone this far. That he's sitting here and talking this out. Sure, he's my captain, and sure, the general good of the team has something to do with it. But that's not his primary moti-vation. As hard as he looks on the outside, he truly cares.

"Yeah." I sigh. "I know. Appreciate it, man."

He nods. "It's going to be a good weekend. We'll kick ass tomorrow, then we'll relax. I can't fucking wait to get my wife in that hot tub."

I ignore the part about his wife in the hot tub. The two of them look like opposites in every way, but they work. "I'm excited about the house. It looks awesome."

"And Hannah will be there," he murmurs, his elbow on the armrest between us.

"Nope."

That single word has me spinning.

My sister walks down the aisle, head shaking, and when she stops in front of me, hands on her hips, she frowns.

"What do you mean *nope*?"

Millie accompanies Gavin as often as she can. Vivi too, though I don't see her. That's concerning. My sister is nicer when her daughter is around.

"I mean nope. As in no, you will not sleep with my friend. No, you won't even think about it."

War barks a laugh, but when Millie glares at him, he sucks it in. "She's serious?"

I eye my twin. It's hard to believe we shared a womb. She's five-foot-two, and I'd be surprised if she weighed more than a hundred and thirty pounds. I'm six-one and weigh two-ten. Regardless of our size difference, her death glare is scarier than my muscles in this moment.

"Hannah's an adult," I say. "If she wants to enjoy the company of me and my glitter dick, who are you to stop her?"

Once again, my mouth and the words that come out of it don't do me any favors. Fuck my life.

Millie bends at the waist, her face only inches from mine. "I told her years ago she could touch you at her own risk. But I'm telling you, if you make things weird with my bestie, I'll talk to your coach, who I'll remind you, I fuck."

A full-body shiver runs through me as she stands tall, her lips twitching into a smirk.

"I thought twins were supposed to be best friends," War mutters as she walks away from us, that evil smile still on her face.

I cross my arms, lean back, close my eyes, and smile. "We are best friends. Didn't you hear? She just gave me the all-clear to fuck her best friend."

He huffs. "Did we just sit through the same conversation?"

"Yup." I chuckle. "I'm not sure if you caught it, but she said she told Hannah she could touch me at her own risk, which means," I roll my head to the side and open my eyes, "that Hannah asked for permission." I tap on my forehead. "Twin telepathy. It's a thing."

"You Halls are fucked in the head."

I smile and close my eyes. Yeah, we are.

# Chapter 5
# Hannah



"Just wait until you see the bikini I bought when I was in Florida. This thing barely has strings."

Lennox gives me a once-over. "You telling me you don't have any tan lines beneath that jersey?"

I let out a long sigh. "Sadly, even if I did, no one would get to see them. I was too busy babysitting the damn rookies during spring training to even flirt, let along lay out in the sun."

Lennox smiles. "Just means your kitty is in need of some attention."

"My kitty isn't getting any attention this weekend. But my muscles are ready to get a pounding from the jets in that hot tub."

My bestie grins. "I love hot tubs."

"I love hot tubs too." Aiden, dressed in his signature Bolts blue suit, appears out of nowhere and nuzzles his wife's neck.

He's the first of the guys to make his way to the friends and family room after the game. The Bolts won 3-1, and Aiden and Noah were responsible for two of the three goals.

"Congrats, Lep. That was one wicked slapshot."

He gives me one of his dopey, lopsided smiles. "Thanks, Han. You ready to celebrate?"

"What I'm ready for is a drink. But I promised Noah I'd wait for him. If you're ready to head out, I'll meet you there."

"You sure? We can wait and ride to the house together."

His offer is sweet, but I'm used to traveling by myself. The girls are always being followed by their men, but I've spent more than half my life by myself. I can't imagine spending that much time with another person and liking it.

"I'm good. I promise. You guys go. But put my bag in a room with a nice en suite, 'kay? I need a hot bath when I get there."

Lennox winks. "You got it, girlfriend."

As they head toward the door, Lennox leans into Aiden. In response, he presses a kiss to her cheek.

In the last two years, I've gone from having two single friends to being part of a group of five women, four of whom are either married or engaged. One by one, they fell in love, and not once have I longed for my turn. Most women would want what my friends have. And hell, I write romance novels; I get the appeal. But I prefer to sleep in the middle of the mattress and hog the blankets. A vibrator can get me off just as well as a man, if not better, and then I can turn over and go back to reading my book without feeling like I'm disappointing someone by not pretending to be interested in what they have to say.

My girls still include me in their couples' trips, and I don't mind being the third wheel—or ninth, in this case. All my besties are with wonderful men who make sure that when they get their girls a drink, they grab one for me too. To be honest, I'm more spoiled than most, since all their guys make a point to watch out for me. It's a charmed life.

"What are you smiling about?"

I look up to find Noah sauntering my way, his black suit hugging his rugged frame and a pair of black-framed glasses perched on his face. Yes, Noah Harrison wears glasses, and it has always made the ladies go crazy. It's the juxtaposition, I think. He looks like a nerdy jock. And he is. He recites random facts and loves doing crossword puzzles. He was meant to be a grandpa, and I adore him for it.

"Just thinking about the steak and the orgasm that are calling my name."

"Jesus." Cringing, he peers around to make sure I haven't been overheard.

I, on the other hand, laugh my ass off. I'm the head of PR for the baseball team. No one is catching me saying shit like that in public. I cover that stuff up.

"Relax, old man. I'm just teasing. I'm definitely having pizza tonight."

With a chuckle, he drapes an arm over my shoulders and leads me toward the door. "Missed you, Han. And Oliver hasn't shut up about your offer to take him to a Revs game when you get back."

I grin as we head out into the tunnel that leads to where the team's bus is parked. "Tell him he can have as many hot dogs as he wants."

Noah frowns. "Let's not do that. The kid has a weak stomach."

"Noted. I wish you didn't have to go back tonight. You sure Liam can't watch Oliver for a couple of days so you can hang with me for the weekend?"

"Nah, I miss the little guy too much as it is. He's been at Jen's all week. I've got three days until our next game, and I'm going to enjoy every moment of them with him."

"You're a good dad."

"And you're wearing Daniel Hall's jersey." Noah pinches the fabric at my shoulder and tugs lightly.

"I'd forgotten that I have another player to cheer for now. I always wear Hall because it'd be weird to pick one Langfield over another."

"What about War?"

"Nah, he's too broody for my liking. Besides, he was your best friend in college. That would have been weird."

Noah hums. "True. But it's not a little strange to show up wearing that when you're staying the weekend with him and a bunch of couples?" He raises his brows like he's insinuating a situation that's far beyond the realm of possibilities.

I roll my eyes. "Camden will be there too. Pretty sure they're sharing a room."

Noah waggles his brows as if to say *the more, the merrier*.

I smack his arm. "Noah, I'm not like that."

"I've read your books."

My heart lurches. "You read my books?" Outside the girls, I don't think anyone in my life has ever read my books.

"Of course. Every time you release a new one, I buy like ten of 'em and give them out to my teammates' wives. I'm still dying to know who the younger sister of those crazy brothers ends up with. Are we ever getting her book?"

Truly shocked that he actually knows the plots of my books and is interested in them, I find myself at a loss for words. But rather than show any kind of vulnerability, I straighten my shoulders and force a cocky smirk. "An author never spills her secrets."

As we stop on the sidewalk, he pulls me in for a hug and drops a kiss to my forehead. The gesture is oddly comforting. "Proud of you, Han."

"Thanks," I force out past the lump in my throat.

"Where's your crew?"

"I sent them ahead. I've got an Uber coming."

Noah grins. "So like I was saying before, you and all those couples—"

"And the manwhores. Don't forget the manwhores."

With a shake of his head, he grins. It's good to see him smiling. "I don't get that impression from Hall. I haven't seen him do anything but practice. Kid seems dedicated, that's for damn sure."

"Yes, well, that's what he is. A kid. And like I tell him every time he hits on me, I'm not looking to be anyone's mommy."

Noah's laughter fills the night air. "For the record, I think you'd make a good one." With a wink, he backs up, then turns and heads for the team bus.

I fold my arms across my chest and mentally bat his words away. That is the last thing I want to think about tonight. I've got twenty-four uninterrupted hours of fun ahead of me before the team gets to Arizona and I'm back to babysitting a bunch of baseball players.

"Oh, and Han," Noah calls from the bus's doorway.

"Yeah?"

"Told you." He lifts his chin. "He's a good kid."

I turn, and when I find Daniel Hall in his black game day suit leaning against the door, arms folded across his chest, watching me, my stomach flips.

I don't know what to make of the intense look this usually happy-go-lucky guy has aimed at me, but for some reason, I know even as I walk toward him that tonight won't go at all as I had planned.

# CHAPTER 6
# DANIEL

In a pair of tight black pants that hug her beautiful curves, and with my fucking name and number on her back, Hannah is my literal dream girl. For three years I've watched her. She comes to the games, then joins us at the bar afterward, and every time, she wears my damn number. I can't help that it's gone to my head, no matter how often she's batted away my flirtation like I'm a naughty boy who needs to be punished.

*Punish me, Hannah. I can take it.*

I'd enjoy it, actually.

God, I'd enjoy anything she'd do to me.

What I don't love is watching her stare at Noah. And I really fucking hate how he just kissed her goodbye, even if it was just on the forehead.

But when he calls out to her as he gets on the bus, pointing out that I'm waiting, my distaste for him wanes. Maybe he's not so bad after all. I don't know what kind of relationship the two of them have, but if he's sending her my way, I'll take a guess and say they're just friends.

At least that's my hope.

When she turns around and surprise lights up in those pretty blue eyes of hers, my concerns evaporate. That's all the confirmation I need. I'm at least in the fucking game.

Tonight I'm not going to think about how I no longer play on the first line with my two best friends. The second line had a good game too. Cam and I set up Keegan for a goal, and the team pulled off a win. That's enough for me. As far as hockey goes, at least.

For now, I'll keep my focus fixed on the woman in front of me. With my hands still in the pockets of my black suit pants, I push off the door and slowly walk toward Hannah.

She matches me step for step, the two of us eating up the distance.

"What are you doing up so late, Baby Hall?" she calls as she gets closer, a tease of a fucking smile on her face.

My stomach twists in anticipation. "Thought maybe I'd ask the prettiest girl at the game to come to dinner with me."

She arches a surprised brow. "Aren't our friends waiting for us back at the house?"

"I'm sure they can keep themselves entertained."

Clearly not nearly as affected by me as I am by her, she lifts a shoulder in a casual shrug. "What do you have planned?"

"You mentioned steak and an orgasm. I can handle one of them right now. The other one might need to wait until we get to the restaurant."

Head tossed back, she laughs loudly.

God, the way that sound fills the night air has my balls tightening. She's so fucking pretty.

"You heard that, huh?"

I dip my chin and let my lips tick up on one side. "Was standing right behind you."

Rather than turn pink or stutter out an embarrassed response, she breaks into a wide smile. "I'll let you get the steak. I can handle the orgasm."

My cock jumps as that last word rolls off her tongue with ease. That's one of the things I like most about her. Hannah doesn't bullshit. She's not coy. She doesn't hide behind a façade, not for anyone, least of all a man. She's unabashedly herself, just like me.

She knows her worth and she demands it. It's fucking sexy as hell.

I've never met someone quite like her, and I'm pretty sure I never will.

At thirty-three, so many women still haven't figured out who they are, but Hannah sure as fuck has. She owns every facet of herself, and with that, she owns all my attention. If she's in the room, no one else exists.

As she takes another step closer, her scent—something sweet and musky, like a spiced French vanilla—swirls around us. And when she presses her palm to my chest, the heat of it instantly warms me. With a pounding heart, I stare down at those soft fingers pressed against my body. I don't think she's ever been this close. And she's certainly never touched me. I'm pretty sure her touch would be branded on my skin if she had. It's official: this shirt is retiring after tonight. I'll never wash it again.

I drag my attention up her arm and across her chest to where the Bolts logo sits, then higher to her glossy lips.

Clearly knowing she's in complete control, she drags her tongue slowly across her bottom one. "I'm not sure I'm dressed for anywhere fancy."

It takes everything in me to keep my hands in my pockets. If I remove them, I'll have her pressed against the wall between one breath and the next, with my fingers buried in her hair and my mouth on hers, taking everything I've ever wanted.

But there's time for that.

First, we're going to have a meal.

I'm going to show her I'm more than a pretty face and a fancy dick.

Affecting the cockiest smirk, I give her a slow, thorough once-over. "You're wearing my name on your back, dream girl. It doesn't get more perfect than that."

She laughs that raspy laugh again. "Okay, Baby Hall. You can buy me a steak."

"Oh, that's not dirty enough," I tell the waiter as he arrives with our cocktails.

Hannah ordered a dirty martini, extra dirty, like she always does, but it's still almost clear.

She shakes her head. "It's fine."

"You hate it like that."

Eyes flicking from me to the drink, she lets her shoulders sink and nods. "Yeah, I'm going to need it darker than that."

"Of course." The man sets my drink on the table before disappearing with her too-clear martini.

"You paying attention to how I take my drink, Baby Hall?" Her voice is calm, completely belying the uncertainty swimming in her gaze.

"You order the same thing every time we're out. I'd have to be an idiot to not know how you take your drinks."

One brow arched, she forces her shoulders back again. "Or just not focused on me."

I don't even address that comment. We both know I'm always focused on her.

She coughs out a laugh. "Then you know I normally send it back when it's not right."

"You do. When you're with the girls. I wasn't sure if you'd do the same thing when on a date."

Lips parting, she once again lets out a low, sexy, sarcastic laugh. The one that emanates from deep in her throat. "This isn't a date."

I pick up my lowball glass of whiskey and take a sip, ignoring that comment.

The waiter returns with her drink. This time, the liquid is perfectly cloudy, with three olives pierced by a martini pick balanced across the rim of the glass.

Only after Hannah takes a sip and gives him an approving nod does he disappear.

I set my drink on the table and lean back in my chair so the front legs are an inch off the ground. "So when does the next book come out?"

Head tilted, she zeroes in on me, as if she's trying to read between the lines of my question. After a moment, though, she shakes her head and bites her lip. "Probably not until the winter. I don't get to write much during the season."

"Are you still working on the stalker series?"

Those lips lift in a smile. "First Noah, now you? Coach making you boys read my books or something?"

My gut drops. So do the legs of my chair. Noah reads her books? Why?

And how the hell does he fit into her life? Yeah, I could ask, but I know her well enough to know she'd respond with a snarky quip. Something about how she collects hockey players or something. I don't want to be lumped in with other guys. Especially my teammates. Especially Noah. So I leave it alone.

"Or something," I reply. "Do you miss it?"

"Miss what?"

"Writing. Do you miss it during the season?"

She sighs, her eyes drifting up and to the side as if this is the first time she's really considered it. "I don't necessarily stop writing. I'm always working on something, but it's hard to give the stories in my mind the attention they need while I'm busy dealing with one PR disaster after another. My brain can only do so much spinning, and unfortunately, I have to save my creativity for dressing up the bullshit Jasper pulls pretty regularly."

I cough out a laugh. "The way you spun that nun thing."

She lights up, blue eyes flashing with amusement. "It was good, right?"

"Hell yeah. I knew the truth, and even I almost fell for it. That he meant to send the picture to the team doctor because he pulled his groin during practice, and, unfortunately, it went to his ex-girlfriend who became a nun after they broke up? Genius."

Hannah breaks into a wide smile that shows all her straight, white teeth. "I wrote fan fic about it that night."

Elbows on the table, I angle forward. "Shut up. I need to read it."

She coughs out a laugh. "Guess we'll see how the date goes."

This time I'm the one grinning, and damn, does it make my cheeks hurt.

Martini pick between her fingers, she stirs the murky liquid in her glass. "Made any plans for this summer?"

"You looking for a second date, dream girl?"

With an exasperated roll of her eyes, she shakes her head.

I take a small sip of my whiskey and set the glass down again. "No, I don't think about what happens after the season. I typically keep my focus on the next game."

"So you want to talk hockey? How are you feeling about the season?"

I lean in, sliding my glass a little closer to the center of the table. "Nah, I don't want to waste time going over talking points we could hear in the media room."

She rests her cheek in her cupped palm, eyes glittering in the low lights. "So what do you want to talk about?"

Angling even closer, I dip my head and keep my voice low. "I want to hear more about this orgasm you're looking forward to tonight."

Another eye roll and a bite of her lip have my cock jumping. "What do you think your sister would say if she heard you talking like that?"

"She's already given me the all-clear so long as I don't hurt you."

Hannah lifts her drink to her lips and takes a long sip of her drink, her intense gaze never leaving my face. "You can't hurt me, Baby Hall. I'm an ice queen."

I'm not so sure about that. I've watched this woman for years. She may come across as tough, impenetrable, but I've witnessed enough of the softness she shows to her girlfriends to know it's a front. She's hiding behind a thick layer of armor.

Tonight, though, I won't push too far. Tonight, I'll let her control the narrative. I'll even give her the rope to lead me with.

"Fine, dream girl. Then I just might need to thaw you out a bit."

Hannah smiles again, the expression sending a bolt of satisfaction through me and strengthening my resolve. "Let's see how dinner goes. Maybe I'll let you warm me up in the hot tub."

"OH, LOOKS LIKE THEY PUT YOU IN THE DEN," HANNAH SAYS FAR TOO loudly as we come banging into the rental house hours later. The lights are all off, and the house is silent, so it's safe to say that no one waited up. Camden sent me a pissed-off text when he realized I'd left him alone with all the couples, but there was no way I was inviting him out with Hannah and me.

Sure enough, my duffel is sitting on the futon. "I'm not worried about where I'm sleeping, dream girl."

She rolls those pretty blue eyes at me again. "Thanks for dinner," she says, her tone softer now as she starts to head for the stairs.

Fuck. There's no way I'll let the night end yet. Even if I don't get to touch this woman, this has been the best night I've had in as long as I remember—laughing, teasing and talking, taking shots, flirting—and I'm not ready for it to end.

I reach for her hand before she can get past me and tug her closer. She doesn't wobble even a little. Thank fuck. If she were drunk, I wouldn't even attempt to put a hand on her. "Hot tub?"

She assesses me, her eyes bouncing between mine and my lips, and then she bites her own. "Okay, give me a few. I'll meet you in there."

Once I've located my swim trunks and toiletries, I head into the bathroom. When I come out again, the house is still quiet. The moon is bright tonight, illuminating the interior well enough that I don't need to turn on lights to find my way to the French doors that lead to the back deck.

From here, the view of the craggy mountain landscape is incredible. Outside, I'm greeted by a peaceful quiet, the only sound the low hum of the covered hot tub. A check of the temperature reveals it's already a warm 105. Perfect. Nothing feels quite as good as a soak in a hot tub after a long practice or a tough game. Except sinking inside a beautiful woman, but that's not on the agenda tonight.

All I want is a little more time with Hannah.

I'm just easing into the bubbling water when my girl appears, an oversized robe hiding her petite curves.

"That looks ridiculously amazing," she says as she undoes the knot at her waist.

Arms spread, I watch her every move, knowing that's exactly what she wants.

Hannah is a woman meant to be stared at. A work of art, the lines of which don't follow any of the rules. Like a Monet, the longer a person stares, the more depth they find.

As the robe slips from her shoulders, my heart stumbles in my chest. I suck in a breath. "That is not a swimsuit."

She looks down at it, a look of faux innocent shock on her face. "It's not?"

I roll my lips and bite down hard. "No, dream girl, it's not."

She's testing my patience. The skimpy slip of fabric barely covers her pussy and the little triangles do nothing to hide the pebbled nipples beneath them.

When she steps up onto the stairs and leans forward to slip into the hot tub, tipping her ass in my face, I have to fight the urge to grab my own cock to ease the ache.

"I think it's perfectly respectable," she says coyly as she slides a thumb beneath the string across her hip and lets it go with a loud smack against her skin.

I expect her to sink into the water across from me. Figure she'll taunt me a bit more, maybe even strip beneath the bubbles and make me cry when she forces me to close my eyes as she gets out.

But Hannah is the definition of unexpected. I should have known better. As soon as she enters the water, she slips beneath the surface, then comes back up like a fucking literal dream, dark hair slicked back, water dripping down her gorgeous face, her lips pressed into the perfect pout. And then she climbs onto my lap and rolls that tiny bikini-covered pussy over my aching cock.

"I was promised an orgasm."

I dig my fingers into the edge of the hot tub, holding on for dear life. If I let go, I'll grab her hips and roll her over me until she comes.

But it's not time.

Heart thundering, I focus on stringing a coherent sentence together. "And you want me to give it to you?"

Lip caught between her teeth, she drags her gaze down my body and then back up again. "Not sure yet. I don't give just anyone a shot at it."

I chuckle. "I see. So you want to make sure I know what I'm doing first?"

Hannah's lips tip up in a slow, delicious smile. "Now you get what I'm saying."

I nod. "Well, oral is a lost art, so yeah, I get it."

Brows lowering, she rears back a little. "What did you say?"

I shake my head. Now is not the time to talk about Calliope. I can't imagine the woman on my lap wants to hear about how another woman taught me how to eat pussy so well that her eyes will roll to the back of her head.

The tutorial came from an article, not from a hands-on experience, but still. Not where we're going with this.

"It's all about the tongue," I tell her. "And the right amount of suction."

Hannah hums, her hands drifting up and down my biceps in a way that sends tingles up my spine. "And are you good with your tongue?"

"Why don't you hop up on the side of the tub and spread those thighs and I'll show you?"

She throws back her head, and the sexiest laugh I've ever heard escapes her. The raspy quality makes my dick jump. "Let's try it with a peach, Baby Hall. Show me your technique, and we'll see if you've got what it takes to move on to the real thing."

Blue eyes sparkling in the moonlight, she tips to one side and picks up a peach she must have brought out with her and set in a built-in cupholder on the edge of the tub. "If you're scared, then I can go first."

Without taking her eyes off me, she brings the fruit to her mouth. She sticks out her tongue and slowly licks at the soft flesh, moaning in a way that sends me dangerously close to coming. It's not a surprise, really, considering that the big guy hasn't gotten any attention since I got pierced six weeks ago.

I haven't gone this long without touching my own dick since I first discovered that it felt good.

Yeah, I like sex. And jacking off. And coming.

But I love eating a woman's pussy even more than all of those things. I could do it for hours.

So if Hannah is giving me a shot at tasting the forbidden fruit, you best believe I'm taking it.

She bites into the peach, sweet juices trickling down her chin. Then, eyes closed, she twirls her tongue and sucks, making the hottest fucking slurping noise I've ever heard.

My chest tightens, along with my balls. God, what I'd do to hear that as she sucked me dry.

"Okay, you've made your point." I swipe the fruit from her, desperate to stop the torture. There's no fucking way she's going to let me eat her out tonight. She's just teasing me, so this game needs to end right now.

Hannah licks her lips and hums, as if she's savoring the taste.

I can't help it. I lean closer, wishing I could lick the taste from her lips.

"You giving up already?" she taunts, rolling her hips over me again.

Abs tightening, I will my hips not to thrust up into her. "Careful, dream girl. You keep looking at me like that, and I can't be held responsible for what happens next."

Her lips part, and though it's dark and the water is hot, I swear her cheeks flush a deeper shade of pink. If she were the kind of person who could be flustered, I'd swear she's a little thrown off. But I know better than that.

"I think you're all talk, Playboy."

I grin. Playboy. Damn right. I much prefer the nickname I've been given on the ice to Baby Hall. While I may live up to the name off the ice too, with Hannah, I can't help but want more than one night.

That's another reason I should stop this before it goes any farther. She'll never give that to me. Hannah is a badass and the most aloof woman I've ever met. I've never seen her go on a date or heard her talk to the girls about one, let alone introduce a guy to her friends. She's like me. When she finds someone she wants to spend her night with, she disappears quietly. Usually after a game when we're out celebrating or drowning our sorrows.

But the guy never makes it to Sunday dinners at War's, and she sure as fuck hasn't brought anyone to the Bolts games she attends religiously.

Yet I can't help but be caught in her snare. Despite her teasing, I could make this woman come in less than two minutes. Calliope's technique is foolproof, though I've yet to try it. It's from a more recent article, and since my dick has been out of commission, I haven't had a chance to put the knowledge to the test.

Calliope's actually the reason I chose this specific piercing. She claims it's the best for female enjoyment. In the months I've been following her, I've learned all kinds of shit. Like how prolonged non-ejaculatory orgasms are really a thing. It sounds fucking amazing. Again, I've yet to try it, since I've been unable to touch my dick for weeks. But as soon as I'm healed, I'll be following her instructions to the T so that I, too, can have a ten-minute orgasm.

Maybe if I give Hannah a ten-minute orgasm using my tongue, she'll let me test out my new techniques in a few weeks. A guy can dream, right?

"Give me that fucking fruit." I grab it and take a bite, sinking into the flesh around the smaller piece she's already taken from it. "Need a bigger playing field. I really like to get into my meal."

The second my tongue laps up the juices of the fruit, Hannah moans and rubs her pussy over my dick.

It takes more willpower than I thought I had to keep from bucking my hips in response. Instead, I close my eyes and focus on the peach. It's sweet and soft, but I know she'll taste better. I suck and lick and circle my tongue, making sure she knows precisely what I'll do to her.

Panting, she yanks the fruit from my hand and tosses it into the darkness. "Okay, audition's over. You've got the job."

She grips my shoulders and shifts, like she's ready to dismount.

Only then do I allow myself to put my hands on her. Clutching her hips, I pull her back to me. "Where you going?"

"I'm going to grab towels so we can get to the orgasm part." She says it like it's obvious. Like she can't imagine I'd want anything more than that.

And hell yeah, I want to taste her orgasm on my lips. But that's not all I want. And if I don't slow us down, I'll never get a shot at what I've been dreaming of.

Fingers pressed into the soft flesh of her hips, I hold her in place. "Slow down, dream girl. We'll get there, but there's no way I'm rushing this."

She frowns. "Rushing what?"

I lick my lips, my focus locked on hers. "Our first kiss."

A crease forms between her eyebrows. "You act like this means something, Playboy, when we both know that nights like this are a dime a dozen for you." As she says it, she straddles my hips and rolls her sweet body against mine. I'd say it was a taunt, only the way she clings to my arms, then rubs her hands down my pecs makes me think she can't help but touch me. It's been like that all night. For both of us. There's this pull between us. This magnetism that I've only experienced with her and have never been able to ignore. I'm certainly not going to start now.

"And what if it does mean something?"

"It doesn't." She lifts her chin, eyes narrowed.

"What if you're wrong? What if we look back on tonight and realize it was the first of many nights? What if—"

"*Daniel...*" Her tone is dripping with confusion, but it hits me then that I'm not sure she's ever actually used my name. Fuck, do I like it.

Arms tight around her waist, I hug her to me, relishing the electricity coursing from her body to mine and back again. "I've never had a night like this before because I've never had my actual dream girl straddling me. So give me a sec to enjoy this. And fuck, Hannah, just let me kiss you."

# Chapter 7
## Hannah

"I've never had a night like this before because I've never had my actual dream girl straddling me. So give me a sec to enjoy this. And fuck, Hannah, just let me kiss you."

All the air leaves me in one whoosh. Why is he like this? Why is he saying all the things and making my belly do the thing it never does? I want an orgasm. Fast and dirty. Hall should be the perfect person for the job. He's young, hot, and in incredible shape. He fucks regularly and without shame.

This should be easy.

But he's making it anything but.

And yet…my heart can't help but stumble over itself when his face softens as he pleads with me. The smooth hue of his brown eyes is just decadent enough to make me want to give in. And it's impossible not to revel in the way he touches me. He strums the backs of his knuckles against my sides, like he's warming me up, stirring my insides until I'm one melty, gooey puddle.

I want to kiss him. And I want it to mean something.

What the fuck is that about?

"You're smooth, Daniel Hall. I'll give that to you."

I inch closer, but when he doesn't so much as smile at my nonchalance, at the teasing tone I force, I suck in a breath.

Because rather than break into a devilish grin like I expect, he holds my gaze, his focus steadfast on the moment.

The moment he says could potentially mean something.

If it did, it would be one for the books. A starry night. The perfect view of the mountains. Nothing but the sounds of the bubbling water around us and our hearts beating wildly. If one were to write a perfect first kiss, it would absolutely begin with a beautiful man waxing poetic about it in a setting like this.

I'd read it.

He's silent as he watches me, his hands on my thighs now.

My lips tingle under his intense gaze, my heart skipping again.

We shouldn't be doing this. I shouldn't be falling for the allure of the moment. There are a multitude of reasons why this can't go past tonight. Why it won't.

Ah, fuck it. I clasp my hands at his nape and pull myself closer. "You want a kiss to remember, Baby Hall? Remember this."

I press my mouth to his. At first it's just a brush of our lips. He stiffens, as if surprised I've actually given in, but in the space of a heartbeat, he's cuffed my neck, holding me in place. And then he feasts. He licks at my lips the same way he licked that peach. His mouth is sweet, his lips soft, as he plunders like a pirate who's finally found the treasure he's been searching for. He's greedy and determined, taking all he can from me, leaving no crumbs.

Of their own accord, my hips grind over his. "Yes," I pant as I pull back and watch the way my pelvis rolls.

"You like that?" He matches my movements, providing the exact amount of pressure I need.

Of course he does. The man knows how to fuck. Yes. This was the right decision. I haven't had a male-induced orgasm in a really long time. It's depressing, really, as a romance author and woman who writes about sex.

But what's the saying? Women who can't do, write?

Yeah, that's me lately.

Tonight, though, I'm going to do. And do and do until we're both exploding.

Desire pools in my belly, and electricity runs through my veins. "Yeah, Daniel. Just like that."

His mouth curves up in a delicious smile. "I love my name on your lips."

I cough out a raspy laugh. "Of course you do. What kind of man doesn't want to hear a woman say his name when she comes?"

He grips my ass and squeezes hard. "Not just any woman. *You*. My fucking dream come true. Do you have any idea how fucking hot you are? How many times I've thought of you when I jacked off?"

A shiver runs up my spine. I'm not sure if a line like that works on other women, but it certainly works on me. "Tell me more. How would you do it? Or better yet, tell me what you'd picture."

"Your hot mouth wrapped around my cock." His voice is like gasoline, and my body is absolutely on fire. He sucks my tongue into his mouth, and I can't hold back the moan that rumbles up my chest and out of me. "Though I'd much prefer my mouth on your cunt right now."

Breath catching, I pull back. "Really?" *That's* gotta be a line.

Yet there's nothing but heat and honesty in his eyes. "Tonight's about you, dream girl. I've got an audition to finish."

I shrug, not one to turn down a good time. "In the hot tub or—"

"No, baby. I need room to work." He stands, taking me with him, holding me easily with one arm as he throws one leg over the side, then the other. There's no hiding the strength he possesses. He may be young, but he's easily the strongest man I've ever been with. I feel small, delicate, as he holds me close, protecting me from the cold. The wall of muscle I'm pressed to speaks of dedication. I run my fingers over his toned shoulders, delighting in the touch. I can't wait to see just how dedicated to other things he can be.

With a grunt, he reaches for a towel. One hand under my ass, he shakes it out with the other and drapes it over me.

"You can put me down so you can dry off."

Silently, he lumbers to the door and eases me onto my feet on the warm rug. Only then does he snag a second towel and quickly dry himself off.

"Let's go to my room since you don't have a bed," I say with a smirk.

Chuckling, he follows me.

My room is one of those pretty ones with a four-poster bed as its focal point. The massive windows let in enough light to see where we're going as I toss my towel and turn so I'm facing Daniel as I back toward the mattress. His gaze is hawklike as he watches me untie the string at my neck, then the one behind my back. And when I shimmy out of the bikini bottoms, he brings a fist to his mouth.

"Fuck, Han. You could give a man a heart attack with a body like that."

Even as I roll my eyes, my chest expands. I'm not the least bit shy or modest, but it never hurts to see a man so affected. "You don't have to keep complimenting me. I'll fuck you either way." I ease myself onto the bed and rest on my elbows.

With a shake of his head, he drops his towel, then shucks his swim trunks.

When I see the impressive package he's been hiding, I can't help but inhale a surprised breath. The piercing is incredible, but it's so much more than that. I'd heard rumors. The idiots who play for the Bolts have mentioned more than once that Daniel has the biggest cock of them all, and they weren't playing. The man is so fucking big I actually think he may rearrange my insides.

And damn am I looking forward to it.

Now, back to the piercing… "Is that an apadravya piercing?" I can't hide the awe in my tone.

He fists his shaft and looks down at it. "It's fucking beautiful, isn't it?"

Normally when a man asks me to compliment his dick, I take it as my cue to leave. Instead, I find myself pushing up off the bed and stepping closer.

"It really is."

The urge to drop to my knees and take the piercing—a barbell that goes straight through his head vertically—into my mouth is powerful. I want to roll my tongue over both ends of the barbell. I want to hear him hiss in pleasure and pain when I tease him with it.

And then I want to experience it for real. Deep inside me while I ride him.

Because an apadravya is for the female's pleasure.

Of course he'd choose this specific piercing. He's such a fucking playboy.

As I continue exploring it from a distance, need drips between my thighs. Damn, I'm in for a treat tonight.

"Can I touch it?" I reach out, though I pause inches away, waiting for permission.

Head bowed, he gives it a shake. "Let me eat you first. I want you soaking the sheets and then my face. Then maybe I'll allow you to please me."

The heat low in my belly ignites. Am I really going to beg him to let me please him?

You better fucking believe it.

"Please, Daniel. Just one little lick?"

With a hissed curse, he squeezes his eyes shut. "How can I deny you?"

"You can't." Grinning wickedly, I drop to my knees and tilt my head back. From here, I get a true understanding of just how big his dick is. Just the sight makes my mouth water. "Want to know a secret, Baby Hall?"

Jaw hard, he nods.

"I love sucking cock. Almost as much as I love riding a man's face. Are you going to let me do both of those things? Will you let me sit on your face until I come so hard I squirt all over you?"

He drops his head and groans, his hands clenching and unclenching at his sides. "And she's got a filthy mouth. Fuck, how am I ever going to get over you?"

Laughing, I lift a shoulder. "Not my problem." Then, without another second of hesitation, I wrap my fingers around his dick. The warmth of him, the smoothness of his skin make me sigh. When I roll my thumb over the new piercing, he practically sings.

"Fuck, Hannah. Fuck, that feels—*shit*, put your tongue on it right the fuck now."

I push closer and do just that. There's no way I'll ever be able to deep throat him. I'd choke on the piercing alone. Forget the size of him. But god do I love a challenge.

Fingers buried in my hair, he thrusts just a bit deeper. Instantly my nipples pebble and I let out a moan that matches his. I'm so turned on; there's no way I won't be crashing over the edge in minutes once we get going. I roll my tongue around his head, playing with his piercing, then lapping at it, sucking hard.

His hold on my hair tightens, then he tugs my head back. "Fuck this. I need to taste you."

In one quick move, he's got his arms under mine, and he tosses me onto the bed. Then he's jumping after me, pushing my thighs apart and sucking my clit.

"Oh fuck, yes. Be a good boy and yup, right there. Oh shit." I don't even try to keep my voice down. I've never shied away from telling a man what I want, and that's not going to change now.

With a hand on his head, I keep him right where I need him, and he eagerly sucks like he's never tasted something so sweet.

He rolls his hips in time with his sucking, pressing his pelvis against the mattress like he could get off just from doing this.

"You like that, Baby Hall? Like eating my pussy?"

Tugging his head back, I flip over. And without instruction, he follows so he's on his back. When I'm sitting on his face, I take control, riding him like he's my own bull.

Daniel grabs my ass and squeezes, and in seconds, I'm coming all over his mouth and chin.

"Yes, lap that up. Drink like the filthy boy you are. You love this, don't you?"

As I come down, he keeps up his ministrations, his licking slowing along with my heartbeat, but even once I've stopped, he keeps going, savoring me, humming and groaning in pleasure.

When I can breathe deeply again, I crawl forward and drop onto my elbows, sticking my ass out.

"Get a condom and fuck me."

"*Hannah.*"

"No glove, no love," I say with a smirk over my shoulder.

He shakes his head. "I didn't plan for this."

With a huff, I drop my head between my shoulders. "There's a condom in my purse over on the dresser. You did plan this. Own it. I know I fucking will."

When he doesn't immediately move, I peer back at him. He's standing at the foot of the bed, staring at me. A heartbeat later, thank fuck, he shakes himself from his stupid stupor and backs away.

Thank fuck. For a moment I was worried he'd really convinced himself this is more than sex. Now he's thinking like me. Finally, I'm going to feel that massive, beautiful cock inside me.

When the bed finally dips with his weight, I sigh in relief.

His warm hand presses against the small of my back, and he hovers close so his lips are at my ear. "Are you sure about this?"

"I'm sure that if you don't rearrange my insides, I'm going to cry."

The mattress shakes as he laughs, but then he's lining up and sliding inside me.

"Holy fuck," we cry in unison.

"You feel—this is…fuck, Hannah."

I press back into him, taking more of his length. I swear I feel him all the way to my throat. "That's it. Fuck me, Daniel. Fuck me so good."

With each thrust, he rocks perfectly against my insides, his piercing reaching parts of me I didn't know existed. It's so good. Exquisite, really. Maybe the best I've ever had, and it only gets better when he brings his fingers to my clit and rubs methodical circles.

"Come on, dream girl. Come for me. Squeeze my cock and make this the best night of my life."

I teeter on the edge of orgasm, my body buzzing, my head floating. An instant before I'm certain I'll shatter, Daniel sniffles. The tiny sound distracts me enough to keep me from hurtling into the abyss.

Eyes closed, I focus on the sensation as he continues to play, and instantly, my body coils tighter, the heat in my core ratcheting up. But then there's another sniffle, and the wave ebbs.

The third time it happens, Daniel's sniffle is followed by a grunt. "I need you to come."

Me fucking too.

But I just…can't. Maybe I need to see him. Maybe watching him fuck me will be enough to push me into oblivion. I crawl forward and flip onto my back, legs spread wide.

As if reading my mind, he loops his arms around my thighs and slides right back inside me. He's returned to his painstaking rhythm, and my core is tightening again when he locks eyes with me. That's when I see it. The sheen on his cheeks. The wetness that pools beneath his lids.

"Are you…crying?" My stomach sinks.

"Just ignore it," he pants as he wipes at a literal tear rolling down his face.

Heart lurching, I grasp his forearms. "Daniel…"

"Don't, baby. Don't use that sweet voice, or I'm going to—" He clenches his jaw, and his movements grow jerky. "Don't come, don't come, don't come."

He's clearly not talking to me, though he might as well be, because there's no fucking chance I will now.

Eyes squeezed shut, he lets out a slow growl. "Fuck." And then I feel it. The pulsing inside me. The jolt of his cock as he unloads. The muscles and tendons in his neck go taut, and he comes with a low moan. It's fucking beautiful. He's fucking beautiful. Even crying.

"I'm so sorry," he says, the look of torturous rapture turning to mortification. "Just give me a few minutes and we can go again."

I shake my head and gently slide my hands down his forearms. "It's all good."

He wobbles, his jaw dropping. "Hannah."

I bite down on my lip. *No. This is good. One night. One fuck. And now it's over.* "Don't get attached, Baby Hall. I told you I'm the ice queen."

With that, I slip out from beneath him and stride to the bathroom without looking back. Because let's be honest, there's no coming back from a one-night stand that involves crying.

# CALLIOPE'S COLUMN



## Almost

Almost, ladies. Almost is the absolute worst word in the English language. You want to know why? Because I almost had it all.

I thought I'd found the unicorn. You know, the kind of man romance novels tell us exists. A man who wined and dined me, said all the right things, waxed poetic about our first kiss, and excelled at using his freaking tongue—so well I'm optimistic the lost art of oral may see a comeback. And to top it all off, he had the kind of dick dreams are made of. Long and thick and blinged out with my favorite kind of piercing…

Sounds perfect, doesn't it?

Only he had absolutely no idea how to use it.

There are all kinds of ways a guy can disappoint in the bedroom.

So often, they last too long, jabbing me over and over until I'm begging them to come so it can be over. Or it's too quick. A one-pump chump, if you will.

This man was a literal god with his tongue. He let me ride his face like he was my personal playground, and let me tell you, I got down and dirty on the playground.

So the minute I saw the piercing, I thought he was the unicorn I'd been searching for.

But he catfished me with those tongue skills. Honestly, if the sex had been better, I wouldn't have let him out of that room.

I would've just chained him to my bed and kept him there so I could do it over and over and over again. Don't worry, I would have taken notes and reported back.

But that's not what happened.

The problem wasn't even that he didn't last. I could have made the best of a quickie, followed by another round.

No, what ruined it for me was the sniffles. Every time I'd get close, the man would sniffle, and it totally threw me off. I imagine it must be akin to having a baby monitor set up beside you while you're trying to fuck your man. What kind of person can orgasm to a soundtrack of sniffles?

I swear I tried to tune them out, and I figured if I changed positions, that would do the trick, but when we were face to face, I found out it was so much worse. It wasn't just sniffles.

He was CRYING!

Yep, literal tears streaming down his face while he tried like hell not to come. There was honest-to-god chanting: *don't come, don't come, don't come.*

Well, I've got news for you ladies, I didn't.

# CHAPTER 8
# DANIEL

No fucking way. She's not...she can't be. Holy shit, is Hannah *Calliope*?

# Chapter 9
# Hannah



"I SWEAR IF SOMEONE DOESN'T BUY ME A DRINK AFTER THE WAY LIFE HAS been fucking me lately, I'm going to need a cigarette."

I glare at my computer, skimming the email from another media source asking for Beckett's comment on the Xander disaster. Beckett owns the Boston Revs—and along with his parents and siblings—just about the rest of Boston. Billionaires like him keep scandals like this locked down pretty well most of the time, but damn, this one is a doozy.

Sara leans into my office and smiles. "Oh, a good fucking. I'm always down for one of those."

I close out of the email as my blue-haired friend steps over the threshold. She dyes it at the start of hockey season every year because she's as superstitious as her goalie fiancé, Brooks. I'm not at liberty to share what I just read with her. It involves the Langfields, though it looks to be centered around the youngest sibling, Sienna. Though I'm sure Sara will find out soon enough, I'm oddly protective of Beckett, and I know for a fact that when it comes to this, he was only trying to do the right thing.

"I haven't had one of those in a long-ass time," I admit, rolling with our usual banter. Talking sex with Sara is a good way to distract her. She's a hoe for a good dicking, just like I am.

Sara's laugh echoes off the walls of my office. "Right. Everyone who stayed in that rental in Arizona with us knows you had at least one good dicking." Arms crossed, she cocks a brow. "Millie hasn't stopped crying about having to hear you chant her brother's name that night."

I never did give the girls details about sex with Daniel. I'm not one to kick a man when he's down, and that boy was very obviously down after that night.

When I came out of the bathroom, he had disappeared. I figured it was in both our best interests to call it a night, and I woke up the next morning with the intention of checking on him in hopes that we could keep things from being awkward, but the man was already gone.

That's when I made the mistake of asking Millie where he was. My friend was pissed.

*"You mean he fucked you all night and then just left?"*

Rather than own up to the disappointment that washed over me when I realized he'd vanished, I pasted on a smile and swore it was exactly how I would have wanted the weekend to end.

After all, I told him I'm the queen of unaffected.

"Please." I scoff. "I'm sure she was too busy chanting Hockey Daddy to even notice." The girl is feral for her husband. I push back from my desk and snag my purse from the bottom drawer. "Are we meeting the girls for lunch, or is it just us today?"

"Just us," Sara says on a sigh. "Ava is leaving early to get Josie to dance, and Lennox is working on a big party for Sienna's birthday, I guess."

My instinct is to wince at the mention of the youngest Langfield sibling. Fortunately Sara's on a roll and doesn't notice.

"Oh, and Millie has a meeting with her dad to discuss her next album."

God, our friends are impressive.

I don't have to ask about Liv, Beckett's wife. Yes, she's our direct boss, but we are close with her too. Today, though, I can imagine she's got her hands full dealing with poor Beckett, who I'm sure is working overtime to fix this disaster.

A disaster I, unfortunately, can't help with. I will, however, lend support when it's time to contain the fallout.

For now, all I can do for them is paste on a smile and pretend I know nothing.

"Sounds good. You've got another away stretch, right?"

Her blue eyes sparkle with amusement. "Already looking forward to having the apartment to yourself?"

I shake my head. "God no. I love having Noah around. And when he's gone, Oliver goes to his mother's, and then my place is too damn quiet. I never thought I'd like living with people, but it's been fun."

"How is Noah settling in?" She tilts her head thoughtfully. "Does he like the team?"

I shrug. "I think so. Honestly, he could get along with just about anyone."

She hums. "I can see that. And he's great on the ice. You coming to tonight's game?"

I haven't been to a hockey game since we made it home from Arizona. Baseball season is kicking my ass. But Noah has been on me about showing up tonight since the season is winding down. It doesn't look like they'll make it much farther in the playoffs, and after this game, they'll be traveling for several days.

The overlap of the two seasons is rough on me. I hate missing so many of the Bolts' games because I'm busy with work for the Revs. Hockey is my first love. Probably because of Noah, and if I could be in the stands cheering at every faceoff, I would.

Once again, I pull out that smile I've become so good at plastering on. "I'll be there."

THE WAITER HAS JUST DROPPED OFF OUR SALADS WHEN MY PHONE RINGS.

Across the table, Sara gives me a conciliatory smile. "The job never ends, huh?"

I turn the device over. I'm going to enjoy this meal before I allow myself to even take a peek at what disaster is waiting for me now. Though, in reality, not a whole lot has changed, this season feels so much worse than the last few. Maybe it's me. Maybe I'm just tired of the constant go-go-go of it all.

Before Daniel asked if I missed writing during the season, I hadn't really thought about it. For so long this career has been my life. My entire personality. Since I was young, I've been hell-bent on being independent. I can take care of myself—as well as the forty men on the roster and Beckett Langfield—thank you very much.

I never wanted to be like my mom—dependent on the man she was with at the time to pay the bills. Dependent on him to make her happy. No man or woman will ever be responsible for my joy, for my wellbeing. I'm more than capable of shaping my life into what I want it to look like all by myself.

But this job has lost its luster. Especially since I'm selling a pretty impressive number of books each month. Though it seems unbelievable, I think that if I could keep up with the readers' demands, I could support myself solely on what I make as an author.

But what would that even look like? I've never been a homebody. I can't imagine the company of nothing but a computer and a cup of coffee day in and day out would be enough.

If my career didn't satisfy me, then would I fall into the rut my mother found herself in? Always searching for something more? So far, I've done well at trying to have a little less. Do I really want to risk throwing my life off balance?

Sighing, I push the thought from my mind and focus on my friend. "Why doesn't your phone go off at all hours like mine? The guys on the hockey team can't really be that much better behaved than my players."

"Brooks just glares at them." Sara shrugs and stabs at her salad. "It doesn't hurt that because we're engaged, I'm always around the guys. They can't get away with anything, and I'm always sure to throw my two cents in before they disappear with a random puck bunny who has drama written all over her."

Suddenly my appetite has vanished. "Hall and Snow must keep you busy."

Sara's fork pauses halfway to her mouth, and her lips quirk up. "You fishing for information? Thinking of going in for a repeat?"

Head dropped back, I bark out a laugh. Instantly, the tension I've been holding in my shoulders dissipates. God, that felt good. I swipe at the tears that form in my eyes. "I don't do repeats."

"Well, either way, no, they don't keep me particularly busy. Hall's been suspiciously quiet this year. They're all a little on edge with the season coming to such an early end."

"Is Brooks upset about it?"

She hums and tilts her head from side to side. "You know, I don't think he is. He doesn't like losing, obviously. But I think they're all ready for a break. Between Aiden's depression diagnosis and then War and Ava almost losing custody of Josie, it's been a tough year. The whole team could use a reset, you know?"

Lips pressed together, I nod.

Shit.

On top of all of that, Brooks and Aiden don't even know yet that their sister's return is *not* going to be a happy one.

My phone pings again, and just like that, the tension is back. Motherfucker. I can't control the media. Might as well suck it up and get to work fixing the team's next disaster.

I flip the device over and unlock it, and when the headline on the screen registers, I hiss.

"Fucking Jasper."

"What?"

"Looks like the man might have knocked a girl up."

"THIS IS BULLSHIT, I SWEAR." JASPER QUINN STALKS BACK AND FORTH IN front of me, his hair wild from the way he keeps tugging on it.

It's nearly four o'clock, and dealing with his bullshit yet again just may cause me to miss the game I promised Noah I'd attend.

Though maybe it would be better if I didn't go anyway.

No. Daniel ruined a good orgasm for me. He's not ruining my favorite sport too.

I'll fix Jasper's disaster, and then I'm going to the game. Somewhere between the two, I'll find a secluded place where I can scream my head off, because god dammit, I need that right about now.

"It would be a lot easier to believe that if you didn't continue to fuck up."

Another tug of his hair. "I heard you last year, Han. I need to clean up my act, and I've been working on it. I met a nice girl. We've been seeing each other. You saw her at spring training. She was there almost the entire time."

I roll my tongue over my teeth. He and I have two totally different definitions of the word nice. He's dating a ball bunny. And really, I've got nothing against ball bunnies. Some really are nice. But she's not exactly helping him clean up his act. She likes to party even more than Jasper does. In fact, at this point, I'm waiting for Beckett to tell me I'm in charge of cleaning up her mess too.

Though I'm guessing she's done with him now.

With a sigh, I prop a hip against my desk. "Like you said, *almost* the whole time. And *almost* is always the problem. There was that weekend when we were in Fort Lauderdale when she had"—I snap my fingers, trying to remember exactly what kind of event he told me she attended—"the Hooters competition. Did she win, by the way?"

Jasper deflates. "Nah, she didn't even place in the top ten. It's bullshit, if you ask me."

Ah yes. It's a real competition. Like Ms. America for Hooters girls. It's in Vegas and apparently a big deal for a waitress to qualify. But I digress.

"That's too bad." I try for a sympathetic tone. Really, I do. "But you get my point. She wasn't there, and this girl claims she was."

I hold up my phone, where I've pulled up an image of the woman who's gone to the press. I really don't get it. Why would anyone want to announce publicly that they hooked up with a baseball player and ended up pregnant? What's her goal? If she wanted money, wouldn't blackmail be more effective? I sure as shit would have paid her to shut up. I've paid a hell of a lot more for peace in the past.

"It's not my kid," Jasper grits out.

"Jasper—"

"No, Han, seriously. Don't you remember? You had those awful cramps when we were in Fort Lauderdale. We stayed in and watched a movie. I even went to the store and picked up chocolate for you."

I frown at the memory of that day. My cramps have always been bad. Truly debilitating. I could barely get off the couch for two days. I'd been in the middle of yelling at him over god knows what that day when one hit me so hard I could barely breathe. And when I stopped yelling, it was the first time I'd ever seen him look truly concerned. The kid can be caring when he wants to be.

"Okay, I'll admit that her rant to the media does seem suspicious. But if she's not pregnant with your kid, why's she coming for you?"

He bends at the waist, hands on top of his head. When he straightens again, he blows out a breath. "Who the fuck knows? I tend to piss people off pretty regularly. Maybe I flirted and then forgot about her?"

"Or fucked her last season and forgot her name this one?"

He shrugs, only looking a little sheepish. "Or that."

With a snort, I set my phone down. "Fine. I'll get to the bottom of this."

Jasper's green eyes light up, and that cocky smile returns. As if he knew he would get his way all along. God, men are infuriating. "You're the best, Hannah."

"Tell me about it."

"Let me know the next time you get your period. As a thank-you for all you do for me, I'll show up with chocolate and movie cuddles." With a wink, he saunters out the door.

I can barely react, though, with my jaw on the floor.

Because fuck, I should have already had my period.

The last time I was graced with period cramps so painful I could only curl up in a ball and whimper was that day in sunny Florida Jasper was talking about.

Before I went to Arizona.

Before I slept with Daniel.

*Shit.*

# CHAPTER 10
# DANIEL

My attitude is shit right now. Hell, my attitude has been shit for weeks. Since Arizona. *"Fuck."*

I slap my locker and wince as the metal reverberates. The need to release this energy is almost unbearable.

Beside me, Aiden kicks his skates off and offers a similar curse.

"I know you're all tired," Gavin starts.

He strides into the locker room, ready to give us *the* chat. The one where he tells us he's disappointed and he knows we're all disappointed. That we played like shit and we can do better. The *it's not over until it's over* monologue he has to give because he's our coach and he owns the team and he can't control any of it because he didn't play like shit today. He's here to tell us we can do this, that he believes in us. That we should trust him when he says it.

But with a look around the locker room, it's more than obvious that as a whole, we agree this season is a loss. We're down 3-1 in this round. If we don't pull off a win on the road this week, we're done.

It's a sad fucking state of affairs, yet I can't be bothered to listen to him. Already, I'm focused on finding another way to release this energy. Something I'm actually good at.

Which apparently isn't sex. Fuck, I can't even look at my dick without blowing a gasket. The piece-of-shit appendage made me fucking *cry* the last time I used it.

Yes, my dick is in dick jail. He hasn't been given even the tiniest bit of love. I knew I shouldn't have let him out to play that night. Fuck, I should have taken things slower. I'd told myself I would. And if I had, maybe I could have had a chance at more than one night with Hannah. By now, maybe he'd be sleeping snuggly inside her warm cunt night after night. And I wouldn't be so fucking irate.

I'd never cried during sex before. But that night, the feelings got the best of me. And no, I don't mean emotionally. I mean the fact that my dick was so fucking sensitive from the piercings that it was this pleasurable pain that I couldn't wrap my fucking head around. It felt incredible and hurt at the same time. And okay, maybe I got slightly emotional over knowing I was finally getting a chance *with her*. Because she's Hannah. My fucking dream girl. And I fucking blew it.

I pound my fist against the locker again, this time hard enough to send pain radiating up my arm.

"Enough." War puts a hand on my shoulder and squeezes. "We're all going out."

"You're going out?" Snow says from my other side, brows pinched.

He's probably as surprised as I am that War would even suggest it. Since he and Ava got married, he's been a complete homebody. I'd do the same too if I had a wife and kids at home. They've probably got much better attitudes than the rest of his team does lately.

"We're all going out." War scans the room, locking eyes with each guy, before turning back to me, his expression hardening. "I know we shouldn't be celebrating, but we need this. We need to remember how to have fun again." He lifts his chin to Noah. "We need the chemistry back."

I'd like to say that his comment makes me feel a modicum better. That maybe he realizes that since Gavin fucked with the lineup, we've been doomed. But I know I wouldn't have been playing any better than Noah has in his position with War and Aiden. None of us are playing like we should, and it's time I get my head out of my ass and take some responsibility for that.

"Fine. But you're buying." I toss the last of my gear into the locker and stalk toward the shower.

Dad: Sorry about the game tonight. You'll get the win in Detroit, though, and bring it back home to finish it out.

WITH A SHAKE OF MY HEAD, I PICK UP MY WHISKEY. IF I WERE A BETTING man, I'd put money on our season ending in Detroit. And there's nothing like losing on another team's ice and having to deal with their happy fans and then all the travel home.

Though losing at home isn't a whole lot better. Letting down our fans is always tough. So is facing the staff who work all year to keep the arena running, win or lose. Yeah. Losing sucks no matter where it happens.

Me: Thanks. We're all at Ground Zero. War says we need to work on our team chemistry.

Ground Zero is a private bar tucked away beneath Langfield corporate offices. It can only be accessed by the underground tunnels that link the arena to the baseball stadium. It's reserved for players and staff and their guests only. A haven where we can relax without being hounded by the media. A spot free of bunnies and fans trying to get a piece of us.

Not that I'm feeling very relaxed now.

Dad: Good. Relax. Enjoy. And then get your head back into it. Only a few weeks left of the season. Make them count. But no matter what, I'm proud of you.

I blow out a rough breath to ease the tightness in my chest. I haven't done a whole hell of a lot to boast about, but my dad has always been proud. So many of the guys on my team have shit relationships with their families, but that's never been my issue.

My dad is one of my best friends and my biggest supporter. I truly wouldn't be where I am today without him. He might stick his nose in my business a little too often, and he and my mom may not have a whole lot of love for one another, but he's always made time for me. He dedicated far more time and showed far more interest in my life than I can even fathom giving to another human. When I was a kid, he was the one driving me to hockey practices. In college, he'd attend as many games as he could. Now that I'm playing for the Bolts, that hasn't changed, and more often than not, he's right here with me after a game. Our whole lives, he's treated us as if we're his entire world.

Until he married Lake, he really never did anything for himself.

Now, seeing him with my youngest brother, Nash, his child with Lake, it's clear he was made for this role.

> Me: Thanks. I'll call you when I head to the airport tomorrow.

I slip my phone into my pocket and focus on the guys around me. Despite War's intentions, there's no laughter. Hell, the group is barely conversing at all.

Determined to get my shit together and help War turn the night around, I straighten and take a quick drink of my whiskey. As I'm lowering my glass, Hannah walks into the bar flanked by Lennox and Sara. Mills probably won't be here. Ava either, since they have kids. But fuck, I wish my sister had shown up with them. At least then I'd have an excuse to go over and say hello.

I haven't seen Hannah since that night, and I've yet to figure out how to get back to the banter we used to fall into without making things awkward.

My mouth waters at the sight of her. She's wearing the same thing she wore the night of our date, a Bolts jersey and tight black pants. She's got on a Bolts beanie that says *Brooks's Puck Bunny*. Yeah, in any other circumstance, that would send me spiraling, her wearing another man's name, but Sara made the hats a couple of years ago, back when she and Brooks were only fake dating, as a joke, so I let it go.

With pouty red lips and a big smile on her face, she's just as gorgeous as the last time I saw her. Only now I know the way those lips feel against mine.

"Let's do a shot." Camden pushes a shot glass filled to the brim with tequila at me.

Head lowered, I pick up the drink. I've got to figure out what the hell to say to her. With a quick inhale, I toss the tequila back, relishing the way it burns.

I look back up at Hannah, now turned away from me, and inhale so sharply I choke on air. What the fuck? There, on the back of her jersey, is the number sixty-nine—not eighteen—and *Harrison* is emblazoned across her shoulders in big white lettering.

Why the fuck is she wearing Noah's jersey?

Also, I'm pretty sure Gavin gave Noah that number just to fuck with me. It's not the number he wore for his previous team, and worse, it's the number I specifically requested when I first signed with the team and was denied.

*Fucker.*

I slam the glass onto the bar, and before I can think better of it, I'm moving.

Jealous rage has me acting blindly.

Maybe this is good. This way, I won't have the chance to bumble through an apology or act awkward.

Without pausing, I clutch her arm and pull her away from her friends.

"What the—"

When I glare at her over my shoulder, she snaps her mouth shut, and rather than fight me, she allows me to drag her along.

Where the fuck do I go from here? Not the locker room. Not the arena, where the janitorial staff is surely all over the place.

I settle for a closet near the entrance to the bar.

It's a small space, but there's nothing actually in it. No coats, no cleaning supplies. Just an empty supply closet. Thank fuck.

When the door snicks shut behind us, we're blanketed in darkness.

*"Daniel."* My name is a whisper on her lips, and fuck, do I like the way it sounds.

I grasp her hips, and when she doesn't push back, my heart thumps. There's no snarky comment. No feisty attitude. Hell, she doesn't even seem pissed. If anything, she's surprised. I know I sure as fuck am. "Dream girl, what are you doing to me?"

She tilts her head, her lips turning down a fraction. "What?"

"The jersey. I get that I screwed up that night, but *fuck*, seeing you in his number? Was it really that bad?"

Fingers tangled in the front of my shirt, she pulls me closer. As my eyes adjust to the dark, I can just make out her facial features. "You smell like tequila, Baby Hall."

"Don't *Baby Hall* me. Tell me what I can do to make it up to you. Tell me it's not too late for us."

She licks her bottom lip and loosens her hold on me. "There is no us." The words are whispered. Like she doesn't actually believe them.

That's all the encouragement I need to grasp her upper arms and squeeze.

"There could be. Give me another shot. Let me make you feel good. And then promise me you'll never wear his jersey again."

She sighs. "This is a bad idea."

It's just enough of an opening for me to take a step closer. I run my nose against her neck and inhale her. "Nothing could be a bad idea when you're this close." I press a kiss to her collarbone, and her breath catches in her throat. Her pulse flutters at the base of her neck, calling to me, so I trace it with my tongue.

She hisses out a breath. *"Daniel."*

"Every time you say my name in that raspy tone, I die a little from being unable to touch you," I murmur in her ear. *"Let me touch you."*

Clutching my shirt tighter again, she sets those pretty blue eyes on my face, studying me. What looks like a thousand thoughts war in her mind. Though I only have one. Getting another shot. Convincing her we're right for one another. Making her come. Okay, so that's at least three, but they all end up the same way: with me inside her, again and again. It's like she reads my thoughts, because her eyes light up and the look of consideration fades. Her chest rises and falls, and she mumbles, "fuck it" before tugging me closer and finally setting her lips on mine.

For a moment everything else fades away. Hockey, the playoffs, the shit season I've had, the even shittier mood I've been in. My stomach swoops and my heart jumps. It's like her kiss set a defibrillator to my life. Cuffing the back of her neck, I pull her closer and explore her mouth. The way she tastes, the soft whimpers that she breathes against my lips. The tongue that stars in every fantasy I've had for at least the last year.

"Need this off you," I rasp against her mouth as we stumble deeper into the closet.

As I yank the jersey over her head, she slips her thumbs into her waistband. And while she's stepping out of her pants, I back up and undress just as quickly. It isn't until my pants are off that I remember that my wallet is in the pocket of my suit jacket. And my suit jacket is sitting on the back of the chair. "Fuck, I don't have a condom."

She shakes her head as she shimmies out of her bra. "It's fine. You're safe, right?"

I nod, zeroed in on her perfect tits. "Haven't been with anyone since you."

She rolls her eyes and mutters, "Same."

That's enough for me. I've got a one-track mind, and all I can think about is fucking her against the wall. About how I'll make her come at least three times. I owe her that and then some.

The next time my dream girl writes a damn column, it'll be about how I rearranged her insides, not about how disappointing tonight was.

I hiss when I grasp my rock-hard dick and give it a single pump, drinking Hannah in.

"You're so perfect."

She cocks her head. "I'd like to say you are too, but I've gotta see how that pretty dick works me over this time before I commit to that."

I chuckle darkly and take a step back, feet planted firmly shoulder-width apart. "Get on your knees and lube me up. We both know you want it."

With a wicked grin, she drops to the floor. When her lips suction over the head of my dick with the most exquisite pressure, my head falls back against the door with a loud thud.

"Don't come," she taunts in a seductive-as-fuck voice. Then she's lapping at me again.

Her mouth feels like heaven, and the vision of her, completely naked, eyes closed as she moans around my length, is sinful.

For a moment, I fall victim to her spell, mesmerized by the sight and sensations. Then she rolls her tongue over the crown of my cock, toying with my piercing, and my eyes roll to the back of my head. Not wanting to risk blowing my second chance—pun intended—and before she has the opportunity to taunt me again, I pull back, scoop her up under her arms, and press her against the wall. Once we're both steady, I line us up and slam into her.

"Holy shit!" she hisses, clenching around me.

I squeeze my eyes shut, willing myself to last. I've never been inside a woman bare. Never would have considered it with anyone else.

But with Hannah? "Fuck, I could live inside you. I may just give up hockey and become your personal fuck toy."

Her loud, raspy laugh rings out in the small space, and she spasms around me again. "Don't tempt me, Playboy." Then her lips are on mine again.

Heart hammering, I lick into her mouth, savoring her as I roll my hips in a steady rhythm. There's never been a moment more perfect than this one. Fucking against a wall is always a challenge. It takes strength and balance I've honed during my years playing hockey. But I'm not trying for easy tonight. The adrenaline from my jealous anger is still pulsing through me, and with each thrust, I expend a little more of the pent-up anxiety.

"You're so goddamn tight, Han." Dammit, I have to distract myself from the unreal sensation of her tight pussy swallowing me up. Is she doing Kegel exercises? Timing them to each of my thrusts? Because I'm so damn close to coming already. And fuck if I'll make that mistake again.

I walk across the tiny space and balance her against a small shelf on the opposite wall. With one hand freed up, I get to work circling her clit.

"Oh, right there," she hisses, spasming even tighter.

I groan at the torturous flood of desire sweeping over me. "Look down, baby."

"Holy fuck. Look at how gorgeous your cock looks as my pussy sucks it in."

"Shit, Han. Your dirty talk."

Those plump lips of hers lift in a devious smile and her blue eyes glitter with excitement. "I want you to fill me with your cum. Make me your little cum slut."

Holy fuck. My balls tighten, and my hearing goes hazy. "Dream girl, you're going to need to come right the fuck now," I grit out.

"You going to come for me, Baby Hall? You're so beautiful when you do." Her voice is like whiskey, smooth and sensual, washing over me as my orgasm crests.

Fuck. Fuck. Fuck. "You don't play fair."

Hannah laughs, the move making her pulse around me. "No, I really don't." She smacks my hand away and brings her own fingers to that swollen bundle of nerves. Her head falls back, and she lets out the most beautiful whimper. "Fuck me, Daniel."

With both hands on her hips, I do just that, pumping into her until she's shuddering and spasming rhythmically and I'm coming in long waves.

When I can finally feel my toes again, I press a kiss to her lips. "Fuck, you are the best sex I've ever had."

Head lolled back against the wall, she pants. "I think you got me pregnant."

I laugh as I ease out of her, making sure she's steady before I bend to pick up her clothes. "I got really deep, didn't I? Fuck, I can't wait to take you home and do it again."

She grasps my arm and squeezes, gesturing for me to stand back up. "I'm serious, Daniel. I haven't gotten my period. I think I'm pregnant."

# Chapter 11
## Hannah

I blow out a relieved breath. God, I'm glad I'm not carrying the weight of it all on my own anymore.

And as a bonus, I'm no longer wound up. That orgasm was fantastic.

"You're pregnant?"

Daniel's panicked voice brings me back to the present.

I shrug as I take my clothes from him. Though he gave me one hell of an orgasm, I, unfortunately, have to put this jersey back on. I can't very well leave the building topless.

"Promise I'll take this off as soon as we get back to my place, but for the time being, I need clothes."

Once I've pulled it over my head, I turn in a slow circle, searching for a paper towel. I find none. What the hell? What kind of storage closet doesn't have at least one random roll of paper towel? Other than an empty shelf, this one is completely bare. So with a sigh, I slip a foot into my pants. I'll just have to walk around a bit sticky from Daniel's cum. Things could be worse.

"Hannah." His tone is more serious now, less dazed. "Look at me."

I drag my eyes up to meet his, and at the shock written across his face, I wince. Poor kid looks the way I felt a few hours ago. "I'm sure you couldn't have imagined I'd tell you something like that when you dragged me in here—it wasn't what I expected when Jasper mentioned my period either—"

He stumbles back. "You and Jasper?"

I have to force myself not to laugh. Boy, is he easy to rile up. It's kind of adorable when he's jealous.

Or it would be if we were actually doing that whole thing where he had any reason to be jealous.

We're not, though.

He may be my baby daddy, but he won't be my boyfriend.

Though it's good to know that if I need to get my rocks off during this pregnancy, he can actually do the job.

"Jasper is just—"

"If you say a friend," Daniel grits out, stepping closer.

A laugh bubbles out of me. "A pain in the ass, and one I'm paid to deal with, at that. Definitely not a friend, nor someone I've fucked." I press a hand to his chest and push him back. God, I need a little space to breathe. "Like I said earlier, you're the last person I was with. Honestly, you're the only person I've been with this year, so don't go thinking you're not the father—"

Daniel's eyes soften, his shoulders falling. "I would never."

With a shrug, I straighten my waistband. "I would understand if you did. Plenty of guys would."

He blinks like he's trying to wrap his head around all the information, then sighs, as if resigned to the confusion. "How far along are you?"

My chest tightens at the thought. "I don't actually know that I'm pregnant."

Eyes wide, he snaps his head up. "What?"

I hold up a hand. "I haven't taken a test yet. But I haven't gotten my period since March so…"

I let the words hang between us.

"It's May now. So we should go get a test." The words are earnest, even.

I can't help but shake my head, confused by how okay he seems. Yeah, he's surprised, but he's not freaking out. "We?"

"We did get into this together, right? So we should probably go to the store and confirm that we're really *in this* together."

Lips pursed, I study him. The boy with the messy hair, a cocky smirk, and one hell of a smolder. The man who flirts incessantly—with me and probably every other woman he comes across in Boston and during all his travels.

The playboy who earned that nickname fair and square.

And yet here he is, looking at me with a warmth in his eyes and kindness in his voice, offering to take me to the drugstore so he can be there for me while I take a pregnancy test.

"You're not who I thought you were," I say softly, heart aching. They're probably some of the strongest words I've ever offered to anyone.

I don't trust easily, and I'm rarely wrong in my judgments.

And in this moment, I hope I'm right in believing that Daniel Hall may not make the worst father after all.

# Chapter 12
## Hannah

Never in my life has anything been more awkward than walking up and down the aisles of Walgreens with my bestie's twin brother, looking for pregnancy tests.

Let me set the scene.

By some miracle, Daniel snuck me out of the bar. He texted Camden Snow and had him snag his jacket—and the keys and wallet inside it. I texted the girls and let them know I was heading out.

The only bump in the road we came to was the moment when Camden saw me in all my walk-of-shame glory, waddling down the hall, trying to keep Daniel's juices from free flowing down my leg.

Yeah, he knew precisely what I was doing. That was evidenced by the way he eyed me up and down, then turned to Daniel and nodded, a smile on his face, and muttered, "Nice."

No. Not nice, Baby Snow. Nothing about this is nice.

God, I might have to stop calling the boys Baby anything if I actually have a freaking baby.

Anyway…

It took a minute to find the correct aisle—much to my shock, neither one of us has ever had to do this before—and now we're staring at a wall of pregnancy test options.

"This one tells you how far along you are," he says, squinting at the back of a purple box.

If it were up to me, I'd snag a couple and bolt. This is mortifying. We barely know each other, and we're shopping for pregnancy tests.

How is this my life?

But Daniel picks up a second box, this one pink, his movements languid and easy.

"This one claims it can detect pregnancy five days before the others." He hums to himself as he considers the two boxes, one in each hand.

With a huff, I snatch both from him and clutch them to my chest. "They look great. Let's go."

"I feel like we should get a few more." He plucks a box from the highest shelf. The shelf I can't reach, yet he doesn't even have to stretch.

Sheesh, he's tall. Will we make a tall baby? Are babies tall? How would a tall baby even fit inside me? I stare down at my short torso, then shake my head, and when I look up, he's grabbing yet another pregnancy test box.

"You're probably hoping for a negative test and think that the more boxes we get, the more likely the chance—"

He whips around, frowning. "It's actually something a friend of mine told me. He and his wife were trying to get pregnant. Took a test, got a positive result. They were really excited, but it turns out it was a false positive, and…" He lifts one shoulder. "Anyway, I figured we'd have a more definite answer if we had a few of them."

I pluck two more from the shelf at random, then pull the one from his hand so we have five total. "Okay, just in case we need to break a tie."

He laughs, and instantly, a little of the tension in my muscles eases. I'm not normally this uptight. And I never care what others think of me—but here and now, I can't help but stress about my every word, my every action. Because if I'm judging him as the potential future father of my child, then it's safe to say he's judging me as the potential mother of his.

I don't have a single maternal instinct. I'm the last person who should be given a child, and before tonight, Daniel would have been the last guy I'd pick to father mine.

But holy hell, has he shocked me tonight. He's handling all of this a hell of a lot better than I am.

"Should we get diapers?" Daniel points to a package to the left of us in the aisle.

I bite back a chuckle. "Those are for adults."

"Why would adults need diapers?" His tone is almost sarcastic, like he thinks I'm the clueless one here. But then he picks the package up and reads the words on the box, and a second later, his entire body shudders. He tosses it back onto the shelf. "So newborn ones?"

"How about we stick to the pregnancy tests for now? Then, if it's positive—" The words hang between us, making it hard to breathe. Other than the painful way my stomach twists, I don't even know how to feel.

"If it's positive," Daniel says softly, taking my free hand and squeezing, "then we're in this together."

I roll my lip between my teeth and stare into his warm brown eyes. How is it that, already, I've developed an instinct to seek them out for comfort? "You're annoyingly cute."

He grins and leans forward, his mouth dangerously close to my own. "Take out the word annoyingly and try again."

With a roll of my eyes, I spin and walk away, but I'm smiling, and I'm pretty sure that was his plan all along.

I BLINK AT THE TOILET, THEN AT THE TEST. DAMMIT. NOW I DON'T HAVE TO pee. I glare at the test again.

If I thought picking them out was awkward, it had nothing on standing in the checkout line with Daniel Fucking Hall by my side. I told him to go outside, that I'd handle paying, and he practically growled, "When I said we were doing this together, I meant all of it."

I drew the line at letting him wait in the bathroom with me while I peed on these sticks. I'm sure he'll regret that position soon enough. There's no way the media hasn't been notified that the playboy winger of the Boston Bolts was buying a cart full of pregnancy tests tonight.

Of course the kid at the counter recognized him right away. Looks like I'll have to enlist Sara's help tomorrow. And that means I'll have to actually tell Sara that I got myself into this position with our best friend's twin. I'm not ready to tell anyone, and yet it's a certainty that I can't keep this secret for more than a day or two.

*Only if it's positive.*

The words are a taunt.

Because if it's negative, this will be nothing more than a funny story I'll share with the girls. Not Millie, obviously. But the rest of them will have a good laugh at my expense.

It's fine. This will all be fine.

"Hannah?" Daniel's voice, followed by a gentle knock on the door, makes me jump.

"Just trying to remember how to pee."

He laughs. "Do you need water? Or soda? You could turn on the faucet. Running water normally works for me."

I sigh. This is absurd. *Just sit down on the toilet and pee.* "I'm fine."

I pick up the test that says it will tell me five days earlier than the others and get to work. Once I've set the stick on the ledge next to the window, I wash my hands and pace.

"*Han.*" Daniel's voice on the other side of the door has my heart rate picking up. Do I go out there so we can wait together? Do I sit here and stare at the test? I don't know him that well. None of this feels natural.

Then again, if he were someone I knew well, like Noah, who arguably knows me better than anyone else, I don't know that I'd feel any more comfortable.

Bizarrely, Noah isn't who I want in this moment. For some inexplicable reason, Daniel is. So I open the door.

Arms up, he's gripping the doorframe above me, leaning forward, eyes roaming over me, like he's trying to decipher my body language. As if that'll give him the answer he's waiting for.

"I didn't look yet."

He nods, dropping his hands to his sides. "Do you want me to look?"

I blow out a breath. "It said three minutes, so we've got at least another two."

Stepping back, he gives me room to move past him. I make a beeline for my bed and drop onto it, causing the Walgreens bag to crinkle. Heart lurching, I turn away from it. The stick I just peed on is one of many I'll have to test.

Though if it's negative, I don't care what Daniel says. I'll chalk this up to a mistake and kick him out so I can take the others by myself.

But if it's positive…

"Isn't it wild how long two minutes can feel when you're waiting for something important? When I'm on the bench during a game, it feels like everyone is moving in slow motion while I wait to get back onto the ice. Then once I'm out there, it flies by."

I offer him a weak smile. "Your life revolves around hockey, huh?"

He shrugs. "Is that bad?"

Head shaking, I pick at a piece of lint on my pants. "No. Work is my life. And honestly, I love hockey."

With a step closer, he smiles, his eyes lighting up. "Yeah?"

"Yeah. I'm glad I don't have to work with you guys, though. All the bullshit the Revs guys pull is starting to make me hate baseball. It's work, ya know? But hockey—I can just enjoy watching the sport."

"I can see that." The bed dips as he settles beside me, pushing the white plastic bag away. "Who's the biggest pain in the ass on the baseball team?"

I snort. "Is that even a question?"

Lips pressed into a line, he shrugs. "I really don't follow the Revs, and I definitely don't read gossip rags."

My eyes roll out of habit. "Of course you don't."

With a nudge of his elbow, he frowns. "What's that supposed to mean?"

"Just that you probably don't follow because you know what they say about you."

"You keeping tabs on me, dream girl? What do the tabloids say?"

My lips itch with the need to smile as I assess the man who keeps pulling them out of me despite the shitty situation we're in. "Another night, another girl. That kind of thing."

Daniel licks his lips as he studies me. "Does that bother you?"

There it goes, another laugh, though I don't think he was trying this time. "God, no. I haven't been pining for you since we last slept together, Baby Hall. I'm not that kind of girl."

Head bowed, he shrugs. "No, I guess that'd be me." Before I can process the words, he switches topics. "So who's the biggest pain in the ass?"

"Jasper Quinn," I say easily. He's the reason I'm here right now. If he hadn't been accused of knocking a girl up, I wouldn't have realized my period was late, and we wouldn't be sitting here right now.

"Okay. And who's your favorite Bolts player?" His lips lift like he knows he has this in the bag.

I bite my bottom lip and peer over at the bathroom door. "I don't pick favorites."

With his lips against my ear, he lets out a low, deep laugh that rattles me all the way to my toes. "Bullshit." He pulls back and stands. "Want me to check it?"

With a thick swallow, I give him a single nod. I don't think I could make my feet move if I tried right now.

He disappears into the bathroom, and when he reappears, he's got the simple white stick in his hand. Face set in a completely neutral expression, he says, "We're pregnant."

# CHAPTER 13
# DANIEL

Is it weird that I wanted it to be positive? That I felt this ridiculous pressure in the center of my chest as I leaned forward, knowing with complete certainty that I was ready for this?

Yes. That's probably delusional. And there's no way in hell I'll mention a word of it to Hannah. It's clear from her expression that she does not feel that way.

Not at all.

"We're what?" She pulls herself from her stupor and jumps up, reaching for the test. "Are you sure you read it right?"

The word *pregnant* in the little window is a pretty good indication that I did, in fact, read it right, but I won't be a dick about it. She's freaking out, and she has every right to. I give her a few seconds to digest the knowledge as she gapes at the most life-changing string of letters in the English language.

"Holy shit," she whispers.

I cough out a laugh. "Yeah, looks like there's more than one hockey daddy on the team now."

Eyes flashing, she snaps her head up, her jaw still hanging open.

Okay, maybe that joke didn't land. But I can't help it. Might as well ride it out. Uncomfortable, I grin. "Can I call you mommy?"

"*Daniel.*" The word is chock full of exasperation.

Yeah, I get it. Clearly, I should shut up.

With a step closer, I grasp her hip, and when she sucks in a breath in response, I waggle my brows, all tease. "I've heard pregnancy sex is fantastic."

The air escapes her in a whoosh.

Oops. Shoot me now. Please. Put me out of my misery. Why I am I like this? Why, when I get uncomfortable, does my mouth take over and say stupid shit? Shit that makes Hannah look at me like I'm nuts.

"I'm sorry." I dip my head so we're eye to eye. "I'm just trying to make you smile."

She bites her lip, attention drifting down and to one side. "Because you're freaking out, right?"

I shake my head. "Don't worry about me. Let's focus on you. This is happening to *you*. So what can I do to make this better? Besides woo you with my awesome jokes."

"Maybe tell less of them," she says, her voice quiet and a little too serious for my liking. Slowly, she pulls away from me and paces to the other side of her room.

"So we're having a baby," she says as she strides back my way. Though if I had to guess, she's not talking to me. It's more like she's talking about me. "You're a hockey player, and I run PR for a baseball team. Neither of us has a job that allows us a whole lot of free time—"

"*Hannah.*"

"I've got five dads—" she turns around and looks at me, *finally*. "Did you know that?"

"Did I know that you have five dads? Um, no, I wasn't aware." Who the fuck has five dads? And how is that possible? Those words swirl in my head very, very quietly, just in case she can read minds. I have no intention of making this worse for her.

Her gaze roves the room, never settling. "One mom who didn't want to be one and five dads. I'm close with four of them." Her eyes finally flit to mine. "You're close with your dad, right?"

I dip my chin. "Yeah. He's my best friend."

Shoulders lowering a fraction, she nods a little manically. "Good. That's good." Then she shakes her head, her lips turning down. "Actually, Millie always talks about how fucked up your family is."

I grip my neck, my stomach twisting. "More like inappropriate. Dad is married to my brother's ex. Millie is married to our dad's best friend. That's the extent of it, really."

She nods. "Now her twin has knocked up an older woman he barely knows."

My heart sinks. So that's what this is about. I walk across the room, and when she turns to pace in my direction, I'm there to catch her by the arms. "We don't have to figure it all out tonight."

She bites her lip, but focuses on something over my shoulder. "Right. It's just kind of what I do. I solve the crisis."

Gently, I grasp her chin and tip it up until she's forced to meet my eye. "This isn't a crisis."

Her lip wobbles, and a vulnerable side of Hannah I never knew existed peeks out. The woman who normally taunts and laughs loudly has the softest center. I knew it. It's endearing as fuck. "You can't really mean that."

Unable to stop myself, I swipe my thumb across her bottom lip. "My dad always says things look better in the morning."

"That's because he wakes up next to a sexy woman half his age." Finally, she laughs.

I can't help but join in, but the moment I do, the sound coming from her turns into a groan.

Forehead pressed against my chest, she sighs. "I'm sorry I'm being crazy right now."

I wrap my arms around her and squeeze. "Not crazy. Overwhelmed. Completely reasonable. Why don't I turn the shower on? You'll feel better after, and then you can get some rest."

Hannah tips her head up and eyes me. "Yeah, you probably want to get out of here."

My chest constricts at the idea. "Can I stay?"

She frowns. "You don't have to—"

"Please, Han. I want to. I know today has been stressful, and I can guarantee I won't say anything right, but maybe if I sit quietly, I could at least be here. We could...I don't know, deal with this together."

I hold my breath. *Please say yes.* She may not need me, but fuck, do I need her. I have to get on a plane tomorrow for our next game.

The idea of leaving this room, let alone the state, has me digging in my heels and wishing the season was over. And I never feel that way.

Blue eyes search mine like she can't quite figure me out. But I luck out. She must see the truth there somewhere, that I want to be here, because she finally relents. "Yeah, I guess that would be nice."

"COFFEE. I WANT COFFEE, AND I CAN'T EVEN HAVE IT," HANNAH whimpers as I press kisses to her collarbone. I woke up cold, so I rolled so I'm half on top of her for warmth. Apparently my girl's a cover hog. Figures.

She hasn't even opened her eyes, but already she's complaining.

"Want me to get you decaf?"

Dark lashes flutter, and I finally get a glimpse of her crystalline irises. "Are you offering to pick up breakfast?"

Propped on one elbow, I grin down at her. "Will that make you smile?"

She purses her lips like she's trying to hold one back right now. "It's a start."

My cock is rock hard between us, but I keep my hips away from hers, hoping she doesn't feel it. I'm not sure what we're doing here, and I don't want her to think I stayed over with the intention of having sex. Not that I'd turn down a little morning action. Especially with my dream girl.

"What else would make you smile?"

She drags her fingers down the center of my chest, sending sparks of desire through me. Abs tensing, I let out a slow moan. Maybe we are going in this direction. Okay, I can get on board.

With a smile playing on her lips, she pushes me off her. "A blueberry muffin and a fruit cup."

I groan at the loss of her warmth and any hope of getting laid. "You're evil."

She laughs, pulling the sheet up to her chin. "Go. Quickly. I'm hungry."

Once I've pulled my pants on, I head for her bathroom. Unfortunately, I'll be wearing my game day suit while I run out for breakfast. If photos of me out buying pregnancy tests last night aren't already circulating, this will give them something to talk about. When I come out of her bathroom, buttoning up my shirt, she's still lying in bed. "Take another test while I'm gone. I heard you get the most accurate results in the morning."

She rolls her eyes, the action one I've seen at least a thousand times since I've known her. "You know too much."

As if it's routine, I hover over her and press a kiss to her mouth. No second-guessing, no hesitation. Her lips are soft against mine, and fuck, I forgot how good she tasted. She moans as I lick at her lips, cradling her head, needing more. With a knee on one side of her, I adjust my weight, ready to straddle her and make this morning even more perfect.

Before I get any farther, she pushes back, face flushed and lit up with sleepy joy. "Breakfast, Baby Hall."

I dart in and bite her lip, then soothe it with another kiss. "Fine. But take the test. And do the one that estimates how far along you are."

She laughs. "We only slept together that one time. I can do the math."

"Do you have a smart-ass comeback for everything?" I call as I open her bedroom door. Her raspy, happy laugh follows me out, lighting me up from the inside as I head for the front door.

I've just disengaged the dead bolt when a male voice behind me has my heart thundering. "Hey, Han. Now that your boy toy is gone, are you hungry?"

I spin, chest tight, and find Noah walking toward Hannah's bedroom in nothing but a towel.

"The fuck?"

Noah freezes, his back straightening, and tilts his head. "Hall?"

"Harrison."

With a laugh, he rubs a hand down his face. "I'm going to go put on clothes. When I get back, I'm guessing you'll be gone." He nods and spins on his heel. "See you on the plane." With that, he's gone, disappearing into the second bedroom.

Hands clenched into fists, I stomp right back into Hannah's room.

"Please tell me you don't live with fucking Noah Harrison," I grit out as I throw the door open with a little too much force.

Her room is empty and the bathroom door is closed.

"Hannah." I say her name again, because apparently, I've lost all control.

She steps out of the darkened room in nothing but a purple silk robe and frowns. "That was quick."

"Are you dating Noah Harrison?" I grit out.

Her face pinches. "Ew, no."

My chest squeezes tighter. Shit. Is this what a heart attack feels like? "What do you mean 'ew, no'?"

"I mean, ew, no. He's like my brother."

I clutch at the front of my shirt, my pulse haywire. "You fucked your brother?"

She stomps across the room and plants her hands on her hips. "*No.* He's my stepbrother. We're not blood related. And I never fucked him."

My stomach churns. "Oh my god, that's so much worse."

"How is that worse?" She tilts forward, eyes narrowed in a look that should have me cupping my balls and backing away.

Instead, I glare right back. "Now I'm a brother fucker."

Her brows knit together, her arms falling to her sides. "You fucked my brother?"

"No." I pull at my hair. "I fucked your brother's sister."

"You fucked—" She tilts her head, lips pursed. "Wait, Noah doesn't have a sister."

"No." I cough out a strangled sound. "I fucked you. I'm a brother fucker."

She shakes her head. "I don't think you're saying this right."

I pace to the window. "Brother fucker. Brother fucker. Brother fucker." When I spin back in her direction, I lace my hands on top of my head. "He's going to kill me."

She shrugs. "Eh. He knows I've had sex. And we all know you have sex with everyone. It won't really be a surprise." She smiles. "And it wasn't even good sex."

My heart lurches. "Let's not lead with that."

With a roll of her eyes, she shuffles back toward the bathroom. "Let's not lead with any of it. None of it matters. I certainly don't intend to tell anyone I had bad sex."

"Last night wasn't bad sex," I call after her.

She comes back into view holding another pregnancy test, and all my anger dissolves. "Well, the bad sex is what made us three-plus weeks pregnant," she says, her smile wry as she tilts the stick in my direction.

On autopilot, I stalk across the room and snatch it from her hand. Like last night, it's positive. She listened to me and took the one that estimates how far along she is. Three-plus weeks. Fuck. We're pregnant. This is real. We're really having a baby.

"Should I take another one?" she says almost too quietly.

I look into her blue eyes, noting the uncertainty and the fear swimming in their depths, and all the energy fueling my anxiety drains from my body. It drains from her too.

"We're going to be parents," I murmur.

She shrugs. "Yup."

"I'm sorry for yelling at you."

With a light laugh, she does that damn eye roll thing again. I'm beginning to realize it's a defense mechanism. She's uncomfortable or unsure. There's a story there, and one day I'll get her to tell me. One day I'll get all the answers. But not today. "It's okay. I didn't realize you didn't know who Noah was to me."

"Are you guys close?"

She smiles. "Yeah. I'm close with all my stepbrothers, but Noah's dad was married to my mom when I was in high school, so we lived together during my teenage years. That quintessential time when everything just felt like more, ya know?"

I nod. Until Mills moved to Paris a couple of years ago, she and I had spent our entire lives nearly attached to one another. And since she came back to Boston, we live in the same building, and she travels with the team quite a bit, so though she's got a family, we're still damn close.

"Is he really going to kill me?"

An adorable little snort escapes her. "Not if you pick up breakfast for me."

"Should I get him something?"

She shakes her head. "You know what? I'd actually rather not do the whole meet-the-family thing this morning. Give me five, and I'll come with you."

I nod. That's good. Great even. Because yeah, I may be ready for almost everything that's been thrown at me, but given the bullshit that keeps flowing from my mouth, the last thing I need to do is have a conversation with Noah this morning.

# CALLIOPE'S COLUMN



## Who Woulda Thought Men Would Care So Much About Clothes?

I'm pretty sure athletes are built different. No, I'm not talking about their muscles or their stamina, although that can be pretty fucking impressive. No, what I'm talking about is the thing they have for clothing. Take hockey players, for instance. The men can wear the hell out of a suit. Other men—like baseball players—don't give two shits about what they wear from the stadium to the plane. But hockey players? They've got special shoes and ties. They style their hair and don the cockiest smirks, knowing that everyone they come across is drooling over the way their pants stretch across their thighs.

And the one thing they're even more feral about? Who's wearing their jersey. *And who's not.*

You want to see whether a hockey man is interested in you? Put on another man's jersey. Holy shit. I had a front-row seat the day one gal wore her husband's friend's jersey to a game. Safe to say he ripped it from her body and replaced it with his own. *My wife, my jersey.* Yeah. That was hot.

But let me tell you, *experiencing* it firsthand? Way hotter.

This hockey player took one look at the jersey I was wearing—one with another man's name emblazoned on the back—and suddenly, I was shoved into a closet, and I didn't leave until I'd received the best orgasm of my life. All because of the name on my back.

Speaking of that night. If a gal goes for a second round with her one-night stand, and maybe a third, does that make it a relationship? What if they just keep sleeping together without putting a label on what they're doing? Can it be considered a continuation of a one-night stand? Asking for a friend.

90

# Chapter 14
## Hannah

Daniel: How are you feeling?

Me: I'm good.

*Two hours later*

Daniel: How are you feeling?

Me: still good.

*A few hours later*

Daniel: Still feeling okay?

Me: I'm fine. Thanks.

Like a tiny tornado, Oliver scrambles into the kitchen holding up a card and wearing the biggest smile on his face. "Dad is taking me to Disney World!"

With as much faux surprise as I can muster, I widen my eyes and let my jaw go slack. *"No way.* Does that mean I'll get the television all to myself this weekend?"

Oliver folds his arms across his chest and grunts. "You control the TV even when I'm here."

A chuckle escapes me. He's right. I refuse to watch cartoons or YouTube videos. SportsCenter feels too much like work, and no one in their right mind should watch the news. That shit is just depressing.

"Don't lie. You like watching Joanna Gaines just as much as I do."

Yup, I force my four-year-old nephew to watch home DIY shows with me. When I was a kid, we never stayed anywhere long enough to develop that sense of home. Even now, there are no pictures on my walls, no memories stashed away. I don't think my mother has a single photo album from my childhood.

Since Noah and Oliver moved in, I've become acutely aware of how different his parenting is from that of my mother's. Then again, it makes sense. His father has photos galore all over his apartment. He even has one of me with Noah at his graduation.

A dull ache throbs in my chest. What type of mom will I be? Will any of that stuff come naturally?

I'll probably be the clueless, delusional type. So far, since I took the pregnancy tests last week, all I've done is ignore everything pregnancy related.

I'm also doing an excellent job of avoiding Daniel.

Can't say my mother never taught me anything.

I clearly inherited her natural tendency toward avoidance and an inability to communicate. Excellent.

To be fair, the man has texted me the same couple of words every few hours, every single day, for the last week. It's awkward. And annoying. I'm fine. Okay, maybe not totally fine, but mostly. I'm not nauseous, I'm not showing. I'm just a woman who can no longer have coffee, alcohol, or sex with strangers.

Basically, I'm no longer me. But still, I'm fine!

"I do love Joanna, but I miss cartoons."

Noah laughs as he joins us in the kitchen. "Are the two of you arguing about the TV again?"

Oliver is incredibly smart for his age. So smart I wonder how he puts up with the rest of us.

"Oliver was just telling me about your trip to Disney."

Noah ruffles his son's silky brown hair, and the little boy peers up at him with a look of total adoration. "*Dad.*"

With a smile down at the kid, he heads for the coffeepot. It's ridiculous, really, but I'm still brewing a pot of regular coffee in order to keep up appearances. Even at work, I use the same coffee pods I always have to avoid drawing attention to the change in my routine. It should be a crime, pouring out so many cups of perfectly good coffee.

"When are you headed out again?" Noah asks as he spins around, holding a coffee cup out to me.

I hold out a hand. "Had one already, thanks. Trying to cut down on my caffeine."

He lets out a loud laugh. "Right. You, not drinking coffee?" He shakes his head and gives me a sly grin.

Ugh. He's so right. I live for coffee. And alcohol. And sex.

Not that I can't have sex. The issue is that the only person I want to have it with right now is the man I'm avoiding.

"We leave for Chicago on Sunday."

"Damn. That's the day we get home from Disney." He sighs.

"I know. My schedule sucks." It truly does. During the season, I bounce from place to place constantly. Though I technically live in Boston, I don't spend more than four days at a time here during baseball season. And the season is *long*. We travel from March through the end of September. If the Revs play well enough, they sometimes travel until the end of October. And the team owns me. I go where they go.

It's exhausting, but I love it.

Or I did.

Last season felt longer than any other before. And soon, my whole life will be changing. I'll show in the not-so-distant future, right? Will I get sick? Will my feet swell? Will I have pregnancy brain and be unable to do my job effectively?

As well as I've avoided most things, I have forced myself to do some reading on what's safe during pregnancy, and the long list of symptoms I came across during that research could very easily make my job a challenge. It seems pregnancy and parenthood don't mix well with the type of job that requires a person to travel for six months out of the year.

And motherhood sounds even less conducive to that.

Just another set of thoughts to avoid for the time being.

"Wish you could come to Disney," Oliver pouts.

Noah laughs again. "That is not your aunt's scene." He eyes me over his cup of coffee. "Kids. Rides. Family time." He shudders, though he's grinning. "Her worst nightmare."

I roll my eyes. He's not wrong. But still…I guess I may need to change that. Right?

"I can't believe the season is over." Millie lets out a long sigh.

Dinner tonight is a subdued affair. The guys lost their game against Detroit last week, which brought the season to an end. They've got seven weeks of freedom before preseason training begins in August, and for a lot of them, that means they'll be leaving Boston. But the guys whose wives and girlfriends are sitting around this table with me will stay in town and be home much, much more.

Lennox smiles. "I, for one, was over it. Aiden was too damn busy. I'm excited to have him in bed with me every night for the next few months."

"Same," Ava agrees. "Especially since we have some news."

Hand resting on my hip, I turn to my best friend. Before she goes on, I know what she's going to say. I assess her stomach, looking for changes. It doesn't look any different, but as if on instinct, she brings a hand to it.

That's all the confirmation I need.

Even so, I lean in close. "You're pregnant?"

Green eyes glistening, she dips her chin. "We wanted to wait until the whole crew was in town before we told everyone."

"Oh my god!" Lennox hoots.

Sara scrambles out of her chair and around the table and pulls Ava into a tight hug.

When she releases her, Millie is there taking her place.

Then it's my turn. I pull my best friend into my arms. "I'm so happy for you."

I truly am. Ava is such an amazing mom to the girls she and War adopted, and to Brayden, the teenage boy who isn't legally theirs but might as well be. This child will be just as blessed as its three older siblings. Ava's challenging childhood—War's too—makes this even sweeter.

Ava squeezes me back. "Me too."

"When are you due?" Millie asks.

"November seventh."

"Wow," I rasp, bringing a hand to my lips.

I've done the calculations, and if I'm correct, I'm due in January, which means Ava and I will be pregnant together. We'll have kids the same age. Our children could grow up to be best friends, just like us. If I weren't so emotionally stunted, maybe I'd share this information with the group.

"I've got news too," Millie says.

"Oh no. Not you too," I mutter without thinking. My chest constricts tightly. Shit. I'm not sure I can take another big announcement. This week has been full of surprises.

Sara snorts. "Took the words right out of my mouth."

Millie shakes her head, but she's smiling. "We've decided we want to try for another baby. I thought I wanted to wait until I was a bit older, but with Gavin being in his forties already—"

"That sexy silver fox Hockey Daddy," Lennox coos.

Millie giggles. "Yeah, that. And it might be nice for Vivi to have a sibling closer in age."

Ava nods. "That's how I felt. I love the idea of Scarlett and this baby only being three years apart."

"Yeah, I'm sure that's what you were thinking when you were begging War to bang you against the door."

Ava turns a rosy pink and hisses, "Hannah."

I laugh. "What? We all know how babies are made. Not one of you is innocent."

Sara dances in her seat, one hand raised. "Guilty. But no babies for me anytime soon. Thank god we've got you, Han. We can always depend on you to be the fun auntie who drinks cocktails with us and talks about dirty sex."

I hold up the glass of liquid I paid the server to make look like a dirty martini and dip my chin. "That's me. The inappropriate auntie."

And the in-denial future mom.

# CHAPTER 15
# DANIEL

It's been seven days. Seven days since I left Hannah after breakfast. Seven days since she's responded to my texts with anything more than *I'm fine*. It's been seven days since we found out we were going to be parents and seven days since she basically ghosted me.

We lost in Detroit, and the season officially ended. Normally I would have gone out and lost myself in alcohol and women. Yes, women.

My reputation never bothered me before. Only in the last month has it hit me that it's a hurdle I'll have to overcome to get Hannah to trust me.

I never believed my dad when he swore that one day it would get old. That one day I'd only care about one woman, and her opinion would be all that mattered.

I never cared what people thought of me. At least not when it came to my reputation off the ice. On the ice? That's different. I've always cared, and I've always worked my ass off.

But now—well, fuck. Now I care more about what Hannah thinks than what Gavin or even my father does.

And that's a big fucking problem since she won't give me the time of day, let alone the opportunity to change her opinion.

Yeah, maybe I asked her how she was feeling one too many times.

But what else was I supposed to say? I was doing my best not to make a fool of myself. I want her to know I'm thinking about her. That I didn't just stop caring about her the second we parted ways last week. But I can't exactly make that known if she won't pick up the damn phone.

The number of times I considered showing up at her apartment this week is embarrassing. I went so far as to get in my car and head for her apartment. I got halfway there before turning around. I'm not ready to deal with Noah. It was bad enough that the way he looked at me changed instantly. I tried to sit down next to him, but before I could, he shook his head. "Focus on the game, Playboy. Talk to me after we win." We didn't. So I didn't.

But if Noah is as important to Hannah as Millie is to me, then I need to make time for that conversation soon.

"Earth to Daniel." Camden waves his hand in front of my face.

Clearly this is not the first time he's said my name. Feigning a calm I don't feel, I dip my chin. "What?"

"You want a shot? That hot blonde sent them over." He points in the direction of a group of women. Smack dab in the middle of them, a beautiful blonde is watching us. Her tits are spilling from her top, her lips are glossy, and her eyes dance with promises of an enjoyable night.

I turn away. "That's all yours."

"She looks like she could be both of ours." Cam tosses back the shot. "What the fuck, Hall? You've been a fucking nun since you got that piercing. Maybe that's why you played like such shit this season. Your dick's off balance."

I shove him, though I can't help but laugh. "My game was not the problem."

Cam holds up his hands. "I know. I know. But seriously, when was the last time you got your dick wet?" He glances at the blonde again, brow lifted in obvious interest.

"Like I said, she's all yours."

My body feels heavy, deflated, as I sip my beer and scan the bar. Brooks, War, and Aiden are here too, sitting in a corner, quietly talking. Every thirty seconds or so, one of them glances at the door.

Suddenly feeling a tiny bit lighter, I turn to Camden. "Do you know if the wives are coming?"

He bows his head and sighs. "Tell me you don't have a thing for one of them and that's why your dick stopped working this year. You can't fuck a wife."

Head dropped back, I groan. "Did you get hit too hard this season? You're fucked in the head."

He shrugs. "I'm just trying to figure out what the hell is wrong with you. You've been quiet all fucking week. You haven't come out. Where the hell have you been?"

I've been hanging out at my dad's house in Bristol, spending time with my one-year-old brother, trying to wrap my head around the idea that I'll have a baby of my own in a few months.

I haven't told my dad yet. Figure Hannah probably wants me to keep it quiet. But I'm going out of my fucking mind. I need to talk to someone.

But not Camden Snow. He's the last person I would talk to about this. He'd whine about how all of our teammates have settled down and now I've gone and knocked up the one girl who probably doesn't even want to be a mom.

He wouldn't be wrong about that last part. It's obvious Hannah's struggling with the idea of being a parent. Maybe I'm an asshole, but I'm thankful as fuck that she's the one I'm doing this with. There's not a single other person in the world I'd want to be the mother of my child. And that's fucked, because I'm pretty sure I'm the last guy she'd choose to father hers.

Hopeless. It's all so fucking hopeless.

"Just spent time with my family. Haven't gotten to see Nash much since the season started, and he was tiny back then. I want the kid to know my name."

Cam sobers. His family situation is shitty. I know the issues center around his sister, but that's about all he's ever shared. If there is one thing that can ground Cam, it's the mention of siblings. "Nice." He turns toward the girls and mouths a "thank you, be over soon." Then he zeroes in on me. "I got a call from Sam."

"Oh yeah?" Sam's his agent.

"Yeah, he said Vegas is still sniffing around. They're looking for a few guys to rebuild the team."

This isn't news. Cam is from Vegas. Last year when we played there, he mentioned this. The team's new owner is willing to spend a substantial amount of money to rebuild a team that has had years of losses. "They want us." Cam's blue eyes are extra sharp, as if he's reading my reaction.

I smile. "Of course they do. We're awesome."

He shakes his head. "I'm serious. Think about it: Noah still has years. War too. We're not going to be the stars of this team until we're at the tail end of our careers."

A sense of defeat I typically keep locked away finds its way out and slithers through me. Even so, I play it cool. "We get equal play."

"But we're not first line."

"There's really no difference."

It's a lie. Yeah, the second line plays almost as much as the first, but no longer playing with Aiden feels like a demotion.

Camden knows this. "That's bullshit. You deserve to be the center of attention. You know it and I know it. What Gavin did this year was shit."

I grind my teeth. "He's married to my sister."

He scoffs, straightening beside me. "And he essentially demoted you."

The barely noticeable ache in my chest flares, but I keep my mouth shut.

"Just think about it. We could help build a team. We'd be the stars. Here, it's all about the Langfields; there, *we'd* be the gods."

"My family is here," I bite out. "My sister *is* a Langfield."

"Right. But you're not." He taps his glass against mine. "I'm going to get the blonde. Offer's still open." With a smirk, he stands. "Both of them. Come with me. *Play* with me." The innuendo is clear. His proposition isn't just about hockey. No, it includes letting loose for the night with the blonde who is clearly interested in both of us.

I don't even have to think about my response. Both of my *no*s are centered around Hannah. Because when I say my family is here, that includes her now too.

"I'm all set. But have fun." I clap him on the back and turn, ready to go hang with the other guys.

Only when I'm on my feet do I realize they're surrounded by women.

But these women are of a different variety, and one of them is the person I've been waiting for.

Hannah.

It's time we had a conversation. And tonight, I won't let her ignore me.

# Chapter 16
## Hannah

I'M NEVER UNCOMFORTABLE. I LIVE BY THE MOTTO THAT I BELONG IN EVERY room. Every person I encounter is lucky to be in my presence. Even if the wives and girlfriends are the ones with excuses to be here—it's their guys who just finished their season, after all—I've never once questioned what I bring to the table. Even as a seventh wheel.

But tonight I'm questioning why the hell I thought it was a good idea to tag along. I can't drink, and hiding that fact is more work than I like. I'm exhausted. Pregnancy is kicking my ass, and the baby is probably only the size of my thumb.

Actually, I have no idea how big the baby is. Once I searched for safety guidelines for pregnancy—and accidentally stumbled upon the daunting list of symptoms—I stopped researching.

Denial. That's where I'm living.

And in my own personal hell. Because while I'm seventh-wheeling, Daniel is sitting at the bar with Camden Snow, accepting shots from a gorgeous blonde on the other side of the room. When he straightens and checks her out, I worry I might be sick.

Swallowing back bile, I tug on Ava's arm. "I think I'm going to go."

"What? Why? I never come out." She pouts. "Please. Just one more drink?"

I laugh. "You can't even drink."

She eyes me. "Then I'll just have the kind of *drink* you had at dinner." The serious glint in her usually so kind eyes has me squirming.

And I never squirm.

I'm turning into a person I don't recognize, and I don't like it. I blame the pregnancy.

Fuck this. I'm not hiding anymore.

"Fine, let's get a mocktail." I loop my arm through hers and drag her to the bar, parking myself right next to the woman who just bought my baby daddy a shot. "Oh, tequila. Love that," I say to her as the bartender pours another round of shots for her and her friends.

The girl side-eyes me, her lips turned down in confusion. "Yeah, it's good."

"Not as good as that guy over there is with his tongue." I nod toward Daniel, who now has his back to us as he and Cam talk.

Ava digs her nails into my arm and forces me to look at her. "What are you doing?"

"Just telling my new friend here how great our hockey boys are." I grin at the girl. "Rumor has it he's even pierced."

The woman bites down on her bottom lip, eyes flashing as she darts a look at Daniel.

Before I can continue, Ava drags me away from the bar. She doesn't stop until we're tucked into a corner alone. "What the heck is wrong with you?"

Shoulders pulled back, I lift my chin. "I have no idea what you're talking about."

Without speaking, she zeroes in on me, using some kind of weird mom power to get me to talk. I may need lessons.

"She was pretty and clearly interested." I wave a dismissive hand. "Just doing the guys a favor by putting in a good word."

"Good with his tongue?" She crosses her arms. "You only know that because you hooked up with him." Her eyes widen, and she sucks in a breath. "It's almost like you're jealous."

I cough out a laugh. "I'm never jealous."

Ava lifts one brow, her lips quirking along with it. "Exactly. But that's obviously changed recently."

I open my mouth to deny it, but the words get stuck in my throat. So I let out a long huff of a breath instead. "I don't want to talk about it yet."

Her expression softens. "We don't have to talk about anything. Just —" She grasps my hand and squeezes. "Don't push the guy you're interested in off on someone else because you're scared."

My stomach sinks. That's so not what this is about. But I don't argue. It's easier to let her believe that than to explain that it's easier to push Daniel away now and plan a future where we're just co-parents than to get attached and lose him later. We aren't destined for a happily ever after. Perfect endings are reserved for fictional characters in fairy tales, though my friends are clearly living theirs, that's not in the cards for me. We're going to raise our child together, and in order to do that, we need to be friends. Nothing more.

And friends look out for one another.

Friends play wingman.

I can be an excellent wingman.

But Ava's right. I'm not feeling it tonight.

Chest aching, I drop my arms to my sides. "Can I go now?"

Ava nods. "Yeah, I'm pretty sure Ty wants to hang out a while longer, but if you need a ride, we could run you home and then come back."

I laugh. "I'm a big girl, Ave. I can get myself home."

She pulls me in for a hug. "I know you can take care of yourself. It's just that you don't always have to. It's okay to let your friends help out sometimes. We *want* to."

Arm in arm, we walk back to the table. Though I prefer taking care of myself, I can't deny it feels good to know there are people in this world who genuinely care about me.

As we approach our friends, she grabs War's attention—as if she didn't have it the entire time we were gone—and motions to me. "Can we take Hannah home? We can come back if you're not ready to call it a night."

With tattoos up and down his arms, the Bolts captain can be intimidating, but the moment he looks at his wife, he's all mush. "Course, Vicious. I wouldn't mind a few hours alone with my wife anyway."

I open my mouth and stick a finger into it, making a gagging sound. "You guys are adorable, but seriously, go have sex or do whatever married people do. I can grab an Uber."

"I got her." My heart thumps in the most ridiculous way at the sound of the voice behind me.

I spin, and a heartbeat later, he grasps my hip, practically pissing on me in a ridiculous grown-up version of calling *dibs*.

"Aw, Baby Hall, I don't want to take you from your playtime," I say, my tone disgustingly sweet.

Despite my best efforts, I instantly lose myself in the deep brown eyes of my baby daddy. My heart rate picks up, and suddenly, it's hard to breathe. And the place where he's still touching me? It's aflame.

Daniel gives me a look that says *oh, we're doing this?*

I simply hold his gaze.

"The only person I want to play with is standing right here."

Ava and Lennox snicker beside me. It takes a shit ton of effort not to glare at them.

"But I put in such a good word for you with the Barbie over there." I nod to the bar where Camden is already deep—and I mean that figuratively, because the flirty looks they're both wearing scream *shallow*—in conversation.

"Yeah, I'm all set with that." He holds my stare, his jaw rigid.

Our friends are silent, and though I don't dare look at them, I can feel every eye locked on us, like they're all waiting for the fireworks to start.

"I'm not in the mood," I grit out.

"It's true," Lennox says from nearby. "She's been in a funk all night."

Before I can turn to her, Daniel leans in and presses his lips to my neck, sending shivers streaking through me. "That's because my girl is needy, and she's been depriving herself."

"Oh, that is totally a thing," Lennox agrees. "I call it hagitated. Horny and agitated. You just need an orgasm or two to set you right."

Straightening, Daniel raises his brows, his attention all on me.

I bite my lip as I try to keep from laughing. "Can I use that in a book? That's gold."

"What is happening here?" Sara says, her voice a little too loud.

Finally, I look away from Daniel, the spell his touch put on me evaporating.

"Nothing. I'm just leaving."

"Yes. With me." The bane of my existence leans across me, one arm still holding me in place and the other outstretched toward War. "I'll get her home. Great first season, Cap. Proud to be on your team."

With a look at me, War slips his hand into Daniel's and smiles. "Take care of *our* girl."

The fucker still clinging to me chuckles as he tugs me away. "My girl, but thanks for caring about her."

As soon as we step outside, I shrug him off. "What the hell was that?"

"Hi, sweetheart," he says, his tone a strange mix of forced sweetness and irritation. "It's nice to see you too. Thanks for returning all my phone calls. I really appreciated that."

I huff out a breath and come to a stop on the sidewalk. "This isn't funny. Now everyone's going to know."

With a purely unaffected shrug, he says, "You didn't seem to care about that when you were screaming my name in Arizona."

My cheeks heat. Dammit. What is wrong with me? I never blush. "That was before."

His jaw tightens, and for the first time tonight, the cocky playboy persona fades. Gone is the smooth man with all the lines. This man is something else entirely. Earnest, serious...hurt? No, that can't be it. I can't quite put my finger on it.

"Yeah, Hannah. Before." He presses closer, engulfing me in his warm, smoky scent. "Before we walked through that pharmacy together and picked out pregnancy tests. Before we found out we're going to be parents." He huffs out a breath and shakes his head. "As in us. You and me. So yeah, I know all those people"—he nods at the door to the bar—"mean a lot to you, but I should mean something too. At least enough to deserve a return phone call."

The words hang between us, and a truckload of shame rolls through me.

"I'm sorry."

Hands in his pockets, he only watches me, waiting for me to elaborate.

I look back toward the bar. On the other side of the window, our friends have gone back to their conversations. Laughing and happy, completely unaffected, while my world has been turned upside down. He's right. He's likely the only person who would have noticed if I'd walked out of that bar without saying goodbye. I should have more respect for him than what I've shown. "I'm having a hard time wrapping my mind around all of this. I"—I shake my head—"I'm not good at this."

Daniel frowns, ducking his head and meeting my eye. "Neither of us is good at this. We just found out, Hannah. Give yourself some grace."

"No, I mean relationships." I shrug. "Regardless of how casual. Considering another person's feelings." I look away from him again. "There's never been a person in my life who's expected me to check in regularly. No one has ever really cared what I'm doing on a day-to-day basis."

No one. Not my mother. Certainly not my father. Sure, my stepdads check in from time to time and my brothers are great, but they're all living busy lives. They check in when they can, but not on any regular schedule.

And outside of a very short, horribly cliché marriage and divorce in college, I have never been in a long-term relationship.

Daniel's dark eyes are fathomless as he assesses me. Like he wishes he could read my mind. But what I've given him already is a hell of a lot more than I've shared with anyone else, and it's all I can get through tonight.

He squeezes my hand and takes half a step closer. "Well, I care. I'm probably going to fuck up a lot." His throat bobs as he swallows. "But if you could just talk to me, that's all I need."

*"Daniel."* My heart pangs painfully. He deserves so much more than that.

With a press of his finger to my lips, he shakes his head. "I can't promise that any of the things I'll say will be clever or right or will make you feel better—in fact, I'll probably babble stream-ofconscious style most of the time and make you question why you're with me…"

I inhale, ready to tell him that I'm not *with* him, but with a narrowing of his eye, he's got me squeezing my lips shut, allowing him to finish.

"But I will talk to you. And that's all I ask of you. Talk to me, Hannah. It's the only way we're going to get through this."

How the hell did I get so lucky? And why has it taken me this long to realize how wonderful this man is? I point to my mouth, and when he removes his finger, I tilt my head. "Can I do that talking thing now?"

He smiles. "Yes, dream girl."

"I have an OB appointment tomorrow. Would you like to come?"

His smile widens so much I can't imagine it doesn't hurt. "I would love to."

"The baby is probably so small we won't even see anything—"

He wraps his arm around me and leads me down the street. "Baby Hall is the size of a grape."

"What?"

With a laugh, he pulls me in closer. "I typed in the date we were in Arizona into this app I downloaded. According to it, the baby is about the size of a grape."

I lift up my thumb and study it. Kind of the same size. Hmm, maybe I do have this mom intuition thing down.

Daniel grasps my hand and kisses it. "What are you thinking about?"

I lace my fingers with his, and while we walk home together, I tell him. Then I tell him about my week. And how I'm feeling. And I make a vow to myself that I'll keep telling him things. Because he's right: that's the only way this is going to work.

# CHAPTER 17
# DANIEL

MY STOMACH FLIPS AS I PULL UP TO HANNAH'S APARTMENT. I'M EARLY. Like thirty minutes early. I didn't want to risk running into traffic or end up having trouble finding parking—yes, it's midday in Boston, so it's probably not actually a concern, but I couldn't stop stressing about it. We're going to see the baby this morning. Our baby.

I did a lot of research online after I left Hannah's last night. Apparently, they typically collect a urine sample to confirm the pregnancy at the first appointment. And depending on how far along the mother is, they may use the doppler to hear the baby's heartbeat.

The minute I read that, my own heartbeat took off. Because from the sound of things, we're far enough into the pregnancy for that. Today we could hear our child's heart. A baby that is mine and Hannah's. My future best friend.

I hope I'm as good of a father as mine is. I hope—fuck, I hope so many things. But really, I just hope our baby is healthy. That everything goes okay today. That Hannah smiles.

My phone rings and I practically jump, feeling caught. Can she see me sitting down here? She probably thinks I'm a fucking stalker, but I figured I'd wait here rather than text her to let her know I arrived and risk rushing her. It's my fault I have to wait, not hers.

But when my dad's name flashes across the screen, I relax and pick up. "Hey, Dad."

"How was last night?"

"It was good. Ending the season that way sucks, but we all need this break."

My father laughs. "Yeah, I'm sure your legs could all use a few weeks on the beach."

I hum, scanning the front of the apartment building. "How are Nash and Lake?"

"They're good. We're going to Miami for Melina's first show next weekend."

"No shit," I laugh. "Fitz must be stoked."

He didn't come out with us last night. Not that he comes out much anymore anyway. Our goalie coach is dating Lake's best friend, who just so happens to be an international popstar. The third member of their throuple is Fitz's longtime best friend turned partner. The guy is the fire chief in Bristol, where my dad lives.

"Yeah, he and Declan flew down with Melina yesterday. I think they're spending a couple of days together before the tour starts."

A chuckle breaks loose. "Bet he's not all that sad our season is over."

"You sound good. Glad you aren't sinking into the depression some guys face during the offseason."

I'm back to watching the building when Hannah steps out. Her long brown hair is pulled up, and she's in a pair of jeans and a white shirt. The woman makes even the simplest outfits look incredible. When she catches sight of me, her face lights up.

"Nothing but good vibes here," I say to my dad as Hannah tilts her head, as if noticing that I'm on the phone, and offers a little finger wave. "I gotta go."

"Okay, kid. Let me know when you're coming down to Bristol again. Miss you."

"Miss you too." As I push the door open, I call out a "bye, Dad" and hit End.

"Aww." Hannah's eyes light up. "You talking to Daddy Hall?"

I round the car and grab her by the ass, pulling her in for a hug. "I'm your only Daddy Hall."

Hannah snorts. "You aren't *my* Daddy anything." Lips twisting, she hums. "Well, maybe my baby daddy."

With a growl, I squeeze her ass cheeks again. God, I like touching her. And I'm fucking ecstatic that she's letting me without an ounce of hesitation. "Not a fan of that term either."

Pushing away from me, she laughs. "Too bad. It's Baby Hall or baby daddy."

I shake my head as I pull her door open. "You sleep okay?"

Her face softens, and she keeps her focus on me as she eases into her seat. "Yeah, I slept okay. You?"

I have to grip the door to keep myself from ducking in and buckling her seat belt for her. Instead, I settle for watching her do it. Once she's safely tucked into my car, I nod. "Slept great."

I don't tell her that I fell asleep watching baby vlogs. The one created by a group of dads hooked me right away. I went all the way back to the first episode and started there.

The ride to the doctor's office is quick, and it isn't until I'm pulling in that I realize I was so lost in my head—trying to come up with conversation topics and worrying about making it awkward—that I haven't said a word since I pulled away from the curb.

Once the car is in park, I clear my throat, ready to apologize, but she's already getting out. I reach into the back seat and snag the gift I brought, now worried that she'll think it's weird.

But she's having my baby. It feels monumental. Like it should be celebrated.

I stare down at the bag and grimace. Fuck. What was I thinking? I should have gotten her jewelry or, I don't know, a car? What kind of gifts are appropriate for the woman carrying my child? It all feels like it's so much. Honestly, every time I'm near her, I have to fight the urge not to drop down at her feet to thank her or scoop her up and carry her around.

But not a single woman arriving for her own appointment is being carried in by her man, so I shake off the ridiculous thoughts and scurry after her, gripping the bag behind my back. I should have left it in the car.

By the time I get inside, Hannah is at the front desk, checking in. She motions me to sit, and although I want to go over there and hand my credit card over to pay for everything, I honestly have no fucking idea how any of this works, so I obey, finding two empty seats together, my knee bouncing as I wait for her.

"First time?" a guy sitting on the other side of a small coffee table asks. He's facing me, waiting just like I am. Probably for his wife.

I nod. "Yeah, you?"

His lips tip up. "Nope. Fourth time."

"Fourth visit to the doctor?"

That gets a chuckle from him. "Fourth child."

"Shit," I hiss.

"You'll be fine." With that, he holds his phone up and scrolls, ending the conversation.

I'm considering asking if he's seen any of the baby vlogs when Hannah sits next to me. "She said it shouldn't be too long."

I turn my whole body to face her, taking in her pensive expression. "It's okay. I've got nowhere else to be today."

She forces a smile. "I have a plane to catch later."

Gut sinking, I deflate a little. "Oh, right. Your season isn't over."

She chuckles, though there's nothing humorous about it. "No. We're just getting started."

"Where are you off to?"

"Philly, then Tampa. Then we're back for a series, then—" She hums, lips twisted. "I think after that, we're in Cali, but don't quote me."

I laugh. "Got it. Do you like it?"

Her eyes widen, the blue of her irises sparkling in the light of the waiting area. "My job?"

"The travel."

"Oh." She shrugs. "Yeah, I do. Though now that I'm tired twenty-four hours a day, I'm not sure how I'll handle it."

"Oh!" I say, a bolt of excitement running through me. "I've got something for that." Bending down, I pull out the bag that I've hidden beneath my chair.

"What's this?" Brows pulled together, she studies the pastel pink and blue bag I hold out to her.

I shrug. "Just a few things I picked up for you. Not a gift, because who would buy a gift for the woman they knocked up?" I chuckle but snap my mouth shut when I realize I sound like Ross from *Friends*. "But also, like, kind of a gift, because, obviously, you deserve all the gifts. Just not only this stuff."

Hannah's lips tip up in a half smile. "You freaking out a bit, Baby Hall?"

I blow out a breath. "That obvious?"

Her expression turns into a full-on grin. "Can you keep a secret?"

I nod. Hell, yeah, and I'm frickin' elated that she's willing to share one with me.

"I am too."

The way her blue eyes appear almost translucent in this moment, like she's just as emotional, just as in over her head, and just as in *this* as me, sends a calming warmth through me.

"Let's see what we've got here." The spell is broken as she reaches into the bag and pulls out a bottle of prenatal vitamins.

"I'm sure you've already got them, but I figure you can't have too many vitamins—" I shake my head. "Actually I should probably google that. Maybe it's possible you can."

With a giggle, she places her hand on my perpetually bouncing knee. "I don't have any. Thank you. And I'll make sure to ask the nurse if it's possible to take too many."

Sighing, I settle back in my seat. "Right. Because we're at the doctor's office. Definitely better than Google." As she pulls out the next gift, I point to it. "That's the tea Lake liked to drink while she was pregnant. She said it helped with her heartburn."

Hannah stiffens, her focus zeroing in on me.

"I didn't tell her." I hold up both hands. "I just remember seeing her drinking it a lot, so when I saw it on the shelf near the prenatal vitamins, I grabbed it."

Hannah smiles softly. "You can tell your family if you want. It's not just happening to me. I get that now. It was unfair to keep you out of the loop this past week. And I shouldn't have made the decision to keep this quiet without your input. I'll do better."

I dip my chin, keeping my mouth shut. I'm done talking, since everything I say comes out all crazy-sounding.

She picks up the next item and tilts her head, a frown marring her gorgeous face. "Is this a butt plug?"

My mouth falls open as I scan the room. There are four couples scattered around the space, and every one of them is staring at us. I didn't notice before, probably because I was too focused on my own insanity. "No." I shake my head and lean closer, voice a low whisper. "It's to put on nipple cream."

"Nipple cream?" she practically shouts.

The woman across from us glares over her magazine.

"Oh, fuck," I mutter, which only makes her scoff. Hand held up, I wince. "Sorry."

Hannah shoves my hand into my lap and glares right back at the woman.

"We're in a doctor's office, and you're pregnant, because guess what? You fucked. Get over it."

With a huff, the woman stands and storms to the other side of the waiting area. A moment later, the man with her eases out of his chair and slinks over too.

Hannah turns back to me without a care in the world. "Continue."

"You're kind of a badass," I whisper.

Those pretty peach lips of hers lift in a wide smile. "Thank you." She holds up the nipple cream applicator. "So nipple cream?"

"I read that they can get sore. This numbs them."

She laughs. "Cool. Thanks."

"There's one more thing—"

The door next to the check-in window opens, and a nurse in blue scrubs calls Hannah's name.

We both straighten, the heaviness of the moment returning.

I'm thankful for the few minutes we've had together. I may have embarrassed the shit out of myself, but it was worth it just to see her smile.

# Chapter 18
## Hannah

"This is easily the strangest first date I've ever been on," I say as the woman leads us into the room.

I just peed in a cup while Daniel stood in the hall outside the door. Again.

The nurse giggles, but Daniel's eyes widen.

"This is not our first date," he murmurs when she turns toward the computer.

I shrug. "If you say so."

He steps closer. "I took you to dinner the night we—" He waves his hands. "You know."

"The night we fucked?"

The nurse is still turned away, but she stiffens, and the clacking of her fingers on the keyboard stops.

Oops. Oh well.

Daniel huffs. "No. The night we—"

"The night you knocked me up?" I grin. "It's okay, Baby Hall. She knows we had sex. That's why we're here, after all."

He exhales loudly through his nose, his jaw pulsing. "You like pushing me, don't you?"

I smile. Yeah, I really do. It's the one fun thing I've got going on right now. Also, if I don't tease him a bit, all his sweetness will get to me. The present? Adorable. The way he showed up thirty minutes early and sat in his car? Not expected.

That's what he is. Unexpected. At every turn.

The tongue, the dick, the sweetness. The way he reacted when I blurted out that we could be pregnant. How he held me that night. All of it. Every minute since the night of our first date—yes, I'm aware it was a date; doesn't mean I can't tease him—has been a surprise.

A very pleasant one.

But I've reached my limit when it comes to surprises. The pregnancy itself is too much. I can't allow myself to get sucked into a fantasy.

Eventually he'll tire of my sarcasm, of my need to push him—just like every one of my stepfathers did with my mother. So when that happens, it'll be better for the baby and me if we're prepared.

"I'll step out so you can change into that gown." The nurse nods at the faded piece of fabric folded on the white paper covering the exam table. "Leave it open in the front. The doctor will be in shortly."

She's gone quickly, probably running for cover, and Daniel settles into a chair, one leg bent at the knee and the other kicked out, his entire focus set on me.

"Not going to offer to turn around?" I tease as I start to strip. I have no shame. He knows that.

His pupils dilate, making his irises look even darker, though his expression remains impassive. It's annoyingly hot. "Nothing I haven't seen."

I pull my jeans off and toss them onto the empty chair beside him. Immediately, he picks them up and folds them neatly.

He takes my shirt before I can toss it as well. Just as I'm backing up to hoist myself onto the exam table, he's behind me. With warm hands on my hips, he skirts around me and lifts me with ease.

For a moment, we're frozen like that: my breaths shallow, his lips parted. Only when a knock sounds from the door do we startle back into reality.

I clear my throat and find my voice, letting the doctor know I'm decent, and a heartbeat later, she strides in, attention fixed on a chart.

And still, my body buzzes. The touch was simple, gentle, quick, but the effect is clearly long-lasting.

"Are you dad?" She smiles at Daniel.

With a nod, he holds out his hand and introduces himself.

She points to a spot near my shoulder. "I'm going to examine her, but if you want to stand over there, you'll be in a good spot."

I blow out a breath as he saunters closer again, eyes locked on me. With every step he takes, the tension in the room ratchets up.

When the doctor turns to her computer, he leans down and brings his lips to my ear. "If it makes it easier for you to push me, I'll play along. But I'm not going anywhere."

With a squeeze of my hand, he backs off. Rather than anger or cockiness, all I see in his expression is open honesty. He sees right through me. He knows I use sarcasm to hide my nerves, my insecurities. He doesn't know the details of the emotional damage of my childhood, but it doesn't matter. He sees me. He understands.

Shit.

"Based on your HCG levels, you're about seven weeks. That means you're far enough along for a sonogram if you want to see the baby."

Daniel angles forward, his hand splayed between my shoulder blades. "Oh, we can get a picture of the baby this way, right?"

I study him over my shoulder. "How do you know that?"

He's still staring at the machine when he replies. "The guys on the vlog talked about it."

"What guys?"

Finally he turns to me, his cheeks an adorable shade of pink, and shakes his head.

I point a finger at him. "You made me promise I'd tell you everything I was thinking. Don't go quiet on me now, Hall."

His face splits into a wide smile. What the hell?

"Why are you smiling?" Despite my best efforts, I can't help but return the expression. His happiness is contagious.

"You called me Hall."

I roll my eyes and turn back. "Dork."

The doctor chuckles and turns from the machine set up next to the table. "You two are adorable. So often, parents come in here scared and quiet."

I glance at Daniel. I'm pretty sure we're both scared, but he doesn't let me go quiet. I kind of love it.

She examines me, and afterward, when she detaches a long device from the sonogram machine, explaining how she'll use it to see the baby, I swear Daniel almost passes out.

"You have to put that inside her?"

I snort and turn my head so I can see him, the paper crinkling beneath me. "I've had bigger dildos. Calm yourself."

The doctor drops her head back and barks out a laugh.

"You're brutal, you know that?" Daniel squeezes my hand again, his tone light, easy.

I smile. "And you're stuck with me for the next eighteen years. That's quite a sentence."

"I'll become a career criminal," he murmurs quickly, like no thought was put into it at all.

Once again, I'm trapped in his gaze, my lips lifting of their own accord.

I only break the expression to press my lips together when the doctor slides her special tool inside me.

Despite my effort to hide my discomfort, Daniel's brow creases in concern.

"You okay?" he mouths.

With a nod, I smile again, hoping to ease his worry.

"Just give me a few seconds." She shifts the object around, and a moment later, a whooshing sound fills the quiet room.

"Is that our—" My heart stutters as I study the image on the screen. It's a little misshapen bean, its heart fluttering along with the beat echoing off the walls. Unbidden, tears prick at my eyes. It's the most beautiful thing I've ever heard.

"That's our baby's heartbeat," Daniel murmurs, his face next to mine.

I look back at him, and his lips brush against my cheek.

"That's our baby," he says, his voice stronger now.

"It is." Despite all my fears and reservations, this moment just may be the greatest of my life. And though I was worried about lingering awkwardness, Daniel's presence is nothing but a comfort.

"Everything looks good. The baby's heartbeat is 178, and you're measuring right at seven weeks. That puts your due date at"—she squints at her computer screen—"January twentieth."

Somehow hearing that date makes it all seem more real. It only now hits me that we've got a finite period of time before our child arrives and upends our entire world.

"Right in the middle of hockey season," Daniel mutters, his tone defeated.

Unfortunately, that's life for both of us. Hockey season and baseball season both seem endless sometimes. There's no way around it. Our lives are going to have to change. Mine will, at least. Daniel can't just take time off from his hockey career.

I've been around long enough to meet many players with families. And every one of them has a spouse who does all the heavy lifting when it comes to day-to-day care. The parent that *isn't* the athlete. I get it. It comes with the territory. But it doesn't make the pill any easier to swallow.

Then again, Daniel is determined to be a good dad. Plenty of men wouldn't be so eager. He'll show up when he physically can. And I have to remind myself that it's more than I could hope for from a one-night stand.

"Could you print a picture for us?"

Daniel's question has me peeking over at the doctor. Is that possible?

"Of course. I'll print out a few."

My breath catches. Pictures of our baby? "I'll have to get a magnet so I can put it on the fridge or something."

Daniel smirks. "That's the last gift."

"A magnet?"

With a chuckle, he presses a kiss to my cheek. "No, a frame for our baby's first picture."

Heart stumbling, I lift up on an elbow and study him. His messy hair, his warm eyes, his easy posture. "You got the baby its own picture frame?"

"I got the baby its own album." His expression is bashful again, but there's all kinds of joy radiating from him too. "Figure we can add pictures of you throughout the pregnancy and of all the ultrasounds. Maybe pictures of our family when we give them the news and find out the sex—"

He ticks off one milestone after another, all the moments he wants to commemorate.

All I can do is stare in complete wonder.

I don't have a photo album to commemorate anything. Not my birth, not my high school graduation. Nothing. Yet Daniel has already started one for our unborn child.

Who is this man, and what do I need to do to keep from breaking him?

# TEXT MESSAGES FROM DANIEL AND HANNAH'S PHONE

Lennox: Did you take care of that little situation last night, Hannah?

Sara: What situation? What did I miss?

Hannah: No idea what you're talking about.

Lennox: Oh, so you weren't hagitated?

Sara: LOL she was so HAGITATED, but I'm sure Daniel handled that.

Millie: What does hagitated mean?

Millie: Actually, if it involves my brother, don't answer that.

Sara: It's Lennox speak for she was in a MOOD because she needed to get railed.

Millie: She was fine at dinner. God, I miss everything when I don't come to the bar.

Ava: She was fine at the bar too.

Lennox: You obviously didn't see what we saw. Probably too distracted by your HOT HUSBAND.

Millie: Oh, I love hot husband distractions. Tell me more about that.

Sara: Nah, I love Daddy War story time, but right now, I need to hear about what happened after Hall called Hannah HIS!!!

Millie: He WHAT?

Hannah: Oh my god, you are all so dramatic. Nothing happened. He drove me home. End of story.

Ava: You ready to talk yet?

Hannah: This is one of those kind of talks that needs to be in person and requires lots of alcohol.

Ava: But neither of us can have alcohol.

Ava: Right?

Hannah: Why do you have to be so smart, sweet girl?

Ava: Not that sweet. Just to you.

Hannah: I wish I didn't have to travel all week. The exhaustion is killing me. Is it killing you too?

Hannah: You know, hypothetically speaking and not actually saying what I'm saying because it needs to be said in person.

Ava: Yeah. I'm exhausted. And Ty has so much freaking energy now that the season's over.

Hannah: I don't know that I can do this. Tell me you think I can do this.

Ava: I know you can. You're the strongest person I know. And that's saying something, because I know some pretty amazing people.

Hannah: I love you.

Ava: Love you too. Call me when you're actually ready to talk. I'm always here.

Mills: What's going on with you and Hannah?

Daniel: Thought you didn't want to hear about my sex life?

Mills: <sick emoji> <crying emoji>

Mills: So that's all this is? Just screwing around? The girls made it seem like it was something more.

Daniel: Hannah was talking about me? What did she say?

Daniel: Mills, pick up the damn phone.

Daniel: Mills…WHAT DID SHE SAY?!

Mills: oh my god.

Daniel: WHAT?

Mills: You are so down bad for this girl.

Daniel: Oh, yeah. That's not news.

Mills: I'm putting Vivi to bed, but I'll call you later.

Daniel: Give my favorite girl a kiss good night.

Mills: I thought Hannah was your favorite girl
<laughing, crying emoji>

Daniel: Hannah is all woman. And yeah, she's definitely my favorite.

Mills: <sick emoji> also <heart eyes emoji>

# Chapter 19
## Hannah



"WHEN ARE YOU GOING TO BE IN BOSTON?"

"We should all plan to be there for the last weekend in June."

"Yes. Oliver and I will be around then. He'd love that."

"I might be able to swing it."

"That should work for me. My dad made me take summer classes, but I can probably leave campus early that weekend."

"Awesome, I'll make dinner reservations."

I look from one little screen to another, my eyes bouncing from brother to brother. Like always, they're all talking at once, making it hard to keep up with the family chat.

Oddly enough, only a few of them are actually related to one another. For most of the guys, the familial link is me. My mom was married to each of their dads at some point, but because they care about me, they all got close. And now, rather than being an only child, I have six brothers.

"Wait a second. I'm not even in town that weekend." I deflate as I double-check the calendar hanging on the wall. I've marked off the days I'm not traveling for the whole season. It's easier to note the ten days a month I'm home than it is to highlight the twenty days I'm gone.

"Oh, shit," Riggs says.

His father was married to my mother when I was in elementary school. He's a couple of years older than I am, but his brother Ash and I were in the same grade. Riggs is married and has kids, so his schedule isn't easy to coordinate, and Ash works security for the Berkshires, who are basically American royalty, so he's rarely in town either.

"What about August?" he asks. "We could come down before the kids go back to school."

"No can do," Tim says. "I'll be back in school by then."

His brother Kevin nods. "Yeah, I start law school the second week of August."

Matt, their older brother, laughs. "So don't plan on seeing Kevin at all for the next three years."

"Hey"—Kevin points at the screen—"just because you lived in the library doesn't mean I will."

"I'll be back to training in August anyway," Noah says. "Besides, Hannah will be really busy then."

I nod. August is one of those months that flies by. Between games and special events, I rarely have a day off. I have no idea how I'll manage that with how tired I already am.

That thought reminds me of why I scheduled this phone call. Because despite how much I'd love to do this in person, the likelihood that I'll get all of these guys in one place is nearly nonexistent.

"You guys should still get together the last weekend in June. I can't be here, but that doesn't mean you can't all hang out."

Six sets of eyes blink at me, and one by one, my brothers offer *yeah, sures*. They're placating me. Not a single one of them will follow up. I'm the glue that keeps us all together. We really are our own strange family. The six of them, plus Noah's dad. Of all my mom's exes, I'm closest to him and one other who doesn't have kids.

"Anyway," I say, dragging out the word. "I didn't actually call to set up a weekend, although I'd love to see all of you when you have time."

They all nod, but they're quiet. They're probably confused. It's not like me to be evasive. I'm a get-to-the-point kind of person. No dilly-dallying. Not a single one of us has time for that.

So here it goes…

"I'm pregnant."

There. That's the old Hannah.

"You're what?"

"Did she just say she's pregnant?"

"Holy shit."

"How?"

"Who's the father?"

"When are you due?"

They all speak at once, and when they finally shut up, I do my best to tick off answers, looking at each of them as I do. It's like handling reporters in the media room. I could do this in my sleep.

"I'm pregnant. Yes, pregnant. Though the how of it would probably require a discussion we don't have time for. Kevin, maybe Matt could have a talk with you about the birds and the bees. The father is none of your business, and I'm due January twentieth."

"He isn't stepping up?" Riggs is the one who speaks, but the other five nod in agreement.

"Just give me a name," Ash grits out.

Head tipped back, I groan. "Oh my god. I didn't call you to enlist a brigade to go after the father. I called you because I wanted to let you know you're going to be uncles again."

Noah, naturally, is the first one to soften, though Riggs is right behind him.

"Aw, Han, I wish you were home so I could hug you," Noah says.

I'm in Detroit, while he's in Boston. That's why I arranged this call. I didn't want to tell him one-on-one and face-to-face because I was worried I'd break and tell him who the father is. And I'm not ready to handle that just yet.

Though I did tell Daniel he was free to tell whomever he wanted. So he very easily could share with the guys on the team. Though, if he'd done that already, I'd have heard from the girls.

"You okay?" Riggs asks softly.

I look straight into the camera, expression easy, and lie to all of them. "I'm perfectly fine. Now tell me how my nephews are doing."

I'M PATTING MY FACE DRY WHEN MY PHONE RINGS AND NOAH'S NAME flashes on the screen.

With a laugh, I swipe to answer the video call. "I figured you'd be calling, but I thought maybe I'd get an hour or so reprieve since it's Oliver's bedtime."

Noah frowns. "He talked me into letting him watch another episode of Joanna Gaines because he says it's educational and I quote 'I miss Auntie Hannah.'"

I laugh. "Total con artist."

He doesn't smile. No, that frown stays firmly in place. "Tell me it's not Daniel."

All I can do is stare at him.

"Jesus, Han." He rakes a hand through his hair. "Does the kid know?"

"First of all, he's not a kid—"

He glares at me.

"Fine, he's a kid. And yes, I'm not an asshole. I told him as soon as I suspected. We took the test together."

My stepbrother hums, his gaze drifting away from the screen.

Unease rolls through me. "What exactly does *hmm* mean?"

He shrugs, his image jostling. "Just surprises me, is all. He slept over that night, didn't he?"

Lips twisted, I lower my chin. "Yeah, he said he just wanted to hold me after we found out."

"That's…" He chuckles, his face finally relaxing. "That's sweet."

"I guess. Whatever." Emotion rises in my throat, but I choke it back. "Anyway, I wanted to wait until after the doctor confirmed before I mentioned it. Now that we have, I don't know, I was freaking out, and I needed—"

"Your brothers," he finishes for me.

Warmth blooms in my chest. "Yeah."

Eyes swimming with genuine concern, he brings his phone closer. "How are you feeling about it all?"

My stomach tightens, and that pesky vulnerability rises in me again. "Honestly?"

"Always."

"Nervous," I admit. So fucking nervous.

"That's understandable. I was beyond nervous when I found out about Oliver."

"I just don't think I'll be very good at this."

He doesn't bat an eye. "You will."

"And I barely know the father."

"He's a good kid."

My only response is a glare.

He laughs. "I stand by the fact that he's a kid. But that doesn't change that he's a good one. He'll do the right thing."

I huff. "Don't you dare go putting any thoughts into his head. I don't want him to feel obligated to do anything."

"*Hannah.*" His tone is the same one he uses when Oliver tries to go for the extra scoop of ice cream or argues about brushing his teeth.

"I'm serious." Shoulders back, I keep my voice even. "No one forced you and Jen to get married. We're not putting that on Daniel. Like you said, he's a kid. I don't need another one to take care of. I'll have more than enough work being a mother of one."

With a sigh, he gives me a comforting half smile. "You're going to be fantastic."

"You're a pain in my ass."

He barks out a laugh. "I love you and I'm proud of you."

"Love you too."

"Call me if you need me." He brings his phone closer again, his eyes narrowed. "Any time."

"Except when you're on the ice."

"Even then, Han. Even then."

I haven't seen Hannah in two weeks, and I'm going out of my mind. Fuck. If this is how the guys' wives feel all season, I'm shocked any of them stick around. I've never been the one at home waiting—and I sure as shit have never had someone at home waiting for me—and I never want to do it again.

She's good about responding to my texts, though she never initiates them. I don't hold it against her. She's the one carrying my baby. I'm the one who should be checking on her. It's just—I want her to *want* to talk to me. I wish she felt the same emotions that are bubbling inside me, threatening to burst out at all times.

Night after night, I use all the restraint I possess to keep from picking up the phone and calling her. When I'm watching a funny show on TV, I want to text her about it. When I find a great pregnancy article or a vlog that really hits home, I want to watch it with her.

But are we even friends? We may be having a baby, but if her lack of interest in communicating is anything to go by, that might be the extent of our relationship. So I don't know how to act. I don't want to push too hard—come on too strong—and risk causing her to shut things down before I even have a chance. A chance to get her to fall, a chance to give our child a family.

Obviously, we'll be a family whether we're together or not, but the last thing I want for this kid is to grow up tethered to two parents who kind of hate each other the way my parents did. The way my mom hated my father, at least. My dad was indifferent to her.

So I don't know how to act.

Which is why I'm rereading our last string of texts, wondering if enough time has passed to ask her how she's feeling.

According to the timestamps, it's been a whopping four hours since the last time I asked.

"You going to join the party?" Millie settles beside me on the outdoor couch at Beckett Langfield's house and peers over my shoulder. "Who's dream girl?"

I flip my phone over on my thigh and shoot her a glare. "Nosy much? How would you like it if I looked at your texts with Gavin?"

A laugh bursts out of her. "Would *you* want to look at my texts with your coach?"

A shudder rolls through me. Unfortunately I'm aware of how kinky my sister and Gavin are, so no, I absolutely want nothing to do with her phone, her texts, or any of the intricacies of her marriage.

Eyes dancing, she flicks my cheek. "That's what I thought. So as I said, who's dream girl? Is that Hannah? Are you guys still talking?"

I planned to tell Millie about the baby today. Later. With fewer people around.

But here we are, surrounded by almost everyone we know. Beckett's family is here, along with all his brothers and their women. War and his family are in attendance too. Apparently Beckett is close friends with Ava. I was included because my sister is married to Gavin.

Secretly, I'd hoped Hannah would show up to the barbecue so we could casually run into each other and I could get a read on how she'll act around our friends.

But she's yet to show up, and I'm too in my head to ask if she's coming.

Last week, she gave me the go-ahead to tell my family about the baby. The guys too. So she won't be mad if I break the news. I just wish she were here for it.

I got an idea from one of the dad vlogs and ran with it, knowing the guys will get a kick out of it. Pretty sure Millie will too.

"I gotta run to my car real quick." I pat her leg and hop up before she can continue with her questions and skirt around the guys gathered around the grill, laughing and chatting.

It takes me all of one minute to locate what I'm looking for. But then I'm staring at the T-shirts, wondering if they'll really react the way I think they will.

"Fuck it." I slip mine over my head and straighten it, then snatch the bag and stroll back through the gate.

Aiden is the first to spot me. Head tilted, he mouths the words emblazoned on my chest in Bolts blue. Eyes going wide, he smacks Brooks with the back of his hand. One by one, my guys notice. None of them move. Only my sister heads my way, arms pumping and her tiny legs moving faster than I've ever seen.

"*Daddy* Hall?" she screeches. "That should say *Danny*, right?" With far more force than she should possess, she pokes my chest.

With a grimace, I pull back and rub at the ache.

"Daniel," she grounds out.

I can't help but smirk. "From now on, you can all call me Daddy."

My sister shudders and gags. "Oh god, I knew this day was coming. Who did you knock up?"

The boys have now made their way over, and from the way War is grinning, he knows precisely who the mother of my child is.

My heart takes off at a joyful pace. "My dream girl."

Millie's face scrunches in confusion. "Who?"

Aiden whoops, startling my twin and me at the same time. "Hannah's pregnant?"

My sister smacks my chest. Once, twice, three times. "You knocked up my friend." Another smack. Her little hands are surprisingly effective weapons.

Thankfully her husband grabs her by the hips and pulls her against his chest. "Stop beating up your brother and let him speak."

She whips around, hands on her hips. "Are you forgetting how he almost punched you when he found out you were dating me?"

I straighten and run a hand down my shirt. "That was justified."

Gavin cuts me a stern look

"What?" I throw my arms out. "I'm not wrong. It's obvious now that you're the only person who can deal with her kind of crazy, but at the time, you were my dad's best friend and my coach. How should I have reacted?"

Gavin only grumbles in response.

Beckett barks out a laugh. "Imagine if Vivi came home with a guy twenty years older than her."

The grumble turns into a growl. "She's not even two. What is wrong with you?"

Hands in his pockets, Beckett shrugs. "I'm just saying."

"Say less." Gavin turns back to me. "I'm not sure how this got turned on me, but did you say you're having a baby?"

Bouncing on the balls of my feet, I grin. "Yeah. Hannah and I are having a baby. Don't worry, I got you all matching T-shirts because you're going to be the best damn uncles around." I toss Gavin his shirt.

He's the first to tug me in for a hug. Then, one by one, I give the other guys their shirts and accept their congrats.

When my sister appears in front of me again, I reach into my bag and grab the hat I bought her. It says *World's Best Auntie.*

Instantly, the shock on her face melts away and her eyes go misty. "Why are you being so cute about this?" Finally, she throws her arms around me.

With her still in my arms, I look down at her. "Because this is literally the best thing that's ever happened to me. I get to raise a baby with Hannah. My literal dream girl."

"So, are the two of you together?" She sounds almost hurt, like she thinks we've been sneaking around behind her back.

As much as it pains me to admit it, I tell her the truth. "No. Not that I wouldn't like that, but I'm not sure she's ready for all of this." I drop my arms and motion to myself.

My sister coughs out a laugh through her tears.

"Congrats," Beckett says, bringing over a handful of cigars.

With a dip of my chin, I take one from him. "Sorry I didn't make you a shirt."

He shrugs. "I probably deserve one more than most of these guys."

He nods at the group who have all pulled their *World's Best Uncle* shirts on. "But it's fine. I don't need a shirt to prove I'm the reason you're having a baby."

Aiden steps up beside his oldest brother and rubs his hands together. "Oh this will be good. How did you make this happen?"

Beckett smirks. "I made Arizona happen."

Frowning, Gavin brings his drink to his lips. "What does Arizona have to do with it?"

Beckett's focus remains entirely on me. "That's when the baby was conceived, right?"

"Pretty sure Hannah would prefer her employer not know that," Liv points out, her brow raised like she's daring her husband to continue.

He shrugs. "I know what I know."

"Even if that were true," Gavin says, his eyes cutting to mine. "How are you to thank for that?"

"Because I made the schedule."

Gavin's loud laugh startles Vivi, who's clutching at his leg like she wants him to pick her up. "Nice try. The NHL and MLB make the schedule."

The way the oldest Langfield brother looks back at him like he's an imbecile makes the entire group of us go quiet.

"You have input into the schedule?" Gavin whisper-hisses, brows furrowed.

Beckett merely shrugs, gaze cutting to me. "You're welcome."

"Is she coming tonight?" I ask him.

Liv smirks. "Her response to the invite was 'and spend more time with Beckett than I have over the last two weeks? No thanks.'"

Everyone laughs, even me, though disappointment settles in my stomach. I was really hoping to see her today.

Millie snuggles beside me on the outdoor couch again as the rest of the group falls back into conversation. "Why not text her and tell her you miss her?"

I frown down at my sister. "Am I that obvious?"

"You're my twin. I can sense these things. I've never seen you like this." She glances at the words on my chest again, and her lips curl into a smile. "You seem really happy about the baby."

"I am." For the next several minutes, I tell her how the last few weeks have been and how I didn't freak out when I found out I was going to be a dad.

"That's how I felt the moment I met Vivi."

Vivi was left on Gavin's doorstep as an infant, and Gavin and Millie officially adopted her last year. She's their entire world.

"But you had Gavin. The two of you—" I shake my head. For as much shit as I give her, it's more than obvious they're soulmates. The way they look at one another, the way they rally and support each other, it's rare. All the guys here tonight have that. Hannah and I are constantly surrounded by a group of inspiring couples.

"You don't think you could have that with Hannah?" My sister pulls back and studies me.

I swallow past the lump in my throat. "I think if she gave me a chance, we could be amazing. I'm just not sure how to get her to give me that chance."

Millie sighs. "You'll figure it out. God, I can't believe you're going to be a dad."

She throws her arms around me, and I allow my twin to ease some of the tension I've been feeling. Maybe she's right. I'll figure it out somehow.

"How did you get Liv to fall for you?"

It's after eight, and the backyard is aglow with twinkling lights. War and Ava took their kids home, but the rest of the women have disappeared inside for dessert while the guys are gathered around Beckett's fire pit with cigars and glasses of whiskey.

Beckett leans forward. "You're looking for ways to woo Hannah?"

"Oh no," Gavin grumbles. "You woke the beast."

Aiden swats at him. "Come on, it's fun to watch Beckett work his magic."

Gavin groans. "Stop feeding his ego."

"It's about little things and the big gestures," Beckett says, ignoring his brother.

I straighten, elbows on the armrests of my chair. "What kind of little things did you do?"

Gavin chuckles. "He got her drunk and conned her into marrying him."

Beckett grunts. "Then I bought a case of the wine we were drinking that night and made sure we have enough bottles to last us a lifetime. The little things like *that* are what keep a woman happy."

"I kept Millie plenty happy when I bought out the bar we were in so we could have some privacy," Gavin says, brow arched.

"You did?" I lean back in my chair and bring my cigar to my lips. "That's romantic. Did she think it was romantic?" Millie didn't tell me this story, though when it comes to the interactions between the two of them, less information is always best.

Gavin wipes at his smile. "Sure. I think she was satisfied by the gesture."

I nod. "Okay, small things and big gestures. I think I can work with that."

"Brooks cut off all his hair." Aiden dips his chin in his next oldest brother's direction.

Our goalie just laughs and shakes his head. "A small thing."

"That stunt led to the NHL raising millions of dollars for a charity that was important to your fiancée," Beckett points out. "Not such a small thing."

"I cloned Lex's phone and read along with her, then acted out her favorite spicy scenes," Aiden says, chest puffed out proudly.

Gavin covers his face. "You've got to stop telling everyone that. Millie has talked to me about some of the books she reads, and now I can't look your wife in the eye."

Aiden licks his lips. "My wife is filthy, and I love it."

"Okay, so presents, dinner, big gestures, and light stalking. Got it."

Gavin throws his head back and laughs loudly at my summation.

Beckett, on the other hand, studies me as he takes another slow drag from his cigar. "How's Hannah handling the pregnancy news?"

In the space of a breath, I go from hopeful to filled with dread. Because I just told her boss that she's having a baby before she broke the news. *Fuck.* I clear my throat. "She's, uh, she's good. You know she's dedicated to her job, so that's her focus."

Beckett nods. "Yes. But that changes now. Kids change everything." He leans forward. "Family changes everything."

I force a smile, certain that I'll never have the ability to do it again once Hannah finds out what I did.

# Chapter 21
## Hannah



"How many pieces did you eat?" Oliver's jaw drops.

Across the table, Noah laughs. "You should have seen her in high school. First time I had pizza with her, she finished five slices without looking up. I always order an extra pie now."

I roll my eyes. He's totally exaggerating. I had four slices that day. Might have even been three. But Noah could house one pizza on his own, which he did tonight, by the way. Oliver and I shared the second one. "You're just lucky you put pineapple on yours so neither of us touched it," I tease.

Oliver makes a gagging noise. "Seriously, Dad. You are the uncoolest pizza eater ever."

Noah tosses his wadded-up paper towel across the table and hits Oliver in the chest. "Go put on pajamas and brush your teeth. Then you can pick a movie."

Oliver sticks out his bottom lip. "Can we play a game instead?"

Noah arches a brow, focus drifting to me. When I nod subtly, he gives Oliver the go-ahead.

The little guy scrambles off his seat, but before he can get far, Noah clears his throat.

"You forgetting something?" he says, holding out his arms.

His sweet little boy runs toward him, his little body darting across the room far faster than I could travel, and launches himself in for a big hug. I breathe out a small laugh as I watch them. Noah is a great dad. Is this what Daniel's relationship with our child will be like? The thought instantly has tears threatening to spill. I suppose it will be similar in the sense that a woman who isn't our child's mother will be sitting with him or her and Daniel during his parenting time. While during my time, I'll probably be right here, doing this—hanging out with my brother and my nephew.

The thought sours my stomach, but before I can think too hard about it, Oliver is launching himself into my chest.

He comes at me with so much force my chair tilts, but before I can go down, Noah steadies it.

"Be careful with your Aunt Hannah." His tone is chiding but soft. He never raises his voice to his son.

I wrap my arms around the little guy and squeeze. When I release him, I run my fingers through his silky hair. "It's okay. I appreciate the hug." More than I can say. I can't remember the last time someone truly hugged me. It melts my heart every time Noah hugs his son. Oliver will always know he's loved, that's obvious.

When he rushes off, yelling that we should set up Jenga while he gets ready, we both laugh.

"He's a good kid." I stand and pick up my plate and Oliver's, then head to the kitchen. Noah follows with his and all three of our plastic cups. That's another thing I love about Noah. He doesn't judge my hatred for doing dishes or my overuse of paper products. With my hectic work schedule, using the dishwasher typically means the dishes sit too long. Sometimes clean, but sometimes dirty, and that is the worst kind of welcome to receive after days on the road.

I close one pizza box and stack it on the other, but Noah bumps me out of the way gently.

"Sit. I'll take care of it."

"I'm pregnant, not injured." Despite my argument, I shuffle back to the table and drop into my chair. After ten days of travel, I am exhausted. It's more mental than physical this time. Probably because of the mental gymnastics I've been doing while I try to come to terms with this pregnancy.

I can't stop stressing over things like whether I'm supposed to call Daniel and make plans to see him. A part of me wants to—maybe a big part of me—but the other part, the girl who knows how this works, keeps coming back around to how unwise it would be to get attached. And it could be so easy to do that. He's just too sweet. I genuinely enjoy spending time with him. But I don't really know him, and he most certainly doesn't know me. He knows the fun, loud Hannah. The person I am out in a crowd or at work, when I'm dealing with the baseball neanderthals. The attitude I have to wear. It's not a mask, per se, because I truly am that person. But that's only one facet of my personality.

And he's truly never seen the rest of me. Not many people have.

"Speaking of that..." Noah says as he shoves the plates into the trash.

I take a deep breath, preparing myself for the spiel he's about to give me. The one about how he thinks Daniel should be here—

"The baby will need his or her own room in a few months, so I have an appointment with a realtor tomorrow."

I panic. Straight-up panic. Nervousness claws at my chest at the thought of them leaving. Of being alone in this apartment again. Of taking care of a child by myself. I don't know how to be a mom. My mother didn't have the kind of warmth Noah shows his son so easily. I thought he'd be here to help, to guide me, to show me how to be a parent.

"The baby can stay in my room."

Noah drops the pizza boxes onto the counter and strides my way. "I just figured you'd want privacy." He settles opposite me, his arms folded across his chest. "And the space."

I shake my head. "I don't."

For a long moment, he's quiet, studying me. Eventually he nods. "Whatever you want. But if you change your mind, just tell me."

Before I can reply, my phone buzzes on the table between us and Daniel's name flashes on the screen.

Noah knocks on the table once and stands. "I'll finish with the kitchen, and then I'm going to get changed."

As he disappears, I pick up my phone, excitement causing my lips to tip up.

*Stop. He's probably just asking how you feel. Again.*

It's his go-to question. He's only reaching out because we're having a baby. If we weren't, he'd have moved on long ago.

Having adequately talked my excitement down, I unlock the screen and read the text.

Daniel: I fucked up.

My stomach sinks and the multitude of wrongs he could have committed filter through my mind. As each enters, I work through a way to deal with it. Until I've come up with a quick plan for them all, I can't reply.

Daniel: Can I come over? We need to talk.

I blow out a breath. It's always better to deal with things in person. That way there's no risk of texts being leaked.

Me: Noah and Oliver are here, but sure.

Daniel: Never mind. We can talk later.

A harsh laugh escapes me.

Me: you can't drop an avalanche on me and then say never mind. Get your butt over here. We're playing Jenga—the big blocks—we can talk, and then you can be on my team.

Daniel: If you still want me to stick around after, sure.

My stomach swirls with nerves as I set my phone down on the table.

Fuckity fuck. What the hell did Daniel do?

FIVE MINUTES LATER, DANIEL IS KNOCKING ON MY DOOR. MAKES ME wonder if he was sitting outside again.

The moment I open the door, I'm hit with the smell of cigar and his cologne. The man standing on the other side wears the hell out of a pair of shorts and a polo shirt. I've seen Daniel in all types of clothing. Suits, hockey gear, T-shirts. Naked. But god, there is something extra attractive about the way the black polo tugs across his chest and how his muscled thighs cause his baby blue shorts to creep a smidge higher than they should be. Not even models can pull the look off like he does. Must be all the skating he does, because his thighs have my mouth watering.

I wave him inside. "Spend the night in a cigar bar?"

Rather than coming in, he takes a step back, his face falling. "Sorry, I changed my shirt and sprayed cologne. Is it too strong? We can do this another time."

I grab his arm and tug him inside. "I like the smell. Stop being weird and tell me how much of a fuck-up this is."

He ducks his head and scans the space. "Where's Noah?"

I roll my eyes. "He's helping Oliver get changed. Talk."

Teeth sunken into his lower lip and his hands in his pockets, he assesses me from beneath lowered lashes. "I told Beckett you're pregnant."

Relief crashes over me like an ocean wave. "Jesus." I laugh. "You had me sitting here freaking out for that?"

He straightens, his eyes narrowing. "I told your *boss* that you're pregnant."

I shrug. "Can't wait to see what the big guy buys to congratulate us."

"Why are you acting so calm?"

"I was worried you were going to tell me you knocked up someone else and that you now had two baby mamas. I was working through ways to not only co-parent with you but some puck bunny, and I—" I shake my head and laugh. "Anyway, of all the scenarios running through my head, this is far, far better."

His brows pinch together. "You thought I knocked up someone else?" He scowls.

"I'm sure one baby mama is more than enough for you." I wave it off, hoping he'll let it go.

He steps so close I can't help but inhale him. "Stop calling yourself that. I haven't slept with anyone but you this year. There's no chance anyone else is pregnant."

Momentarily off balance, all I can do is gape. Seriously? He hasn't slept with anyone else this *year*? We're almost six months in.

Maybe I'm not the only one who presents only one part of who I am to the public.

"Are we good?" he asks, gaze sweeping over me.

Without my permission, my attention slides to his lips, and when he wets them, I whimper.

At the sound, he leans in, but before we make the catastrophic mistake of falling victim to the sexual chemistry again, a little voice interrupts us.

"Who's that?"

Heart stuttering, I pull back. "Oliver, this is my friend Daniel. He plays hockey with your dad. Daniel, this is my nephew Oliver."

Daniel crouches so he's eye to eye with Oliver and holds out a hand. "Nice to meet you, buddy."

The little guy scrutinizes him through narrowed eyes but takes his hand. "You smell funny. Like my dad does sometimes."

Noah laughs as he approaches, hand held out to Daniel. The move is friendly enough, even if he's assessing Daniel just as intently as his son was. "Hey, Hall. You joining us for Jenga?"

"Why'd he call you Hall?" Oliver squints at Daniel, then me. "Why do hockey players have so many names?"

The three of us burst into laughter, the moment of levity thankfully easing some of the tension in the room.

"It's my last name," Daniel tells him. "You can call me whatever you want."

Lips pursed and pushed to one side, Oliver peers up at each of us again. Then he shrugs. "Aunt Hannah calls you Daniel, so I will too."

It's on the tip of my tongue. I so want to tell my nephew to call him Baby Hall.

Daniel quirks a brow like he can read my mind, but his lips tip up. "Yeah, your aunt is pretty smart, so that works for me."

We settle in the living room and take turns sliding Jenga blocks off the tower. When the whole thing topples on Daniel, Oliver giggles so hard he falls over too, and with him, he takes the last bit of tension between the adults.

At bedtime, Oliver doesn't need a reminder to give hugs, and when he doesn't hesitate to offer Daniel one too, Noah smiles at me.

"I'm going to take this one to bed, so I'll say good night now." He nods at Daniel and then he and his little guy disappear.

"I didn't know he had a kid," Daniel admits.

"Really?"

He shrugs. "I tried really hard not to pay attention to him when he got here."

My chest aches for him. I can imagine it was hard. Noah was traded late in the season, and then Gavin moved Daniel from the first line to second. "You guys seemed to get along tonight, though." I can't hide the hope in my tone. Noah is the closest thing I have to family, and for some reason, I want the two of them to like one another.

With a smile, he rubs his hands down his thighs. "Yeah, now that I know he isn't trying to date you, we're all good."

My stomach lurches. "Ew."

He laughs. "My sentiments exactly."

Silence descends as his laughter dies. Then we're just looking at one another. Will he leave now? That's what he should do. We dealt with the alleged emergency, and he stayed for the game. But, ridiculously, I don't want him to go.

He angles closer and sweeps my hair behind my ear. Then his warm palm falls to my neck, his thumb brushing the skin there, sending shivers down my spine with every move.

"What are you thinking?" I whisper as he holds himself still.

His lips hook into a half smile. "That I really want to kiss you, but I don't know what the rules are anymore."

Instantly, my instincts kick in, and I can't help but taunt him. "Since when do you care about rules?"

He licks his lips and inches closer. "Since I started caring about the outcome."

My stomach swoops, my words barely audible. "And what outcome are you hoping for?"

He hovers even closer, and just when I think he's going to kiss me, he rests his head on my shoulder and pulls me in for a hug. My heart squeezes at the unexpected and ridiculously sweet gesture. I have to suck in a breath to keep my emotions in check before I hug him back.

"Can I take you out tomorrow?" he asks.

"Out?"

"Yes. I'd love to spend more time with you, but it's late, and you need your rest."

A hint of sorrow threads through my veins. I don't want to rest. I want Daniel to kiss me and then carry me to my room and make me forget every single obligation, every responsibility. If just for a little while.

I don't tell him that. He hugged me. He didn't kiss me. I don't know what that means, but I do know that I want to spend more time with him too, so I nod. "Okay. We can do something tomorrow."

His face lights up in a mixture of delight and surprise, like he thought I'd say no. He pulls me in for another hug, this time hauling me onto his lap. When he stands, a jolt of excitement hits me. It quickly fizzles out, though, when he sets me on my feet. With a kiss on my cheek, he heads for the door.

"Night, dream girl." He steps out into the hall and gives me a small wave.

"Good night, Daniel."

# CHAPTER 22
## DANIEL

Everything is set. I've confirmed with the restaurant and the liquor store. My shirt smells like detergent and a hint of cologne. No cigars or any other odor. And a look in the mirror in the hallway confirms there's nothing in my teeth.

"You've got this. Small moments, big gestures."

I give myself a final once-over in the mirror and then knock on Hannah's door.

At the sight that greets me when it swings open, my heart stutters. She's fucking gorgeous. Chestnut waves cascading down to the tips of her shoulders. A long, yellow, silky dress that highlights her curves and her damn cleavage, which has my mouth watering. Glossy lips that lift in one of her knowing smiles.

"They look good, don't they?" She peers at her tits, then, eyes on me, she cups one and whimpers. "They're supersensitive too."

My dick kicks at my zipper and saliva pools in my mouth. I'm literally going to drool if I don't get it together. I push a multicolor gift bag toward her and step into the apartment.

She tugs at the paper, revealing her gift, her expression morphing into one of confusion. "Tequila?"

I bob my head. "The first shot we ever did together. I got you a lifetime supply of it. So you never forget me."

With a hand on her stomach, she laughs. "Pretty sure you already gave me a gift that'll last a lifetime, Playboy, but thank you?" Her voice lifts at the end, almost like that last part is a question. "I'll, um, go put this in the liquor cabinet since I can't drink it just yet." She steps away, then quickly spins back. "Unless you want some before we go?"

My gut churns. Dammit. A lifetime supply of tequila for a pregnant woman. What was I thinking?

I shake my head. "Nope. Just for you."

As she disappears, I berate myself. Should I call and cancel the lifetime supply? No, I already told her about it, so—

"You ready?" she asks as she reappears.

My breath escapes me this time when I get a look at her. She's so pretty.

"Your dress," I croak.

She glances down at it, her brow knitted. "Too fancy? Figured it won't fit much longer, and who knows how my body will change after this pregnancy. Might be my last shot at wearing it." She slides her hands down the glossy fabric.

I itch to do the same. "It's perfect, Hannah. *You're perfect.*" I flex my hands at my sides. "Sorry. I'm already screwing this up. I meant to tell you that you look beautiful, but I lost my words when you opened the door."

She holds out her hand, and when I grasp it, I swear I'm shocked by a current of electricity. I've always had a thing for Hannah. Always felt a pull to be near her, a rush of sensation in her proximity. But this is more. She's having my baby. We're going on a date. She dressed up...*for me*. The sensation floating around inside me now is more than just a casual affection. But I don't want to get ahead of myself.

"I'm not sure what you think you could screw up. No expectations. Let's just have a good time tonight." She steps closer and presses a kiss to my cheek. Before she can pull away, I yank my phone from my pocket and snap a picture of us. When she giggles at my antics, the nerves that have held me hostage melt away. Practically floating, I lead her out into the summer night.

On the way to the restaurant, she tells me about her visit to the park with Noah and Oliver and mentions stopping at the salon to get her nails and toes done. When I ask her what she's got coming up and she tells me about the next away stretch, my shoulders droop. I shake it off quickly, intent on focusing on the time we have together. As we approach the doors to the restaurant, her eyes widen with excitement. When she says she's always wanted to try this place, my chest expands with pride.

I hold the door open for her, and when she walks into the empty room, she turns back to me. "Are you sure they're open?"

Hand on her back, I smirk. "Yup. I paid the owner to close it down so we could have the place to ourselves."

Glossy lips pressed together, she glances around the eerily quiet steakhouse. "But there's staff here, right?"

I smile. Of course there's staff. I survey the place, and when I don't spot a soul, I start to worry. I take out my phone and text the owner. "Gavin told me how he closed this place down for Millie once. The guy said he'd give us the same treatment."

Hannah snorts and brings a hand to her mouth. "Wait—you do know why he shut down the restaurant that night, right?"

The twinkle in her eye has me taking a step back. "Do I want to know?"

She coughs out a laugh and points a pale yellow nail toward the bar. "No, you most definitely don't want to know that your twin sister experienced her first ever O right there on that bar top after Gavin paid a hundred grand to get her alone."

My stomach roils violently. "I'm going to be sick."

She doubles over. "You brought your pregnant baby mama to the restaurant where your twin *got it on*." She wheezes out a breath. "Oh god. I'm all for reenactments, and we know I love my orgasms—" She rights herself, swiping at the tears streaming down her face. "But I'm hungry, and I'm guessing there's no kitchen staff, either, is there?"

My phone buzzes in my hand, and I groan as I read the text from the owner telling me it's empty, as he promised. "Fuck."

Hannah bursts into laughter again, the sound filling the quiet restaurant where I am very clearly not going to feed her.

All I can do is stare in awe. She doesn't seem the least bit upset that I've screwed up this date more than once. And damn, I love the sound of her laugh. Maybe I've made a fool of myself, but it's worth it to be enveloped in her delight. My body warms at the sound, my heart pounding and my toes tingling too. If I could only hear one sound for the rest of my life, I'd want it to be that.

Her happiness brings me a joy I didn't know existed. If she's laughing—even if it's at my expense—I'm smiling.

Even as her laughter dies, a smile remains on her lips. She reaches for my hand. "Come on, Playboy. I've got dinner covered."

Shoulders back and head held high, she leads me out onto the busy Boston street, looks left, then right, then up at me. "How do you feel about hot dogs?"

I tilt my head. "Hot dogs?"

She hums. "I've been craving the ones from that vendor right outside the stadium. What do you say?"

"Yes." Already, I know it'll be my go-to answer when it comes to her. Hannah doesn't know it yet, but she owns me. And if I'm lucky, maybe one day I'll own her heart too.

"So does it live up to your expectations?" We're sitting side by side on a bench in the park across the street from the stadium, hot dogs in hand. Hannah got two with everything on them. She added ketchup and mustard, but when she got to the relish, she hesitated, biting her lip and eyeing me. When I asked if it was because she didn't like it, she told me she loved it, but she said she worried that if things were heading in the direction she hoped, she didn't want to have bad kissing breath.

My heart fucking floated in my chest.

So I dropped a glob of relish on mine and told her to go crazy, that we'd both taste the same.

Now she pops the last bite of her hot dog into her mouth with a hum, and I stare like the lovesick puppy I am.

"It's so good." Wiping her hands on her napkin, she turns to me. "Can I ask you something?"

"Anything. That's what we promised, right? Complete transparency and honesty. It's the only way this will work."

She sets her napkin down and takes a sip of her lemonade. The freshly squeezed drink was another must have, and damn am I glad I listened to her. It's incredible. "Why did you buy out the restaurant like Gavin did for Millie?"

I shudder again. If I never have to see that restaurant again, it will be too soon. "It's stupid, really."

"Complete honesty, Daniel," she chides, bumping her shoulder into mine.

I wipe my mouth, hiding my smile. I always seem to be wearing one around her. "Last night, I was talking to the guys about what they did to get their women to fall for them."

Her brows raise, but she doesn't speak.

So with a deep breath in, I continue, hoping she won't focus too much on my motivation. "Beckett said small things like paying attention to the drink he and Liv had the night they got married—"

"The only red they ever serve at their house," Hannah says with a knowing smile.

I nod. "He says he bought a case and replenishes annually."

"He's cute when it comes to Liv." Her tone almost comes out wistful. It's unlike anything I've heard from her before. *Interesting.*

"Gavin mentioned the restaurant—"

She laughs. "Not investigating what happened in that restaurant before you paid so we could have it to ourselves was an epic error on your part."

I hold up my hand. "You've got to stop."

The laugh turns into a manic fit of giggles.

Desperate to avoid hearing any more about my sister and her husband, I continue. "Brooks cut his hair, so I considered a buzz cut—"

She shakes her head. "No, you don't have the forehead to pull that off."

My jaw drops. "Excuse me?"

"You're very pretty, Daniel Hall, but please don't touch your hair. I'm a fan."

A fan? Noted. "The last Langfield cloned Lennox's phone and reads along with her books. I was thinking"—I waggle my brows—"maybe I'd clone your computer so I can read what you're writing."

The glare she hits me with is almost powerful enough to knock me out of my seat. "I'll kill you."

"Jeez. Touchy." I return the look with a grin.

Her expression smooths out. "There's a reason writers tend to be protective of their works in progress. They normally suck."

I shake my head. "Pretty sure nothing you write could ever suck."

"Because you haven't read my books before they've been edited. I'm telling you, they're garbage until my editor works her magic."

*She's* magic. This moment is magic. Learning anything about her feels special. I'm so glad we promised one another honesty. I don't know if I would have admitted the truth if we hadn't.

"If you ever want to share it with me, I'd love to read anything you write."

She smiles coyly. "Maybe one day. Oh, did I tell you that I received a gift from Beckett today?"

I groan internally. I'm still beating myself up for not thinking before I told him about her pregnancy. "Oh yeah?"

She wipes at her lips with her thumb, catching a little mustard, then pops the digit into her mouth. "Flowers and ginger cookies. Apparently Liv loved the cookies when she was pregnant with the twins. He sends his congratulations."

"That's nice of him."

Dammit. Why didn't I think of ginger cookies? They would have been a much more appropriate gift for a pregnant woman than tequila.

Her nose scrunches. "I tried one of the cookies—not my favorite."

I laugh. "We'll find another dessert for you."

She places her hand on my thigh, and my cock jumps. "Please tell me I'm your dessert."

"Is that what you want?" I turn and bury my face in her hair, my lips at her ear. "You want me to eat your delicious pussy for dessert?"

I pull back, but she stops me by fisting the front of my shirt.

*"Daniel."* Blue eyes wild, she pleads with me. "My nipples are ready to poke out of my dress. They're so needy. Please take me somewhere and fuck me...*quick.*"

I snag our trash from the bench and pull her to her feet. "Where do you want to go? Your place or mine?"

"That's too far." Her lips twitch and her eyes dance with mischief. "Are you up for an adventure?"

A thrill races through me. "You name it; I'm game."

She bites her lip and tips her head. "I've always wanted to have sex on the field."

Electricity bolts down my spine. *"Lang* Field?"

"Yeah, I have keys. What do you say?"

I toss our trash in the garbage behind the bench, then clutch her hand. "You're going to get us fired."

"Nah, I put out the fires."

# CHAPTER 23
# DANIEL



"Who did you text?"

Hannah, who's still focused on her phone, stands at my side just outside the door that leads to the field.

As soon as it lights up with a response, she tugs the door open and saunters away. "Security. I told them a VIP wants to get on the field and asked for complete privacy. Told him to shut down the cameras for the next thirty minutes."

I chase after her, heart racing. "They'll really do that?"

Hannah giggles, the sound floating into the night air. "Guess we'll find out." She peers over her shoulder as she tugs on the zipper of her dress. "Think you can make me come before our thirty minutes is up, Playboy?"

Her voice is sexy as fuck, raspy and taunting.

I chase after her as she strides toward the field. "Oh, there's no question whether I can. It's a question of how many times, dream girl. And the answer is however many you want."

She glances at the field. "An orgasm a base?"

Fuck. Dick thickening, I toss my shirt toward home plate and drop my pants. "You're on." When her dress falls to the green grass and she stands in nothing but a pair of nude panties, her breasts heavy, nipples pebbled, I rush her, and with my hands on the globes of her ass, pick her up. Without stopping, I run toward first base. It's dark, but the night sky provides enough ambient light to make out most of the details of the empty stadium.

When we hit first base, I press my lips to hers and sink to the ground. The second my ass hits the base, I roll her hips over my hard cock.

"Oh god, that feels good." Hands clutching my shoulders, she moves her pelvis to the rhythm I set. "My nipples," she moans, straightening and pressing her chest forward.

I shake my head. "First base is kissing only, pretty girl. So ride me while I make out with you. I'm gonna make you come like this."

Eyes lit up, she glances around the field. Yeah, she's figured out my plan.

Cuffing her neck, I bring her mouth to mine. As I lick at her lips, devouring her needy moans, she doesn't slow her movements. Never have I ever dreamed of fucking around on a baseball field, but already, this is one of the hottest experiences of my life. She's already soaked her panties and through my boxers. The sensation is fucking euphoric, but I'm trying hard not to get too swept away. I refuse to come until I'm inside her and we're at home base. When she whimpers and throws her head back, I pull her pelvis against mine with more force. Cheeks flushed, tits swollen, she babbles through her orgasm. She's still chanting when I'm on my feet again and carrying her toward second base so I can touch her magnificent tits. The instant I'm on the ground again, I suck one perfect peak into my mouth.

She hisses out a curse. "Holy fuck. That's—holy shit, *Daniel.*" My name is a long, drawn-out whine.

Feeling fucking unstoppable, I clutch her by the waist and flick her nipple with my tongue.

"Oh my god. Don't stop. I think I can come like this."

"Yeah, you can." I nip at her other nipple.

She yelps, her head falling back. "I swear pregnancy is worth it just for the way my tits feel right now."

I love her like this. Uninhibited. Taking what she wants. Chasing her orgasm. Fuck, her attitude alone is enough to have me dangerously close to embarrassing myself again. Forget how gorgeous she looks while she does it.

She rolls her hips again, her knees coated in the orange dust from the baseline.

"Look at you getting dirty, chasing your orgasm." I flick one nipple with my tongue while pinching the other one. "Work for it, baby. Ride me and let me lick it up when we get to third base."

Back bowed, she cries out, and as she goes over the edge, I alternate between her nipples, lapping and sucking and nipping, relishing the way her legs shake. When she drops her head to my chest, heaving breaths in and out, I jump up and run.

At third base, I lay her down in the dirt and get on my knees for her, pulling her panties off and throwing them toward the outfield.

She lets her thighs fall open and watches me, waiting. "Please, Daniel. Please suck my clit right now."

I don't make her wait for my mouth. She's glistening, and I'm hungry. With my hands beneath her ass, I pull her closer and lap at her sweet pussy. "Fuck, you taste good."

She bucks her hips, chasing the pressure, so I use one hand to roll her clit while the other holds her up. "Oh god," she whimpers. "You are a fucking god with that tongue."

Pride swells inside me. I love getting this woman off. I live to bring her pleasure.

As her pussy begins to flutter, I spear her with two fingers, giving her something to grip while she rides out her third orgasm of the night. "That's it, baby. Come all over my fingers." Good fucking god. My cock pulses, my every muscle coiling tight. This woman will be the death of me. "Make a mess. Fuck, you're the hottest woman I've ever met."

She convulses around my fingers, arching her body back.

This time I don't rush to the next base. I'm too busy licking her clean. I want every delicious drop.

"Oh god, it's too sensitive." She fists my hair and tugs.

Damn, I like that. When I don't stop licking, she pulls harder. Fuck, the move brings with it the best kind of pain.

"I need you to fuck me," she begs.

I press a kiss to her clit and then her pubic bone, then meet her eye. The sight of the desire on her gorgeous face almost bowls me over. "Only because you asked so nicely."

As I carry her to home plate, she wraps her arms around my neck and nuzzles into me. We're both covered in the orange dust, but I couldn't give a fuck. With one hand on her ass to keep her in place, I slide my boxers off and kick them out of the way. Then, without preamble, I slam into her.

"Holy shit, Daniel," she pants, clinging to my neck. "You don't want to sit?"

Head shaking, I tighten my hold on her ass. "You did enough work. I'm going to bounce you on my dick until you come, and then I'm going to fill you up."

"God, yes." She spasms around me, and stars dance in my vision. "I love that you can come inside me. It feels so fucking good."

"You have no goddamn idea," I grit out. I love fucking this woman. Love the way her hot, tight pussy squeezes me every time I slide inside her. "Fuck, Han. I'm not going to last. I almost came eating you."

She chuckles, causing those spasms to intensify. "We'll work on making you last next time. I want you to come, Daniel. Come right now."

No way am I coming until I get her off one more time. I lower her to her back with an apology for how filthy she'll be after this. Then, on my knees, I grip one of her ankles up on my shoulder and slide home again. It's the most intense, incredible torture. Spine tingling, balls tightening, teeth gritted, I rub her clit in rhythmic circles as I roll my hips slowly so she feels my piercing with every thrust.

"Oh god. Yes, right there."

She cries out, and my world comes apart. With a low groan, I unload inside her, pulse after pulse. My vision is only just returning when a light on the far side of the field turns on. Then another.

"Holy shit." Hannah drapes her arms over her torso, trying to cover herself.

I yank her to her feet and grab her dress. Thank fuck we made it back to where we began. Then I pick her up and dart for the door, snagging clothes from the ground as I go. We've just pulled the door open when a deep voice bellows, "Security."

Safely on the other side, once again out of breath, I sort through the clothes I picked up. I've got shorts and her dress. That's it. "Fuck, we definitely left stuff on the field."

Hannah is covered in a light dusting of dirt. Her hair is a complete mess, her lips swollen and mascara smudged, but she's laughing so damn hard. I don't know that I've ever seen such pure happiness.

"Holy shit, we almost got caught having sex at my work." She covers her mouth, doubling over with laughter.

"So much for texting the security guards," I mumble as I push her toward the locker room across the hall.

Hannah disappears, her hips swaying as she goes, like she doesn't have a single worry in the world. When she returns, she holds a towel out to me. "Clean off the dust. Don't want them to see us on a camera in the concourse and figure out that the panties and shirt they find are from us."

A scoff escapes me. "Hannah, I don't have a shirt. If they see us on the cameras, they're going to know we were the ones out there."

She shakes her head. "Give me a little credit, Hall. I'm good at my job."

And I'll hand it to her. She pulls me into the locker room and procures a Revs shirt. Then she leads me down a hall where she assures me there are no cameras. We slip through a secret door that leads to the tunnels beneath all the Langfield facilities. We pass by Ground Zero quickly. Though there's no game tonight, low music rumbles from behind the closed door, which means there are at least a few players there. When we finally hit the arena, relief washes over me. I could move through this space with my eyes closed, and if we stay in the tunnels, we can make it to the players' parking garage without being seen.

By the time we step out into the warm night air again, we're grinning at one another.

"Think you'll be hearing from security?" I ask as I walk her back to her apartment.

She shrugs. "I'll figure it out if I do. I'm good at thinking on my feet."

I wrap my arm around her waist, keeping her close. "On your knees, on your back, on your feet." I kiss her head. "You're good at everything, dream girl."

She throws her head back, laughing. "Right back at you, Playboy."

Outside her building, she pulls me to a stop. "Can I ask you something?"

I nod, lost in the depths of her beautiful blue eyes.

"The tequila bottles, the restaurant—" Her brow creases. "Why were you trying so hard?"

With a sigh, I stroke her cheek. "I want you to like me."

Her face lights up in amusement. "I like you enough, Daniel."

I push in closer. "I want you to like me more than that."

Lip caught between her teeth, she studies me. "Why?"

"Because I really like you." I angle in close and brush my lips against hers. Instantly, need consumes me again. It always does when I'm this close to her. Fingers wrapped around the back of her neck, I pull her mouth to mine, inhaling her.

I want her to more than like me. I want her to crave me the way I crave her. Maybe I'm doing this wrong. Maybe I should be holding back and playing some type of game to keep her interested, but I can't find it in me to do that. I want her to want me. Not because she's having my baby. Not just because our sexual chemistry is out of this world. Those are only the tip of the iceberg when it comes to our potential.

That thought has me pulling back. I need more from this woman, and if I keep kissing her, she'll think I only want one thing. "When can I see you again?"

She whimpers, chasing my lips, but I grasp her arms and hold her in place.

"You can come up," she says, motioning to the door.

I shake my head. "Not tonight. I want to take you out again. I need a redo."

She giggles. "Personally, I thought this was an epic date. Not sure you can top it."

Forehead pressed to hers, I squeeze her arms. "Let me try."

"I'll be in town again next week."

"Next week it is." Straightening, I hug her tight. Then, with a final kiss to her forehead, I say good night.

I'm not sure anything I did tonight got me farther in my quest to win Hannah's heart, but I'll figure it out one date at a time.

# TEXT MESSAGES FROM DANIEL AND HANNAH'S PHONE

Sara: HANNAH. We've all been good. We've patiently waited for you to tell us, but PLEASE put us out of our misery.

Hannah: LOL, what?

Lennox: Don't WHAT us.

Hannah: You obviously already know.

Ava: And we're very happy for you.

Sara: Stop being so nice, Ava.

Sara: Hannah!

Hannah: Fine. I'm pregnant with Daniel Hall's baby. Happy now?

Sara: ECSTATIC. But the better question is how are YOU?

Hannah: Tired. Overwhelmed. Tired. Nervous. Have I said tired yet?

Ava: Lol. Pregnancy is exhausting.

Millie: Congrats. I can't wait to meet my niece
or nephew. Let me know if you need anything.
Or if my brother's being an idiot. Or maybe
don't, because that's probably a daily
occurrence.

Hannah: Haha. Thanks. He's been great.

Sara: Lunch to celebrate when you get back,
please. I want to hear every little detail.

Hannah: I assure you, you don't. But yeah,
sounds good. And sorry I didn't say anything.
Still getting used to this.

Lennox: You got this, girlfriend. And you have
us <3

Sara: The best aunties ever.

Millie: They really are :)

Sara: Aw, Mills. Can I come over and hang with
Viv today? I miss her.

Lennox: Oh, I want to come!

Daniel: How are you feeling?

Hannah: Good. Just getting into bed. The
game went extra long today.

Daniel: I was watching. Twelve innings? Fuck.
At least they pulled out the win, though.

Hannah: Didn't realize you watched baseball.

Daniel: Didn't really until you.

Hannah: I don't play.

Daniel: But you're somewhere there. Makes me feel closer to you.

Hannah: I'm not an emotional person, but that's really sweet.

Daniel: Nah, just being honest.

Hannah: Well, it's honestly sweet. Thank you. Can't keep my eyes open. I'll call you when I'm back in town.

Daniel: Sweet dreams, dream girl.

# CALLIOPE'S COLUMN



## Knocked It Out of the Park

I've always admired people who set goals and stick to them, whether they aspire to run a 5K or lose weight or hit a professional milestone. I've got my own list of things that I want to accomplish in my life—a bucket list, if you will—and every time I tick an activity off, the satisfaction that hits me rivals a really good orgasm. Pressing the pen into the paper and creating that little check mark is so, so gratifying.

And last week, I experienced double the satisfaction. Not only did I check off a major item from my bucket list, but said item involved multiple orgasms.

I really knocked it out of the park, and I'm not speaking figuratively. I had sex on a baseball field, a personal bucket list moment of mine.

We'll call it a win-win.

But crossing off this particular item got me to thinking: as I get older and am forced to be more responsible, will I have a chance to tick off the rest of the items on my bucket list? Does growing up mean giving up the fun things in life?

# Chapter 24
## Hannah

I'VE JUST HIT SUBMIT ON MY ARTICLE WHEN THE ALARM ON MY COMPUTER chimes, signaling it's time for my Zoom meeting. When I finally load the app—which, of course, needs updating, when does it not?—the squares are all filled with familiar faces.

The dads.

My stepdads, to be more precise. The four I sent the meeting invite too. My mother is supposed to be on the call, but as usual, she's late.

I smile and say hi, all the while holding my phone beneath the desk and furiously typing a reminder text to my mother. Every other person who's logged on has an actual job. They have better things to do than sit around and wait after being summoned like this, but my dads have never once blown me off when I ask to talk. I see them all individually here and there, but during the summer when I have no free time, we normally group chat. It's better than nothing.

The text I sent shows that it's been read, but when she doesn't respond, I sigh and focus on my dads. Looks like she doesn't plan to make an appearance. It's not really a surprise.

"Is Langfield working you too hard?" Pierce asks. He's Riggs and Ash's father. He knows Beckett's family, though I don't remember how.

"No, I'm fine." I wave a dismissive hand. "Just my mother."

In unison, all four men nod. They know the reality of life with Marilyn almost as well as I do. I'm honestly not convinced Marilyn is the name her parents gave her. My suspicion is that she changed it when she turned eighteen, but she'll never admit to it.

"You should come with Noah and Oliver the next time they come for dinner," Noah's father, Liam, says, his gaze assessing. "You look like you could use a good meal."

"Yes, I probably could. And I'll take you up on that."

"Is there a reason for the call, or did you just miss us?" Kevin, Matt and Tim's father—Ryot—teases. He's a lawyer, and his firm is extremely busy. He's not rushing me—or he doesn't mean to—but his time is valuable, so I get right to it.

I clear my throat and sit straighter. "Uh, yeah. The reason I set up this call is—"

"Oh, hello, boys!" My mother's flirtatious voice drowns mine out as she appears on the screen. Her picture appears smack dab in the middle of the group of them. I know the layout is Zoom's default, but it makes my eye twitch either way.

"Marilyn," Pierce says, his tone firm. "Hannah was just filling us in on what's going on in her life."

My heart squeezes at the way my dads always show up for me. Even small things like putting my mother in her place mean so, so much.

"Oh, Hannah, darling, of course we are so excited to hear about your life." Though she's speaking to me, her gaze is wandering. Clearly, she's more interested in checking out all of her ex-husbands than actually listening to what I have to say. The woman is shameless.

I let out a quick breath and paste on a smile. "I wanted to tell you all that I'm having a baby."

Like with my brothers, the dads speak at once. The questions echo the ones my brothers asked almost verbatim. After assuring them that I'm happy and that the father is a good man who wants to be involved, Pierce reminds me that he'll make him be involved—he is prior military and scary as fuck, just like Ash. Ryot says he'll set me up with the best family law attorney in Boston so I can make sure he pays child support and then some. Liam tells me he'll sit that boy down for a chat right away.

Hands held up, I reassure them that none of that will be necessary.

Bryce, the only man in the group who doesn't have his own kids, tears up, going on and on about how excited he is to be a granddad and how he can't wait to visit when the baby is born.

I'm not an emotional person, but my eyes get hot, and I have to blink away the mist clouding my vision.

Ryot is headed into mediation—the timing couldn't be more perfect —so we say our goodbyes. I promise to send them all the next sonogram picture and to keep them updated when I find out the sex. If Daniel and I decide we want to know. My guess is that he'll be eager to find out, and I'm a planner, so the more information I have, the better.

The second I log out of the meeting, my phone rings. To my surprise, when I see my mom's name on the screen, relief settles over me. She didn't say much on the call, and to say that didn't hurt would be a lie.

I accept the FaceTime request and smile. "Hey, Mom."

"Oh, Hannah, a baby!" she coos.

"Yes, I know it's unexpected, but I'm really excited."

Though I may still be terrified, it's true. I never planned to be a mom. Never played with dolls when I was a little girl. Never imagined holding a baby who looked anything like me. And I certainly didn't sleep with Daniel with any intention of becoming his baby mama. But as I splay a hand over my stomach, something I find myself doing more and more often, I can't help the excitement that bubbles up at the thought of our child.

"Yes, quite unexpected. Liam looked good, didn't he? Do you know if he's still single? Maybe I should come visit you." Her eyes light up. "You probably need my help, right?"

"Because of the pregnancy?" I ask, choking back a huff. "I'm okay, Mom. I'm traveling a lot. No need to come anytime soon."

Shoulders back, she humphs. "That can't be good for the baby."

What the hell does she know about what's good for kids?

"It's fine." I imbue all the firmness I usually save for Jasper Quinn into my tone. I find it's best when dealing with my mother too. She doesn't take hints. "The doctor says I can travel for the majority of my pregnancy without any problem."

Her lips turn down in concern. "And then what will you do?"

My heart clenches. Could it be possible? Does she actually care about my well-being?

"I can come and stay with you then. Maybe Liam and I will bond over our first grandbaby."

My stomach rolls. Never mind. There's no concern for me in that calculated tone. "Oliver is the first grandbaby."

"Well, he's not mine." She waves a hand.

I sigh. "Right. Listen, I have to go."

"Okay. Think about what I said. I'll give Liam a call and see what he thinks about getting together when I visit with you."

Right. Then, when Liam shows zero interest in her, she will show zero interest in coming to visit me. That's fine. Easier, even.

Once I've ended the call, I cradle my stomach again. "I won't be like her. I won't be like her." It's my mantra. One I haven't uttered in a long time. In college and during my ridiculously short marriage, I chanted it almost constantly. A few months into the marriage, when I gave up on the institution, is when I realized I was exactly like her.

I'm not cut out for marriage. But that doesn't mean I'm not cut out to be a mom. I'll be better.

*I won't be like her.*

"WE NEVER SEE YOU ANYMORE," SARA WHINES. LUNCH ON THE SEAPORT was a must after so many days spent traveling. The last thing I wanted to do with the couple of days I have in Boston is spend my lunch hour in Langfield Corp's lunchroom. Beckett Langfield doesn't half-ass anything, so it's the nicest lunch facility in corporate America, I'm sure, but if I see any of the baseball players in the next hour, I may rip their eyeballs out. The guys are in rare form this season. With a bunch of rookies on the roster, the mid-season itch is strong.

And Jasper. Fucking Jasper. Every time I give that kid some rope, thinking he can handle the responsibility, he goes and tangles himself up in it like a stupid dog.

"Baseball season," I mutter as I stare longingly at the sangria Lennox and Sara ordered. They offered not to drink, but both Ava and I waved them off. Millie didn't order a drink at first, and for a moment I wondered if she'd be making an announcement soon, but when the server brought the sangrias, she asked for a mimosa, so I guess I've just got baby on the brain.

"How was Canada?" Lennox asks Ava.

She and War just returned from a three-week visit to Canada. He wanted to show the kids where he's from. After that, they made a stop in Nebraska to see Ava's parents.

This is the first time I've seen the girls since I announced my pregnancy. It's safe to say I missed them something fierce.

With a fifty-two series schedule from February through October, it's just the way it is. There's little time to stop. Though the pregnancy has made it harder to handle. I'm tired all the time and cranky because I miss my bed and my friends.

And if I'm honest, I miss Daniel.

Thank god next week is the All-Star break. Four baseball-free days. I might sleep for three of them.

"It was so good." Ava is glowing. I've literally never seen a prettier pregnant person. Her wavy red hair is like a halo highlighting her rosy cheeks, and her green eyes are bright like she's getting lots of rest and sex. She's probably having all the sex with her hot hockey player husband.

I'm jealous as fuck of my best friend.

Normally, I'm all for my friends having great sex lives. I'm never jealous. If I want something, I go out and find it.

But now that I'm barely having sex, that green-eyed monster keeps rearing its ugly head. I can't very well just call Daniel for a hookup when I'm in town, can I?

Though I normally don't give a shit about rules, I find that, with him, I overthink far more than I ever have.

I sip my water, and when I set it back down, every eye at the table is on me. Oh. Oops. Clearly I spaced out and missed the complete breakdown of Ava's trip. And by the expectant looks on all the girls' faces, one of them asked me a question.

"Hmm?" I ask, feigning like I didn't quite catch it.

Millie giggles. "Lennox asked how you're feeling."

"I probably shouldn't say horny?"

Ava blushes, and Millie folds her lips in.

Lennox, of course, squeals. Decked out in head-to-toe pink—including her hair—she bounces in her seat, a huge grin splitting her face. "Why shouldn't you say that? Is it true that pregnancy sex is better than normal sex? I read that all the blood is centered down there, so it's supposed to be incredible."

I peek over at Millie. Typically, I have no shame, but I worry about making her uncomfortable. I guess I want her to like me for her brother. It's odd. I know. I'm not with her brother. But I'm her future niece or nephew's mom, so rather than overshare, I just shrug.

"Don't be shy on my account," Millie says quickly. "I know my brother."

"Speaking of her brother," Sara says, her tone full of mischief. "What's going on with you two?"

I shake my head and swallow down the lump in my throat. "What do you mean?"

"He hasn't shut up about the baby since he told us. Right, Mills?" Sara looks at her sister-in-law for confirmation.

Millie nods. "He's very excited."

My cheeks heat. I know he is. At last week's OB appointment, Daniel made sure we got a good fifteen images of the baby for the baby album. He framed his favorite and set it on the bookshelf in my living room next to the first. I imagine he's done the same at his apartment, but I can't confirm, since I've never been there.

"He's been nothing but helpful since we found out."

Lennox scrunches her nose. "Helpful? Toothbrushes are helpful. Tell us the good stuff. Are you guys a couple? What are you going to do when the baby is born?"

Sara nudges her roughly in the ribs. "Shush."

Though a hint of unease swirls in my stomach, I laugh. "It's fine.

Honestly, we barely know one another. I like him. He's a great guy." I turn to Millie. "He's going to be a great father."

She nods, though her smile is forced. She knows as well as I do that Daniel doesn't do relationships, and that if I weren't pregnant with his kid, he'd likely be doing a different woman every night during his offseason.

And if I weren't pregnant, I'd be sleeping with a different man in every city while traveling with the team.

Like two peas stuck in the same pod for the rest of our lives.

"Anyway," I say lightly, returning to Lennox's sex question. That's what I'm good at, after all. "My nipples are oversensitive, and you're right—the orgasms are out of this world."

"I knew it!" Lennox hoots, and the girls all dissolve into giggles. The focus turns to Ava, who's bright red, as they press her for confirmation.

Though Millie's gaze quickly wanders back to me. And I have to wonder, what is Daniel saying in response to these questions? Is anyone asking him what his intentions are? Should I?

# CHAPTER 25
## DANIEL

*But crossing off this particular item got me to thinking: as I get older and am forced to be more responsible, will I have a chance to tick off the rest of the items on my bucket list? Does growing up mean giving up the fun things in life?*

For the last two weeks, the final lines of her column have been beating like a drum in my head. Just the thought of crossing that item off her bucket list has my heart pumping. It makes me irrationally happy. It's stupid, really. Especially since she just texted, canceling on me for dinner tonight. She's exhausted. I understand that. Obviously I told her it was fine and to rest.

She promised she was taking care of herself on the road and made sure to remind me that our next OB appointment isn't until the end of August—when we can find out the sex of the baby if we want.

She doesn't expect to not see me again until then, does she?

I miss her. Not the woman having my child, but Hannah herself. I miss her, and every time I think we're taking a step in the right direction, she leaves the damn state, and it feels like we're starting back at the beginning again.

To top that all off, Camden's trade is official. He left for Vegas last week. It hasn't sunken in. Not until tonight. Gavin is hosting a team dinner for the guys who are in town, and for as long as we've played together, Camden has always been here for these.

I survey the guys in attendance. Brooks, Aiden, and Gavin are gushing over Vivi, while War and Noah are in deep conversation about god only knows what. Keegan and I have been shooting the shit, but even that kid has a girlfriend, so when his phone rang a few minutes ago, he stepped out into the hall to talk to her.

With another look at Hannah's text, I consider begging her to let me bring her something. Anything. But that's pathetic. If the woman wanted to see me, she'd tell me. She never has difficulty telling me what she wants.

"Yeah, we find out next week," War is saying as I stuff my phone into my pocket and shuffle over to where he and Noah are standing by the bar. He's holding a small piece of paper out. One that I've become all too familiar with.

"That the baby?" I ask, peeking over at the sonogram picture.

"Sure is." He grins down at the image. "He's a handsome guy, isn't he?"

"Thought you weren't finding out the sex until next week?" I ask.

"Oh, we aren't, but we're positive it's a boy. All the signs point to it."

I slip my wallet out of my pocket and pull out a picture of our baby.

Noah takes it and gives it a thoughtful look. "Is that one different from the one on Hannah's shelf?"

"I've got, like, six, so maybe?"

War takes it next. "It's wild. We're going to have babies at the same time. Ava's thrilled about it. How's Hannah doing now that she's had time to process?"

Though he's looking at me, I focus on Noah. He's more likely to have that answer. I'm pretty sure Hannah tells him everything.

When Noah realizes I'm watching him, he's gracious enough to respond without making it weird. "You know Hannah. She goes with the flow and makes everything her bitch. She's handling the pregnancy like a pro."

"Are those pictures of the babies?" Aiden appears, and then we're surrounded by the rest of the guys, all studying our two blobs and commenting on whether they think a certain angle makes it clear the babies are boys. Leave it to a group of men to see penises in every abstract image.

In all honesty, I don't care whether the baby is a girl or a boy, though the idea of a son causes this strange pressure in my chest. Maybe because I'm so close with my dad, or maybe because I'm just more comfortable around guys.

I couldn't begin to guess either way. The longer the conversation goes on, the less I realize I know.

War, of course, knows precisely how his wife is carrying—high—whether she's got heartburn—she doesn't—and what her cravings are —salty foods.

Luckily, the guys don't ask me. Probably because they realize I won't have the answers. We're just sitting down for after-dinner drinks when my sister strolls into the apartment, her cheeks flushed and her gait relaxed. The moment Vivi sees her, she squeals. "Mama! Mama!"

With their daughter in his arms, Gavin gets up and greets my sister at the door. In this moment, I know what I'm witnessing is exactly what I want. I want to be greeted by my excited child when I get home. I want to share that home with Hannah. And if I don't figure out how to make that happen, these are the moments I'll miss out on. Every night.

"How was your afternoon with the girls?" Gavin asks her as he ushers her inside. It may be guys' night, but he welcomes her happily. That's the kind of guy he is. Wherever he is, Millie and Vivi are welcome. If someone has a problem with that, they can leave. He's a family guy, a great coach, and a genuinely good person. Thank god my sister didn't listen to me when I told her seeing him was a bad idea.

Eyes glassy, she appraises the lot of us. "I feel like I'm tattling if I tell you." She cups a hand to one side of her mouth, and in a loud whisper, says, "All their husbands are here."

Noah holds up his hands and barks out a laugh. "Not married, so don't look at me."

She peruses the group again, this time more slowly, making eye contact with Aiden, Brooks, and War. "But they all are," she whisper-shouts.

"Did you have a few drinks, Peaches?" Gavin murmurs.

My sister's dark, curly hair bounces as she giggles. "Not pregnant yet, so might as well!" As the laughter dies down, she catches sight of me, and her eyes go wide. "You! You're in trouble!"

"Why am I in trouble? Also, what do you mean not pregnant *yet*? Are you guys trying?"

Gavin presses a kiss to Millie's neck. "We're always trying. Right, Peaches?"

I gag and have to choke back bile. Otherwise I risk puking on the guys' shoes.

"Nope, you don't get to change the subject." Millie shakes her head wildly. "Hannah is sad."

My gut plummets. "She's what?"

"Sad. You made her sad. You are very bad." She giggles, the sound ending with a hiccup. "That rhymes. Look at that, Aiden. I'm almost as good as you are with bad lyrics."

"You're a songwriter," I grumble. "You're better than Aiden—"

He huffs, but before he can disagree, I shoot him a glare to shut him up. "What do you mean Hannah is sad?"

"She doesn't know you," she says in that tipsy voice. "She should know you, Danny. Although, I wouldn't have slept with you"—the room erupts in a chorus of groans, but that doesn't deter her—"but she seems to like you, so you need to fix this."

"Fix what?" Chest tight, I look at Noah.

He only shrugs. "I have no idea what she's talking about. Hannah seemed fine when I saw her a couple of hours ago."

"Mills, baby. Why don't you go take a shower?" Gavin passes Vivi to Brooks and grasps his wife by the upper arms.

I step in front of them. Hell no. I'm not done with this conversation. "What exactly did she say?"

Millie tilts her head, her face scrunched in concentration. "It was her eyes. They looked sad. She said you're a good guy, but she doesn't really know you." Millie's dark eyes—the same color as mine—bore into me, and that twin sense kicks in. That look is all it takes for me to understand exactly what she sensed when she saw Hannah.

"But how do I get her to give me the time to get to know me?"

I step back and scan the group. I need all the help I can get. I'm fucking trying, but between Hannah's busy schedule, my reputation as nothing but a playboy, and her obvious distrust of men in general, what I'm facing is the definition of an uphill battle.

One guy after another rattles off generic advice.

Noah, on the other hand, purses his lips in concentration. "Ya know," he says when the other guys have quieted down.

I lean forward. If he's got an idea, then I'm all ears.

"You should take her on a *have a day* trip."

Millie nods, her expression lighting up. "Oh yeah!"

My mind spins as I try to decode what they're saying. "A what?"

"A have a day trip. It's a thing Hannah talks about all the time. She has a fund for it," Millie explains, like her words make perfect sense.

Noah grins. "She made me go on one when Jen got pregnant."

Beside me, War crosses his arms. "Oliver's mom?"

Noah nods.

"But you're not with Oliver's mom. So the trip obviously didn't help." Shoulders sagging, I drop into my chair.

"Oh, I didn't go with Jen." He joins me at the table. "Hannah came up with the idea when her mom got divorced the first time. She wanted to cheer her up, so she took all the money from her piggy bank, and they spent the night in a hotel. Hannah's convinced there's something magical about hotels." He laughs as if hit with a memory the two of them probably share.

Dammit. I hate that I'm hearing this from him and not her.

"Anyway," he shrugs. "She saves money, and when someone she's close to has a breakup or a big life change, she makes sure they *have a day*. It doesn't have to be fancy, but the point is to take a step back from real life and splurge a little. She sent me on one when I found out about Oliver."

His expression turns wistful then, like he's lost in thought.

"Alone?" Brooks asks.

Noah shakes his head like he's forcing himself back to the present and sighs. "Yeah, I went alone."

"Why do I get the feeling there's more to this story?" Millie leans forward so far that if it weren't for Gavin holding her up, she'd probably fall over.

"Okay, you sound like Beckett now," Gavin grumbles.

"There was a girl. It was a good week." Noah wipes the smile from his face and looks back at me. "Hannah's got a few days off next week."

"Oh, yes! The all-star break," Millie squeals.

My heart thumps with anticipation, but my brain won't stop spinning. "How will I get her to agree to go away with me, though?"

"You ask," War says, his blue eyes more piercing than ever. "You're Daniel Fucking Hall. You ask, and if she says no, you beg."

Brooks chokes out a laugh. "Yeah, I have a feeling Hannah would love to see you on your knees."

"Ew!" Millie groans and flops back against her husband.

"And with that, I'm out." Noah stands, shaking his head. "If you get on your knees, just please don't be loud." He shudders.

Millie groans again. "Hannah's the loud one."

"Please stop." Noah roughs a hand through his dark hair.

She giggles. "Oh, I love having someone new to taunt. Hannah's always taunting me."

"Okay, Peaches. We're going to bed." Gavin picks my sister up and heads down the hall. Over his shoulder, he calls, "Brooks, you got Vivi?"

"I got her," he calls. Then, to me, he says, "Go get your girl."

BACK IN MY QUIET APARTMENT, I LIE IN BED AND STARE AT THE PHONE. IT'S now or never, right?

> Me: How was your bath?

Dream Girl: I would have preferred one with jets, but the warm water felt good.

Me: Hmm, so you prefer hotel rooms with jacuzzi tubs?

Dream Girl: that sounds dirty.

Dream Girl: But also, yes.

Me: lol. You up for another adventure?

Dream Girl: Tonight?

Me: No. (Though I'd gladly venture over to your apartment right now if you said yes.) I'm talking about next week. I heard you have a few days off.

Dream Girl: Yeah, for the all-star break

With a steadying breath, I type the next message, and then I go for it.

Me: Come away with me.

Dream Girl: Huh?

Me: A road trip. I've always wanted to go on one.

Dream Girl: You have?

Me: Yeah, what about you?

Dream Girl: It's on my bucket list, actually.

SATISFACTION COURSES THROUGH MY VEINS. BINGO.

Me: That same bucket list that included sex on a baseball field?

Dream Girl: <smirk emoji> I can't tell you all my secrets.

Me: If I ask, you have to share. We made a pact.

Dream Girl: Damn you and your honesty pact.

Me: LOL you don't have to if you don't want to.

Dream Girl: Promise you won't tease me.

Me: Never. I love teasing you.

Dream Girl: Dammit, but I'll share it anyway.

Me: On our road trip.

Dream Girl: What kind of music do you like?

Me: What kind of question is that?

Dream Girl: If we're going to be in a car for hours at a time, I need to make sure we're musically compatible.

Me: Lol, musically compatible.

Dream Girl: It's a thing.

Me: Hannah, we're compatible.

Dream Girl: You don't know that. You barely know me.

My heart thuds heavily. I'm tempted to type out a list of all the things I know about her just to prove her wrong. She knows me too. Though I can't say I don't want to learn more. There isn't a thing I don't want to know about Hannah.

Me: So get to know me. Let's go on a road trip together. You can ask me whatever you want during the trip.

Dream Girl: Whatever I want?

Me: Whatever you want. I'm an open book. Part of the honesty pact.

Dream Girl: Fine. But I control the music. And you drive.

I chuckle. Like I'd ever let her drive.

Me: Done.

Dream Girl: Seriously? Just like that.

Me: Yes, just like that.

Dream Girl: Why?

Me: You'll understand eventually.

Dream Girl: I'm tired, and you're talking in riddles, so I'm going to let you win this one.

Me: Okay, dream girl, get some rest.

Dream Girl: Okay.

Dream Girl: Daniel.

. . .

My chest warms. Fuck, I love when she uses my name. I can practically hear her throaty voice saying it.

Me: Yeah?

Dream Girl: I'm really excited about our trip.

Me: Me too, baby.

# Chapter 26
## Hannah



"Why did I agree to this?"

I'm sweating as I rush around my apartment, confirming I have everything I need. Or hoping like hell I do. I don't even know where we're going, so it's hard to know what those things might be.

We only have three nights, and he said road trip, so we aren't flying. That means we aren't going terribly far. So I went with summer clothing. I packed a few bathing suits, some leggings in case we're hiking, shorts, a few maxi dresses…and I might have tossed in a sexy piece of lingerie or two, just in case.

I have the tiniest bump. It seemed to pop over the last week.

Will Daniel notice? And if so, what will he think?

"Because everyone deserves to have a day," Noah answers.

The question was rhetorical. I didn't even realize he was home. Typically, when Oliver is with Jen, Noah is out moping around. He hates being away from his little guy during the summer, knowing he'll be gone so much the rest of the year, but Jen is strict about their parenting time, believing it's best to keep Oliver on a schedule.

I can't argue with that.

That's one more facet of life Daniel and I will eventually have to figure out.

Maybe while we're driving to who knows where.

"What are you talking about?" I say as he stops in the doorway.

"Who do you think suggested this little road trip?"

I smack him. "Ass."

He chuckles. "Please, you and I both know you're thrilled to have a few days away with your boy toy."

"He's not my boy toy. He's my—my—" I scrunch my nose and have to fight the urge to stomp my foot. The jerk called him that on purpose. He's trying to make me put a label on it. "Never mind, you. Why would you suggest a trip?"

Head tilted, he gives me a placating smile, like he thinks I'm an idiot. "You're always the one who plans trips for the people you care about. Let us take care of you this time, Han."

I sigh, shoulders falling. "I feel like you're meddling."

"You sent me on one when I found out about Oliver."

"Yeah, without your baby mama. It was a week away to get your head on straight before you had a kid. And you could drink. And have sex with strangers."

"You want to have sex with strangers?" he asks, brow creased in genuine curiosity.

No. I really don't. The idea of touching anyone but Daniel makes my stomach roll. And the idea of another woman touching him? It makes my chest burn like I need an antacid. I haven't had heartburn a single time during my pregnancy, so I can't even blame it on the baby. No, it's all because of Daniel and the intrusive thoughts suddenly plaguing me. Rather than answer his question, I change the subject. "Did the trip help?"

His eyes flutter shut and his lips tip in the smallest of smiles, like he's disappearing into a memory. "When things got really tough that first year"—he opens his eyes—"I'd think of that trip, and it was enough to get me through."

"I still don't understand why you didn't look that girl up afterward."

Though he didn't share many details, it was clear that their time together was more than a week-long vacation fling. But he refused to speak about her then, and years later, he's still holding strong.

He grabs my suitcase and rolls it to the door. "Do me a favor?" He doesn't turn around, like he's not yet ready to face me.

"Name it."

He turns, his expression serious. "Give him a shot. For the next few days, get to know the father of your baby."

"Like you did with Jen?" I tease, willing my nerves to remain steady.

He rolls his eyes. "Jen and I never had the kind of connection you have with Hall."

I don't even know what that means. Why the hell does every one of my friends swear there's more going on between us than there is?

Not interested in arguing, I duck my head and rifle through my purse, double-checking that I have all I need. "Fine. I'll be open-minded."

Noah sags in relief. "Thank you."

We're still hovering near the door when a knock sounds from the other side.

When Noah pulls it open, we come face to face with Daniel, who's wearing a smirk and a black shirt with *daddy* scrawled across it.

"Harry!" He holds out his hand, and then the two of them do some weird slap-grab-bro-hug thing. When they're finished, Daniel zeroes in on me, his lips tipped up in the sexiest smirk. "Ready for our next adventure, dream girl?"

I huff like I'm being put out, even as a zing of excitement courses through me. "You going to tell me where we're going?"

He steps past Noah, drinking me in. His perusal comes to a halt at my stomach. Then he's reaching out, hand splayed, like he can't stop himself. Just before his fingers brush my abdomen, he pulls back a fraction. "May I?"

My lower belly coils tight in response. God, why is that hot?

*May I?*

Fuck.

I suck in a breath and nod.

When he gently presses his palm to my stomach, tears burn my eyes. It's too much. The way he looks at our connection, the reverence in his gaze. Dark eyes on my face again, he gives me the softest, sweetest smile. Like he knows exactly what I need. Exactly how to handle me in this moment. "Our baby's in there," he whispers.

I suck in an unsteady breath and nod again. There's no way I could speak right now.

He tugs me to him, hugging me with the perfect amount of pressure. Tight enough to imbue me with the comfort I need but not too tight. "You got that list for me?" he murmurs in my ear.

I nod against his shoulder and clear my throat. "It's a note in my phone. I'll share it with you."

He releases me and pulls his phone out, clearly eager to get his eyes on the bucket list I added to last night. Some of the items are ridiculous. Others are simple but still meaningful. I put a lot of genuine thought into all I hope to accomplish in my life. It's absurd, really, but typing it all out was therapeutic. Like putting it into the universe made it hold less weight.

I hit Send, and an instant later, his phone buzzes. My stomach flips as he unlocks the device, my nerves a mess. I've given him yet another piece of me, and part of me wants to unsend the message before he can open it.

For a solid minute, he uses his thumb to scroll through all the bullet points. Finally he peers up at me, his messy hair hanging over his forehead. "Give me until the end of the list."

I tilt my head, lips turned down in consideration. Does he mean what I think he means? "Why?"

"You want to get to know me, and I want to get to know you better. Give me until the end of the list."

Tongue pressed to my cheek, I step closer. "There are quite a few things on that list, Playboy. You sure you're up for it?"

With a grin, he cups my face with one hand. "For you, always."

Stomach swooping, I lean in. God, I want to kiss the ever-loving shit out of this man—

"I'm going to get out of here," Noah says, his voice like a bucket of ice water.

Oops. Poor guy. If he hadn't spoken up, there's no telling what would have happened next.

My cheeks flame in an unfamiliar way, and I turn my face into Daniel's palm, hiding. "Bye, Noah."

When the door shuts behind my stepbrother, Daniel chuckles and presses a soft kiss to the side of my neck. "Come on, dream girl. We've got a list to attack."

"You really aren't going to tell me?" I ask for what has to be the fifth time since he merged onto I-95 headed north. I don't often travel from Boston by car, so I don't have the faintest clue where we could be going.

As promised, he's let me control the radio the entire time. We're currently listening to Tom Petty with the windows down and the warm summer wind whipping my hair all around. I couldn't wipe the smile from my face if I tried.

Daniel tips his head in my direction. The way he holds the steering wheel, with one hand, his arm relaxed and yet somehow the muscles still bulging, is so damn sexy. "Do you trust me?"

"I got in the car with you, didn't I?"

He arches a brow, doubling down on his question. "Do you trust me?"

With an exhale, I relax against my seat. "Yes, I trust you."

Daniel's expression softens. "Then let me surprise you. Okay?"

Though my natural reaction is to argue, to demand I have at least a little control, I give in. "Okay."

He switches arms and grasps my hand, giving it a squeeze.

It's impossible not to smile down at them. I've never held hands with another person in a car, at least not that I remember. His hands are surprisingly soft for a hockey player's, though they are huge in comparison to mine.

"Did Ava tell you they're finding out the sex of the baby next week?"

I blink out of my rumination and focus on his face. "Oh yeah, she mentioned that at lunch."

He licks his lips and peeks over at me quickly. "Do you want to find out what we're having?"

"Yes," I blurt out, and when he laughs, I straighten. "What? Don't you?"

He nods. "Yeah, I'd like to know." He clears his throat, his focus fixed on the road. "Do you have any feelings that make you think you know what we're having?"

On instinct, I cradle my stomach with my free hand and close my eyes. It's simple, in this moment, to allow myself to let go of all the stress I usually carry. Right here, with no work to worry about and Daniel's hand in mine, the music playing and the sun warming my face, I feel nothing short of happy.

"I think it's a boy." I roll my head in his direction again and open my eyes. "What do you think?"

Daniel presses his lips together in the way he does when he's concentrating. He sucks on them, making his dimples deepen.

I'm beginning to think this expression is one of his tells. Something he does when he's trying to temper his words.

"I don't really know what kind of symptoms you're having. War said Ava hasn't had heartburn, that she craves salty food, and that she's carrying high—" He darts a look at my abdomen, sucking in a breath like he still can't believe what he's seeing. That, or maybe he's overwhelmed. "I don't even know what any of that means, though."

With my head resting against the seat, I study him. The man I find myself more and more fond of every time we're together. He's nothing like the playboy good-time guy I thought he was.

"I always prefer salty over sweet, so I'm not sure that says much about anything. No heartburn, and as far as how I'm carrying—" I look down just like he did and shrug. "I have no idea. Probably too early. I guess maybe it's not so much that I think it's a boy but that I secretly hope it is."

The happiness radiating from him as he smiles at me is so pure, so comforting. "You want a boy?"

"I wouldn't be upset if it was a girl," I say, glancing out the window at the scenery. "I just never had a great relationship with my mom, so I guess I'm nervous that if I have a daughter, we'll have that same type of relationship. I worry that I don't really know how to be a girl mom."

Daniel gives my hand another comforting squeeze. "You'll be a great mom, no matter what we have. I have no doubt."

"You have to say that."

"I had a pretty easy relationship with my mom," he says instead of arguing. "But for our whole lives, she tried to turn my sister into what she considered the perfect daughter. She could be harsh and unkind to her, and she always pushed her own agenda rather than allowing Millie to pursue what made her happy. Honestly, I think what Millie went through has made her a better mother." He lifts a shoulder. "Yeah, Vivi is only two, but already, it's clear that Millie always has her daughter's best interest in mind. She works hard not to be our mother, and I have no doubt you'll do the same."

Heart thudding, I have to focus on my breathing to keep the tears at bay. "Thank you, Daniel." I look past him, focusing on the dense forest we're passing. "My mom isn't all bad. She's just selfish."

Maybe that's downplaying it, but it's hard to admit some of her worst attributes. Despite that, I find myself wanting him to understand me better, and I guess a part of that includes who I am because of my mother.

"And your father?"

"Not like Daddy Hall," I say breezily.

Daniel snaps his head to the side and glares. "Don't."

I giggle. "Sorry, habits die hard. And you've got to admit, you've got one hot dad."

He groans, pushing his head back against the seat. "Hannah."

"You should be happy about that. Good genes. You'll probably look just like him when you grow up."

He coughs out a laugh. "I am grown up."

"Nah, you're still a baby."

He shakes his head, but he's smiling. "So you're close with your stepdads?"

"Yup. And unfortunately, you get to meet them all. Don't worry, only one of them owns guns and knows how to use them."

He grips the wheel tighter, making it creak, and hisses out a *Jesus*.

"Honestly," I say with a grin, "he's the last one you should worry about. The rest own guns and don't know how to use them. Far more dangerous."

"*Hannah.*"

I shake with my silent laughter.

"You're evil, you know that?"

"I do."

An easy silence falls between us as the sound of Billy Joel's voice fills the car. When we hit the sign for New Hampshire, Daniel pulls over to the side of the road and tells me to get out.

I turn to him, my back pressed to the door. "Damn, what did I do to make you mad enough to kick me out of the car?"

He steps out and rounds the hood, hand outstretched when I throw my door open. "I want to get a picture in front of the sign."

I glance at the Welcome to New Hampshire sign. "But why?"

He shakes his head. "Do you always ask so many questions?"

"Yes. So like I said, why?"

He ducks into the car, looming over me, and unbuckles my seat belt, then tugs me by the hand. I follow him away from the whizzing cars and toward the sign, still confused.

He positions me in front of it, then backs up and pulls his phone out. "For the baby album," he says, holding it up. "I want to show him or her where we took them for their first road trip."

The smile I wear as he snaps the picture might be the most genuine ever to be caught on camera. It reaches my soul.

He does this again when we reach Vermont, only this time, I ask him to join me in the picture, and we take a selfie. "Our first real picture," he says quietly as he studies it.

"Can you send it to me?"

He looks up, his brows lifted in surprise, but without a word, he forwards it through text.

"So are we crossing the border?" I ask. If we're headed to Canada, then I'm going to have to stop at a bathroom first.

"Nah, our destination is only a little farther."

In the car again, he takes my hand like it's a habit and heads back onto the highway. I open up the text from him and examine the photo of the two of us. Suddenly I can imagine sitting on the edge of a toddler bed, listening to Daniel tell our child all about this trip. I can visualize him with a photo album on his lap, pointing at this exact picture.

It's the two of us together in that room. Parents. And maybe something more.

I allow that thought to settle in my bones. To take up residence in my heart. To warm me from the inside out.

Forget the promise I made to Noah. I'm doing this for me. For our child. I'm going to open my heart to the possibility that, just maybe, Daniel and I really could be more.

# CHAPTER 27
# DANIEL

"The moment of truth," Hannah says as I pull out the key to our room. It's a legit brass key. Of course it is, because we're staying at a classic New England Airbnb. While Hannah enjoys luxuries, I can't help but think the author in her would prefer the feel of this spot over an impersonal hotel room, even at the Ritz.

Aside from the romantic vibe, there's a forest behind the house with trails that lead to a waterfall. I don't know whether she's into hiking, but if not, there's plenty to do without wandering into the woods.

I quirk a brow her way. "The moment of truth?"

"Yes, in romance novels, there's a moment when the couple opens the door to their hotel room to discover there's only—" She stops, brows lifted, so I swing the door open and step aside. As she walks in, her shoulders slump almost imperceptibly. "Two double beds," she says, her tone a bit softer.

I inspect the room from the doorway. It seems clean and airy. The forest is framed perfectly in a picture window, and the bench built into it is cozy. I was certain she'd love that part. Yet I swear she's trying to hide her disappointment. "Something wrong with the beds?"

She smiles and shakes her head. "Nope. I'm going to use the bathroom really quick. I've had to pee for, like, ten exits."

I wave her deeper inside, then set our bags on the small benches at the end of each bed. Hands in my pockets, I shuffle to the window and take in the view. When the bathroom door opens, I spin around and pat the bench. "Come join me over here for a minute."

The second her ass hits the cushion, I pull her closer. For a moment, we just breathe together, holding one another. In this moment, I'm more relaxed than I've been in a long fucking time. It's easier, I've noticed, to settle when I'm with her. Sitting quietly with Hannah like this is a gift, doing so with my hands on her, a dream. With my baby inside her? It's fucking otherworldly.

How did I get so damn lucky?

"You sure the room is okay?" I nuzzle against her neck. "You seemed upset by the two beds."

Hannah tilts her head up, her blue eyes sparkling with humor. "You noticed that, huh?"

With a hand under her chin, I smooth my thumb over the little divot that feels like it's just for me. "I notice everything when it comes to you."

She worries her bottom lip, her soft breath fluttering against my fingers. How is it possible that such a tiny wisp of air could send blood rushing straight through me?

"Don't look at me like that unless you intend to do something about it," she practically purrs.

I angle in, my lips brushing hers. "We have nowhere to be and nothing that has to be done for the next three nights."

"With two beds," she sags in my arms.

My lips curve up. "You really hate that second bed."

"I really do."

"It's a good thing we've got this bench, then." Without pulling my face from hers, I pat at it.

She sticks out her tongue, and instead of licking her bottom lip, she laps at mine, and fuck does that make my toes curl.

Unable to hold back, I pull her closer and suck her tongue into my mouth.

Fingers digging into my thighs, she matches my fervor. Soft whimpers have me pulling her onto my lap, trying to get her closer.

"God, I'm so horny," she mumbles against my mouth as she pulls at my shirt.

With a laugh, I break away so she can yank the fabric over my head. "Way to make a guy feel special."

"I'll make you feel special. I'll make you feel so special your eyes roll to the back of your head," she teases as she drops onto her knees and pushes my thighs apart.

I bury a hand in her hair and tug gently. "What are you doing, dream girl? I should be on my knees for you."

Brows waggling, she grins. "We're going to work on your stamina."

She's already tugging on my shorts, so I lift my hips to make it easier. "And how are we going to do that?"

"I'm going to blow you until you're seconds from coming, then you're going to stop me."

"That sounds like an awful idea." My tone is all tease as I give my cock a firm tug and brush the head over her lips. She wants to teach me how to last longer, and there's no way in hell I'll stop her. She knows what she's talking about. My fucking Calliope.

She purses her lips and literally blows warm air against the head of my dick. I let out a rough exhale at the tingling sensation coursing up my spine. And when she flicks her tongue over my crown, taunting me, I resist the urge to force her mouth open wide.

She cups my balls and squeezes, focus fixed on my face. "It will be incredible. Because, eventually, you'll have the ability to orgasm multiple times, just like me." With a long lick up my shaft, she finally takes me into her mouth.

I slump back, my head bumping against the window, eyes closed. "That's the dream, Hannah. You are a fucking dream."

She hums around me, the vibrations sending electricity straight to my balls. I ease up straight again so I can watch her. Hannah's blow jobs are a performance art. She doesn't just suck. She fondles and deep throats. She hums and moans. She jacks me and then squeezes, and when I signal that I'm close, she holds me at the precipice. Over and over, she does it until I'm panting and begging.

"You're such a good boy." She licks my sac and sucks my balls into her mouth. It's heavenly. Euphoric. Transcendent.

Until she falls back, leaving me hard, aching, ready to burst.

On instinct, I reach for my dick, desperate to ease the ache, but she bats my hand away.

"Don't touch."

"Fuck, baby. I don't know if I can—"

She tugs her shorts off and spreads her thighs, and goddamn, I fall to my knees, crawling to get to her, my mouth watering. My aching dick all but forgotten.

"I need to touch you," I plead, holding myself back until she gives me permission.

She spreads herself with two fingers, unabashedly showing off that gorgeous, drenched pink flesh. "You've been a good boy. You can eat now."

Just like she taught me through her column, I lick and suck until she's a puddle, crying out for me to fuck her. When I finally slide inside her, still avoiding either of the fucking beds, we let out matching sighs.

"I could live inside you," I tell her, thrusting slowly. Each time I pull back, she tightens her thighs, bringing me closer, as if she can't stand the distance.

"*Daniel*," she moans. Gripping the hair at my nape, she pulls me in for a kiss. Our mouths stay fused like that until I'm once again on the precipice. She's writhing and panting like she's right there with me.

Before I can plunge in again, she pulls back, and I have to fight the whimper that rolls up my throat.

"Please, dream girl," I pant. "Please let me come."

With her eyes fixed on the space where we're joined, she gasps. "Do it, Daniel. I want to watch you pulse as you empty inside me. I want you to fuck me so good I could get pregnant again. Fill me up and don't you dare let a drop escape."

Fuck. This woman. The need to see my release dripping from her spurs me on. I piston my hips, quickening my pace until I'm unloading every ounce of pleasure inside her. And when I pull back and admire the way my length is coated in a mixture of both of us, I can't fight the urge to thrust back inside her, pushing it all back in.

"Yes," she yells, her voice hoarse.

Every nerve ending in my cock sparks. *Fuck.* The pleasure is almost unbearable. I pull out and replace my cock with my fingers, pushing my cum back inside her. Finding the exact angle my girl needs, I curl my fingers, hitting that magic spot, kissing her through her orgasm. I keep kissing her, and I don't stop, even as the kisses become softer, more affectionate rather than passionate. I kiss her because I can't pull away. Then I lift her up and set her on the bed closest to the bathroom while I run a bath for her.

We spend the afternoon soaking in the tub, talking and getting to know one another even better. She tells me about every town she lived in growing up. We talk about the towns we've both traveled to with our respective teams, comparing our favorite sights, discovering that we like a lot of the same restaurants and bars. Each time the water cools enough to become slightly uncomfortable, she turns on the hot water with her toes, and we drain a little of the cold out.

By the time we emerge, the sun is dipping behind the mountain.

"I ordered room service," I call from the bed.

"I feel bad." She appears in the bathroom doorway, wearing a fluffy white robe just like I am.

I pat the spot next to me, and she pads over and then settles close.

"Why?"

"You planned a special trip, and we haven't left the hotel room."

I tilt her chin up so she's looking at me again. "Are you having a good time?"

Her lips curve into that beautiful smile I'm starting to become addicted to. Oh, fuck, who am I kidding? I'm well and truly deep in my addiction by now. There's no starting involved.

"The best."

"Then I'm happy. My goal was to give you a few days away from real life so you could relax. You've been going nonstop, and I'm about to do the same since training starts next week."

She hums contentedly. "I appreciate it. Did Noah tell you this is what I did for him when he found out Jen was pregnant?"

"He did. Though he didn't say much more than that. Just that it's something you do for people."

*"Have a day* trips." She leans against me. "I started the tradition after my mother's first divorce."

I let out a low hum, hoping she picks up on my interest. I'm completely infatuated with this woman, and I don't mind admitting it one bit.

"She was so depressed. She wouldn't get out of bed. Wouldn't get dressed. He was the only husband to ever leave *her*. And she never allowed that to happen again." She shakes her head subtly, like she still doesn't understand it. "When I was young, if I had a bad day, she'd tell me we should have a day. It meant shopping, treating ourselves. She did it on her ex-husband's card back then.

"When he left her, that was no longer possible, but I wanted to cheer her up like she'd always done for me. So I counted up all the money in my piggy bank, and we spent the night at a local hotel. We ordered room service and laid in bed, watching movies for hours." She gives me the smallest of smiles. "The next day, she perked up. God, I was so relieved. I can see now that it wasn't so much the hotel but that she realized it wasn't right to fall apart like that when she had a child to take care of. I think it hit her how sad it was that her daughter had to orchestrate the scenario to get her moving. Or at least I'd like to think that's what it was. Anyway." She shrugs. "From then on, any time a friend or family member hit a rough patch, I'd take money that I'd set aside and we'd go *have a day*. I've had far more of those days with my mother. One after each of her divorces. Then another after my own divorce."

Without my permission, my body tenses. *Divorce?* This is the first I'm hearing of it.

She peers up at me through her lashes, worrying her lip. "That's a story for another day, please?"

I give her an easy smile and squeeze her hip. I'll wait as long as she needs. "I'm glad that we're having a day," I say softly, "But, Hannah, our reality isn't something I need a break from. I understand if you don't feel the same way, but honestly, this is easily the best thing that's happened to me."

She pulls back, eyes wide. "How can you say that?"

An ache blooms in my chest. I want to pull her in again, but it's better that she looks me in the eye so she knows I'm serious. "Do you trust me?"

She nods. "I really do. It may not seem like I'm giving you much, but for me"—she motions between us—"*this is* a lot."

I get it. The last few hours in the bath—hell, the last few weeks— she's been slowly opening up to me in a way I don't believe she does with others. Now that I have a little insight into her history with her mother and the smallest tidbit of information about her divorce, I can't blame her for holding her cards so close.

I press a kiss to her head. "You'll understand eventually, but for right now, just believe me when I say that I don't have a single regret about what led us to where we are."

She settles against my chest, her warm breath tickling my neck. "Can I sleep in your bed tonight?"

With another kiss to her crown, I chuckle. And my heart does this strange flippy thing that I've never experienced before. "Yeah, dream girl. You can sleep in my bed any night you want."

"I might hold you to that."

# Chapter 28
## Hannah

"I WISH WE NEVER HAD TO LEAVE." I SUCK IN A LUNGFUL OF FRESH mountain air and tip my head toward the sun. It's peeking between the trees as we hike the path toward what we're told is a beautiful set of falls.

We had breakfast with the owner of the inn and a few other guests. It was nice, really—dining with strangers. It gave us the opportunity to try out interacting like an actual couple. Though it kind of felt like we were pulling one over on the other guests, since we still haven't defined what the hell we're doing—other than having a baby together.

I can't say it wasn't magical. Daniel wrapped his arm around my chair and tugged me close. He filled my plate with a little of every-thing set out for us, then fed me bites of each while we chatted with the other guests about where they were from and what they were hoping to do here. From what I could tell, no one recognized him, and we were able to steer clear of questions about our occupations. It might have been the most relaxing morning I've ever had.

"We can't accomplish that monster of a bucket list if we're stuck in one place."

I giggle and crack my eyes open. "We don't actually have to do everything on it. I know some of them are ridiculous."

He cocks a devilish brow. "Yeah, I don't think we'll be running with the bulls anytime soon."

"Fine. We can remove that one, but I still want to do a gondola ride in Venice. And karaoke."

"Karaoke is not a bucket list item. Just go out with Aiden on a Friday night or hang out in our locker room before a game." He shakes his head. "Actually, no. Don't do that."

"Oh, come on. I've always wondered what you boys do in the locker room. Swing your dicks around, I'm sure."

He swivels his hips aggressively. "Obviously."

"So who's the biggest?" I ask, trying my best to bite back a smile.

Head dropped back, he guffaws, the sound so loud he startles the birds in a nearby tree, and they take flight. "Is this really even a question?"

It's not. I've got it on good authority that the honor goes to Daniel. From my personal experience with it, I 100 percent believe the rumors. The guy is hung, but I've never hooked up with any of the guys on the hockey team and have zero intention of ever doing so. I have, however, heard the guys talk about their dicks on more than one occasion. I swear that's all they do, and every freaking time, they talk about how hung my man is.

*My man.* My heart stutters right out of my chest. *Whoa. What the hell was that?*

When I don't reply, Daniel grasps my wrist and tugs me into his chest. He tips my chin up with one finger and leans down. "Do I need to remind you of just how big I am, or can you still feel me between your thighs?"

My body pulses with a desire that never seems to wane when he's around. I lick my lips, hungry. No, famished. It must be his age. I've never met a man who could keep up with me the way he can. "We could cross off another item on the bucket list."

He brushes his lips against mine. "Which one?"

I bite down on his lip softly, then in one quick move, dart back and take off at a run. "Skinny dipping!" I yell as I head straight toward the falls ahead.

When the forest opens up and they come into full view, I pull up short. Holy fuck. All around, there's nothing but lush greens, a flowering mountain, and the heavy, thundering rush of water. The way the sunlight glints off the water makes the whole clearing glow. Like an oasis. Like a mirage. It's too beautiful to be real.

Daniel barrels into me, sweeping me off my feet and heading straight to the edge of the water. "I'm going in first to make sure it's safe." He sets me on my feet, then gives me the sternest expression he can manage. "Seriously, if you listen to nothing else I say, let this be the one thing you do."

I smile. "Aw, you want to protect the baby."

With a grunt, he yanks me in for a kiss. It's not a brush of lips. No, he goes for it, his tongue massaging mine as he holds me in place, forcing me to accept what he's trying to tell me. Then, just in case I didn't get the message, he pulls back and ducks so we're nose to nose. "I want to protect *you* and the baby. You are nonnegotiable in that equation. You get me, dream girl?"

"I'm beginning to," I say, the words barely audible with the way emotion clogs my throat. He's told me again and again that I'd eventually get it, and now, I think that maybe I'm beginning to. "Now strip." My voice is a little stronger now.

With a slow, cocky smirk, he grasps the hem of his shirt, and with a ridiculous amount of teasing, he inches it up his torso, showing off his abs. He dances to nonexistent music, swinging his hips in a way that would have his dick rolling if he was naked.

I scan the area to make sure we're truly alone before I egg him on. "Take off the pants, Hall. Remind me what we're working with here."

He unzips his pants, and when he whips out the goods, I have to bite down on my lip to keep a moan from slipping out.

The way his eyes flash tells me he caught the reaction. "All right, dream girl, stay on the shore," he reiterates as he steps to the edge and dips his toes in. "Shit, it's cold."

"This is almost worse," I whine. "I think I'd rather jump in. Get it over with quickly."

"Not happening." He growls at me. But in the next heartbeat, he does just that. When he lands with a big splash and then stands up easily, he swipes the water from his face. "Okay, hot girl. Now you can come get wet."

"That's what she said," I mutter.

Daniel's laughter is like a balm for my soul. Every moment of this day has been. I make a show of undressing for him, and like the good boy he is, he hoots and hollers until I'm running toward the edge and cannonballing into the water beside him.

When the ice-cold water hits my body like a million pinpricks, I surface and practically throw myself into his arms. "Holy shit, you said it was cold, not frigid."

"How long do we have to stay in here for this to qualify as skinny dipping?" He palms my ass and lifts me.

Automatically, I wrap my legs around his hips. Like we're two pieces of a puzzle, his dick slots perfectly between us. "Wait a second." I wriggle against him. "How in the fuck are you hard right now?"

"Um, you're naked."

"The water is freezing."

"Yeah, the rest of my body will probably go into hypothermia because all my blood rushed to my dick the second I saw your tits."

With a laugh, I whack his chest. "Shut up. That's not science."

He rolls his hips. "Then how do you explain this?"

I open my mouth to quip back, but I've got nothing, so I snap it shut again.

"You could keep me warm," he suggests, pressing kisses to my chin.

"Oh, could I?"

"Public sex was on your bucket list."

"Pretty sure we covered that at the stadium," I murmur even as I lick across his lips.

He slips a hand between us and lines his head up with my entrance. As he pushes himself in to the hilt, we moan in unison. "Fuck, you're perfect."

"No, we're perfect," I breathe as he fucks me, keeping his dick buried deep and his movements small. God, how is it possible he feels this good?

How can everything with him always feel so good?

"I watched this episode of *Grey's Anatomy* where a couple went skinny dipping, and the guy got a worm in his penis."

Daniel grabs his dick and sucks in a breath. "Take it back."

I take a long, dramatic lick of my ice cream.

We're in downtown Enchanted Falls, Vermont, and as the name suggests, everything about it is absolutely magical. After our afternoon romp, we had a picnic—another one of my bucket list items—and took a nap. I woke feeling rested but also bad about wasting so much of what little time we have together sleeping.

Daniel, of course, responded with something like "There's no such thing as wasted time as long as you're in my arms."

He might be making it really hard not to fall for him.

We have dinner plans in an hour, but I mentioned craving something sweet and salty, and Daniel was ecstatic about being around when a craving hit, so he forced me to put on my shoes and dragged me to the fudge shop, insisting we could have dessert before dinner. He's going to make a fabulous father.

"You should probably check the anaconda in your pants and make sure it's the only thing there."

With a shiver, he surreptitiously eyes his crotch.

Head tossed back, I laugh. "Men are so easy to rile up. Dicks, women, and sports. That's about all you think about, isn't it?"

"I can't speak for all men, but for me, yes."

"Great."

"With one caveat," he adds, holding up a finger.

"I'm all ears."

"It's not women, it's *woman*." He drapes an arm over my shoulders. "You."

"Such a romantic," I tease him, even though I'm swooning internally. It's pathetic, really.

Daniel slides his hand down my body and links his fingers with mine. "So you were a *Grey's Anatomy* fan?"

"Oh god, who wasn't? I binge watched every episode of the first ten seasons after my divorce, and I've been hooked since."

He side-eyes me, though he doesn't turn his head.

I huff and take another lick of ice cream. "You want me to tell you about the marriage?"

All I get is a simple shrug. "Only if you want to, and only because I want to know you."

I lean my head against his chest, making sure to hold my cone out so neither of us wears it. "There's not a lot to tell. It's a simple story about a girl who'd been told all her life that if her mother just found the right man, she'd be happy. My mother's happiness was dependent on one man or another for years. You'd think that would have made me run in the opposite direction of love"—I glance up at him—"And it did eventually, but back then, I went to college intent on finding a man and falling in love, certain that if I did that, then life would be perfect."

"I'm guessing it didn't work out like that?"

I take another swipe at my ice cream. "Not at all. I married my professor. Very cliché. He was older, obviously. I thought it was this grand love affair." I shake my head. God, I was so naïve. "He wanted me to drop out of school so we could start a family right away. It's funny, because I went to school not really caring about the actual education, but once I was there, I fell in love with it. My dreams were bigger than just being his wife, and well..." I shrug. "We fought a lot, but I figured that was normal for people who were just settling into marriage. I didn't expect to end up divorced so quickly. But when my mom called me about her fourth divorce, I planned a *have a day* trip with her. I booked a couple of nights at a hotel, and Mom planned to come to town. Rafe, apparently, took that as his *get out of jail free card*."

He growls, his whole body going rigid.

All I can do is shrug. "My mother was supposed to meet me at the hotel, but she texted a couple of hours after she planned to arrive to tell me she'd met someone at a bar and that I was off the hook for the night. I went back to my house and—" I squeeze my eyes shut; this part is hard to admit. "I don't want you to hate my mother, because even I don't hate her."

Daniel winces. "Fuck, please tell me she wasn't at your house."

"I wish I could." With a deep inhale, I force myself to get the rest of it out. "She'd never met my husband or been to my house. I'd gotten married on a whim that semester. It was this big, fun, secret love affair, and it was all mine." I let out a sarcastic laugh. "Until it wasn't. She still doesn't know she slept with her daughter's husband. The second I saw them in bed, I turned around and walked out of the house. I never said a word."

"That asshole." Daniel holds me tighter, his eyes burning with anger. "Please tell me he had a heart attack and died. Or that you stabbed him. Yes, that. Tell me you stabbed him and he's rotting in the basement of your old house."

I bow my head and bite back a grin. This man. "No. I told him I knew he'd slept with another woman—I didn't tell him she was my mother, because once again, how fucking embarrassing is that? He tried to gaslight me, telling me it was my fault for gallivanting around town with my mother when I should have been at home working on our marriage. Whatever. He's a dick, and no, I have no idea whether he's alive or dead. I signed the divorce papers and never looked back."

Daniel sighs, probably realizing just how uphill his battle is if he really wants to keep pursuing me. I can't blame him. I don't trust easily. Though I do trust him. He's proven time and again that I can, and it's not in my nature to hold the sins of another person over his head. I give people the opportunity to show me who they are. But that doesn't mean I'm not still tending to emotional scars. I'm wary, yeah, but I can give this a chance. I'll let Daniel decide whether this is something he can truly handle.

"I'm sorry that happened to you." He pulls me to a stop in front of a small restaurant.

A handful of small tables are scattered around the patio out front. The ambient lighting and the music from the solo guitarist make for the perfect low-key spot.

"I'm not," I say, chin lifted. "Because if he hadn't screwed up all those years ago, I wouldn't be standing here with you. And Daniel?"

He presses his hand to my cheek, his eyes warm with adoration. "Yes?"

I one-up him and cup both his cheeks. "I'm really happy I'm here with you. And I'm really happy we're having this baby." I swallow down the emotion bubbling up inside me. "What you said last night about this being the best thing to happen to you? Well, *same*. I can't say I ever would have written this into my own story, but I know now that I'd have been missing out. So thank you for giving me the time to get here. And thank you for this." I peer around us. "This place, these past few days, they've meant everything to me."

He leans down and kisses me gently.

When he pulls back, I smile up at him. "Seriously, how did you find such a perfect spot?"

Hands at my hips, he turns me so I'm facing the restaurant. "You can actually thank your brothers for this one."

That's when I realize I recognize two faces on the patio. Riggs and Ash are sitting across from one another, grinning at me.

With a squeal, I charge toward them excited to spend the evening laughing and talking with two of my favorite people. All thanks to the man who is climbing the ranks and not so slowly unseating everyone else for that title.

"I still can't believe you're both sitting here with me," I say to my brothers, still in shock.

Ash gives me that knowing smirk that he's so famous for. He's cocky in a way most people simply cannot be, because his cockiness is backed up by years of experience as a Navy SEAL. The man has seen and done things that I know have left him both scarred and a bit weary of the world, but somehow, he never manages to let it affect the people around him. He's aware of the darkness in the world, not grumpy. And I'm a hell of a lot happier that he's now on this side of the globe, even if I still rarely see him because of his demanding job. "We couldn't leave it up to Noah to let your boy know he better behave."

I roll my eyes, even as Daniel chuckles easily. For as much as he shouldn't be comfortable around my brothers—two men who are trained to kill in more ways than I'd like to imagine—he is completely at ease. "Like I told you on the phone, I'd cut off my own hand if I hurt her." He lifts our hands, which are joined on his lap and brings it to his lips, his eyes never leaving mine. "She's safe with me."

"We'll be the ones to decide that," Riggs says, dragging an annoyed sigh from me.

"Everyone can stop with the *I've got her* thing." I arch an unimpressed eyebrow at both of my brothers. "You all know that I've got myself. I don't need a man to protect me." I dart a glance at Daniel, and the tension in my body releases. "But I like this one, so be nice."

Daniel squeezes my fingers, and Ash blows out a breath. "Fuck, never thought I'd see the day that Hannah was *nice*."

I think Daniel is about to tear Ash's head off—even if he is a dangerous motherfucker who's not to be messed with—but when I bark out a loud laugh, he relaxes and shakes his head. "You guys are all brutal," he mutters.

Riggs chuckles. "You're part of the family now. Get used to it."

I bite down on my lip hard as a realization hits. I want it. I want it so bad I can taste it. But I'm scared to want it at the same time, so I change the subject before I can focus on the way Daniel's cheeks have gone a warm red, like he's both surprised and pleased with that idea. "Speaking of family, how are my nephews?"

Riggs pulls out his phone and gives us a play-by-play of all the sports the boys are now involved in and how Pierce—their father—is already itching to teach them how to shoot. I shake my head. I hate guns, but I know it's a big part of life in rural Vermont. Especially for my brothers, who work in security.

"How's Teddy?" I ask Ash.

My brother's fists clench slightly, a tick that most would have missed, but I know him too well. When we were kids, he had a crush on the middle Berkshire girl, and I don't know that it ever faded. I'm not sure if anything ever happened between the two of them, but she was married by the time he left the SEALs, and I've never seen him date or even mention another woman.

"She's fine. Her daughter's first birthday is this week and they're doing some big celebration at the estate. Whole family is going to be in town. That's how I knew we could make tonight work."

I smile. "Give her my love."

I've met Teddy a time or two over the years, but I feel like I know her far better than those limited interactions allowed because Ash has always talked about her, even if he never realizes it. It's sad to think that they never got their chance.

That thought has me turning my focus back to Daniel.

I'm glad we're getting this chance. I'm glad he's giving it to us. Not just for our child, but because I'm starting to realize I could see a future with him. And I don't want to look back years from now and wonder what would have happened if I'd spoken up, or what would have happened if I'd been brave enough to try.

As if he somehow knows precisely what I need, he wraps an arm around my chair and tugs me closer, pressing a kiss to my forehead. Then he turns back and answers question after question, acing the interrogation my brothers have thrown together.

I don't bother to try to shut them down. I know better. Plus, I know that, to him, I'm worth it.

# CHAPTER 29
## DANIEL

Brooks: How's operation make Hannah fall for you going?

Aiden: God, I love love. We should add Beckett to this group. He'd have some input.

War: Guys, it's 7 a.m. Why the hell are you up?

Snow: 4 a.m. in Vegas, and I haven't gone to bed. At least not my own.

Brooks: LOL. We miss you, buddy. How's Vegas?

Snow: A dream. You guys gotta come visit. The women here…fuckkk

Me: Talking to a group of guys who are all obsessed with their women.

Snow: Aw, shit. Even you?

Me: Even me. Miss you, bro. Call soon.

Smiling, I plug my phone into the charger, then turn all my attention on my current obsession.

"Okay, peanut—yup, that's the name we're going with, since your mama tells me you like the salty stuff, just like her." I gently press my lips to Hannah's belly, careful not to wake her. Though I'd gladly watch her sleep for hours, I have to get her up soon so we can hit the road. But before that, I want a little more time with my child. Once we get back to Boston, I won't have unfettered access like I've had for the last few days. "Here's the deal. I don't get to talk to you as much as I want since mama's got an important job and has to fly all over the country, but that doesn't mean I'm not thinking of you always." I rest my head on her thigh and close my eyes. "And wishing I was with you both."

The last few days have been nothing short of perfect. Even a year ago, my ideal break from hockey included bars, beaches, and hooking up. This vacation couldn't have been more different. Yet the mere idea of spending time with another woman makes me sick. There's comfort in the softness of this woman. In the way she lights up when she smiles, in the spark in her eye when she's gearing up to sass me. I love when she does it too. The teasing and the sex. Everything with her feels right.

Two nights ago, when she opened up about her divorce, it struck me that there really is potential here. I've known for a while that Hannah is my endgame, but I think she's finally coming to terms with it too. Maybe even wanting it. A guy can hope, right?

Watching her interact with Riggs and Ash was far more satisfying than I could have imagined. Their presence unlocked a side of her I hadn't seen, and it had me dreaming of being part of her family one day.

They're the reason I brought Hannah to Vermont. Noah mentioned that Hannah had been trying to schedule a time to get together with Ash, but because of all the traveling he does, along with her intense schedule, it's next to impossible. So when he said they'd be home for the week, I figured Vermont was the perfect place for our road trip.

Ash is thirty-three, like Hannah, and I couldn't get enough of the stories he had to tell about his job. He works for a security firm and has been assigned to the Berkshire family, who are basically American royalty.

Riggs is a few years older and has a few kids who are already excited to meet their cousin. That's when reality really set in. Our baby already has a whole slew of aunts, uncles, and cousins.

Fuck, more than anything, I want our child to have two parents who are present. I don't want to be a part-time dad. I don't want to be away from our child at all. I don't want to be away from Hannah either.

Our jobs make that impossible, and I can't change that. But I can make sure we spend as much of our time off together as we can.

So my goal over the next few months is twofold: to make Hannah fall in love with me and to create the family of my dreams with my dream girl.

"All right, peanut, good talk. I love you. Now I gotta focus on waking up your mama." As I press a kiss to her belly, her fingers slide into my hair, and she tugs.

"I think the baby can hear you."

A bolt of excitement courses through me. "Why? Did you feel a kick?" I press my hand to her belly.

She smiles. "No. Should I be able to?"

I crawl up her body and brush my lips over hers. "Morning. And no, the books say you'll probably notice it around sixteen weeks. You're only thirteen."

With a sigh, she slides a leg over mine, cuddling into me. "You're so good at this stuff."

A peace I've never known before settles into my bones as I stroke her hair. It's a gift, the simple ability to touch her. "I just like to read. Like to be in the know."

She smiles. "Yeah, what else do you like reading?"

"Articles about hockey. Articles about sex."

Does she have any clue that her articles in particular are the ones I love to read? Should I tell her? If she wanted people to know she was Calliope, she'd say so, right? For now, I'll keep the knowledge to myself. "Now most of the articles are about babies. I've been following a vlog created by a group of dads. It's really interesting."

Hannah hums. "It's good one of us knows what's going on."

At the flat tone of her voice, I tuck my chin and assess her. She looks almost...*lost*.

"What if the baby moves and you're not there?"

As much as it pains me to admit, it's probably better to be realistic about it. "You travel a lot, Han. That will probably happen."

She peers up at me from beneath dark lashes. "But I don't travel all the time."

Cautiously, I eye her. "No, you don't."

She bites down on that plump bottom lip of hers. From what I can tell, it's always swollen. How can it not be with the way she's always gnawing on it? "So if I'm at home and the baby kicks, maybe I wouldn't have to call you. Maybe I could just reach over—" She walks her fingers across my abdomen and grasps my hand, then places it on her tiny belly.

Every cell in my body is dancing with excitement, but I'm doing everything I fucking can to hide behind a calm façade. I don't want to scare her, but fuck do I want that. So I just nod, attention locked on where my hand rests. "It would be amazing if I could be there for that."

"But it doesn't happen for at least another few weeks? So—"

My heart stutters. "The guys on the vlog say it varies. Some of their partners felt it a couple of weeks earlier."

When she looks back at me, I swear I see a flicker of hope in her pretty eyes. "Yeah?"

I glide my hand across her stomach, soaking in her warmth. "Yeah, and you're so tiny to begin with. I bet it'll be easier to feel smaller movements."

"Right, and we wouldn't want you to miss that," she whispers.

Staring down into her gorgeous blue eyes, I swallow down the emotion threatening to spill out of me. "I don't want to miss anything."

"I don't want you to miss anything either." She's quiet for a moment.

Damn, I wish I could read her mind. Is she thinking what I'm thinking? Does she want me around for it all the way I'm desperate to be there for every milestone, no matter how small?

"So maybe when we get back to Boston, you'd consider staying with me for the night?"

My stomach swoops, and I swear my heart doubles in size. "I'd happily stay the night at your place any time you want me there."

Her lips twist. "That would help when I get cravings, I suppose."

Eager for any excuse to be near her, I nod. "Yeah, I'm more than happy to run out to get whatever you're craving. Are you craving something right now? I can head into town before we go."

With a grin, she slips a warm, soft hand beneath the waistband of my boxers. "Not the kind of craving I was referring to," she says as she strokes me with just the right amount of pressure.

And then the girl of my dreams slides down my body and proceeds to give me the best morning head any guy has ever received.

# TEXT MESSAGES FROM DANIEL AND HANNAH'S PHONE

Sara: Don't kill me, but Brooks and I decided to move up the wedding.

Hannah: Okay, when?

Sara: This weekend.

Ava: What???

Sara: I don't want to wait another year to marry him and Sienna is in town visiting and the guys start practice again next week, so it's now or 340 days from now. The season is so damn long, and the second I heard War growl wifey in Ava's ear, I knew I had a new kink and we can't test it out until we're married.

Ava: <side eye emoji>

Millie: Oh my god ,you are ridiculous.

Sara: Says the woman who has more kinks than I have fingers.

Millie: Thank you.

Sara: <wink emoji> You're welcome

Sara: So, are you guys in?

Hannah: Wouldn't miss it for the world. Or a baseball game. So I'll be asking for the night off.

Sara: We already cleared it with the owner.

Hannah: Haha. I'm sure you did. I'll still chat with Liv and make sure we've got everything covered.

Sara: Thank you. It wouldn't be the same without you girls there. And you know I love you all, but since we're throwing this together in a matter of days, we're keeping things simple and only having Ethan and Lennox in the wedding.

Millie: How did Aiden handle that?

Lennox: He's singing sad ballads about how he's unwanted and unloved. So it's going well.

Hannah: hahaha. Thank you for not making me put my pregnant ass in a bridesmaid dress. When I can have a cocktail again, I'll make a special toast just for you.

Hall: Where's the bachelor party?

Beckett: Why am I in this chat?

War: Yeah, you can't get married without a bachelor party, Brookie ;)

Brooks: You did.

Gavin: I heard Sara and the girls got a male stripper.

Brooks: No strippers.

Beckett: Obviously.

Gavin: I don't know. Could be fun.

Hall: Millie, did you steal Gavin's phone?

Beckett: That makes so much more sense.

Gavin: You ruin all my fun, Danny Boy.

Beckett: I feel like Aiden should be planning this.

War: He's still moping in the corner and singing to himself.

War: <picture of Aiden sitting on the floor in the corner of the weight room with a gallon of ice cream in his lap >

Beckett: I'll have a limo pick you all up at Ground Zero.

Hall: Nice!

War: That sounds better than what I planned...

Beckett: That's because you boys have no business doing a man's job.

Beckett: And no, I'm not insulting Ethan. This is about all of you.

Gavin: Love you, Beckett! Take care of my man tonight.

Hall: Millie, please stop. It keeps getting weirder.

Daniel: I hate that I can't see you tonight.

Hannah: I'm so tired. I'm not sure how I'll hang at Sara's bachelorette party. Thank god Ava is pregnant too.

Hannah: Also, I miss you too.

# Chapter 30
## Hannah



"You look good, mama." Noah lets out a long whistle.

I assess the black dress that took more effort to get into than I would have liked. The silk used to drape over my curves in a flattering way. Now it hugs them. Also my boobs. My boobs look spectacular. "I look pregnant."

Oliver looks up from the blocks he's got set up on the coffee table, his tongue pushing at the inside of his cheek. "Yeah, there's definitely a baby in there."

"Oliver!" Noah and Liam say in unison.

My stepdad is here to hang out with Oliver while Noah and I go to the wedding. He came early so we could visit, something we haven't done in far too long. He did tell me my mother has been texting here and there, apparently inquiring about how I'm doing. He suggested meeting for dinner this week so he can assure her he's been checking in. It's humorous, the thought of her texting him rather than me, but more than anything, it's pathetic. But Liam genuinely cares about me, and I enjoy spending time with him, so I was more than happy to agree.

"It's fine." I wander over to him and run my fingers through his silky hair. "I *am* pregnant. Always best to be honest, Ollie."

Noah shakes his head. "Careful what you wish for. He told the coffee barista his pants were too short, his pre-k teacher she needed to brush her teeth better, and Jen's husband that life isn't a competition, but if it was, he'd be losing."

Oliver just shrugs. "Was any of that wrong?"

God, I love this kid.

Noah crouches next to his son and pulls him in for a hug. Then he whispers in his ear, probably telling him to be good and listen to his grandfather.

TEARS COAT MY LASHES AS SARA WALKS TOWARD BROOKS, HER ARM looped around her little brother's, a cascade of flowers peeking through the wavy strands of her long blond hair. I wondered whether it'd be blue, since the preseason is right around the corner. Either way, she is gorgeous. Brooks wears the biggest smile on his face. Before Sara and Ethan have cleared the front row, the groom steps forward, reaching for his bride. He's been gone for her for so long, and I'd place bets on that never changing. He's always eager to have her by his side and most content when he's touching her.

For a last-minute wedding, the decorations are exquisite. Lennox, the event planner slash matron of honor, surely had something to do with that. We're all gathered in the ballroom at Lang Corp. I figured the location was by default, since they literally threw the event together in days. It wasn't until we were walking past the wall that Brooks bought for Sara when he proposed that I understood. Every one of us had to pass an adorable painting of the two of them. In it, she's sitting atop his back while he does his famous set of pregame push-ups. It started as a joke when they were fake dating and quickly became a Bolts tradition.

Noah slides a handkerchief from his pocket and pushes it toward me. "This is a happy occasion," he mutters.

I elbow him in the ribs.

Beckett begins the ceremony—I'm not surprised he's officiating; it appears he's been deemed the honorary wedding officiant since Millie and Gavin's wedding—and I search the room for Daniel.

He spent the morning with the guys. Honestly, it was a relief knowing we didn't have to do the whole walking in together in front of our friends thing. They surely would have embarrassed us with their catcalling and hooting and hollering.

There's no doubt we'll have to suffer at some point, but for now, I've got a little more time to figure out how I want to react.

Daniel must be behind me, because I've yet to lay eyes on him. I don't want to be rude and turn around, so I focus in on the ceremony instead.

When Brooks and Sara exchange the vows they wrote to one another, my gentle tears turn to full-on sobs.

Lennox mouths, "Keep it together."

I try. I really do. But holding it in only results in an unladylike snort that has half the people in the room looking at me.

When Beckett introduces Mr. and Mrs. Brooks Langfield, Sara squeals and jumps into her husband's arms, then lays the most inappropriate kiss on his lips.

Beckett's son Finn yells "get a room," and Sara barely takes a breath to pull away and respond with "Oh, don't worry. We did!"

Brooks carries Sara up the aisle. God, the photos are going to be pure gold.

"Now, that's a wedding," Noah says to me as he stands and holds a hand out to help me up.

"I don't know," I say as I ease out of my seat. "The way Ava and War did it was ridiculously romantic."

Noah's brows knit together. "Wasn't theirs a contract?"

"Well, yes." I lift one shoulder. "But it was just the two of them at city hall. I don't know, there's just something about the simplicity of it, doing away with the whole pomp and circumstance, that I love. Just two people pledging to do their best for one another."

Noah's eyes warm. "That is beautiful, Han. Spoken like a true romantic."

I laugh lightly, ignoring the flutter of nerves in my belly. "I'm an author. Not a romantic. I don't actually believe in all that stuff."

With a smirk, he shakes his head. "Sure you do. You write love stories for the most improbable couples. People who overcome their own traumas who don't have to change who they are to find the love they deserve."

I stare at him, kind of gobsmacked. "That's what you get from my writing?"

"Actually," he says as we wait for a line of guests to move past our row, "it's how Daniel described it when he was telling the guys about you during morning skate last week."

I'm kind of speechless. Not only does Daniel read my books, but he talks about them and *understands* them maybe better than anyone else ever has.

Kind of like how he understands me better than anyone ever has.

Chin lifted, I search him out.

It only takes a minute to spot him. He's leaning against a door to one side of the exit, his black suit tailored perfectly, accenting his forever impressive physique, his attention fully on me.

The smolder he wears has my entire body heating. "Dream girl," he mouths. He brings a fist to his chest. "Fucking perfect."

I tilt to one side and tell Noah I'll be back, but he's frozen, his face ashen, his attention locked on the front of the room where Beckett is talking to Gavin, Liv, and Sienna.

Beckett has a possessive arm wrapped around Liv, as always. Gavin is grinning from ear to ear. Sienna, the youngest Langfield, and the most fashionable, is smiling brightly as she regales the three of them with a story that probably has to do with her work in the fashion industry in Paris.

I squeeze Noah's arm. "You okay? You look like you've seen a ghost."

His Adam's apple bobs as he swallows audibly, and with a shake of his head, he finally looks away from the group. "Might have." He rubs a hand over his face. "I'm going to splash some water on my face."

"I've got her." Daniel appears at my side, his deep voice sending a shiver down my spine.

Noah nods and disappears without another word.

"He's acting weird," I say as I watch him bolt from the room.

"Weddings tend to affect people in one of two ways," Daniel says, holding out his arm.

I take it and let him lead me up the aisle and toward a wall of windows that overlooks the ocean and the dazzling sunset.

"Really?"

"Yes. Some people get stuck on the what-ifs. What if I'd settled down? What if I missed out on the one? What if I married the wrong person?"

I hiss out a dramatic breath. "Scandalous."

He smiles. "And others latch on to the maybe. *Maybe* I'll meet someone tonight. Maybe I'll get lucky. Maybe I *should* propose."

I turn to face him, the windows at my back. "And what kind of person are you?"

His brown eyes twinkle. "I'm definitely a maybe guy."

A thrill zips through me. "Are you?"

He nods and leans down. "Absolutely."

"And what's your maybe?"

"Maybe I should ask my dream girl to dance. Maybe she'll let me hold her hand tonight. Maybe I could kiss her in front of all our friends."

Arms draped over his shoulders, I pull him close, my lips a breath from his. "There's only one problem with your theory."

He closes his eyes like he's relishing the closeness. "Oh yeah, what's that?"

"I'm neither of those."

He smiles, his lips brushing mine as he does. "And what are you?"

I press my mouth to his, my tongue seeking his. Grabbing his hair for purchase, I deepen the kiss, licking and sucking, making it clear to every person here that Daniel is all mine.

Our friends break into cheers just as I knew they would. But this way, it's on my terms and not the least bit awkward. We're breathless and panting when we finally pull apart.

"I'm a doer, Baby Hall. I'm in this. So take me out onto that dance floor. There's no maybe about it: you're coming home with me tonight."

# CALLIOPE'S COLUMN



## Hard Truths.

Cold hard truth time: our moms were right. Sex is better when it's with a person you know and trust. Slow sex with a stranger? Can you imagine how awkward that would be? But staring into the eyes of the person you're fucking can be the most intense experience. The orgasm is stronger, the toe-curling pleasure immeasurable.

Now maybe that's not what our moms meant when they said to wait to have sex, but I'm here to tell you, you should wait to have sex with someone you know, *because it's better*.

And I don't mean that having sex with the same person repeatedly will get you there. It's the intimacy that comes from actually opening up to them. Sharing your secrets. One of the best things my new guy has done was ask me to tell him exactly what I'm thinking. I've never been the kind to sugarcoat my thoughts, but this goes beyond being blunt. This is being honest for the sake of being honest. There's no guesswork. It's been eye-opening. I dare you to try it. Tell the person you're dating the complete truth and watch how amazing your sex life becomes.

# CHAPTER 31
# DANIEL

"Do your boobs hurt?" With a grimace, I rub at my nipples.

It's week three of training, and we're still finding our groove now that Camden is gone. We've been adjusting the lines, and from what I can tell, Noah has settled in well with Aiden and War. That means I'll most likely remain on the second line with Keegan and one of the rookies. I'm putting effort into remaining positive, focusing on becoming a dad rather than on the changes in my career I can't control. Which, I guess, is why I'm rubbing my sore nipples in front of my teammates.

Standing in front of the locker next to mine, War glares. The look says *go fuck yourself* and *you're an idiot* all at once. It's impressive, really.

"And the heartburn. It's fucking killing me." I move one hand to the center of my chest and push on it like the guys on the vlog suggest. It helps. I swear it. "Tell me I'm not alone here."

Brooks looks up from lacing his skates. "Uh. Shouldn't the pregnant person in your relationship be the one having heartburn?"

"Nah, they're called sympathy symptoms."

I can list every one of Hannah's symptoms front to back now that she's no longer hiding from me.

"So the two of you are spending time together?" Brooks asks.

War's still watching me out of the corner of his eye like he can't figure me out.

"Yeah. When she's not traveling, we're together. Though it feels like she's never off the clock. Does Sara ever stop?"

Brooks straightens, brows pulled low. "What do you mean?"

"She's dealing with an emergency just about every night. If it's not one of the rookies, it's fucking Jasper Quinn. I never considered myself a jealous guy, but the way she runs when his number flashes on her phone is concerning."

"I'd kill any of you if you caused Sara headaches like that," Brooks says without so much as blinking.

War nods. "Yeah, I'm not against bodily harm if it means my wife sleeps at night."

"But this is *Hannah*." My girl is a bit crazy. And not in the same way Sara is. Sara's harmless, while I'm pretty sure the term *she could kill a bitch* was coined just for Hannah. "I don't even know if we're actually together *together*," I add because it seems pertinent.

I sleep over there when she's in town—and sometimes when she's not because Noah and I have been hanging out, and he and Oliver have been teaching me how to play Dungeons and Dragons—the kid version, obviously. Besides, her bed is softer than mine, and it smells like her. I haven't actually told her that I sleep there when she's not there. I'm afraid she'll think it's creepy, or that it goes against the agreement we've made—which is that I come when she calls, and then she comes. Sorry, I had to, and besides, it's true. It's a guarantee: within an hour of walking in the door, my girl is writhing beneath me.

"What are you going to do when the baby is born?" Aiden bounces on his toes, stretching his muscles.

"What do you mean?"

"She can't possibly do her job with a newborn," War points out.

I roll my eyes. "She's Hannah. Of course she can."

"Does that mean you're going to quit your job and stay home with the baby when she has to run out at all hours of the night to deal with bullshit?" War cocks a thick, dark brow. "What about when she's traveling for thirty weeks out of the year? Our seasons overlap. How's that going to work?"

Gut twisting painfully, I eye Brooks. Sara and Hannah both work in PR, just for different teams. "What will you do when that happens?"

"We don't plan to have kids yet. Neither of us wants to give up what we do."

I turn to Aiden, my chest tightening.

He shakes his head. "Lex and I are enjoying our baby-free lots-of-sex marriage. I'll let ya know if the plan changes."

Short of breath, I focus on War. "You have kids. Hell, you're about to have *four* of them, and you're making it work."

"My wife's job doesn't require her to travel. That's how we ended up married in the first place. I needed someone home with the kids."

"You sure you want to phrase it that way?"

War doesn't look the least bit ashamed. "It's our story. Can't change it, and honestly, I wouldn't. I love my wife, but the truth of the matter is that had I not been trying to figure out how to raise three kids on my own, I doubt we would have ended up together. The kids are part of our love story, and I'm okay with that. Now your child is part of your story, so what do the two of you have planned when it comes to raising him or her?"

I shrug and inhale deeply, forcing my nerves to settle. "I guess we probably need a nanny."

"I guess you should probably talk to your baby ma—"

I point at War with a glare. "Do not finish that sentence."

War smirks. "Thatta boy."

"I'll talk to Hannah."

"You do that. And while you're at it, do not complain about any of those pregnancy symptoms. You sound like an idiot."

I blow out a breath. The guys on the vlog would understand. "They're called sympathy symptoms. Maybe I'm just more in tune with my woman than you are."

He turns and faces me full-on, shoulders pulled back. "You don't even know if you're in a relationship with your woman. I promise you, the two of you are not more in tune than me and my wife."

Deflating, I yank my jersey from its hanger. He's right. And I fucking hate that he can use that term so freely, while I can't even call Hannah mine.

Because she is. She just doesn't know it yet.

"OH, GOD. RIGHT THERE. YES!" HANNAH WRAPS HER LEGS AROUND MY head and bucks her hips, chasing her orgasm.

She's on the precipice, clenching around my fingers, when her damn phone rings.

She growls and slaps the mattress, her thighs relaxing as she reaches for it. "Hello?"

I swipe at my face and suck in the first deep breath I've had in a good ten minutes.

Hannah's expression darkens. "No, Jasper. Don't do that. No, dammit. I'll handle it. Just"—she pulls the phone from her ear and glances at the screen—"give me thirty minutes." She slides her legs off my shoulders and settles on the edge of the bed as she ends the call.

"What's the problem?" I'm proud of myself for keeping my tone even when all I want to do is fucking growl.

She reaches for her robe, her words clipped. "Jasper got into a fight at a bar. I need to go down there and take care of the security footage and the guy he fought with."

"Absolutely not," I grit out, sitting up.

Hannah tenses and slowly turns my way. "Excuse me?"

Maybe I should be scared by the death glare she's wearing. Maybe I don't have any sense of self-preservation.

"There is no way my pregnant girlfriend is getting out of bed at ten p.m. to deal with some asshole in a bar." I hold out my hand. "Give me your phone."

She rolls her lips in like she's fighting a smile as she drops the device into my hand.

"And yes, I called you my girlfriend. You're going to have to deal with it."

Tongue in her cheek, she averts her attention. The girl who always has something to say has suddenly gone silent. I laugh. I'm a fucking idiot. She's clearly my girlfriend, and she doesn't mind when I take control, yet I've been too afraid to try until now. Too afraid to push the relationship boundaries.

I pull up Jasper's information and text him. I remind him not to say a word to anyone and just hang tight.

"What did you say?" she asks, her expression guarded.

"I told him exactly what you did. That I'll be there in thirty." I also told him to make sure his baseball buddies stick around. I'm only doing this once.

Hannah studies me, lips turned down. "The bar is around the block. If you went right now, you could be there in five."

"Right, but I'm not leaving until my *girlfriend* comes."

She shakes her head but at the same time drops her robe. "This is very unprofessional. It's my job that you'll be doing."

With a growl, I pull my naked girlfriend onto my lap. "Baby, my job is to take care of you. Can you let me do that, please?"

Biting her lip, she grinds against me. "Call me your girlfriend again."

I flip over, laying her flat on her back, and push her thighs apart. "Look at how beautiful my girlfriend looks begging for my cock." I line myself up and fill her in one thrust. "Can my girlfriend be quiet?"

She moans loudly in response. "Fuck no."

Chuckling, I grab the headboard with one hand and cover her mouth with my other. "Then I'll just have to find a way to keep my girlfriend quiet." I thrust into her warmth again, relishing the way she tightens around me. "Don't want your brother to hear."

The vixen moans loudly—she loves being loud—and nips at my palm. "Oliver isn't even home."

I slam into her hard enough to make the bed shift. Luckily, I'm gripping the headboard hard enough to keep it from hitting the wall. "Yes, but Noah is," I grit out, trying to regain some sense of control. "I can't look him in the eye when I walk out of this room if he knows I've been in here fucking you."

She bucks her hips, chasing her orgasm. My eyes roll back, and a tingling sensation starts at the base of my spine. She feels so fucking good. So tight and hot. But it's those blue eyes and the way they stare into mine, the way she's begging for me to claim her, that have me releasing my hand so she can scream as she does it.

I tweak one nipple, then the other. Her tits are a full size larger now and even more sensitive. I twist and pull on them in the way that sends electric bolts straight to her core. She squeezes so hard around my cock, stars dance in my vision. Breath held, I rein myself in and slide my hand down to her clit. I set a languid pace, rolling the little bud in time with my thrusts until she's shattering around me again. Only after she's come for a third time, and yelled about it, do I finally unload inside her.

WHEN HANNAH COMES OUT OF THE BATHROOM, ASKS FOR A KISS, THEN curls up in bed while thanking me for handling Jasper, I'm pretty sure I've slipped into an alternate reality. Either I fucked the sass right out of her, or she really is tired of dealing with the guys.

Either way, I take the win and head out of her room, determined to handle this once and for all.

Light filters out from beneath Noah's closed door, so I suck in a lungful of courage and knock.

"Come in," he hollers.

He's propped up against his headboard, black-framed glasses perched on the bridge of his nose, a book in hand and headphones on the mattress beside him.

And the world's sourest expression on his face.

I hold up my hands. "Don't blame me. She's insatiable."

He shakes his head. "Yeah, I'd really rather not hear about it."

"Good, I don't kiss and tell. Now grab your shoes. I need your help."

To his credit, Noah doesn't hesitate to hop out of bed and follow me.

As we take the elevator to the lobby, I fill him in on our task.

His eyes are wide. "You actually got Hannah to agree to let *you* handle her problem?"

I waggle my brows as I hold the door open for him. "I'm very convincing."

He gags.

"And you're welcome. She would have been a hell of a lot louder while I did all my convincing if not for my efforts."

Noah strolls by me, giving me a wide berth. "A week after we moved in, I got noise-canceling headphones. For me and Oliver."

I chuckle as I run to catch up with him. "Mind if I ask why you stay?" His presence doesn't bother me at all. I actually love it. Gives me somebody to hang out with while Hannah's traveling, and Noah and I actually have a lot in common. We like the same shows and we've gotten into the habit of working out together. And since we have friends in common, it's easy to hang out in a group setting. The relationship he and I have created is exactly what I used to wish I had with my older brother, Paul. But Noah doesn't *need* to stay here. Guy makes way more money than me, so I'm not sure why he hasn't found himself a nice big apartment with a view.

"Hannah needed me." He jabs a finger at me. "And don't you ever tell her I said that."

I hold up my hands. I'm not saying a thing.

"But now that you're around…" He hums, side-eyeing me. "We'll see. You stick around and prove you can take care of her, and I'll think about getting my own place."

"I'm not trying to get rid of you." Shit, I hope he doesn't think that. "But I intend to do all those things, so when the time comes, you don't have to worry about her. I'll be there for her and our baby."

Hands in his pockets, Noah nods. "I'm beginning to believe that."

As the bar comes into view, I smile. "Ready to go scare a few base-ball players?"

# Chapter 32
## Hannah

I'm going to blame the way I folded and let Daniel do my job for me last night on the pregnancy. I was too tired. I *am* too tired. Constantly.

Before I got knocked up, I'd heard about morning sickness, swollen ankles, and strange cravings, but no one told me about the bone-deep, mind-numbing exhaustion. I walk around in a fog for nearly half the day. The other half, I'm horny as fuck.

Seriously. I'm sprinting through a sex scene that's finally come to me after suffering from writer's block for too damn long, and I have to clench my butt cheeks to keep from humping my office chair.

Yes, I'm doing work for one job while at another, but with as often as I field calls and put out fires after hours, Beckett owes me a few thousand personal minutes, so I'm cashing in a few now.

*She pulses*—no, delete that—*she spasms*—yes, much better word —*around his huge, throbbing, pierced*—

"Knock-knock."

With a growl, I shut my laptop and glare at the person interrupting my sexy scene. Now that the mood has been killed, the scene will have to be completely rewritten. One day I'll finish this book.

"Jasper." I nod to the chair across from me and grip my armrests to keep myself from lunging over the desk and strangling him.

"You're motioning for me to sit, but your eyes are telling me you're planning my death—and it looks painful—so I'm not sure I should."

"Sit the fuck down."

With a grimace, he practically throws himself into the chair. "I just want to say that it wasn't me."

"Save it. Beckett warned you that you had one more chance." I hold up a finger. "*One*, Jasper. Give me one reason I shouldn't call him right now and tell him you blew it. I have no idea how Daniel got the kid to agree not to press charges or how he got the bar to let you go without calling the cops—"

He grins. The kid fucking grins at me. "Your boy is the man."

I blink and shake my head. "My what?"

"Your boy. *Daniel.* Ya know, your baby daddy. He's awesome."

With a sharp inhale, I will my muscles not to lock up. "I'm going to pretend you didn't just say those words—baby daddy—or boy—and we're going to start over."

"It wasn't me." He holds up both hands. "It was Leggs. But the kid freaked out and started crying, so I pushed him into a booth and tried to talk to the guy he punched. It was a big misunderstanding. But then the bartender got involved. I hooked up with her once, and it didn't end well, and, you know, things just got a little"—he scrunches up one side of his face and scans the wall behind me—"confusing, if you will."

"I won't."

"Listen, I just came in here to tell you that I'm sorry."

"You're what now?"

"I'm sorry. Daniel made a good point last night. It's up to us to represent Boston, and I realize now that we're doing a shit job of it."

It takes all my willpower not to fling myself back in my chair and growl. Those are the words I've repeated time and again. He hears them from a man one fucking time, and suddenly, they're brilliant. "What else did my *brilliant boyfriend* say?"

Jasper smirks. "He told us that if we didn't respect the mother of his child, we'd be dealing with him from now on."

My panties practically incinerate on the spot. Oh, that is so inappropriate when I'm sitting across from the fucking bane of my existence. "He said *what*?"

Jasper leans forward. "Kid's in love with you. You know that, right? Don't fuck this up."

I ignore that little dig because it's way too on the nose. "I'm going to need you to repeat what he said, verbatim."

I have a feeling I'll be using it to get myself off during the next away stretch. Holy shit. I've never wanted to be anyone's mother, but god, being the mother of Daniel's child…yeah, that's hot.

"He asked us what we thought of you. We all agree you're awesome. The best. That's when he made his first good point." He scratches at the back of his neck. "He said we're doing a shit job of showing you that, and if we respected you at all, we'd clean up our act. And then, like I said, he glared at all of us—*practically made Leggs shit a brick*—and said, if we didn't respect the mother of his child—then he smacked his fist to his hand like this"—Jasper mimics the move—"we'd be dealing with him."

Yeah, just as hot the second time. Would it be weird to ask Daniel to recreate the moment? Maybe stand over me and smack his fist into his hand as he demands respect for the mother of his child?

Oh god, the heroine of my work in progress should be pregnant, shouldn't she? Is this hot? Do I think this is hot? Yeah, I really think it is.

"You've got to go." I open up my laptop, and my hands fly over the keys. I don't hear him leave. I don't hear anything except the click-clacking of the keyboard as the story flows from my fingers.

"If we ever go three months without a girls' brunch again, I'm going to revolt," Lennox says as she holds up her drink.

"I'll drink to that." Sara taps her glass against Lennox's and eyes me.

"I'm not the only one who's pregnant." I point at Ava. "She probably gave it to me."

She giggles, green eyes sparkling. "It's not contagious."

"Maybe pregnancy isn't, but you were walking around talking about your sex god of a husband, and I got so horny I fucked her"—I throw a thumb in Millie's direction—"brother."

Daniel's twin gags, and I wink at her. I love us so much.

"Speaking of sex gods." Sara grins. "I heard a certain daddy threatened the baseball players last night."

I hiss out a breath. "Yeah, as head of PR, letting him handle it was definitely not the best move I've made."

Sara cackles. "I've been using Brooks to do my dirty work for years. Why shouldn't you?"

Millie nods. "My brother needs to be good for something." She rolls her eyes. "Something that doesn't involve his dick, at least." With a groan, she drops her head back. "Did I just say that out loud? Hannah, look what you're doing to me!"

I giggle. "But seriously, I should have handled it myself. It sucks being interrupted in the middle of the night, but that's the job. I deal with emergencies. Even if I'm fucking over telling the imbeciles not to use their fists to have conversations—*or their dicks.*"

"Ugh, so true," Sara agrees. "But I'm serious. You did yourself a favor by allowing Daniel to chat with them. Guys are annoying in that they only listen to other dudes."

"Right?" I throw my hands up. "Jasper literally showed up in my office today and yammered on about how, when Daniel said they represent the city of Boston and that they're doing a piss-poor job of it, it really stuck with him. Um, I say that all the time."

Lennox licks her lips. "It's a good thing Jasper is so freaking hot."

Millie shrugs. "I prefer my men older."

Sara cackles, and Ava nudges my foot. "But things are good with Daniel?"

There's no tempering the smile that spreads across my face. I love coming home and finding him in my bed. I also love coming home and finding him playing games with Oliver. Or hanging out in the kitchen with Noah. In summation, I guess I just love coming home to *him.* Rather than freak out when he declared me his girlfriend, I all but melted. I want to be his girlfriend. I want to be his anything, really. I just want to be *his.*

And I don't know when that happened.

Fine. Maybe that's not exactly true. It began the night he wandered through Walgreens at my side, searching for pregnancy tests. The sensation only grew when he didn't freak out about how my pregnancy would affect his life. He just handled the situation with grace and care—and in turn stopped me from freaking the fuck out.

Normally, I'm the one cleaning up messes, but despite his age and his playboy reputation, Daniel has never once made me responsible for his decisions. No, he's constantly looking for—and finding—ways to make my life easier. It's refreshing, and damn if it's really hard to remain unaffected by all of it. So I'm choosing to uncomplicate things. I can accept that I'm going to fall for him, and I'm certain it will all be okay.

"We're good," I promise my bestie. "Honestly, my only complaint is that I never have time to write now."

Ava tilts her head, studying me. "You've been working on your book again?"

I shouldn't be surprised that my friends don't follow the socials associated with my other career. Even so, it stings a little to get confirmation.

They cheer me on when I talk about what I'm doing. That *should* be enough, and I'm mortified by the reality that it's not. It's expected, really, that they'd be more curious about my relationship with Daniel and this baby than they are about my books. It's a societal thing. We're raised to believe who a woman dates and when she decides to have kids are the most interesting things about her. And while I certainly find Daniel and our baby interesting, I've kind of stumbled into this place in my personal life, to these things that are happening to me. Whereas my career as an author is something I've worked hard for. An achievement I've put blood, sweat, and tears into.

"Of course she's writing again." Lennox smiles wide. "And I for one can't wait to find out which guy the sister ends up with. Or maybe it's a why-choose situation." She bounces in her chair. "Oh, tell me we're getting Melina'd."

"Why can't it be Fitzed?" Sara asks.

I laugh. "This sister will definitely choose. Could you imagine how her older brothers would react if they found out she'd been surrounded by that many dicks?"

Lennox sighs. "Oh, but what a fun scene that would be."

I'm smiling when my phone lights up on the table.

Daniel: Hi, dream girl. Hope you're having fun with my sister and the girls. My dad asked if we were available to meet for dinner. What do you say? Want to meet the parents?

"Oh my god," I practically shout. It comes out kind of like "ermeegawd," though my friends all give me concerned looks, clearly getting the meaning.

"What?"

"Daniel just asked me to meet his parents."

Ava huffs out a laugh. "You've met them before. I don't get the big deal."

"He just asked me to meet the parents," I say again, my tone dead serious.

I glance at Sara. I can't be the only one realizing this.

She's doing the math, her face doing all the talking. Her mouth opens, her lips go limp, and then she drops her chin as she points at me. "Dude."

I nod.

"Dude!" she yells again.

Millie shakes her head. "I don't get it."

"She's meeting the freaking parents."

"I know. He's my dad. It's not a big deal."

Ava sighs like she's catching on. Lennox nods in agreement.

"What?" Millie snaps.

"Lake fucking Paige is married to your father," Sara whisper-yells.

Millie scoffs and picks up her water. "Yeah, that's not news."

"Lake fucking Paige is going to be my baby's grandmother!" I shout.

This time, Millie's mouth drops open too. "Oh my god, that's too funny. I mean, she's Vivi's grandmother too, though."

I shake my head. "Yeah, but you were all *Lake is the devil* when Vivi came into your life, so you didn't get excited about it. I'm about to have dinner with Lake Paige because she's my boyfriend's stepmother."

Sara shakes her head. "It never gets less shocking, no matter how many times we say it."

Millie laughs. "You guys are ridiculous."

Lennox gasps. "Did you just call Daniel Hall your boyfriend?" Her voice is far too loud for such a public place.

While I don't have a problem oversharing with my friends, I don't exactly want all of Boston to know my business. Although, at this point, the whole restaurant probably knows that *Lake Fucking Paige is going to be my baby's grandmother*.

I arch a brow at Millie. "Earmuffs."

She rolls her eyes, but she cups her hands over her ears and rests her elbows on the table.

"Last night, when Jasper called, Daniel said, and I quote…" I shake my shoulders and lower my chin so I can deepen my voice. "'There is no way my pregnant girlfriend is going to get out of bed at ten p.m. to deal with some asshole in a bar.' And when all I did was bat my lashes at him, he added, 'And yes, I called you my girlfriend. You're going to have to deal with it.'"

Lennox fans her face while Millie pouts, pulling her hands down from her ears. "You seriously made me cover my ears for that? I've heard you moan my brother's name like a banshee in heat."

With a lick of my lips, I fight a smirk. It's no use. "And not only did I not argue with his terminology, but I made him say the word over and over until I came three times."

"Oh my god," Millie whines.

I smile at my boyfriend's twin sister. "I warned you."

# Chapter 33
## Hannah

THE RIDE TO FORD AND LAKE'S HOUSE IS A BEAUTIFUL ONE. ESPECIALLY IN late summer, when the sky is almost iridescent magentas and fuchsias and the air is balmy against my sun-kissed skin. After brunch, I took a nap on the roof of the Langfield Corp building. It's surprisingly quiet up there when there's no baseball to be watched.

On game days, it's a great spot to catch the game, not that I've ever had the opportunity. I'm always in the stadium, available for whatever may arise.

With no game until tomorrow night and the lecture Daniel gave the boys, I'm hopeful the evening will be a relaxing one.

The drive to Bristol is an hour, and though we're quiet, Daniel peers over at me every few minutes.

"Are you nervous?"

Because, god, he's making me nervous.

"No." A slow smile spreads across his face. With a hand on my bare thigh—I'm wearing a sundress since I'm meeting the parents tonight and it felt like I should be dressed up for that—he squeezes. "Just trying to figure out how I got so damn lucky."

"*Daniel.*"

"Baby, don't say my name like that. You know it makes me hard, and I can't walk into my dad's house hard."

I giggle. "I'm sure it wouldn't be the first time. Lake Paige is your freaking stepmother."

He shrugs. "Honestly, you might not believe it, but I never really crushed on her."

He's right. That's impossible. Every human on the planet under the age of forty—and plenty over forty, including her husband—has a crush on Lake Paige. Even me. She's the biggest popstar of our generation. She's absolutely brilliant when it comes to music and she's freaking gorgeous. How could Daniel spend so much time around her and not have a crush on her?

Not that it matters. Lake is obsessed with Ford, and Daniel is clearly obsessed with me.

My man is not a cheater, nor has he ever made me feel like he's interested in another woman. In fact, if I think back to every moment since I met him, he's always made it clear he's only got a crush on me.

"How long have you liked me?" I shift in my seat and study him.

Lips tipping up, he side-eyes me. "Ah, she's catching on."

I cough out a laugh. He does that often. Takes me by surprise. Makes me light up with joy.

"I guess I am a little nervous," he admits, though his smile is still firmly in place.

"Yeah?"

"This only happens once. Bringing *the* girl home to meet the parents for the first time. This is a big night, Han."

A bolt of anxiety shoots through me. "Damn. I wasn't nervous before."

Daniel keeps saying I'll catch up, and every time I think I have, he goes and moves the goal post a little farther. This man is playing the long game. I'm not complaining. How could I? Who wouldn't want to be adored by a man like him?

Even so, if I put too much thought into it, it's all a little overwhelming.

"Don't be, dream girl. That's the thing about being *the girl*. You don't have to be anyone but yourself tonight. And there's not a damn thing you could say or do to change how I feel about you."

I try hard to come up with some type of response to this man's swoony statements, but even the writer in me is completely speechless.

DANIEL HALL ON THE ICE IS HOT, BUT HE'S GOT NOTHING ON DANIEL Hall with two babies in his arms. Nash, Lake and Ford's son, is in one arm and Vivi is in the other. Vivi is two, but Nash, who just celebrated his first birthday, is a chunky, happy baby who's nearly as big as his… niece? Every time Daniel turns his head in his direction, he lights up. And when Daniel looks at Vivi, the little guy pouts dramatically and grabs Daniel's face with his chubby hands.

My ovaries are screaming, and I'm pretty sure our baby is itching for his or her daddy's attention. I think that's what these tiny flutters in my belly mean.

We'll find out what we're having this week, but as I watch him with both kids, I know for certain that I couldn't care less what the doctor tells us. Daniel will be a great dad no matter what.

"Come here, bestie. Your uncle is being a brat." With a grin, Millie takes her daughter out of Daniel's arms.

"You've got to stop pointing that out, Mills. You're going to give Nash a complex." Daniel lifts Nash into the air and gives him a raspberry on his big ole belly. The little boy scrunches forward, giggling and squirming.

"You're slobbering all over your brother," Millie replies. "It's never not going to be weird."

Pure contentment settles over me as I watch them. Daniel and his twin absolutely kill me with their dry banter. And Millie is right. It'll always be strange that Nash has a niece who's older than he is. And soon he'll have a niece or nephew who's only a year younger than him.

But every person here glows with happiness, despite the non-traditional family dynamic. Ford is pressing a kiss to Lake's neck as if he doesn't even notice any of us are watching, or maybe he just doesn't care. Gavin—who is Ford's best friend—is motioning for Millie to settle on his lap with their daughter. If anything, they're all watching Daniel and me like we're the new, shiny toy—Daniel, reformed play-boy, having a child after a one-night stand with the older divorcée he's been crushing on for years.

Yeah, I can imagine that's how our story could easily be spun. And might be, if the media takes interest.

But every one of us is in a happy, committed relationship. I have a feeling our children will be more well-adjusted than most kids born into traditional families. So I'll take our crazy any day of the week.

Lake murmurs in Ford's ear, then straightens. "Have you registered yet?"

Suddenly, every eye is on me, every smile directed my way. "Um, I haven't had a chance to even think about it, actually."

My stomach sinks. Shit. Mothers are supposed to be excited about shopping for their child's nursery, but for me, it feels like one more item on a long list of things I don't know how to do. And with every day, that list gets more daunting. What do babies need? Can the local baby store provide a checklist so I don't forget anything?

Daniel settles beside me and rests a hand on my thigh while still holding Nash. He's such a cute kid, with big blue eyes, dark brown hair like his parents, and the rosiest cheeks. "We can check out the stores together when you're back in town next week."

"I can help put together a list of the must-haves if you'd like," Lake offers with a kind smile. "But I don't want to overstep if either of your mothers has already done that."

I snort. The idea of my mother even thinking of my child's nursery is comical. She knows less about babies than I do, and she certainly hasn't reached out to check in about my pregnancy since the day I broke the news.

Daniel's eyes widen in response to the unladylike noise. Shit. I cover my mouth, hoping they'll all assume I was choking. Choking on what, I don't have a clue, since I haven't had anything to eat or drink in quite a while.

Clearing my throat, I straighten. "We'd love any help you can offer."

"Yeah, since you guys are the only ones with a newborn we know, I'd say you'll be more helpful than either of our moms," Daniel adds.

Ford squeezes his wife closer to him. "Lake researched every car seat, every bottle, and every diaper brand. I'm sure she can give you the pros and cons of it all."

Lake's cheeks go red. "I just want the best for Nash."

I rub the little guy's arm. "As you should. Seriously, though, with how busy I am at work, I'll take all the info I can get."

"How are the Revs doing this season? I haven't made it into Boston to watch a game." Ford, bless him, changes the subject.

Is it because he can see how unprepared I am? God, I hope not. I don't want the grandfather of my child to think I'm incapable, or worse, that I don't care about this pregnancy or my baby. It's all just so overwhelming, and I'm still trying to come to terms with all the changes that are sure to come.

With a deep breath in, I push all my fears away and force myself back to the conversation. "They're doing well. We'll see how September goes. So much of the season will be determined in the next few weeks."

"Do you travel with the team?" Lake asks.

"Unfortunately," I hedge, my attention flitting to Gavin. His family owns the team, and I'd hate for him to think I'm complaining about my job. "But I don't mind. I like to travel."

"Me too," Lake says. "But when I was pregnant, traveling was a nightmare. God, all I wanted to do was sleep."

I nod. "The exhaustion doesn't make it easy."

"I wish I could say it's only a pregnancy thing. The truth is, having a newborn is even more exhausting." She chuckles.

Breath held, I assess the rest of the group, searching for signs of judgment. Do they see how unprepared I am? Do they know how hard my life is about to become?

But I don't see a single shred of censure. In fact, Gavin launches into a lighthearted tirade about how exhausting kids can be while Millie nods along. Ford plants a kiss on his wife's cheek. Here I am again, in my head. I have no fucking idea what I'll do about my career when this baby is born, but I'm too scared to put my concerns into words.

Once again, Daniel's warm palm finds another part of my body. With an arm around me, he pulls me against his chest. "We'll figure it out together," he mumbles in my ear.

While I know that he can't possibly be around every day once the baby is born, somehow, I believe him.

HOURS LATER, DANIEL'S PROMISE IS STILL ECHOING IN MY HEAD.

I enjoyed myself today, despite the realities I was hit with. Millie and Lake are wonderful mothers. Neither showed an ounce of judgment, and it took minutes in their presence to realize that they'll be great role models for me as I navigate this new season of life.

It's wild, how easy it was to spend the afternoon with the biggest popstar in the world. Lake's incredibly down-to-earth. So much so that on more than one occasion, I had to remind myself of who she actually is.

I swear she was even a little shy and uncertain when she asked if she could throw a baby shower for us. Listening to her and Millie talk about who our child might favor, whether he or she will play hockey, and about how fun it will be once all three of our kids can play together made it all seem so real. I could picture all of those things, and none of them seemed scary.

Daniel walks out of the bathroom in nothing but a towel, and my mouth goes dry. My sex drive has always been on the high side, but now that I'm pregnant—and now that I'm in such close proximity to this man so often—it's practically out of control. When I'm near him, all I want is for him to fuck me hard.

I'm just about to tell him that when the strangest flutter-roll-spasm thing happens low in my belly. "Oh!" I cup my abdomen and press my hand to where I'm pretty sure our baby has just kicked me.

Daniel rushes to me, concern written all over his face. "What's wrong?"

Though my eyes well, there's no tempering my wide smile. "I think the baby just kicked."

"You think?" He kneels between my thighs and blows on his hands to warm them. Holding them inches from my bare belly, he peers up at me, hope swimming in his eyes.

I slide my fingers through his and drag his hand to the right spot. For the first time in a long, long time, I don't feel lost. "I don't think," I tell him. "I know. Our baby just kicked me hello."

"Hey, peanut," Daniel murmurs, dipping his head close to my stomach. "Can you give me a fist bump? I'd really like to feel you."

I can't help but watch him, in awe of his gentleness. He's folded over me, our hands melded together, his focus so earnest. And when our baby does it again, a tear slips down my cheek.

Daniel laughs. "Oh my god. I just felt him. That's our baby, Han." He blinks up at me. Then, with a shake of his head, he's back to concentrating on my belly like he's waiting for another kick.

"We don't know he's a him," I tease, though my words come out a bit garbled because of my emotions.

Glassy brown eyes meet mine, but there are no tears. No, it's all wonder. "You think he's a him too, and you're never wrong."

I bite my lip, my heart fluttering. "I guess we'll find out next week."

While his head is bowed again, his focus intent on our child, I work up the nerve to bring up his comment from this afternoon.

"Did you mean it today?" With my free hand, I run my fingers through his dark hair.

He leans into my touch and lays his head against my stomach. "I mean everything I say to you, but be more specific."

Warmth spreads through my limbs. Not just because of his words, but because of the way he says them. Because of the way he's holding me and our child. His mere presence has the ability to settle the chaos in my head. He knocks down my walls before I have a chance to erect them. I've never been so comfortable with a person in my life.

Tears clog my throat, but I force the words out. "That we'll figure it all out together."

"Yes. Of course we will." He nuzzles my stomach. "Right, peanut? It's not all on your pretty mama. We've got this."

That's what does it. That's what sends the tears cresting over my lashes and rolling down my cheeks. It's so natural, the way he loves on us both. In this moment, I know I've fallen in love with the father of my child. The feeling hits me smack in the chest, the overwhelming tidal wave washing away every insecurity.

The *hows*, the *what-ifs*, the *can we reallys*?

In their place is this certainty.

An overwhelming knowledge that, no matter what happens, I'll be okay. *We'll be okay.* And it's all because of him. Because of the way he looks at me. The way he holds me. The way he *has* me.

"You're going to be an amazing dad," I rasp.

Daniel peers up at me, his throat bobbing. "Yeah?"

With a swipe at my cheek, I nod. "You were so incredible with Nash and Vivi today. I couldn't stop thinking about how you'll be with our baby. How, in a matter of days, we'll know what we're having and…you're just going to be so good, Daniel. I'm so happy you're the father of my child."

I have so much more to say. There are so many words beating wildly against my breastbone. But they remain lodged there. I'm too overcome to let them out.

Daniel kisses my belly, whispers something to our little peanut, then climbs up my body. "Can I ask you a favor?"

"Anything." I ease back, rapt by him.

He hovers over me, his elbows planted on either side of my head. "I feel like we missed out on the excitement of announcing our pregnancy because—"

"Because it was more *oh shit, we got pregnant*." I laugh.

He nods. "But now it's more like *oh shit, we're pregnant*." The words are the same, but his tone is full of wonder. He strokes the hair from my face and cradles my cheek in his warm palm. "And I want to celebrate that we're having a baby with all our friends."

My heart trips over itself. "What do you have in mind?"

"Do you trust me?"

My response is immediate. "Always."

"Then let me take care of everything, dream girl. I want to do a big gender reveal. Is that okay?"

"So we'll find out with all our friends there?"

He nods and presses a kiss to the tip of my nose. "I promise I'll make it fun. You'll be happy."

I pull him to my chest and hug him tight. "I already am. But yeah, we can do it your way, Playboy."

# CHAPTER 34
# DANIEL

"So I'm the only person in the whole wide world who knows?" Lennox wears the biggest grin as she peeks inside the white envelope again.

"Well, you and the ultrasound tech, likely a nurse or two, and the doctor." Eyes narrowed, I study her expression, looking for any hint about what's printed on that piece of paper.

Fuck, it's hard to be patient. I want to know whether Hannah and I are right. More than that, I can't wait to find out what we're having so we can pick a name and I can stop talking to my child like it's a snack. But I refuse to peek. I want Hannah at my side when I find out. I promised one epic reveal, and I intend to give it to her.

Tonight.

I wrangled Lennox, the queen of event-planning, into helping me.

I've been told she can keep a secret. At least for a few hours.

"This is so exciting." She bounces on the balls of her feet. "I can't wait to tell Sara that I know."

*On second thought.* I reach for the envelope.

With a giggle, she waves it above her head. "I'm just teasing. I won't say a thing. Should I plan on getting Hannah to the rink, or will you handle that?"

"Millie's got it covered."

My sister wasn't happy when she discovered that Lennox would know before her, but she changed her tune when I told her that she had a more important role. That I was counting on her to get Hannah here for the surprise. It helped that I let her in on another secret, one that not another soul knows.

Now I've just got to settle the knots in my stomach and convince myself this is the right thing to do. That she's ready.

I thank her and say my goodbyes. I've just rounded the corner leading to the locker room when my phone lights up. When I see that it's because the note Hannah shared with me—the one containing her bucket list—has been edited, my heart leaps.

She's been doing that a lot lately.

Adding items to her bucket list

I have until the end of this list to make her fall for me, and at this rate, she'll never be done with me.

It's hard not to hope that she's adding ridiculous things like *jump out of a plane* and *swim in the Dead Sea*—things she can't do while pregnant—because she wants this list to last forever just like I do.

My phone rings in my hands, startling me, and instantly, my mood sinks. It's my agent, and it's not his first call. I've been avoiding him because I'm nervous about what he'll say. I signed with the Bolts three years ago, which means this year, I became a restricted free agent. Because I'm under twenty-seven and have less than seven years in the NHL, the league rules provide that other teams can approach me, but the Bolts can exercise certain rights to keep me if they choose.

Vegas is interested; that's abundantly clear. Camden Snow was an unrestricted free agent, so when the offer was made, he went happily. I don't know whether Gavin negotiated to keep him. And I don't want to know what will happen if Vegas makes a real offer. Will the Bolts exercise their rights in hopes of keeping me? And what if they don't?

A year ago, I couldn't have imagined worrying about any of this. But now that Noah is playing with Aiden and War, my position feels much more precarious. How important am I to the team? If Vegas offers what I've been told they might, would Gavin risk the salary cap to match it? Can he? I hate talking money. Maybe that's absurd, considering the kind of wealth my family has. Now, though, it seems perti-nent, and I fucking hate that.

I just want to play hockey with my friends. I want to win. I want to be useful to my team. But as I listen to what my agent has to say, it's never been more clear that we don't always get what we want.

# Chapter 35
## Hannah

"Oh my gosh, oh my gosh, oh my gosh." Phone in hand, my thumbs fly over the screen. If I don't get this scene out of my head, I'll forget it, and that would be a travesty, because the words the hero just whispered in my ear are literally making me melt. I never thought I'd love a swoony man so much—I always leaned toward the bad boy, the forbidden, the age gap—but god, this story is writing itself, and it's all because the man is such a hidden cinnamon roll.

"Are you in pain?" Millie offers me an arm while simultaneously scanning the hallway of the hockey arena.

I wave her off without speaking. If I do, I'll lose the plot.

"Are you calling 911? Do you need me to get Daniel? *Daniel!*" She hollers like a lunatic.

Shit. If I don't calm my baby's aunt down, a slew of huge hockey players are liable to come running out on their pointy knife shoes.

"I'm fine," I huff. All I can do now is hope I got enough of the sentence down to spur the memory of the words that just came to me. This book is begging to be written. The couple won't stop talking to me, but finding time to write it is damn near impossible.

I can't wait until this season comes to an end and things are a tiny bit less hectic. Though will they be? Daniel's season will just be ramping up, so I'll be busy cheering him on at home games or wallowing in self-pity when he's traveling.

The opposite seasons are going to be a major hurtle, though if I'm lucky, maybe I'll actually get some writing done while he's on the road. My goal is to get this book edited and published before this baby arrives in January. If I don't, then I worry that it'll never happen.

"Are you sure?" Millie grasps my arms and inspects every inch of me.

I roll my eyes and shake her off. "I was working on my book. I know it's crazy, but if I didn't get the words down, then I would have forgotten them."

Millie smiles knowingly. "I get that. When I get a lyric in my head, if I don't write it down, something ends up lost, and I'll stress for months about how it's not quite right, and a year later, after I've recorded and can't make changes, the original lyric will come to me."

"Yes, that!" Excitement courses through me. This girl gets me. "Do you have a note dedicated to random lyrics?"

Millie pulls out her phone and taps on the app. The first note on the screen is filled with words. Half-written songs. Ideas. Bits of songs I recognize from her last album. Millie is a goddess. She somehow managed to write and record an album while parenting an infant.

My chest tightens. I hadn't thought about how challenging it must have been for her, but it gives me hope. If she can do it, then maybe I can figure out how to be a mom and have a career.

"Want me to distract Daniel so you can get the scene done?" Millie offers. "I can tell him all about what Gavin did to me last night in the locker room after practice."

With a laugh, I shake my head. Oh god, her poor brother would be horrified. "Nah, I think I'm good."

Arm looped with mine, she tips her head in my direction. "Okay, but the offer stands. I'm always happy to torture him to buy you more writing time."

"Appreciate that." I lean into her.

It's the absolute truth. Especially because our little moment distracted me from the nerves that have been plaguing me all day, not knowing exactly what Daniel has been up to.

When we step into the arena and I spot all of my girlfriends hanging out by the bench while the guys skate, all in casual clothes rather than their hockey gear, my stomach does a somersault, and this time it's not because the baby is kicking me.

He or she has been doing it more and more every day. Especially when I stop moving like I am right now. With a hand over my stomach, I take in the scene. So many of our friends showed up to find out the sex of our baby. And—my heart expands almost painfully—my brothers. Every single one of them. Even Ash.

I have to blink back the tears at the show of support.

Never in my life have all of my favorite people been in one room. Most certainly not for something for me.

"Surprise," Millie whispers as she pulls me toward the ice.

Likely noticing the way the chatter in the arena quiets, Daniel slows to a stop and spins. When he spots me, his face lights up. "Hey, dream girl!" he yells like a complete lunatic.

I shake my head, but warmth blooms in my chest. The man has no shame.

"Hi, Playboy. What are we doing here?"

My brothers get to me before Daniel can, each pulling me in for a hug. It takes far more effort than I'd like to admit to hold back the tears as I squeeze them all extra tight. "I cannot believe you're here," I say to Ash as he releases me.

"Wouldn't miss it. Besides, your boy threatened bodily harm if we didn't show up." His lips kick up on one side, his eyes twinkling.

I peer around him, focusing on Daniel—sweet, young Daniel, and look back at my brother—a former Navy SEAL who's as tall as the guys on skates and knows seventy ways to kill a man. Maybe more.

"Listen, anyone who has the balls to threaten me in order to keep my sister happy deserves my respect," Ash mumbles.

"He is always full of surprises," I whisper, mostly to myself. I'm still processing the scene.

He waves me over to the boards, and with Gavin's help, lifts me and settles me on my feet on a length of Bolts blue carpet that's been rolled out on the ice, leading to the center where the puck is normally dropped.

"Hi, dream girl," he says.

I shiver, not only because of the affection in his tone, but also because it's cold in here, and I stupidly didn't even bring a sweatshirt. I rub at my bare arms as I take inventory of all our friends, and I'm immediately warmed when he wraps me in a hug and holds me close.

"All my brothers are here," I tell him, like he doesn't already know it.

He chuckles as he drags his knuckles down my skin, sending goose bumps rushing across my flesh. "Yes, they are. I wanted to share the excitement with everyone. That okay?" He peers down at me like this is really a question. As if this isn't already one of the best days of my life, and nothing's even happened yet.

"It's more than okay." I press a kiss to his lips.

Behind me, Lennox shouts, "Drop the puck already!"

Daniel turns me so we're facing our friends. Everyone but War, Brooks, Aiden, and Noah—who remain on the ice with us—has gathered on the other side of the glass.

Daniel clears his throat. "Thank you all for coming—"

Aiden zooms past us, and doing his best Britney Spears impression, croons, "Oh baby, baby."

"Oh fuck." Daniel hangs his head.

I choke on a laugh, but it's cut off when War skates in front of me and sings, "We really want to know."

Brooks is next, scowling, his words more of a mumble than a tune. "The sex of the baby."

Across the ice, Sara screams, "Yeah, Brookie. Sing it!"

All three guys spin on their skates facing us, their arms outstretched, and then start singing the rest of the song.

*"Oh, baby, baby,*
*We're your uncles and we need to know-oh*
*And now is the time, yeah.*

*Tell me, are you a boy baby,*
*Or a girl, 'cause we need to know now,*
*Yeah, we do.*

*Your dad's cool, but your mom's the best, and we,*
*We must confess, we still don't know (don't know)*
*When Playboy shoots, we'll all find out,*
*So take the stick.*
*Hit it, Playboy, just one time."*

DANIEL TOSSES HIS HEAD BACK AND LAUGHS, STILL HOLDING ME TIGHT.

War eases forward and holds out a hockey stick.

With a kiss to my lips, Daniels murmurs, "Ready for this?"

I push him away, eager to see what happens next.

As he takes the stick, Noah appears at my side and drapes an arm over my shoulders to keep me warm.

I smile up at him, and he presses a kiss to my forehead.

The guys skate, maneuvering pucks back and forth between them. Then, in unison, they pull back and slap their sticks down.

An instant later, a cloud of bright Bolts blue erupts.

With a whoop, Daniel spins, skates toward me, the biggest smile on his face, and scoops me up. "We're having a boy, baby! A fucking boy."

The joy pulsing through my veins is so powerful I feel like I'll erupt. "I knew it," I murmur, hugging him tight.

He sets me on my feet, and without a word, pulls his jersey over his head and yanks it over mine, instantly encasing me in his warmth and scent.

Around us, our friends and family hoot and holler, but all I can see is Daniel. I pull the neck of his jersey up to my nose and inhale, closing my eyes, and sink into the comfort only he could provide. When I open them again, Lennox is holding out a small pastel pink and blue bag.

He takes it and holds it between us. "Baby's first present."

My throat grows tight. "Our son's first present."

Dark eyes glassy, he nods.

We're going to have a *son*.

With a strengthening breath, I pull the blue sparkly paper from the bag and toss it at Noah. My heart thumps as I grasp fabric and pull the tiny Bolts blue jersey out. When I hold it up, the entire crowd goes wild.

"So the little guy can cheer for his daddy," Daniel says with the shiest grin.

The expression tugs at my heart, like maybe the baby is in there pulling at my heartstrings.

I turn the tiniest jersey I've ever seen around, and when I find a number 18 and the name *Hall* emblazoned above it, I grin so wide my cheeks hurt.

"Wanted my family to have matching jerseys." The low rasp claws at my defenses.

"And I'm your family?" I ask, heart thundering.

God. This is it. I think I finally get what he's been trying to tell me all along.

With an arm around my waist, he pulls me close. "Yeah, dream girl. You and our baby are my family." He ducks and examines my face, his lips tugging down. "Why are you crying?"

I hadn't even noticed I was, but I don't even care. "Because I just—" I shake my head and cup his cheek. "Do you love me, Daniel?"

He blinks at me, a deer in the headlights.

"Because," I sniffle, "I think I may be head-over-heels in love with you."

"Holy shit." He leans into my hand.

Tears continue to fall, my smile only growing, along with my heart. "No. Actually, no thinking. I'm in love with you, Daniel. And I'm really happy you're my family."

Forehead pressed to mine, he sucks in a deep breath and closes his eyes. When he blinks, tears crest his lashes. "I don't think I've ever been so happy in my entire life. I've been in love with you for a long time, dream girl. I'm so crazy in love with you I don't even know what to do right now." Then, straightening with a jolt, he yips and holds up my hand. "I love this woman!"

My chest expands, like it's carving out a permanent space for him as the people gathered cheer.

I lean my head against his chest, plastering my body to his, the tiny jersey fisted in my hand pressed between us. "I can't wait to come to the games with our son and cheer on my favorite Bolts player of all time."

He kisses my forehead. "Say it a little louder. I'm not sure everyone heard you."

Laughing, I tip my head back and rest my chin on his chest. "You're my favorite person of all time."

"Fuck, Han. I'm getting hard, and your brother is *right there*."

A zap of electricity arcs through me. "Take me home, Playboy. I want to make love to my favorite hockey player of all time."

# CALLIOPE'S COLUMN



## The Art of Getting What You Want by Speaking (or Texting) Up

One of the hardest struggles women face is telling others what we want. We can complain to our friends about what our significant other isn't doing. And hell, we might even be able to tell them what we wish he would do. However, the moment most of us are sitting in front of the person who is asking *what do you want?* we freeze.

This is tenfold when it comes to sex.

Maybe it's because we're taught to be demure, to be quiet, to be appreciative of what we've been given.

Fuck that.

Men don't have a problem telling us to get on our knees. They don't struggle with dirty talk. So why should we?

Need practice? Try phone sex. Think about it. You need to say precisely what you want your partner to do to you. It's a fantasy spoken out loud. If you're apprehensive, start with sexting. Try telling your guy exactly what you want him to do to you. Tell him what *you* want to do to *him*. I promise your man will deliver the next time you see him.

Also, say it with me: "You're such a good boy for me when you're on your knees."

# Chapter 36
## Hannah



"You're doing so good, baby. God. Watching you makes me so fucking hot."

Daniel's eyes are heated, his pupils blown wide. "I love when you coach me through it. Spread your legs wider, dream girl."

I angle the phone down, giving him exactly what he wants. This stretch of away games has felt like a lifetime. It doesn't help that our trips overlapped. I haven't felt Daniel's body against mine in far too long. Thank god for phone sex, or I'd be one pissed-off woman.

He works himself over, his piercing peeking out with every stroke. Each time that metal glints, I slide the vibrator inside me, mimicking his movement.

"Fuck, I'm going to come," I tell him.

Daniel slows his jacking. We've been working him toward a non-ejaculatory orgasm, but we're still on step one. He needs to jack off for at least ten minutes without coming, but every time I come, he does too.

"Strangle it," I whimper as the orgasm takes me under. My back arches, and a cry slips from my throat. Covered in a sheen of sweat and a smattering of goose bumps, I come down, working to catch my breath. The orgasms are so much more intense now that I'm pregnant.

Daniel keeps a firm grip on his cock, eyes closed as he sucks in sharp breaths.

"Such a good boy," I murmur, my eyes heavy. "You make me so proud."

When he opens his eyes again, the intensity is palpable, even though he's states away. "Say it again."

"Good boy." This time my voice is clear.

He works his hand over himself again, a man possessed. Like he can't stop. Within seconds, his jaw flexes, and he loses the battle, coming with a long groan.

He disappears to clean up, but not before making me promise I'll stay on the phone.

This is always my favorite part. When we're sleepy and a little uninhibited after a good orgasm. We talk about everything and nothing until one or both of us fall asleep. I've woken up to his sleeping face, the FaceTime call still connected, more times than I can count. He never hangs up if I fall asleep first. Apparently, he prefers to watch me until he dozes off.

God, I love this man.

"Get any writing done today?" he asks as he settles the phone on the charging dock next to the bed in his hotel room and lays his head on his pillow, facing me.

I mirror the position, hand tucked under my face. "Just a few hundred words."

Daniel frowns. "I'm sorry."

I shrug. "It is what it is. The season will be over soon. I'll have a lot more time then." Just the thought makes my chest pang with longing for days where I can sit in front of my computer, uninterrupted, for more than thirty minutes. This season has proven harder than any other, and I'm beginning to see that it's not just the pregnancy. I no longer enjoy it the way I used to. The thrill of fixing other people's problems, of being needed and important, is almost nonexistent these days.

Maybe for the first time in my life, I feel wanted, important, valuable somewhere other than at work. I no longer want to be needed by a bunch of overgrown boys dressed up as baseball players.

For so long, my life revolved around my career. I was fine on my own for more than a decade, feeling complete as a single woman. Now, I'm struggling with this side of me that's been hiding since college. The side that craves Daniel's arms and his affection.

It's so damn tempting to pull back. To put up walls so that it won't hurt so much if he gets tired of me.

But then I see his face, or hear his voice, or unlock my phone and find a text that reads something like the one he sent the other day. A text that literally said *It still amazes me that you exist. That you're having my baby. That you're mine.*

Since I was a little girl, my mother's life has centered around men. If the man she was with was kind, she'd be happy. If he was miserable, she was miserable. I don't want to be like that. Is that what's happening here? Daniel's happiness is influencing mine? Because, god, does he make me happy. I can't imagine a time when he won't.

So I'm determined to give this a chance. To keep my heart open. As long as we continue to be honest with one another, as long as he talks to me, tells me what he needs, and I do the same, I really truly believe we can do this.

Even so, he can't be my whole life. I need my career. My own identity. That's where my mom always got it wrong. She had nothing but the man she was with.

And me, though I was never enough.

Our child will never, ever feel the way I did. The way I do.

"When will you be home again?" I don't even bother to hide the neediness in my tone.

"I'll be home in time for your birthday," he reminds me.

Nose scrunched, I grunt. I'll be thirty-four in a matter of days. I swear it feels like only a year or two ago, I was a twenty-one-year-old college student, depressed and hiding after my divorce. Now I'm in my *mid-thirties* and pregnant.

Dating a twenty-five-year-old.

At least he'll keep me young.

"I thought maybe we could go to Pottery Barn and check out that baby furniture you like," I tell him.

Daniel grins. "Oh, you finally checked out my Pinterest board?"

I snort. Seriously. This ridiculously sexy twenty-five-year-old hockey player created a Pinterest board and filled it with nursery decorating ideas. "Yeah, and you forgot to make your other boards private."

Daniel chuckles. "Baby, there are no secrets with me. You want to see my dream kitchens, the man cave I'm planning for the house I want to build, or the vacations I want to take you on, then be my guest."

I roll my eyes, my heart flip-flopping. "We all have secrets, Daniel. Just because it's not hidden on your Pinterest board doesn't mean there aren't skeletons in your closet."

"Password to my phone is 041825. Code to my computer is Iluvhannah. Bank card pin is—"

Breath catching, I sit up, taking my phone with me. "*Daniel.*"

He laughs, his dimples peeking out at me. "I've got nothing to hide from you. Was I a playboy before we got together? Yes. I couldn't hide that if I wanted. But since the minute you gave me a chance, on April eighteenth, you've owned me."

"Oh-four-eighteen-twenty-five." I shake my head, breathing through the shock.

"Yeah, Han." He leans closer to his phone, his expression open, his eyes dark pools of sincerity. "You're my world. That day, our first date, the night we made our son, was the best day of my life."

"*Daniel.*" Tears flood my vision, and a love so big it can't be contained fills me.

He makes it impossible to be scared of the future. Impossible to not believe that we have a future. That I can have it all. A family. A career. An epic love that not even I could write on the page.

"I love you," he says, voice thick.

"I love you too."

# CHAPTER 37
# DANIEL

"You're sure you know how to cook?" Balanced on the stool beside me, Oliver gives me a wary look.

I angle in so we're eye to eye. "It's pie. How hard could it be?"

I survey the Oreos laid out in front of us.

"Have at it."

"If you say so." He raises the hammer over his head and brings it down in one quick swish.

I almost lose a finger as I reach in to stop him before he smashes the granite counter into pieces. "Jesus, kid. You've got to be ducking kidding me."

Frowning, he tilts his head. "Ducking?"

*Dammit, Hall.* I exhale a loud breath. "Don't tell your aunt I said that."

"Ducking? What's wrong with ducks?"

I shake my head. If the kid hasn't figured out what that's a substitute for, I'm not about to tell him. Jeez, maybe this dad thing is harder than I thought.

I spin the hammer and tap it against the cookies, making them crumble into big pieces. "Can you do it like this?"

He shrugs. "Pretty sure Hannah will be home before we finish the cake if we do it like that."

This kid. He's always got a comment. I like it. He's smarter than any four-year-old I've ever met. And while they aren't blood, he'll be my kid's cousin. An older boy to look up to and learn from.

"It's pie, not cake."

Hannah doesn't like cake. She mentioned it at dinner in Vermont. It's the consistency. She prefers creamy things. Yeah, you heard that right, and of course I went there the second the words registered. She laughed her ass off, because she and I have the same sense of humor.

I scan the recipe on my phone, double-checking that I have all the ingredients.

A little banner appears at the top of the screen, a text from Camden, and instantly I grind my teeth.

Camden: If the rumors I'm hearing are true, the gods will be back together in no time.

"Put them in a plastic bag before you smash them."

At the sound of Noah's voice, I snap my head up, ignoring what-ever Camden is hinting at.

Noah strides into the kitchen wearing nothing but a damn towel.

Already on edge, I can't stop a growl from sneaking out. "We've been over this."

Noah shakes his head. "She's like my sister."

"*Like* your sister. Not really your sister. And you are naked."

Though he's a good decade older than me, he's in incredible shape. I'm not generally a jealous guy, and I know what I bring to the table, but I'm not an idiot. The last thing I want is a naked hockey player—*like a brother* or not—walking around my girl's apartment.

"She told me about your brother ducker comment," he says under his breath.

I glare at him. "It was a perfectly reasonable reaction when I discovered you were living here."

Side-eyeing me, he pops an Oreo into his mouth. "So ducking good," he mumbles.

"Why do you guys keep talking like barn animals?" Oliver asks, head tipped back so he can see his dad. "Mommy always says we don't live in a barn."

Noah barks out a laugh while I dump the Oreos into a Ziplock bag.

"You're making her favorite pie." Noah hums in approval.

My chest expands with pride, but outwardly, I play it cool and lift a shoulder. "She doesn't like cake."

"And you know that how?"

I squeeze the bag, pulverizing the Oreos. "Because I listen."

With a grin, he holds a fist out to Oliver. "Hear that, buddy? Always listen." He spins on his heel and heads toward his room. "All right, I'm going to get dressed, and then I'll come help you."

"Who says I need your help?" I call.

"You almost let my kid take a hammer to Hannah's counter, and the oven's on fire," Noah yells.

I whip around, heart plummeting, to discover the oven isn't even on.

Oliver points at me, eyes dancing. "Made you look!"

I cough out a laugh. Yeah, having a son will be cool.

"Baby, I'm home." Hannah breezes into her apartment, absolutely glowing. She spent the afternoon with the girls at the spa, and we're meeting the whole crew for dinner in an hour.

I scan the kitchen one more time, making sure I've gotten rid of all the evidence from our pie-making activities.

Noah took Oliver to Jen's and will meet us at the restaurant. With any luck, he'll meet someone at the bar and go home with them so we have the place to ourselves. Though I doubt it, since I've yet to see the guy even flirt with a woman, let alone go home with one. We've got to work on that.

I hold out my arms, and Hannah sinks into them. "How's my birthday girl doing?"

"Perfect. We went shopping after the spa." She props her chin on my chest and smiles up at me.

My whole being lights up. There's nothing better than having her attention. Than having the ability to hold her and know this is exactly where she wants to be.

"Oh yeah? Get something pretty to wear to dinner?"

"Nope. I got something pretty for you to wear to dinner."

Nerves skitter down my spine. Knowing Hannah, I have every right to be concerned.

"Want to see it?" she asks, her teasing tone confirming my suspicions. Eyes sparkling, she pulls back.

I follow her into the living room and find her holding up a tiny black plastic shopping bag.

"Nothing that small will fit me, babe." I chuckle as I approach.

She arches a brow. "Wanna bet?"

*No.*

That's what I should say.

Better yet, *fuck no.*

But this woman is pregnant with my child, and it's her birthday. Even if it wasn't, I'd do just about anything for her. She could tell me to punch myself in the face for her own enjoyment, and I'd do it. I live for her smiles.

Hands in my pockets, I sigh. "Sure."

The way her pretty blue eyes light up has my mood lifting. It's unreal, the way her joy feeds mine. I never knew it was possible to be this happy.

As slowly as she can, she pulls out a rubbery blue ring.

Head tilted, I frown. "What is that?"

"It's a vibrating cock ring." She twirls it around her finger. "It's charged up and all ready for you."

My dick jumps. "What do we do with it?"

"You're going to wear it to dinner and"—she leans closer, brows raised—"you're *not* going to come."

The air leaves my lungs in a whoosh. "Hannah, I'm crazy about you, but I'm not wearing that to dinner with our friends." I cross my arms, hoping like hell she'll back down but knowing better.

She pouts.

I shake my head.

She tosses it to me, and as I catch it, I growl out another no.

I stare down at the vibrating toy for another second before I shove it into my pocket.

Five minutes later, we sit side by side on the couch. One by one, little boxes on the screen appear, each filled with the face of a man near my dad's age. Liam has been here more than once, hanging out with Oliver and Noah when I'm here, but this is the first time I'm meeting the other dads.

"Happy birthday." The first man to speak has dark hair and looks just like Ash.

"Thank you."

The others echo the same sentiment, but quickly, every eye is on me.

"I was going to wait for mom before doing introductions, but who knows where she is." Hannah lets out a tight laugh and glances down at the phone in her lap, where she's typed out a reminder message to her mother.

My stomach sinks. From here, I don't see a happy birthday message in the chain of recent texts. I'm going to give her the benefit of the doubt and assume it's because she called Hannah instead.

"This is Daniel," she says, straightening. "Daniel, these are my dads, Pierce—"

The man who looks like Ash waves at me.

"Ryot."

A well-groomed guy in a suit nods.

"Bryce."

This guy is in a suit too.

"And you already know Liam."

Liam smiles. "How'd your afternoon with Ollie go?"

I grin. "We accomplished what we set out to do."

Hannah shifts to face me, but I keep my focus fixed on the screen.

"It's nice to meet the rest of you."

Ryot—the lawyer, I think—eyes me. "I'll be in town next month. We can discuss the custody arrangements then."

Hannah flinches. "That's—*no*." She drops a hand to my thigh and squeezes. "We don't need any agreement. We're together, and we'll figure this out together."

Though she's clearly worried Ryot has upset me, I'm actually ecstatic that she has people in her life who care enough about her to give me shit.

"Hannah and our son mean the world to me. Anything she wants, she's got."

"That's what everyone says before—"

Liam clears his throat. "Ryot, don't forget we promised Hannah we wouldn't let our divorces affect her."

"I'm protecting her," Ryot mutters.

Bryce nods. "I agree with him. There should be formal documentation."

I lean forward, unbothered. "Type it up. As long as it's what she wants, I'll sign it. But it won't matter. We're not breaking up, and there isn't a scenario where I won't provide everything she and our son want or need. But if it makes you feel more comfortable to put that in writing—"

"It does," Ryot presses.

I shrug. "Then fine."

"No," Hannah grits out.

"Han." I scoot closer to the edge of the couch and turn her way. "I'm not worried."

"Neither am I." She assesses her dads, her expression stony. "I love him and he loves me, but even if that weren't the case, I know he loves our child and he'll always do the right thing."

My heart cracks open and love pours out, filling me to the brim. She's sticking up for me. For us. And it only deepens what I feel for her.

I'm ready to end the damn Zoom call and drag her into the bedroom when Liam holds up his phone and gives it a shake.

"Your mom says she has spotty service so she can't hop on the call but she wishes you a happy birthday."

Hannah's attention drops to her lap, where she hasn't received a response from her mother. She doesn't want me to hate her mother, but the woman makes keeping that promise pretty damn hard.

My girl plasters on a smile and shifts the conversation, launching into detail about how we want to decorate the nursery. Every one of the guys stays engaged for the next twenty minutes. They clearly love her.

But despite her smiles, she can't hide the hurt from me.

I'd do anything to make her feel better, so the moment she shuts the computer, I pull out the cock ring and dangle it between us.

"Dude, why the fuck do you keep moving around?" War grumbles.

On my other side, Hannah does a shit job at tamping down on the giggles.

I glare at her, then, focusing on breathing steadily, turn back to War. "Just can't get comfortable."

It's not a lie. I can't get comfortable because Hannah is using a fucking remote control to change the strength and speed of the cock ring's vibrations, and it's pure torture. My dick has been painfully hard since she sat down.

When she turns it up as I'm bringing my first bite of steak to my mouth, I growl. "If you want me to last later, I need to eat."

War chokes on his drink and slams the glass onto the table. "Aw, is Baby Hall having a hard time keeping it up?"

I shove him so hard his chair tips. Fortunately, it goes backward. If I'd made him bump into Ava, he would have beaten the shit out of me.

"I'm not having a hard time with anything," I say through gritted teeth.

Hannah rubs my back, and I shudder. Just her touch sends tingles up my spine. I grimace and inhale deeply through my nose, trying not to explode in my pants.

"Daniel is learning how to have multiple orgasms without ejaculating." Hannah breaks into a devilish smirk.

Eyes closed, I shake my head. This conversation is going to go off the rails now. I'm not the least bit ashamed of it. Hell, I used to tell the guys all about Calliope's column. But in the middle of dinner with all of our closest friends and my girlfriend's goddamn brother? *With* a cock ring vibrating my dick?

Yeah, even saying that sentence back in my head makes me say *what the fuck?*

"What the fuck is the point if you don't ejaculate?" War demands.

I swear to god the entire restaurant goes silent.

Down the table, Lennox and Sara perk up.

"What now?" Sara asks.

"Tyler," Ava hisses, her cheeks a bright shade of red. "Do *not* say ejaculate."

He smirks at his wife. "Yeah, scratch at me, Vicious. You know I love it when you get angry."

Poor Ava sighs and shakes her head. "I'm eight months pregnant. What more could you want with me?"

He looks directly into my eyes, his blue irises icy. "I want to fill you with my cum. Because that's what I do when we have sex. I ejaculate."

My body shudders so violently I almost fall off my chair. Swallowing back bile, I steady myself. "Don't look at me when you say those words."

Holy fucking shit. Did I die? Am I in hell?

The pressure in my dick immediately deflates a fraction, and for a second, I'm actually almost thankful for the man beside me. The one I'll never look in the eye again. Because for the first time in a solid forty minutes, I feel relief.

That sensation vanishes quickly, though, when Hannah laughs in my ear and sets the toy to a pulse setting.

Back to rock fucking hard, I groan and drop my head against hers. I'm losing the battle here. And her fucking smell doesn't help. Neither does the way I know she'll taste. "Fuck," I curse as I squeeze my eyes tight, fighting the impending disaster with everything I've got.

"Oh my god!" Sara slams a hand to the table, making all the cutlery rattle. "Oh my god, oh my god, oh my god."

You can say that again. I'm focused so intently on my dick I can't speak.

The pulsing stops. The vibrating stops. Fuck. Also, thank the hockey gods I didn't just come in my pants.

"What?" I think that's Lennox responding. My brain is too scattered to be sure.

"He's wearing it, isn't he?" Sara shouts.

My eyes snap open.

"Oh my god. You totally are, aren't you?"

"What are you talking about, crazy girl?" Brooks squeezes her shoulder to center her. The girl needs that type of grounding every once in a while.

Lennox snorts. "He's not."

Noah frowns, his focus fixed on me. "What's she talking about?"

Hannah opens her mouth, but before she can speak, I slap a hand over it and bring my mouth to her ear. "I love you, baby, but if you tell your brother I'm wearing a goddamn cock ring right now, I'll kill you."

The table erupts in laughter and questions while I beg the floor beneath me to open up and swallow me whole.

Fuck. My. Life.

FOUR HOURS. FOUR FUCKING HOURS. SHE'S HAD ME LOCKED IN HER bedroom, chained to the bed, fucking me through one orgasm after another. I never thought I'd wish a sexual encounter was over. Never thought I'd be seeking the sweet relief of this pie right now, but fuck, my dick hurts.

I stare at it, really stare at it, and consider what I'm so damn tempted to do.

It's Hannah's birthday pie. This could be grounds for murder.

She deserves this chocolate cream pie.

She's having my baby.

*She's having my baby, and she deserves this pie.*

Oliver and I made this pie together.

It's probably fucking delicious.

But my dick hurts, and it looks so soothing. It's cold but not too cold. The inside is probably soft. It'll swallow my dick in a perfect hug. The kind of hug Hannah used to give me with her perfect pussy. Before she became this sex-crazed demon. The mother of my child is insatiable, and my dick hurts.

Every time I've seen her over the last three weeks, she's immediately jumped me. If I'm not traveling or playing hockey, she's riding me. For the first few days, I was certain I'd died and gone to a horny man's heaven. Hannah loves me and I love her. We're having a kid together. I love sex. She loves sex. We're both really good at sex. Win-win-win-win-win.

Head hung, I frown at my poor dick. It's tired. I'm tired. I just need a little relief.

There's no way in hell I'll tell the woman who is carrying my child that I can't fuck her. That if she slides down on my dick one more time, I'll cry.

I just want Hannah to be happy. We've been so happy.

But…I'm in pain.

Wincing, I step toward the pie.

This is so wrong.

I peer over my shoulder. She's asleep.

Oliver's at his moms.

Noah went to the bar after dinner. I think he's still out.

No one will know.

It's like this was meant to be. She doesn't even know about the pie since she dragged me into the bedroom the second we returned from her birthday dinner. I'll get up early and make another one.

But for now I'm desperate for relief.

Fuck it.

I unzip my pants, and with one last look over my shoulder, I let them fall to the ground. Butt-ass naked in the kitchen, I reach for the tin pan. The whipped cream winky-face I added mocks me.

Yeah, motherfucker, I'm about to destroy you.

Without another second's hesitation, I slam it to my groin.

"*Ahh.*" The groan comes from deep inside my chest. Fuck. This is the most soothing sensation I've ever experienced. "God, yes." It feels incredible. So good I can't help but clench my ass cheeks and thrust, making sure to totally submerge my raw dick in the cool cream.

"Okay, I've put up with the loud-as-shit fucking—"

Lungs seizing, I spin, because what the fuck is wrong with me? And now I'm holding a tin pan to my dick, pants at my ankles, as I stare at my girlfriend's brother.

Noah's eyes bore into mine, his lip curled in disgust. "I even sat across from you at dinner while you did kinky shit with her and a cock ring, and I kept my mouth shut, but I have to draw the fucking line—"

"It's not what it looks like." The words are a little higher pitched than I meant for them to be. Fuck. I sound pathetic, even to my own ears.

"You're cheating on Hannah with a chocolate cream pie?"

"Okay." Shoulders slumping, I whimper. "It's exactly what it looks like, but you don't get it."

He drops his head to his hands. "Have some fucking respect for yourself and at least turn away from me, man."

"You're right," I say meekly, shuffling toward the counter, pants at my ankles.

"Oh, fuck. Now I can see your hairy ass."

"I don't have a hairy ass." Chin to my shoulder, I peek down, but damn, it's a challenge to see one's own ass. "I don't think. Do I?" I glance up at him and shake my head. "Don't answer that."

"What the fuck is wrong with you?" He stalks past me, heading for his bedroom.

Shit. He probably thinks I'm a lunatic. Is he going to tell her?

I hop after him, holding extra tight to the pie tin so it doesn't fall. "She's just so horny. Always so horny."

"Stop talking." He slams the door in my face.

Dropping my forehead to it, I croak out an "I'm sorry!"

"You need help!" he hollers. "Be a man and tell Hannah to give you a break."

I straighten and shake my head. Nah, I'll just soak my dick for a little longer. And then I'll make another pie.

# CALLIOPE'S COLUMN



## Can You Have Your Cake and Eat It Too?

Can women have it all?

I know it's a bit existential for me. But before you hit that X and close out of this article, answer the question. Seriously. Can we?

Can we have successful careers and still make time for dating?

Can we use dating apps, or go on dreaded first dates, or finally tell our long-term boyfriends we want more, and still have a career?

Can we get pregnant during a one-night stand, then—in the best interest of the future child—take the time to get to know the baby's father and, oh yeah, still have a career and goals and dreams for ourselves?

Can we choose not to work so we can focus on being moms?

Can we have kids and still have the career and the husband and the friends and the life and somehow balance every one of those things?

Can we have it all?

The truth is, I don't know. But I'd really like to have my birthday cake—or, in my case, pie—and eat it too.

And I will.

So grab a spoon and dig in, because we're going to figure it out.

# Chapter 38
## Hannah



"Knock-knock."

Biting back a growl, I save my Word document and close it out. I'll get back to my characters later.

"Is now a bad time?" Liv asks from the doorway.

Exhaling, I wave her in. "Never."

It absolutely is, but it's probably best not to tell my direct supervisor that I was in the middle of writing a scene where my heroine is getting railed by the single dad with a choking kink. The season might be over, but my job with the Revs is year-round and does not include writing spicy books during office hours.

The Revs didn't make it to the World Series, so our season has officially come to an end. Liv and Beckett spent a week in the Florida Keys, so her cheeks are rosy and her smile is bright. God, how I would love a real vacation. Maybe after the baby is born, sometime between Bolts and Revs games in the spring, we can find two to three days to get away.

Who am I kidding? The All-Star break is literally the only time each year we'll be off at the same time. That thought is sobering.

And really sad.

Liv settles across from me, crossing one leg over the other. "How are you feeling?"

Instinctually, I settle a hand on my stomach, where our son is pummeling my bladder. He hates when I sit still. "The exhaustion has gotten better, and now I'm just—" I snap my mouth shut before the word *horny* slips out. Liv may be awesome, and I'm sure Beckett keeps her satisfied, but it's probably not appropriate to talk about my sex life with my boss. "I'm ready to have this baby."

"Yeah, when I was pregnant with the twins, I was over it by the end of the sixth month. Now, sometimes I'd like to just slip them back inside so I can get some peace and quiet." She chuckles. "When's your due date again?"

"January twentieth."

Liv nods. "I thought I'd check in to talk to you about what you're thinking for after maternity leave. You plan to take the full six months Langfield Corp offers, right?"

A gasp escapes me before I can stop it. "You offer six months?" I probably should have checked the employee handbook sometime during the last five months, but I just…didn't.

"Yeah, Beckett changed the policy right after I had the twins. I don't think he understood how difficult taking care of newborns can be until I tried to come back to work after three months."

Shit, was she really out for six months? I was probably too busy cleaning up after Jasper to notice. "Wow. Well, yeah. That's great." I clear my throat. "I'll look into a day care, and I guess Daniel and I can figure out where to go from there."

"Hannah," Liv says, her voice gentle as she leans forward, "daycares don't keep babies overnight."

Hackles rising, I splay my hands on my desk. "I'll figure it out. You have five kids, and somehow, you did it."

Liv shakes her head. "No. I was head of Langfield PR. I only traveled with the team here and there—and only because Beckett demanded it back when, apparently, he was obsessed with me and I didn't have a clue. I couldn't have traveled all season and raised my kids. It's a job meant for someone without a family." She shrugs. "Or a man."

A mixture of fear and frustration and, yeah, a little anger, swirl in my stomach. "Can you even say that?"

She frowns. "No. Not as your employer. But we're friends too, and I want to be honest with you. Certain jobs are impossible when you have young kids. You can't travel for two-thirds of the year once you have this baby."

Chest tightening, I blink back tears. "So am I going to lose my job? That's illegal, isn't it? You can't fire me because I'm pregnant."

"Honey, no." She leans forward. "After your maternity leave, you'll transition into another role. A role that doesn't require nearly so much travel. That's what I'm going to offer you, at least. It's up to you to decide what you want to do."

I inhale deeply, then let the breath out a little at a time, willing my nerves to settle. "Can I think about it?"

"Of course. This isn't a demotion. We value your work above all else, and no matter what you decide, you'll always have a spot here. You can have it all. I promise. But sometimes having it all looks a little different once you have a family. Does that make sense?"

I nod. She's right. I can't continue to travel like this. But even if I haven't loved my job so much these days, and even if I miss Daniel when I'm gone—and know it will be ten times worse to leave him and my child next season—I don't know if I can step away from the job I worked so hard for.

I wander Boston for far too long, avoiding my apartment while a war rages in my head. I have to have a plan in mind before I talk to anyone about this. But before I come up with a plan, I need to process my feelings about the loss of my career. Or the massive overhaul of it, at the very least. I have to come to terms with all the changes coming down the pike.

Because whether or not I'm ready, they're coming. Fast.

Something Liv said stuck with me. She said my job isn't a good fit for women with children, yet she implied that a man could do it. She's not wrong. I haven't heard a single person mention to Daniel that he can't play hockey now that we're having a baby. In our society, we assume that the mother will be the one to give up her career.

Even if I'm not happy at work at the moment, I'm still angry at the societal expectations. Those two things can be true at the same time. I'm allowed to not want to do this anymore while also being annoyed that I *can't* do this anymore.

I won't even get a proper goodbye. The season is over, and when it starts again, I'll be on maternity leave. I'll never travel with the Revs as their PR rep again.

But no matter how I slice it, there's no way I can travel with the team. I can't rush out in the middle of the night to deal with problems, especially when Daniel is traveling.

These are just facts.

Facts that make me irrationally angry.

Which is why I'm still walking after seven when my phone rings and Noah asks if I plan to be home for dinner.

Shit. I try to spend evenings at home when he and Oliver are there.

He and Jen have made it work, but I wouldn't be surprised if Jen harbors some resentment about Noah's busy schedule.

I ball my fists and growl in aggravation. Why does this have to be so hard?

I'm angry at Daniel over something that isn't his fault. If I told him how I was feeling, he'd tell me if I wanted to keep my job, we'd figure it out. He'd hire a nanny to travel with me. And if that didn't work, I wouldn't put it past him to give up his dream so he could be home with the baby while I'm gone.

I shake my head and blow out a breath. My muscles relax a fraction as that truth registers with me. Sometimes I forget that I'm not doing this alone.

I head home to talk to Noah before I call Daniel and say something I might regret. I know that man will put me first, so I better figure out what I truly want before I let him do that.

"Why are you looking at me like that?"

I push the plate of pasta Noah set in front of me to the side. It takes effort, because Noah's pasta is homemade. He's kind of a genius in the kitchen, so not diving in when my mouth is watering is a feat of its own.

"I need to talk to you."

I fold my arms across my chest. "So talk."

He settles across from me and smiles. He's not the kind of guy who smirks, but if he were, he'd probably do it right now. I'm being a brat. Luckily, he knows how to deal with me.

So, with that simple expression still on his face, he hums. "You okay?"

Leg bouncing, I wait for the bomb he's going to drop. I can feel it in the air. Everyone is dropping bombs today. "Get on with it. What do you have to tell me?" I force a smile. It's not his fault I'm having an atomic bomb kind of day. "*Please.*"

Angling forward, he rests his arms on the edge of the table. "I found an apartment."

My back goes ramrod straight. "But you live here."

Brows creased, he tilts his head. "Hannah, you need the space for the baby."

"Is this because of all the sex?" I huff. "I know I've been obnoxious, but I can actually be quiet."

He drops his head and laughs. "No. I got headphones a long time ago. And I know how you are. I'd never want you to change," he adds when I scowl. "You and Daniel need your own space." He reaches across the table and squeezes my hand. "The two of you are doing this, Hannah, and I'm so fucking happy for you. You're creating a family, and that man? He loves you so fucking much that I have no concern that once I'm gone, he'll take care of you."

I look away, hiding the tear sliding down my face. What he's saying is true. Every single thing. But everything is changing, and it's happening so fast.

"I'll just miss you." I inhale deeply, wipe at my cheek, then force myself to look at him. "And Oliver. As it is, I barely see him."

Noah grins. "I forgot to tell you the best part about the apartment. It's right across the hall."

The heavy despair pushing down on me lifts. I scramble to my feet and throw myself into Noah's arms. "Oh, thank god."

He rubs slow circles over my back. "You've got this. You are going to be the best mom, and Daniel is going to be one hell of a dad. And I'll be right across the hall if you need me."

I suck in a breath. Just like Liv said, some things have to change. Having it all will look different from now on. I can either embrace it or fight it. And there's no sense in fighting. Not when the baby will be here soon, whether I'm ready or not. And I'd rather be ready.

# CHAPTER 39
# DANIEL



I'VE NEVER BEEN SO EXHAUSTED.

Probably because Keegan and the new kid, Smiles, and I aren't clicking.

No, Smiles is not his last name. And no, he doesn't actually smile. War gave him the moniker the first week of camp. Probably trying to get the kid *to* smile. It didn't work. He scowls every time Aiden breaks into song and generally looks pissed off at all times.

I could deal with all of that if he'd just talk to Keegan and me so we could all be on the same page. But so far, he only communicates in one-word grunts. It's not boding well for our season.

At this point I just want to go home, take a hot shower, and curl up in bed with Hannah.

I'm headed out to do just that when Gavin leans out of his office. "Hey, Daniel, got a minute?"

I stop and turn. I always have a minute for my coach, regardless of whether he's my brother-in-law too. "Everything all right?" I ask as I head in his direction.

Gavin nods, though his brows are furrowed in a way that makes me think it really isn't. "I just got off the phone with your agent. Let's talk about Vegas."

IF I WAS TIRED BEFORE, I'M DEAD ON MY FEET AS I STEP INTO HANNAH'S apartment much later than I hoped.

A sniffle stops me in my tracks, and when I find Hannah sitting at the table, tears streaming down her face, the rest of the world, all my worries that don't concern her, falls away. "Baby, are you okay?"

I drop my bag at the door and rush to her. Dropping to my knees between her legs, I search every inch of her, looking for injury.

She grips my shirt and pulls me in for a hug. "It's just the hormones. I'm fine," she says, her voice shaky.

My heart sinks. This is so unlike her, even at her most emotional. Has she teared up more than I ever thought she would? Sure. But she's pregnant. This? This isn't that.

"Talk to me," I plead, hands on her thighs. "What's going on?"

"Noah's moving out," she sobs, hands covering her face.

Oh. Yeah. He showed me the apartment listing this morning and mentioned that he planned to tell her.

But his new place is across the hall. It seems a bit out of character for her to be crying this much over that. "He'll be right across the hall." I stand and pull her into my arms. When she wraps her legs around me, I stride to the couch. I get her settled on my lap, running my hands up and down her arms and murmuring comforting words.

"Everything's changing," she whispers against my neck.

I sigh. It really is. And she doesn't even know the half of it. But now isn't the time to talk about that. She doesn't need another thing to worry about.

I pull back and tip her chin so we're eye to eye. "But it's not all bad. It's a lot, and I know I can't possibly understand how much it's affecting you, since on top of all that's going on, your body is changing and you are literally growing a human."

Hannah nods even as her lips wobble. "It is a lot."

I hate to see her cry, but she is so fucking adorable in this moment.

Pushing her hair back, I study her. "I don't know if I've said it yet but thank you. Thank you for doing it all. I'm sorry I can't do more."

Lips tugged down, she hiccups. "You do everything. If you weren't so good to me, I'd be really crying. On the floor, wailing and begging Noah not to leave me. But you—" She shakes her head, a pathetic whimper escaping her. "You make it all better. I was just sad because I missed you today and I hate that we barely get any time together."

I pull her to my chest and hug her tight. "I'm sorry, baby. I wish I could be around more."

She nuzzles into my neck. "It's not your fault. I just wish I could come with you. I wish I could be a little groupie. One of your puck bunnies."

A rumble of a laugh rolls through my chest. "Hannah Prescott, you are my one and only puck bunny."

She rests her chin on my chest and peers up at me through wet lashes. "Really?"

"I couldn't possibly keep up with anyone else. You are the love of my life and the best sex I've ever had."

She snorts. "Obviously."

"This is when you're supposed to say, *and you are mine, Daddy Hall.*"

She pushes against me with a huff. "I'm not calling you Daddy Hall."

I grab her wrist and press my lips to it, focus locked on her misty blue eyes. "Oh, you will."

"How do you do it?" She sighs.

I press another kiss to her wrist, then loop her arm around my neck and rest my hands on the globes of her ass. "Do what?"

"Make everything better."

My heart stumbles, and a wave of confidence washes over me. "Because I love you. If I can make it better, I will. Anything. So what can I do to make this better? Want to go shopping for new furniture? Make this place feel more like *our* apartment?"

Head tilted, she giggles. "You trying to move in with me, Playboy?"

"I'm not sleeping anywhere else when my girl and my baby are here, so we can play this game where we don't call it what it is and I'll pretend that I'm just visiting, or..."

She arches a brow. "Or?"

In one quick move, I flip her so she's on her back and I'm hovering over her. "Or we can do it the fun way. I get rid of my apartment. We stop living life with one foot out the door, and we admit that we're doing this. You and me and eventually our little guy…" The last word sticks on my tongue. I'm ready, but is she? Either way, I swallow and push it out. "Forever."

"That didn't sound like a question," she whispers, studying every inch of my face.

"It wasn't. I'm telling you what I want. A question implies that I'm unsure. *I'm not.* I'm sure about us, Hannah. I'm sure that in fifty years, I'll be coming home to you. Whether this is my home or not, *you are.*"

Her lips lift in the most magnificent smile. "Okay. Let's go shopping tomorrow."

Pushing my luck, I add, "Come with me to Vegas for the game next weekend. I know you can't travel with me all the time, but we can fly out a day early and stay an extra night."

Lips parted, Hannah blinks at me. "You think the team will let you?"

I nod and swallow down my nerves. This wasn't the reason I planned to go a day early, but now I can kill two birds with one stone. "Already cleared it with Gavin. So what do you say? Want to come to Vegas with me?"

Hannah throws her arms around my neck. Based on the kiss she gives me, I'm pretty sure that's a yes.

# CALLIOPE'S COLUMN



## The Greeks Really Did Know Best

This should come as no surprise, but Calliope isn't my real name.

Don't get too excited. I don't have any intention of stepping out from behind the pseudonym. I prefer the anonymity. It gives me the freedom to say exactly what I want without censoring myself.

However, I want to share the reason why I chose the name Calliope. I thought I was creative, if I'm being honest. Maybe it's the writer in me, but I wanted to use the name of a Greek goddess, because hello, if you don't believe yourself worthy of goddess status, what are you doing with your life? And Calliope is the perfect goddess to represent me. Or at least the me I show the world.

Unlike the other goddesses, she wasn't a virgin. She was divorced. Like me.

Though the true reason I went with the name is because she is the goddess of the arts and the chief muse.

I truly believed that my only partner in life would be writing. That nothing and no one could compare to the words I dream up.

That books would be my first and only love. That I didn't need a man or a love story of my own.

Oh, how foolish I was.

Because of course a woman who writes about epic loves truly craves one for herself. I was just too scared to admit it.

And then I fell in love with my greatest muse. The man who will likely be the inspiration for many columns going forward. The man who is about to give me the best love story of all as we prepare to become parents.

This column may look a little different going forward. Or maybe it won't, because who says moms can't have epic sex lives?

# Chapter 40
# Hannah

Shit. He crossed another item off the bucket list.

"Daniel." I sigh, shoulders drooping.

"Yes, dream girl?"

"I'm going to tip the gondola."

Head thrown back, he laughs loudly, the sound echoing off the ridiculously tall ceiling painted to look like the sky. The people in line watch us with mostly amused expressions.

I rest a hand on my ever-growing belly. At seven months, I swear it gets bigger by the minute. The baby is sitting high, making it convenient to rest my arms on my stomach. Though I haven't been able to see my toes in a month. The last time I tried, Daniel laughed at me. That didn't end well for him.

I'm always hungry, but even a single bite of food feels like it's sitting in my esophagus—probably because my stomach starts rounding just beneath my boobs—so finishing a meal is impossible. It's cruel, really. I want to order one of everything on the menu, yet I can't eat more than a few bites.

With tears in his eyes, he doubles over, still laughing.

I smack him. "You're rude."

Straightening, he clears his throat, doing his best to compose himself. Then he wraps his arms around my belly and smiles down at me. "Baby, you're beautiful and I'd never let anything happen to you. Besides, the water's like two feet deep. If we tip, I think we'll survive."

This time I swat his abdomen with the back of my hand. "Rude."

"Come on, Han. It's on your list. I promise I won't let you fall in."

"A gondola ride in Venice, Daniel. This is not Venice. This is Vegas."

"We're in the Venetian Hotel, baby. You can't fly to Venice, and I swore I'd help you cross off every item."

Arms crossed, which gets harder every day, I frown. Why is he so determined to cross shit off my bucket list? Every time I add something, he comes up with a creative way to get it done. I was sure that including experiences that could only be accomplished in other countries would slow us down, but no. The man brought me to Vegas, and in a single day, he's crossed off more activities than should be possible.

"This doesn't count," I grind out.

His lips curl in a smirk. "So you don't want to do it? Or how about this? We do this today, but we don't cross it off until we go to the real Venice someday."

I clench my jaw, but there's no stopping my smile. "Promise?"

I'm being ridiculous. I don't even recognize myself sometimes. All of a sudden, I need reassurance that he loves me every minute of every day. I've never been that woman. It has to be the baby. When my son is older, I'll be sure to tell him about all the outrageous things he made me do. Well, maybe not *all* of them.

Daniel pushes my chin up with his finger and practically folds himself in half to get close now that my belly sticks out so far. "Promise."

The moment his lips touch mine, my body heats. I wrap my arms around his neck and push in as close as I can, deepening the kiss.

A loud throat clearing breaks us apart. I drop to my heels, slightly dazed, as Daniel steadies me.

"So are you coming on the ride or can the next couple go?"

Daniel breaks into a wicked smile. "We're coming."

After he's helped me back out of the gondola, he doesn't check it off the list. I breathe a sigh of relief. Good. I don't ever want it to end.

"You sure you'll be okay?" Daniel leans over me as I snuggle in bed. After the gondola ride, we had coney island hot dogs in New York and crème brûlée in Paris, and if I don't take a nap now, there's no chance I'll make it to the Top of the World for dinner.

"I will miss you, but I do promise I'll be fine."

He's headed to a meeting, so I'll have the bed all to myself.

Daniel smirks, still hovering silently. It kind of gives me the creeps.

"Why are you making that face?" I ask him.

"Do you have any idea how good it feels to hear you say that so freely?"

"Say what?" I ask, keeping my tone soft. My emotions are all over the place. Currently, I'm annoyed by his smirking and simultaneously melting at his words.

"That you'll miss me. Sometimes it's hard to believe you're really with me. That you want me around."

My heart cracks at the rawness of his voice. "*Daniel.*"

Eyes warming, he smooths a thumb across my cheek. "You're my dream, Han. Sometimes that's exactly what all this feels like. I swear I'll wake up, and you'll be back to calling me Baby Hall when I flirt with you, telling me I've got no shot at the woman of my dreams."

"It wasn't like that."

He lets out a sardonic laugh. "Oh, yes it was. You were unattainable."

"And yet here I am, carrying your child, begging for your cock day and night, constantly asking you to tell me that you love me."

Daniel's smile grows so wide it can probably be seen from outer space. "Begging? I don't remember any begging."

I pinch his stomach, and when I dig my fingers in and tickle, he squeals. In seconds, we're panting and laughing, but the sounds quickly turn into moans. His lips find mine, and then I'm pulling his shirt off, and he's sinking into me.

"Tell me you love me," I whimper as he lifts my leg so he can get a better angle.

With a grunt, he thrusts deep. "I love you."

Electricity ricochets through me when his piercing hits that spot deep inside me only he can find. "Tell me you need me as much as I need you."

He presses his thumb to my clit and rolls it slowly. "Need you so fucking much. God, Hannah, you feel like heaven."

With every week that passes, my nerve endings become more sensitive. So when his piercing drags against my walls in just the right way, I unravel quickly. Toes curled, I squeeze my eyes shut and give in to the wave of ecstasy washing over me.

"Open those eyes, beautiful. Neither of us is dreaming right now. This is real. You're mine, and so is every one of your orgasms."

It takes effort, but I force my eyes open. Like this, I watch Daniel go over the ledge with me, the pulsing of his thick cock forces his piercings to dig even further into me, sending me straight into another orgasm.

He's right. This is real. Yet knowing that our real life *is* his fantasy brings me a peace I never thought I'd find.

An hour later, after I've given up on napping—despite my exhaustion, I can't fall asleep; thanks, pregnancy—I'm lying in bed, scrolling Instagram, when my phone rings.

The moment I slide my thumb over the screen to answer, a yawn catches me by surprise.

"Did I wake you up?" Millie asks.

"No," I say on another yawn. "I'm just always tired."

She giggles. "I'm guessing all the running around Vegas Daniel had planned isn't helping."

I smile. "He's sweet, and the day has been perfect. But yes, I forced him to bring me back to the room so I could nap. Pretty sure I've walked ten miles already today. Though now that I'm lying in bed, I can't sleep."

"Aw, well, tell him to rub your back or order you a cup of tea."

I arch my back, but when I can't get comfortable, I turn to my other side. I always end up in this position—with a pillow between my thighs and another tucked beneath my bump. "Can't." The word is muffled because of my new position. I adjust, patting the pillow. "Sorry. Can't ask him because he's not here. He had a meeting."

"Oh with the team in Vegas? God, I really hope he doesn't love it. Is it wrong of me to say that?"

"Huh?" I'm too groggy to follow.

"It's just—I want you guys to stay in Boston. I want to be near my nephew, and I want to raise our children together."

Feeling suffocated by the damn pillow, and still so damn confused, I push myself up. "Why wouldn't we stay in Boston?"

"Um—" The line goes silent for a beat too long. "What?"

"You said you want us to stay in Boston." My voice sounds funny. Distant. And my heart thuds in my ears. "Why wouldn't we stay in Boston?"

"Because Daniel has an offer from Vegas. Since he's a restricted agent, the Bolts would need to match it if they want to keep him. Hasn't Daniel talked to you about any of this?"

My heart flops to the floor as my world crashes around me. I shake my head, but the words don't come out.

"Fuck," she hisses, the sound making the line between us crackle. "I shouldn't have—he should have—*fuck*."

I nod. All of those things are true. "Does he want the trade?" I ask. My voice is so quiet I'm surprised she can hear me.

"I don't know," Millie says softly. "He didn't talk to me about it. Gavin told me. I guess he wanted to prepare me if—" She sighs.

He wanted to prepare his wife in case her twin brother chose to move across the country. Because that's what partners do. They watch out for one another. They communicate.

I blink back tears. Why didn't Daniel say anything? Does he think I won't support him? Does he…

"It was hard on him, you know, when Gavin moved Noah into his spot with War and Aiden," Millie says, breaking me from my spiral.

Swallowing thickly, I nod again. That makes sense. But I didn't know how hard it was on him. Truly. He rarely talks about hockey when we're together. He's always talking about topics that matter to me. The baby, my books, his obsession with me.

And I never asked. God. I never ask. "You think he brought me here to see if I'd like it?"

"I think Daniel wants you with him, no matter where he is," she says. "And I'm sure he has a good reason for not telling you about the possible trade."

Once again, I nod, but I say nothing.

Daniel loves me.

He isn't planning on going anywhere without us.

So I'll give him the benefit of the doubt. I'll trust that whatever his plan is, he'll clue me in when he's ready, and then we'll figure it out together.

# CHAPTER 41
# DANIEL



"AND THIS IS THE PRACTICE FACILITY."

Holy shit. The place is incredible. Everything I've seen this afternoon has been. Just like Camden said it was.

"Since we're playing you tomorrow," Coach Bexley says, "I'm going to have to end our tour here."

With a smile, I hold out my hand. "I really appreciate you showing me around."

"Was my pleasure. Think about what I said." With that, he's gone.

I slip my hands into my pockets and take another minute to survey the space. It's been a wild few days. Hell, it's been a wild year.

Sometimes when I think back even to last fall, I swear I must be remembering someone else's life. I was still part of the dream team, still on the first line with War and Aiden, but even then, something was missing. My life had no depth. No meaning.

Hannah provided all that by just existing.

And then she went and made me a dad.

Hockey is no longer my sole focus. Even still, it means a hell of a lot to me. Without it, I wouldn't recognize myself.

But the Bolts aren't my family, Hannah is. Every decision I make going forward has to be with her and our child at the forefront of my mind. And honestly, I wouldn't know how not to put them first. Since she gave me a chance, she's been my first thought and my last.

I start my trek back to the hotel, gearing up to make an important phone call.

"I still can't believe you guys are going to be parents." Camden shakes his head as he sips his soda water.

I bring Hannah's hand to my lips and press a kiss to the back of it. "You better get ready to call me Daddy Hall, because that's what I'll be in two months."

My girl rolls her eyes and yanks her hand away.

Sputtering on his soda, Camden bolts upright. "Don't hit me with your sex talk. Save that for the hotel."

Hannah coughs out a raspy laugh. My favorite kind. "He wishes I'd call him Daddy Hall."

"You will," I say as I snag her hand again and settle it in my lap. "It's only a matter of time."

"How are you liking Vegas?" Hannah asks, changing the direction of the conversation.

We're at dinner at the Top of the World, and I won't lie, it's really fucking nice to see Camden. Hockey hasn't been the same without him. He laughed his ass off when I filled him in on the new guy, Smiles. He doesn't think the kid will last with the Bolts, and I couldn't agree more. He belongs in New York with the rest of the assholes, but I guess I can't say that about a teammate.

My buddy leans back, stretching his arm across the empty chair beside him. "It's awesome. Like I told your boy, if he'd said yes, he'd be a god on the ice here. But it looks like I'll have to rule Vegas all on my own."

While he's chuckling at himself, Hannah's hand goes limp within mine.

And my gut sinks. Dammit.

"Right," my girl says, her tone flat. "Sounds amazing. Will you excuse me? I have to use the bathroom. The baby's sitting on my bladder."

I brush her arm as she stands, desperate for her to look at me, but she avoids my gaze, and since I don't want to make a scene, I let her go.

Once she's out of earshot, I hiss an aggravated breath through my teeth and push back from the table. "Fuck."

"What happened?"

Jaw locked, I shoot him a glare. "I never told her about the trade."

Camden scowls. "The trade you didn't take?"

I toss down my napkin. "Yeah. But it doesn't matter whether I'm taking it or not. The issue is that I never talked to her about it. Now she thinks I'm hiding shit." I duck my head and yank at my hair. I should have just told her. But she's been so overwhelmed, and until a few hours ago, I truly didn't know how it would turn out.

And I didn't want to risk fucking things up until I had all the information. Things with her have always been so delicate. She has so much baggage. And the people who were supposed to care about her most have treated her like crap her entire life. Her absentee father. Her absolute disgrace of a mother. An ex who made her believe she couldn't have real love. I've worked so hard to do everything right, and I was terrified of rocking the boat, but fuck, I think I might have screwed it all up anyway.

I never had any intention of leaving Boston. I would never have uprooted our lives weeks before our baby is due so I can play hockey.

But it hurt, being moved to second line, being separated from the two guys I have such good chemistry with. And yeah, I was embarrassed. Angry even.

How could I not be when Gavin made the changes? The guy isn't just my coach, he's my brother-in-law.

When he brought Noah on, it fucked with my head. Made me feel inferior. I could practically see the writing was on the wall.

"Fuck." I push back from the table and stand. "I've got to go talk to her."

Camden nods. "Do what you need. I'll see you at the game tomorrow."

I feel like shit leaving him here before we've even ordered. "I'm really sorry." With a deep inhale, I glance toward the hall where the bathrooms are.

Is that where Hannah really went? I wouldn't be surprised if she left. I'd deserve it.

Fuck, fuck, fuck.

I head for the bathrooms, my hands balled at my sides, blood pressure rising, head pounding. So unbelievably pissed at myself for fucking this up.

When the door to the women's bathroom swings open, I'm ready to hustle past the person exiting, but I almost tip over when Hannah is the one who comes barreling out. Her eyes are red and puffy, but her face is dry, as if she cleaned herself up so she could return to the table and act like nothing is wrong.

It isn't until I step in front of her that she notices me.

"Daniel?" Her eyes go wide, and she says my name on an inhale, like she's surprised to see me, her hand going to her chest. Quickly, her expression morphs into a glare.

"I should have told you." I step right up to her, keeping my hands to myself for now.

"We can talk about it later. Let's get back to dinner." She takes a step to the side.

Before she can skirt around me, I grab her arm and tug gently. "I told Cam we wouldn't be coming back."

She lets out a derisive snort. "Great. Another steak dinner I missed out on."

The lead ball in my gut sinks farther. "I'm sorry. I'll make it up to you. I'll order ten steaks from room service."

With a sigh, she leans against the wall, her entire demeanor wary. "Why didn't you tell me about the offer from Vegas?"

"I was never going to take it." I make sure each word is clear and concise. The last thing I want is for her to believe there was ever a chance I'd leave her and our child in Boston.

"Why?" Her voice is soft, yet it pierces my heart.

I step closer, pressing her against the wall and cradling her cheek. "Hannah, we're having a baby. Your job is in Boston. Your life. You've given up enough because of this pregnancy. I refuse to ask you to give up more."

She presses her hand to my chest, but rather than push me away, she grips my shirt. "You're my life." With her free hand, she slides my hand from her cheek and settles it on her stomach. "You and this baby. You told me home wasn't a place. You said I was your home. And you're mine."

I take half a step back and shake my head. "Wait, you're not mad at me?"

She huffs. "Oh, I'm mad, all right. I'm upset that you thought you could make a decision like this without me. I'm furious that you thought so little of my love for you, that you assumed I wouldn't do exactly what you do for me. If this is going to work, you need to talk to me. You need to *trust* me."

Heart thundering, I grasp her hip. "I do trust you."

She shakes her head. "Not enough to talk to me about this. Not enough to see that I'm in this with you."

I bury my face in her hair and inhale, letting her scent soothe me while I collect my thoughts. She's right. I guess I didn't trust that her feelings for me are as strong as mine are for her. In the back of my mind, there was always this concern that if not for the baby, she never would have given me a real shot. That maybe she was with me because she felt like she should be. It's unbelievable, honestly, to think that she'd give up any more than she already has just so she could be with *me*. Not for the baby, not for us, but just for me. I pull back, exhaling slowly. "You'd really leave Boston? Your job?"

She dips her chin once. "I planned to talk to you after your game tomorrow. I'm going to give Beckett and Liv my notice next week. After the baby is born, I want to stay home and write. I do *not* expect you to support us—"

I bark out a laugh. "Might as well stop right there. You better believe I want to take care of my wife and the mother of my child."

She blinks up at me, her lips parting. "Your wife?"

"Yeah, Han. Eventually I'm going to ask you to be my wife."

Though the uncertainty that's lived inside me all these months bubbles up, I choke it down and own the statement, standing taller. "You ready to run yet?"

She looks down at her feet. "I'm not moving, am I?"

"What about tomorrow?"

I need to know this is for real. For so long, I've been terrified to make a wrong move, certain I'd lose her. But I made the wrong move tonight, and she's still here. So maybe she's in this. Maybe she's always been in this. Maybe I couldn't let myself believe it, because for so long, she felt unattainable. She was unattainable. Older. My sister's best friend. Confident and intelligent and unimpressed with my flirting. But now?

"And the day after that, and the day after that. For all the days of our lives," she whispers.

I shake my head. Fuck. I'm in awe of this woman. "I'm so fucking in love with you, dream girl."

"And I'm in love with you too, *Daddy Hall.*" She breaks into a smile. "So tell me, where do you want to live for the next few years? Because if it's Vegas, I could get used to all the lights."

Desperate to be as close to her as I can get, I press my lips to hers. This life we're creating is already so damn beautiful. Day by day, piece by piece, we're going to build it. Together. And she's right. We have to make these decisions together. I inhale her. Drunk on her. Light and excited. Energized in a way I've never been.

"Boston," I breathe out. "I want to raise our son in Boston. As long as you want that too. I want him to have a wicked thick accent, and I want to take him to Revs games with his pretty mama because she loves the hot dogs there—"

"The buns aren't terrible to look at either."

Growling, I nip at her bottom lip. "I want to spend weekends at my dad's house so our son can bond with my baby brother. One day, they're gonna be best friends."

Hannah grins. "So taboo."

I run a hand down her hair, smoothing it away from her face. "I want to hang with my sister and her family and spend time with Noah and Oliver. I want our kid to spend time with all his cousins, and I want to give him brothers and sisters."

Her eyes dance. "Oh, a big family?"

"Yeah, Han. I want a big family with you. I want to sink inside you every night. I wanna fill you up over and over until you're pregnant again. And again and again."

With a waggle of her brows, she hums. "I definitely like the practice."

I slide my tongue into her mouth, and when she moans, I swallow the sound, savoring it. When we come up for air, I can't help but push some more. Now that I'm on a roll, I can't help but ask for it all. "I want a lifetime with you, and I want it in Boston."

"What about hockey? If you're unhappy with the Bolts, and Vegas is offering you everything—"

Heart thudding, I pull back and frown. "I'm not unhappy playing for the Bolts. I promise. But how do you know about the offer?"

Her lips twitch like they always do when she thinks I'm being a fucking idiot. The look makes me hard as steel every damn time. "I have my sources."

Hand snaking behind her neck, I tug on her hair so her face is tilted up. "Boston matched it."

Her eyes go wide. "What?"

"When Vegas made the offer and my agent called Gavin, he suggested I come out here and visit with management. Said he wanted to give me the opportunity to see what other teams had to offer. Didn't want me to feel obligated to stay, I guess." I lift a shoulder. "Apparently he did the same thing with Aiden and Brooks, but that was before my time, so I had no idea. Said he understands that it's hard for me, not playing with Aiden and War, but he reminded me that Keegan needs a strong winger, and separating War and me made the most sense. This way pushes Keegan to work hard so he can keep up with Aiden. And he will one day. The kid is great. And I'll have years left to play when War and Noah retire."

I didn't know how much I needed this push from Gavin until I talked to him after I met with Vegas's management. When he called me into his office last week and told me to come to Vegas, to see what they would bring to the table, I was devastated. I was certain he was pushing me out the door. Terrified he'd trade me but hoping he wouldn't, knowing Millie would be devastated. All I could think was that he was betting on me initiating the trade request so he wouldn't have to be the bad guy.

I should have known better.

I should have trusted him. Just like I should have trusted Hannah. I've known Gavin most of my life. He told me while I was still in high school that I had what it takes to make it to the NHL. He showed up at games when he had far more important things to do.

Or maybe not. Maybe it's time to acknowledge that I was one of those important things.

By giving me the opportunity to see what other teams would offer, Gavin showed me how lucky the Bolts are to have me. He proved that I'm a valued member of the team.

And he flat-out told me that I'm the future of this franchise.

With that statement coming from a man I respect tremendously, as family and as my coach, I have every confidence that this season will be different. I'll figure out how to make it work with Smiles and Keegan because I'm that fucking good.

I know that now. I truly see it. Thanks to Gavin.

"You are still a baby," Hannah teases. Her smile slips, and she cups my jaw. "But seriously, I just want you to be happy. That's what I realized when Liv came to me about my job."

"She did?"

She sighs, sliding her hand to my chest. "I guess I can get off my high horse, since you aren't the only one who didn't share about big changes in your career. That's one of the reasons I was so upset last week. She was wonderful. She always is. But she pointed out how difficult handling PR with a newborn—"

Spine stiffening, I growl low in my chest. "Can she do that?"

Hannah huffs out a laugh. "I said the same thing, and technically, no. But she meant well. It's hard to walk that line when she's not only my boss but my friend. She wanted me to think about the challenges I'd face, and she assured me that I could transition into a different role. But I realized that I'd rather write my books. It's what I've always wanted to do; I was just too scared to give up on a career that I worked so hard for—"

I stroke my thumb against her cheek. "It's not giving up; it's going after your dream."

Her lips lift. "See? You get it. Just one more reason I love you. You get me."

I press my lips to hers. "I do." Eyes closing, I blow out a breath. "So we're okay?"

"We're okay." She leans against me, giving me her weight, and I steer her toward the exit. "Man, I really thought you brought me here to convince me to move to Vegas. I was ready to do it too."

I laugh. "No. I had to come out a day early for that meeting, and I didn't want to be away from you any longer than I had to be. Plus, I figured we could cross off half the things on your bucket list here. Ya know, keep ya wild while we still can."

She grins up at me. "I'll keep you safe. You keep me wild."

She says it so flippantly, but the truth is, she knows it's exactly what I needed to hear. She'll keep me safe because she loves me. She really fucking loves me.

"Deal." I squeeze her tight. And damn if that isn't the best damn thing I've ever agreed to.

# CALLIOPE'S COLUMN



## New Year, Same(ish) Me

With a new year upon us, I find myself reflecting on what I've accomplished in the last twelve months and what I've yet to do. The accomplishments of others can be inspiring. But they can also be daunting. They can make you feel like a failure just as easily as they can motivate you. As they say, comparison is the thief of joy. But so is complacency. It's easy to stop moving forward when life feels daunting. To freeze and believe that since doing it all feels like too much of a challenge, you might as well not try.

That's a place I never want to wallow in.

No, I may never be a New York Times bestseller, but maybe I will. I won't know if I don't try. It's quite possible I'll never travel to half the places on my bucket list, nor experience all I want to in my life, but there is still so much I can do.

Maybe bungee jumping will be removed from my list, but I'm adding things I never thought I would. Like marriage and a house. And a book signing.

These aren't items I'm actively working to check off my list yet. But one day, I will. It's wild, how much I want them, these things I never thought I was interested in, let alone believed I could have.

Along with all of that, though, I want to stay a bit wild.

And remind myself that I can have it all, even if having it all looks different from what I once imagined.

# Chapter 42
## Hannah

I FUCKING DID IT. ONE MONTH OF BACK-AND-FORTHS WITH MY EDITOR. Round after round of furiously working through edits. Zero sleep. But today I published my sixth book.

I lean back into the couch as I scroll through the social media posts early readers have created. I'll never get over how a person I've never met can so perfectly visualize characters I created. So many of the images tell my story perfectly. It's incredible. And seeing my words quoted? Reading posts from readers who fell in love with my words or the characters or the world I created? It's surreal. Each one makes my heart grow a little bigger.

The only thing that would make it better would be if I had the actual paperback in my hand. Unfortunately, author copies take weeks, so all I have is the e-book. It's trivial, I guess, and nothing could bring me down today.

Since we were in Vegas a month ago, we've settled into our relationship even further.

Ava and War welcomed their son Beckham the day after Thanksgiving, and I've spent every moment the guys are traveling over at her house, helping with laundry and dishes and dinner while also soaking in every lesson I can so when my baby boy is here, I can put it all to use. Ava is a natural. This is her first experience with a newborn, but she had a leg up, since she's been raising three children with War for the last year.

I never could have imagined being so comfortable holding a newborn, but the first time my best friend put her baby boy in my arms, a switch flipped in my brain. And when she asked me to be his godmother, I just about lost it.

Now I'm even more anxious for our son to arrive.

Noah and Oliver officially live across the hall, and Oliver is obsessed with his new room. While he was at his mom's, Noah and Daniel decorated it—hockey-themed, of course—as a surprise. The kid was doubly excited when he realized his little cousin's room across the hall would match his. Hockey wasn't quite what I had in mind when I told Daniel he could decorate the nursery—don't they ever get sick of it?—but the joy on Oliver's face is worth swimming in a sea of Bolts blue every time I step into the room.

I insisted on a gray rocker and gray furniture to keep the blue from being too overpowering.

"Why are you still laying on the couch?" Sara asks as she breaks into my apartment.

Okay, maybe that's a bit dramatic, since the door was unlocked, but she could have at least knocked.

"You're going to be late for your own baby shower."

I look pointedly at the clock on the wall—the clock with hands that don't move; it's merely decorative, but I want to make a point. "The baby shower that starts in six hours?"

When Daniel left for morning skate, I figured I had at least an hour to lie on the couch before he returned and cuddled me. Sex and cuddles—now, that sounds like the perfect way to celebrate a book release.

Being accosted by a friend at eight a.m. and bullied into getting ready for a baby shower? Not so much.

"Come on, I've got strict instructions to keep you on schedule. Daniel said to tell you *don't fight it.*" Her last few words come out frighteningly deep.

Head tilted, I study her. Her blue hair is up in a ponytail, and she isn't wearing a stitch of makeup. It's cold out, but the woman is bundled up like she's ready to head out into the wild for a week.

"Why are you here?"

The smile that splits her face is the manic one that means she's up to something. "Because Daniel knows I'm the only one crazy enough to drag his baby mama out of her cozy apartment for his surprise."

I roll my eyes. Old habits die hard, I guess. Acting unimpressed by the things this man does for me is my go-to response—a defense mechanism, if you will—but inside, I'm bubbling with elation that could make even my pregnant whalelike figure take flight. "Why would I leave this apartment? It's twenty degrees out."

"It's seven degrees, actually, but who's counting?" She wraps her arms around herself and shivers dramatically.

"Me. I'm counting. Why are we going outside? How about you take off that jacket and snuggle under this blanket with me? We can discuss how to make your man come without coming."

She narrows her eyes at me, but she toes off her boots and hangs her jacket on the hook by the door. "Why would I want him to come without me?"

I toss back the blanket and pat the spot beside me. "Not him without you. Both of you, together, without the mess."

She licks her lips, eyes flashing. "But what if I like it messy?"

"Oh, you'll get there, hunny. But if he comes without ejaculating, then you can just keep fucking."

"Oh my god, you are evil." She taps her phone screen. "You're trying to use my love for sex to keep me from dragging you out into the cold, aren't you?"

Head dropped back, I cackle. "Is it working?"

She plops down on the cushion and pulls her feet up. "Obviously. But you've got ten minutes. Then we're heading to the spa. Daniel told me to get here early. Our appointment isn't until nine."

My chest warms. The man knows me so well. And the spa? God, I love him.

THE TECHNICIAN GRINDS A KNUCKLE INTO THE BALL OF MY FOOT, PULLING a totally inappropriate groan from me. My feet are like sausages these days, and though Daniel is in the thick of hockey season, he massages them religiously on the nights he's home. Elvira's fingers aren't quite as big or warm, but she's working some magic right now.

"Yes, right there. You're doing so good."

Millie gags. "Every time you talk, all I can imagine is you talking my brother through another orgasm."

Sara giggles. "She told me all about how he does it without ejaculating. I'm determined to try this magic."

The horrified look on Millie's face is gold. "Why in god's name would anyone want to come without ejaculating?"

While the women working on our feet snicker, the two older women who are getting their hair set gawk in disgust.

I shrug. Eh. It's sex. Surely the old biddies were getting some back in the sixties. Everyone was having sex in the sixties.

"Do you like having multiple orgasms, Ava?" She chose a seat at the other end of the row of chairs—probably to get as far away from our loud mouths as she could—so I have to shout.

When she walked in, I literally squealed. I didn't think she'd come. She's barely left Beckham's side since giving birth four weeks ago. War was very excited to bring him to morning skate today, so he encouraged her to get out of the house.

From the sound of things, the guys all brought their kids—babies wrapped in carriers and little ones in skates and everything. Shit. I hope to god there are no pictures. If I see evidence, I'll lose my street cred and break down in crocodile tears. Just thinking about it has my nipples tingling and my tear ducts opening.

Ava's red hair curtains her face. The woman is seriously pretending she doesn't know us.

"Come on, my pretty, pretty princess," I tease. "Tell us all about the orgasms your husband gives you on the daily."

When the women under the hair dryers huff, I can't help but taunt them by rubbing my belly with my left hand, highlighting my bare ring finger. I definitely can't see my feet now, even propped up like this. Even so, my man loves my body, and I'm not the least bit ashamed of how much we like sex.

"I'm pretending I don't know you," Ava mumbles.

"Too bad I'm your best friend and favorite person ever—after Josie, of course."

Ava's lips twitch, and her green eyes light up. "Love that you put yourself above my three other children *and* my husband."

"Daddy War will not be happy," Sara cajoles.

"I bet Daddy War likes multiple orgasms, and I'll be his favorite too when I tell Ava how to give them to him." I settle back in my seat, content to know I'm right.

I like being right.

Daniel tells me I'm never not right.

If there's a single thing the guy *isn't* good at, it's keeping me humble, and I'm okay with that.

One of the hairdressers approaches the women across the room and turns off the dryers. The woman who continued to huff stands, straightens her clothing, and with a glare at us, stalks toward the bathroom.

The other one glances down the hall to where her friend disappeared, then shuffles our way.

"Oh, this should be good," I mumble.

She stops directly in front of me. "I couldn't help but overhear…"

"That's because this one"—Sara throws a thumb my way—"is loud."

With a nervous smile, the woman shuffles around the technician in front of me, moving closer. "Do you have any suggestions for men who are"—she clears her throat—"older?"

"How to help him get it up?" I ask, making sure there isn't an ounce of judgment in my tone.

She shakes her head. Her gray hair doesn't move an inch as she does. "Oh, he does just fine in that department. The, uh…" Another step closer. "The multiple orgasm thing."

Lennox stifles a giggle and Millie mutters a "Jesus Christ."

I have to tighten all my core muscles as well as my butt cheeks to keep from peeing myself. My son's favorite spot is tucked up right against my bladder.

"Ya know, I actually don't. But—" I hold up a finger and pull out my phone. "If you follow this woman's column, I'll make sure she gets an answer to that question as soon as possible."

Millie leans over, peering at my phone where I've pulled up the Instagram page for Calliope's Column. "Oh my god," she groans. "Not you too."

I frown, willing myself not to snap at my friend. "What?"

"Daniel's obsessed with that column. If he'd ever met Calliope, you'd have some serious competition."

A thrill works its way through me. "You don't say?"

Daniel never stops surprising me. Obsessed with my column, is he? Could I love the man more?

At two o'clock sharp, the girls and I are standing outside the door to Ground Zero. We've had our bodies massaged, our nails painted, our hair curled, and our faces done up. I laughed and smiled and genuinely enjoyed every moment of our girl time. Even so, I have to fight the urge to grimace at the door in front of us. "He chose the *bar* for the baby shower?"

When Millie smiles this brightly, she looks so much like her twin. "Just give Danny Boy the benefit of the doubt. He did good today."

With a dramatic eye roll—gotta keep up with the persona—I step forward and yank the door open. "Whatever you say."

The moment I step inside, the room erupts in an eardrum-shattering "surprise."

It's not the number of people who are here that genuinely leaves me speechless. I was expecting a celebration, after all.

What I wasn't prepared for—the reason I cup a hand over my

mouth like Daniel does to keep me quiet during sex—is the table in the center of the room. It's covered in stacks and stacks of books. *My* books. There's even a six-foot sign with an enlarged photo of the cover of my new release and my pen name scrawled across it. "What's happening?"

Millie nudges me forward. "Told you he did good."

Daniel appears in front of me, a big smile on his face, wearing one of his game day suits and holding out a flute filled with what I assume is a mocktail. "Congrats, dream girl. Welcome to your very first book signing."

I blink away the tears blurring my vision. I don't want to miss a single moment of this. This is the good. The point of no return. That moment in a love story when finally, *finally*, everything the couple has been through makes sense. Because all their tribulations led here.

*Here* to a book signing I thought was a baby shower.

*Here* to the man of my dreams making another one of my bucket list ideas come true. He never stops. And I don't think he ever will.

We're here. My happily ever after, an ending I never thought I wanted, and we haven't even had the baby yet. Because though our son may have been the catalyst, he may have brought us together, the foundation of our love story is built around us. Around Daniel and me. We're as much a part of it as that one crazy night.

Daniel is my happy, and I think it's fair to say I'm his.

I was sure I got it before. I was wrong. If I thought his feelings for me were any smaller than this huge display of his love, then I never really understood. I'm his dream girl. And he's a wish I never could have dreamed up.

I laugh, sinking into this delirious sensation. The air must be lighter on the other side of happily ever after, because I feel drunk on joy.

"This isn't a baby shower?"

There isn't a baby item in sight. This is all about me. God, that realization only makes me laugh harder.

Like the man understands precisely what I'm laughing about—and I can all but guarantee he does; he knows me better than I even know myself—he steps into me and cups my cheek. "Baby showers are overrated. We're celebrating your book baby today. We'll celebrate our little guy when he's born."

"But don't think for a second that you don't get gifts!" Lennox yells from somewhere behind me.

Daniel rubs his finger against my lip, his dimples on full display.

"What's she talking about?"

"They sent gifts to my dad's house. We can pick them up later and open them whenever you want."

Legs wobbly, I cling to him. "Have I told you lately that I love you?"

It's not that baby showers are exactly awful, it's just that they are absolutely awful. I've been dreading the minute I had to sit and open gifts and coo at every item, diapers and bottles and all. Baby clothes? Sure, I can get behind cooing at cute outfits. The rest? I'll happily let Daniel put each item in its proper spot. Let's be honest, he's the one with all the knowledge since he spends all his free time either giving me orgasms or watching the daddy vlogs.

"I love you too, Hannah. But since I get to see you all the time, I'm going to drag you over to your table so you can meet your fans."

I roll my eyes. These are my friends and their spouses, our families, and yes, maybe just about the entire baseball team and their wives. I wouldn't exactly call them fans.

When he drags me over to the table, though, I can't help but gawk at the stacks upon stacks of books. My books. My book baby, my new release, the novel I don't even have a copy of yet, is even here.

"How did you—Where did you—" Words fail me as I pick it up and turn it over, reveling in the weight of it, in the smoothness of the matte cover with the beautiful man on the front. The man Sara and I giggled over just a few months ago. He's hot, but so were like ten other guys we were looking at.

"These are your preorders," he says, hands in his pockets like it's no big deal that there are literally one hundred books stacked high on a table. Books *I* wrote yet haven't seen before today.

"Would you sign these too?" Wren Wilson appears on the other side of the table with a stack of books.

Her husband, Tom, is the head coach of the Revs. While he's in his forties, I think Wren is a few years younger than I am. She and Coach Wilson's daughter have been best friends for years and years. When she started dating Avery's dad, it was the scandal of all scandals.

Obviously I loved every delicious minute when details of their clandestine affair came out. Now, like Lake and Ford and Gavin and Millie, they fit right in. They're no different from any other married couple. Though Wren is a little wild like me, so I can only imagine how dirty those two are behind closed doors.

Daniel pulls out a chair so oversized it might as well be a throne. Once I'm settled, he hands me a rose-gold sharpie, and with a wink, he tells me to enjoy myself and backs away.

"Tell me the truth," I whisper hiss as Wren leans in close. "Did Daniel force everyone to show up and pretend they want my books?"

"Are you kidding me?" She pulls back, brows pinched. "When he mentioned your new book was coming out, Avery and Jana and I down-loaded the first in the series. I think Gianna did too, but she'd never admit to being a softie for romance." She lets out a throaty laugh. "I finished it in a day, then made it through all six of them in a week. I am dying for this one. And now I have signed copies of them all? My followers are going to freak when they find out I know you. I posted about coming here on my socials, and the number of people who commented about being jealous was wild." She gives me a pointed look. "Girl, this book is blowing up!"

I shake my head, hands trembling. When she pushes her stack of books toward me, I have to shake them out.

I don't know how he did this—I don't even know what is happening right now—but I'm going to enjoy every crazy minute of it.

I sign all one hundred books—yes, every damn one—and after at least a hundred pictures, the last one being one of Daniel and me and my book—a photo he tells me is totally going in the photo album—I'm finally seated by the bar, my feet resting on a chair in front of me, with a jug of water by my side. I'll probably have to get up and pee ten more times before we leave, but I can't seem to get enough water today.

"Oh, I forgot to tell you." Sara leans against the bar next to me. "Lennox told me she knows the cover model."

My jaw drops. "No fucking way."

Lennox shakes her head, but she's laughing. "I told you not to tell her."

"Tell her what?" Ava asks as she shuffles over. I slip my feet off the chair so she can sit, then settle them in her lap once she's settled.

Millie lifts her chin, eyeing us from across the room. With a kiss to Gavin's cheek, she waltzes in our direction. "What did I miss?"

Sara holds up her copy of my book. "Lennox slept with this guy."

Ava's eyes go wide, Millie squeals, and I practically drop my water. "You *what*?"

Lennox glares at Sara, the pink-on-pink outfit taking away from the serious look she's wearing. "Do you have a death wish? If Aiden hears you, he'll burn this place down with all the pretty books in it."

Sara pulls the book to her chest, lip stuck out. "But he's so pretty." She turns him around, petting the man's eight-pack.

"Unfortunately the drapes don't match the carpet," Lennox mutters.

"The what?" Ava shouts.

Every one of us freezes and looks at her. The only time I've ever heard her voice reach that volume was the night she found the ridiculous contract for her marriage in War's office.

"The outside doesn't match the inside," Lennox says, enunciating each word.

"Huh?" Millie's face scrunches in confusion. "Can you speak English rather than Lennox-and-Aiden talk."

My pink-haired friend grins. "His dick isn't nearly as big as Hannah described it in the book." She flicks the cover of Sara's copy. "And he had no idea what to do with it. There were no three orgasms on the beach or on any woman's desk, I assure you."

I chuckle. "What can I say? The book is always better."

As the girls laugh and chatter on, I look around at my real life. I can't say I've ever read a book that's as good as the story I'm living. With a hand splayed over my belly, I silently tell my son how lucky he is to have such a good daddy.

"He's pretty amazing." Sara nods at Daniel.

He's standing across the room with his father and Gavin, holding Nash, completely comfortable with a baby in his arms.

Chest expanding, I sigh. "He is."

"Have you discussed what comes next?" Lennox asks.

It takes effort to tear my attention away from him so I can look at her. "Next?"

"Yeah, like marriage?" Ava breaks into a slow grin.

"Just because you propose to every hot man with a baby in his arms," I tease, "doesn't mean I need that."

Millie's golden eyes swim with earnestness. "Have you talked about it?"

Only if writing about it in my column counts. He hasn't mentioned anything about marriage since that night in Vegas. That conversation was so emotionally charged, I can't hold him to the comment.

It's too soon anyway. It's not like there's any rush—

"Oh," Sara says, drawing out the single syllable. "You have talked about it."

"Huh?"

"You zoned out. Because you're thinking about it. Am I right?"

I shrug. "We barely know one another."

Millie slaps the bar, startling me. "That line is getting old. We all see it. You know my brother better than anyone, and I could say the same about him."

I glance back in Daniel's direction and find him staring at me, his lips tipped up softly. When he realizes he's been caught, his dimples deepen, and he winks. "Having fun, dream girl?" he mouths.

I shake my head, though there's no hiding the way my face splits into a grin. Because yeah, I'm having fun. Every single moment I spend with this man is fun. And I really hope I get many, many more moments with him. Hopefully the rest of my life.

# CHAPTER 43
# DANIEL

There are few things I enjoy more in life than hockey. I can say without a doubt that a year ago, hockey was my number one priority, the thing that mattered most, and very few things came close to competing. It was my entire existence. Hockey was my identity and the one thing that brought me true joy. I spent all my time on the ice or hanging out with my friends who were also hockey players. The reason women wanted to date me? It was hockey.

Not a moment of tonight had anything to do with hockey. Not even a flicker of the spotlight flashed my way. It was all about my girl, and yet it was easily one of the best nights of my life. Hockey doesn't hold a candle to her. If I had to choose between my career and hers, it'd be a no-brainer. I'd gladly stay home with our son and support her in every way I could.

I'm not sure when it happened, or even how the hell it happened, but it's the god's honest truth. Fortunately for me, Hannah doesn't want me to choose. She seems genuinely excited to stay home and enjoy our son while following her passion, and I get to play hockey and spend time with my family when I'm in Boston and maybe even bring them along when I travel sometimes.

When we got home, I started a bath so Hannah could relax. I'm doing the same, waiting for her in bed, looking through all the photos our friends tagged her in on Instagram.

She is gorgeous in every picture. Her tight black cotton dress hugged her perfectly, and her red-painted lips were always tipped up in a smile.

When a FaceTime request from Camden pops up on my screen, I smile and tap Accept.

"Hey! We missed you tonight—"

When his expression registers, I snap my mouth shut. His eyes are red and glassy, his face pinched in pain.

"What the hell happened?"

"I saw Tara." The words come out gruff and slurred. He rarely speaks her name, like it hurts to form the word. Tara was his high school girlfriend. His sister's best friend.

"Shit."

"Bound to happen," he slurs, head lolling to one side.

"Where are you?"

Is he in public? If so, I need to make some calls and get him home. Or is he home? If that's the case, should I find someone to stop in and check on him? I've got contact info for a few of his teammates, so I could probably figure something out.

"She has a daughter. Did I tell you that?" He leans against a wall, eyes drooping.

My chest pinches. Fuck, his heart's gotta hurt right now. "Yeah, Cam, you told me. Where are you?"

"Thought it was my kid for a minute. Could have been." He breathes heavily.

He's known for a long time that Tara's daughter isn't his. Turns out she belongs to his former best friend. When Cam caught Tara and that asshole together, they admitted to having been cheating for a long time.

To make matters worse, his best friend was dating Cam's sister at the time. The four of them had been inseparable for years. He was devastated, but he kept his knowledge of the affair to himself. Eventually, Cam's sister found out. She packed up and left Vegas and never came back. When she discovered that he knew and hadn't told her, she cut off all contact.

That's why Camden never went back home during the offseason. And why I was shocked when he chose to return to the area that haunted him. But unlike me, he's got nothing but hockey. I guess the belief that he could be something more there outweighed the concern he had for the demons he'd have to face. Until now, that is.

"She's not yours, Cam. You had the DNA test. Where are you right now?"

"You should have a DNA test done."

My heart fucking stops when his garbled words register. "'Scuse me?"

"Make sure the baby is yours," he says, clearly not picking up on my anger. "Don't want to be like me and get your hopes up, only to find out you're wrong. I mean, are you sure she didn't hook up with fucking Jasper Quinn?" He stares at the screen, his bloodshot eyes unfocused.

Blood boiling, I focus on keeping my breathing steady. He's fucking lucky we aren't talking face to face.

"Ya said she's always running when he calls—"

"I'm going to say this once," I grit out. "You're goddamn lucky I don't tell you to go fuck yourself, then block your number. If you weren't hurting so bad right now, you better believe I wouldn't hesitate. But if you ever say a damn word about the mother of my child—" I suck in a breath, tempering my anger, and blow it out again in one long gust. "She's the love of my life. Say something negative about her again, and you and I are done."

Camden's silent, his eyes momentarily clear, his breathing heavy. "I'm sorry. I was out of line."

"Yeah, you were." The words tear at my throat like glass. "Get your life together. You have a real shot to make something of yourself out there. If you can't handle being in Vegas, then come back home. We'd all understand if this is too much."

He angles away from the screen, his face crumpled. "Vegas was my home."

"Yeah, but we both know Boston is now. Come back, dude. Smiles's attitude sucks. You and me, we could be gods together *here*."

He blinks, his attention floating to something beyond his phone. Or maybe the ghosts are keeping him company. "I gotta go. But I'll think about what you said."

He hangs up before I can respond.

I toss the phone down, still vibrating with anger over his comments.

"Hey." Hannah's voice startles me. Heart still pumping, I look up and find her standing in the doorway of the bathroom, her belly peeking out from beneath the belt of her gray silk robe.

"Hey, c'mere." I hold out an arm. "How much did you hear of that?"

She settles on my lap, as close as she can get, lips twisting. "Pretty much the whole thing."

Fuck.

Stomach clenching, I stroke her damp hair. "He didn't mean it."

She gives me a soft smile. "He did. And he's not wrong. You should have questioned whether the baby is yours. Can you imagine the money I could have taken you for?" She's teasing me, I know this, but I don't like the way she's talking.

"Hannah."

"You're a big, famous hockey player, and I'm just—"

I tug on the ends of her hair. "A big, famous author."

She snorts. "Not quite."

"Did you see yourself today? Did you see the line of people who showed up to see you? That all want to read your books? Don't get me started on all the social media hype."

Her lashes flutter in acknowledgment. She's got nothing to say. I know she's proud of herself, and I'm bursting with pride for her.

"Also," I say, angling her face so she's completely focused on me, "it wouldn't have mattered if he wasn't mine."

"*Daniel.*" Her voice is chiding.

God dammit. She should know by now that tone only makes me hard.

"I'm serious. You could have told me you weren't sure or that you were sure and he wasn't mine, and I still would have said I'm in this if you'll have me. I've wanted you for so goddamn long, Hannah. My feelings for you have nothing to do with the baby. He just came along and made all my dreams come true a little earlier than expected."

Tears coat her lashes. "You say that now, but what if—"

I shut her up with a kiss. "I look forward to all your what-ifs, dream girl. Just gives me more opportunities to prove you wrong."

Her unshed tears make her blue eyes brighter than usual. "You do love a challenge."

I cup her cheek and bring my face close to hers. The air between is charged. Wrought with emotion. "No, I love *you*. The challenges are fun. These adventures and the bucket list, it's all been fun. But *you*—" I stroke the smooth skin of her cheek with my thumb. "You're the reason I keep fighting. If it wasn't with you, I wouldn't enjoy it. So like I said, with or without this baby, I would have loved you. I just would have had a harder time getting you to give me a chance."

"I always liked you." She presses her lips together, gathering her thoughts.

I slide a thumb across the straight line of them, urging her to keep talking to me. When she sighs in defeat, or maybe relief, her warm breath tickles my face. "I didn't think you'd be like this. I had no idea what I was missing."

"You are getting smarter," I tease. "People change. Priorities change. *Bucket lists change.*"

Like her new additions. The secret ones.

*Marriage and a house. A book signing.*

One brow arched, she eyes me. "How long have you known?"

"Known what?"

"That I'm Calliope."

I grin. "Since the bad sex column."

Hands covering her face, she flops back on the mattress and laughs. "Oh my god. I'm so sorry."

I lie down beside her and grasp her wrists. "It's okay, baby. It was like a little peek into what you were thinking for all those months when I had no idea how to get you to open up to me."

"That's kind of cheating," she says, her light tone belying the criticism.

"I'm not above cheating if it means you're the prize. Besides, someone has to keep you wild."

She takes a swing at me.

Dodging the attempt, I catch her wrist and kiss the back of her hand. "Not cheating on you. Cheating for you. Like I promised you before, you keep me safe, and I'll keep you wild."

"What if I need you to keep me safe too?" she says in that tone that reminds me of just how vulnerable my girl can be. It's the tone that speaks of all the people who have let her down in the past.

I won't be one of them.

"You're safe with me, Hannah. Your heart, your body, and your future."

She smiles. "Are you going to ask me to marry you one day?"

I nod.

Her eyes dance back and forth between them.

"But not right now," I tell her. "Today we crossed off one more bucket list item. Book signing. We'll get to marriage and a house. *I promise.*"

She rolls into me and hides her face in my chest, groaning in what sounds in mortification.

Yeah, my girl really just asked me to ask her to marry me. While she may be embarrassed, I'm fucking elated.

I'll do it soon. But today is about her books, and I'm not taking a damn thing away from that.

# CALLIOPE'S COLUMN



## The Art of Learning to Use a Pen...No, It's Not a New Toy

I have a secret. I've discovered something even better than sexting.

Handwritten letters.

My god, there is nothing hotter than seeing my boyfriend's handwriting scrawled across a piece of paper. Especially when the words detail everything he loves about me. What he's going to do when he sees me again. How he dreams about me when he's gone.

There's no filter. No backspace button. His handwritten notes give me direct insight into what my man is thinking, but even more than that, it's a tangible piece of him I can hold when he's away. Knowing that he sat down and took the time to handwrite his thoughts makes me feel closer to him. I've started writing back, and if I have my way, we'll do this for the rest of time. It's the one benefit of being with a man who travels so much.

Do yourself a favor. Take out a pen and paper and try it out with me...

# Handwritten Letters from Daniel to Hannah

Dream girl,

WILL you do me a favor? Tonight when you crawl into bed and lay your head on your pillow, will you think about what you really want from this life? Not just in your career. Not just with our child. All of it. Make a real bucket list. Fill it with what you really dream of. The place you want to live. How you want to spend your days. And everything in between. I want to know every one of your dreams. It's only fair, since you are every one of mine. I love you and can't wait to be home with you.

Sweet dreams.
Yours,
Daniel

Dream girl,

YOU have the most beautiful smile. I hope our son inherits it. And I hope he has your eyes. And your laugh. I really hope he has my athletic ability, because let's be honest, the only time you participated in a sport was around the bases with me, and we'll never be telling him about that. I've been thinking about names. I know you like the idea of naming him after me, but I want him to be his own person. He'll face challenges growing up with a famous author and a hockey god for parents. I really hope he inherits his humility from both of us, because damn, we have none of it.
I love you, baby. Miss you and can't wait to hold you in my arms again.
Always yours,
Daniel

Dream girl,

MARRY me chicken. It's what's on the menu this week. Millie promised she'd make it for you on the same night we'll have it in Chicago. Also, I snuck an Oreo cream pie into her freezer before I left. Make sure she takes it out for dessert and doesn't hide it for herself. She had one bite of your birthday pie—the one I didn't massacre—and I think she's more hooked than you. Only a few more weeks until we meet our son. I can't wait until I'm with the both of you. I love you.

Forever yours,
Daniel.

# CHAPTER 44
## DANIEL



"Can you taste it?" War yells.

The already wild energy in the locker room ramps up.

"Can you *feel* it?" He pounds his palm against his chest.

He's half dressed. Most of us are, as we gear up for tonight's game.

Our response is a resounding "Yeah Cap!"

"It's January, boys. We're halfway there. And we're number fucking four. Do we want to be number fucking four?" Red-faced, he stalks through the center of the room, careful to avoid the Bolts symbol in the middle. Hockey players are superstitious; the emblem is protected at all costs.

"Fuck no!" one of the rookies shouts.

The rest of us clap and cheer.

War steps in front of the rookie, skates on, his jersey still on the bench. "You're damn right we don't. So what are we going to do today?"

"We're going to win!" the kid replies.

War spins and stomps back toward his locker. "Fuck yeah, we are. Forty-one games down, boys. Forty-one to go. But we aren't only playing forty-one, are we?"

I grin at Smiles, the fucking grumpy winger beside me. Not only did he take Camden's spot on the ice, but he was assigned to his old locker. Though it hurt like a bitch, it's to be expected. In hockey, players come and go. It's what happens while they're here that matters. Guys like War, Aiden, Brooks, and Cam, they'll remain my friends for life. Even if Hannah and I weren't together, I'd like to think Noah and I would have gotten to where we are now. He's good people and one hell of a hockey player. That alone would have garnered my respect.

Then there are guys like Smiles. I wouldn't mind if I never saw him again, but since he's my teammate—and especially because we're on the same line—I'm trying.

"No, we're going to the Cup!" Keegan yells.

"Fuck yeah we are," War replies. "Okay, Lep, you're up."

Aiden is already buzzing with so much energy his entire body is shaking. Dressed in his pants and pads, he jumps up onto the bench and starts his rendition of Ludacris's "What's Your Fantasy?"

> *"We want to win, win, win, win, win, from now to June,*
> *And we want to move from number four to-to number one*
> *And we want to ah-ah, it feels so good we'll want to repeat*
> *Because us Bolts are living out all our fantasies."*

THE GUYS IN THE LOCKER ROOM ARE DROPPING IT DOWN AND CLAPPING and humming. The momentum is fire. No one gets a team amped up like Aiden.

The winger next to me? He's literally glaring.

"Come on, Smiles. Not even you can put me in a bad mood today."

He grunts. "How disappointing."

With a wave, I turn back to the guys. The kid isn't long for this place. It's too bad too. He's good on the ice, but with an attitude like that, he'll be gone by next year. That type of spirit will break down the camaraderie our team is known for. No player—no matter how talented—is worth sacrificing the good of the team.

That's what I learned this year. The team comes first. Not one of us is irreplaceable when it comes to Boston.

Which is why hockey is no longer my primary focus.

That role is reserved solely for Hannah. Speaking of which…

I pull my phone from my locker, and when I don't have any new texts, I type out a quick message.

> Me: Hey, dream girl. You get to the arena okay?

Dots dance on the screen, then a picture appears. It's Hannah from the back, head turned so I can see her profile, my last name across her shoulders. The rink is in the background, and my sister is next to her, smiling big. Fuck, I love my life.

> Me: Fucking prettiest girl in the entire world. Can't wait to strip every other article of clothing off you and fuck you with only my jersey on.

> Dream Girl: For every goal you score, you'll earn one orgasm.

Beside me, Noah groans. "The fuck kind of kinky shit are you and Hannah doing now?"

"Why you reading my texts, Beauty?"

"I saw the picture of Hannah and Millie. Figured it was safe. Who the fuck sexts while they're standing next to their boyfriend's twin?"

I give him an *are you fucking kidding me?* smirk. "Your *'like a sister.'*" I use air quotes to emphasize the stupid term they always use.

He grimaces. "You guys are meant for each other."

"You know it." I shoot him a grin. "Besides, how can I be expected not to get hard when I see my last name on her back? You can't tell me you've never imagined a special girl wearing your jersey."

Jaw flexing, his eyes dart to one side. Interesting. Nothing riles the guy up. Nothing. What the hell has him so sensitive today?

"When are you going to make her last name your last name?" he says.

I grab my own jersey and pull it over my head. I'll let him get away with the subject change, but I'm not done with that conversation. "I have a plan. But you can't rush perfection."

Noah clasps my shoulder, pulling me in close. "Hope she says yes. Then you'd be *like a brother* to me too." He whispers the *like a brother* part seductively.

I scrunch my shoulders, my whole body shuddering.

"I'm already hard from your sister. Don't make it weird."

He pushes me into the locker and spins away.

Like I said, I love my life.

I SCORE MY FIRST GOAL LESS THAN FIVE MINUTES INTO THE GAME. THE moment the biscuit hits the back of the net, I spin on the ice and find Hannah in the stands. She's screaming her freaking head off as I skate toward her and bang on the glass. I blow her a kiss, then skate backward toward our bench. I used to moonwalk across the ice after I scored. This is so much better.

I sink the puck again during the second period. We're up 4-0. We're on fucking fire. This time, I moonwalk to the glass and spin toward my girl. Only her seat is empty. Millie's too. My smile falls, along with my shoulders.

Keegan grabs my jersey and yells at me to be heard over the crowd. "We're going for a motherfucking hat trick, Playboy. Tonight's *your* night."

Normally, I'd push him away and tell him not to jinx it. Players don't mention the fucking hat trick until the game is over. Amateur. But I'm too focused on finding Hannah to bother. Instead, I shrug him off and skate for the boards.

Gavin points at center ice where the play is ready to begin again.

I shake my head. "Can't find Hannah."

He throws a hand up, then jabs a finger toward the ice again, with a whole lot more force this time. "We're in the middle of a fucking game, Hall. Get on the ice."

I'm already climbing over the boards. "Put someone else in. I've got a bad feeling." I drop my gear, then toss my gloves, searching the bench for Sara. She'll figure out what's going on.

When I spot her, she's got her head bowed over her phone, and she's typing furiously. When she finally looks up, it's written all over her face. Something is wrong.

# Chapter 45
# Hannah



"WHO ARE YOU TEXTING?" WITH A GRIMACE, I CLUTCH MY BELLY AND settle on the bed. Goddamn, this hurts just as much as I'd expect it to.

Rather than answer, Millie continues tapping away at her phone's screen.

"Hello, lady in labor, here. You can't ignore me."

When she finally snaps her head up, she at least has the decency to give me a sheepish smile. "Sorry." She slips her phone into her back pocket and shuffles closer. "How are you feeling? What do you need?"

Even as my stomach tightens with the start of another contraction, I have the wherewithal to sense that Millie is hiding something. "*Who were you texting?*"

She looks away, like she really thinks I'll let this go.

I hit the bed with my palm. "Dammit, Millie. Just tell me."

"Sara."

My lungs seize up. Or maybe it's a contraction. I don't know. "I told you not to say anything yet. Daniel needs to remain focused. We've got hours. You heard the doctor."

The cramps started this morning. Maybe I should have mentioned it, but I was certain they were Braxton Hicks contractions. There was no way I'd show up at the hospital just to be told I'm having gas pains, so I figured I'd wait it out. And I didn't mention it to Daniel because I didn't want him to be preoccupied on the ice.

But minutes after the game started, the cramps got intense, and after Daniel scored, the pain only compounded. Maybe it was the jumping up and down—not that the movement was all that abrupt; let's be honest, I'm nine months pregnant; if I'd done more than bend my knees and bounce, I would have wet myself—or maybe it was the sharp contraction that hit just as I was sitting, but I was hit with an irrational fear that if I didn't book it out of there, I'd be giving birth in Bolts Arena. And while I'm sure Beckett would swear that giving birth on any property owned by the Langfields was good luck, I wasn't going to risk it.

"He scored again."

"Great," I grit out. "Now he can go for the hat trick and then come have a baby with me."

Millie stares at me like I'm a toddler throwing a tantrum. Or maybe just a pregnant woman whom she thinks is being unreasonable. She's about to patronize me with kind words, hoping to reason with me. I can see it in her eyes. "My brother would never forgive me if I didn't tell him what was going on."

"*Millie.*" I drag each syllable out as another contraction rolls through me.

Even though I want to yell at her, I take the hand she offers me and squeeze.

"Breathe," she says, her tone gentle, as if she's speaking to Vivi.

Is there a single word in the English language more annoying than that for a woman in labor?

I'm trying to take a breath, but there's an anvil working its way through my body. How am I supposed to suffer through the sensation *and* remember to breathe? When the pain from the contraction recedes, I fall back against the pillow and glare at the ceiling.

Millie hovers over me, her curly dark hair backlit by the dim lighting above her, and in that same voice she uses with her two-year-old, she says, "You've made Daniel the happiest I've ever seen him. You are going to be an incredible mother, and I'm so happy you'll be my nephew's mom. But I don't keep secrets from my brother."

I scowl at her, though my anger has evaporated. "Except when you were banging his coach."

She laughs. "Touché."

Ridiculously, I can't help but smile. "Let's get some rest before hurricane Daniel arrives."

She laughs along with me, no doubt knowing exactly what I'm talking about. That man is sure to be in a tizzy until he sets his sights on me, and then he'll be overbearing until he knows I'm all right.

As I rub my belly, tears prick my eyes. After today, I won't feel this little guy kicking at my insides anymore. By this time tomorrow, I'll have a baby in my arms instead. I'm going to be a mom.

# CHAPTER 46
## DANIEL

I SNAG MY SHOULDER ON THE AUTOMATIC DOOR AS I RUSH INTO THE LOBBY. Out of breath and out of my mind, I come to a sliding stop in front of a glass window. The pair of nurses who are chatting behind the desk pause and eye me. The older of the two holds up a finger and turns back to the younger nurse.

I'm sucking in a breath, preparing to launch into a tirade about how there's no way in hell I'm going to wait while they catch up over coffee, but before I get a single word out, the other one's mouth drops open. "Aren't you Lake Paige's son?"

Normally, I'd make some sort of face over this. Lake is only five years older than me. I am *not* her son. But if this woman wants to call me Lake Paige's son or Baby Hall or any other thing, I'll go with it. As long as it means it will get me back to Hannah faster. So I give her my best smile and nod. "That'd be me."

"Oh my god," the other one says.

"Listen, I'll get you whatever signed memorabilia you want. Hell, I'll even have Lake come say hi to you tomorrow, but what I need right now is Hannah Prescott's room number."

The woman on the left squints, suddenly suspicious. "Did you just come from a fight? Do you need to be seen by a doctor?"

Only now do I even consider what I'm wearing. During my grand exit from the game, I threw my jersey at Gavin. Then I walked straight out of the arena in my skates and pads. Thank god Sara chased me down with my wallet and my keys. She must have darted into the locker room after she filled me in on Hannah. I'm a sweaty mess, and the only reason I'm not barefoot right now is because I had an extra pair of shoes in my truck.

"Hockey game. I'm fine. The room number?" I inhale deeply, holding tight to the last thread of patience I possess.

"Are you family?" the other woman asks as she taps at her keyboard.

"Yeah, I'm her husband," I lie. I should have done it before. I should be her husband. What the fuck was I thinking waiting for some perfect plan to come to fruition?

I was thinking a perfect proposal is what Hannah deserves, that's what. She deserves to know that I want to marry her because I love her, not because she's pregnant with my child.

Soon she'll be the mother of my child. No longer pregnant. My heart rate skyrockets at the thought. Shit. I need to be with her. Now. Is she in pain? Is she giving birth already?

"I'll walk you back," the one who called me Lake's son says. I'll definitely bring her an autograph tomorrow.

She tries making small talk as we wander down the long, sterile hall, but I can't hear anything over the buzzing in my ears. The adrenaline left over from the game has nothing on the second round that shot through me when I realized that I'm about to become a father.

As we reach the door, I wave at her, mumbling a thank-you. For a second, I press my forehead to the solid wood and focus on breathing. When my heart has slowed a fraction, I peek in.

Millie is sitting on the hospital bed, her focus on the television, but she's alone. "Where's Hannah?"

She hops to her feet, her face lit up. "Wow, hi to you too." As she gets closer, her smile turns into more of a grimace. "Didn't you stop to change?"

I shake my head. "Hannah?" I grit out.

A door near the corner swings open, and Hannah, dressed in a hospital gown and gripping her stomach, waddles out.

Don't ever tell her that I described her that way. She'd rip my balls off.

"Fuck, Mills. Giving birth feels a lot like needing to take a shit, only nothing comes out—"

Her words cut off sharply and her eyes go ridiculously wide when she sees me. "Oh my god." She slaps a hand to her face. "Please tell me you didn't just hear that."

I stride up to her and pull her in for a hug. The movement is stopped, though, when she pushes against my chest. "What is that smell?" Cringing, she looks me up and down. "Did you come right from the ice?"

Behind me, Millie laughs. "Yeah, SportsCenter keeps playing the minute he hopped over the boards and tossed his gear."

She points to the television screen, and sure enough, there's footage of me tossing my jersey at Gavin.

Huffing, I look back to Hannah. "Of course I did. You were supposed to tell me when you felt anything."

"You were a little busy," Hannah sasses.

"There is nothing," I say, stepping close, "*nothing* more important than you."

She pushes me back again, nose scrunching. "A shower is more important." Face buried in the crook of her elbow, she turns away. "Seriously, go home and shower, then come back."

"I'm not leaving."

"Oh my god," my sister shouts. "The two of you are so annoying. Daniel, you can shower in there." She points to the bathroom. "You can't expect *anyone* to deal with your stinky ass, let alone your pregnant girlfriend who is literally about to give birth." She eyes Hannah. "You. Your boyfriend just wants to be there for you. Stop being a bitch."

Fucking seriously? I know she's my twin, but if she is going to call my woman a—

Hannah lets out a throaty laugh, the sound instantly soothing my fraying nerves. "I love you, Mills. Sorry. I'll be better. I promise." She turns to me, hands on her hips. "Go. Your sister's got me until you're clean. And since she's your twin and you've got that whole ESP thing going on, it's practically the same as if you were here yourself." She nods once like a single word she's just spoken makes any sense.

But because the two of them are terrifying, I take a step back and leave them in peace while I take the world's quickest shower.

I'm just slipping into a pair of scrubs Millie tossed into the bathroom while I was rinsing off when Hannah screams.

I throw the door open and scurry to her side, heart hammering. "What can I do? Fuck."

"Get her ice chips. She's nauseous," Millie says from the other side of the bed. She pats Hannah's hand. "You're okay. You've got this, mama."

I rush into the hall, arms flung out to steady myself as I whip my head one way, then the other, searching for an ice machine. "Ice! Where's the ice?"

A nurse peeks out from another room. "Room number?"

"Um—" Fuck. "I don't know. I need ice. Please get me the ice."

With a roll of her eyes, she nods. "Just go back to your room. I'll bring it in."

I shake my head. No way. I can't walk back in there without ice. "Just tell me where to go. I can do this. Ice is my specialty." It really is.

She sighs and waves me over. "Follow me."

On wobbly legs, I step into a legit kitchen behind her. As soon as I have ice in hand, I turn and take off.

"Don't run!" she yells.

I basically skate back to the room, and as I step inside, Hannah screams again.

From there, time creeps by while also moving far too quickly. Every time Hannah is hit with a contraction, I want to die. The way her face contorts as she tries to breathe breaks me. Every second that she's in pain is an eternity. But the time between contractions seems to get longer, and as the hours drag on, I worry she'll never make it through this.

"We need a doctor," I say, pacing the room, hands on my head.

Hannah's relaxed, focused on an episode of *Love It or List It* with Millie.

"I'm fine," she mumbles around an ice chip.

"Want me to go look for one?" Millie offers, shifting off the bed.

Hannah clutches her arm. "I want the calm twin. You can go." She barely looks in my direction as she holds my sister hostage.

Shrugging, Millie settles beside her again. While part of me wants to be the one snuggled up with Hannah, I can't just sit here. I'm a doer. I need to *do* something.

Hands fisted at my sides, I stride out of the room. I have no plan in mind other than to walk the halls. To release some of this pent-up tension.

During my third lap around the floor, a familiar laugh echoes down the hall. I follow the sound until I find the waiting room. It's crowded with hockey players. Aiden is in the center—of course—making everyone laugh, and Gavin's sitting in the corner, chatting quietly with Noah.

War is the first to notice me. "Daddy Hall!"

The room goes silent, and every head turns my way. They're all in their game day suits, lounging around the waiting area on the birthing center floor. To say I get choked up at the sight is an understatement. When War stands, I get a peek at the shirt under his jacket. It's not a typical Oxford.

No, it's a tee.

"*Best Uncle*?" I croak, my chest going painfully tight.

Breathing through the ache, I take them all in. Fuck. Every single one of them is wearing a matching shirt.

Gavin stands. "Well, is he here?"

I shake my head and throw a thumb over my shoulder. "Nah, she kicked me out."

The low rumble of chuckles is palpable.

"Were you having sympathy pains again?" War throws his arms out and wraps me in a hug.

"No, it's just so hard to watch her in pain. How did you do it?"

He probably didn't even break a sweat holding Ava's hand.

He releases me, but he keeps his head next to mine and whispers, "I cried the entire time."

My eyes snap to his. "You did?"

He nods. "If you tell anyone, I'll kill you."

I yank him in for another hug. "Thank you."

He claps me on the back. "You've got this. Now go. Hold Hannah's hand and soak in every second." Head bowed, he swipes at his nose with a knuckle. "Greatest fucking moment of my life." He shakes his head. "Fuck, I can't even say that. But it's definitely tied with the moment Josie was officially ours. And the day I brought Scar home. When Bray called me dad for the first time. And when Ava said *I do*."

"Fuck, we're just a bunch of softies aren't we?" I say on a laugh.

War nods. "Abso-fucking-lutely. But if there's anyone worth being softies for, it's our girls. Our fierce women who put us to shame. Go watch her put you to shame. It's breathtaking."

I turn, my determination renewed, but Noah stops me with a hand on my shoulder. "How's she doing?"

"She's giving me shit and taking no prisoners."

He smiles. "Awesome. Tell her we can't wait to meet the little guy. You guys pick a name?"

Nope. We thought we had more time. But ready or not, he's coming. And I'm not going to miss it. On my way out, Sara hugs me tight. Her shirt says *Best Auntie*. With a huge grin, she tells me the guys all wore the shirts during the press conference tonight.

With a final goodbye, I jog down the hall, headed back to my girl. We're going to have a baby.

It's another few hours before the action really starts. When a howl comes from Hannah's mouth, Millie meets my eye, and just like Hannah suspected, our twin intuition takes over, and I'm suddenly in Mills's spot, holding my girl's hand as she screams through another contraction. The doctor is summoned then, and nurses rush in.

"It hurts," she cries.

I lean my body across hers, holding her to me, wishing I could somehow take the pain away. "You're doing so amazing, Han. Just a bit longer."

Tears stream down her face as the on-call doctor examines her. "All right. He's crowning," he says. "I'm going to need you to start pushing."

Hannah's blue eyes widen in terror, but in that moment, all I feel is calm. It's like in the middle of a game, when the crowd is screaming, but I hear and see nothing but the end goal. We're almost there.

"It's okay, baby. Squeeze my hand and push."

She grinds her teeth, and I'm pretty sure she tries to break my hand, but she grunts through a push.

"Good job," the doctor cajoles. "Just two more, and he'll be out."

"Fuck that," Hannah mumbles. She squeezes my hand so tight it goes numb, and this time she roars through another push. And holy shit. There's a whir of action in the room as they announce that he's out. Because, of course, Hannah had to go and prove another man wrong.

At 2:08 a.m. on January eighth, I became a father. I have to wipe the tears from my eyes to get a good look at my son as the doctor places him on Hannah's chest. After we're given only seconds to meet him, the nurses whisk him away to clean him up, and Hannah squeezes my hand, her eyes tired and her cheeks streaked with tears.

"You did so good," I murmur, brushing her hair from her face. I've never been more in love. More in awe. Just more. "I love you, dream girl." I press my lips to hers. "I love you so goddamn much."

She grips my shirt and holds me against her as we both cry, waiting for our son. The moment he's returned to us, bundled up in a white blanket with blue and pink stripes, my heart expands. I was wrong when I said I'd never been more in love. Already, with my son in Hannah's arms, it's compounded. These two…they're my entire world.

"We need a name." Though her eyes are still filled with tears, she smiles up at me.

"I was thinking…"

Hannah kisses our sweet boy's cheek. "Oh yeah?"

"I want to name him after you."

She breathes out a laugh. "Your daddy has lost his ever-loving mind," she says to the tiny bundle in her arms. "I think he needs some sleep. We can't name our son, Hannah, baby."

I brush my fingers against his cheek. He's so soft. He's got a full head of dark hair, just like Millie and me, and with any luck, his big blue eyes will remain that color, just like his mama's. "Maverick."

"Maverick?"

"Means independent. Unconventional. Mavericks don't do what's expected of them." I meet her gaze. "And they're maybe a little bit wild."

She peers down at our boy again. "Maverick. What do you think, baby? You like that?"

Obviously he does absolutely nothing in response. Even so, we grin at one another like loons, and Hannah declares, "Maverick, it is."

# CHAPTER 47
# DANIEL

"How are we ever going to put him in his crib?" Hannah says as the two of us lie in bed. We've been home for one night, and she's currently got Mav on her breast, nursing. Every moment for the last two days has been like this. Perfect. Quiet. Sure, Mav gets fussy, but the moment he latches, he's content for at least another hour, sometimes two. I get it. That's my favorite place to be as well.

Our whole crew came to the hospital in shifts. Mav has a ridiculous number of honorary aunts and uncles. At three a.m., when I finally made my way to the waiting area, my dad had made it in from Bristol. He and Millie were the first to meet our guy. The rest of our friends and family visited the next day, bringing breakfast and lunch for the staff and making us the most liked and well taken care of guests in the hospital. Then Lake showed up, and from what I heard, more than one nurse had a panic attack. Hannah cackled when she pointed out that Lake is Mav's grandmother. Mills chimed in with "That's what happens when you marry an old man."

Hannah was in great spirits, even if her mother didn't show. Noah's father brought Oliver up to meet his cousin, and her other dads checked in via FaceTime throughout the day. Her brothers too. Even now, we still haven't heard a word from her mother.

"I'll never understand how my mother could miss this," she whispers, almost like she's reading my thoughts, her blue eyes filled with emotion. "I love Mav so much, and I've only just met him. How could she not care?"

I press a kiss to her bare shoulder and brush a finger down Mav's cheek. "You're nothing like your mother, Han."

Her responding nod is resolute, like she's finally coming to terms with that truth. I think parenthood does that. Puts things into perspective. We only have so much energy, and using it on a person who isn't putting any energy back into a relationship is a waste. "I know," she says quietly.

"I'm going to refill your water. Want a snack too?"

Without taking her eyes off Mav, she mutters, "I want a slice of chocolate cream pie."

I chuckle as I press a kiss to Mav's forehead. As I pull back, he scrunches up like an angry old man, probably worried I'm going to interrupt his feeding. "Okay, dream girl." I brush my lips over hers. "I'll be back with your pie."

She's too enamored with our son to pay me any mind.

Taking advantage of her distraction, I collect all the supplies, along with my letter and my surprise. When I return, our little guy is on her shoulder, being burped. "Here, baby. Let me take him."

I pace the room, patting his back, giving her time to use the bathroom and eat her pie.

"What do you think, Mav? Can you give Mama and me a few minutes so I can ask her an important question?"

Mav nuzzles into my chest like he thinks he's getting more milk.

I'll take that as a yes. "Awesome." I press a kiss to his soft head and inhale deeply, soaking in his sweet scent. Swaying, I walk out of the room. I don't stop moving until he's fast asleep. Then I do the unthinkable and put him in his crib. When he doesn't stir, I smile. It's like he's giving us his blessing.

When I return, Hannah is holding up the letter, and her pie plate is empty. "What is this?" she whispers.

I smirk. "Read it."

She bows her head over it, sniffling.

"Out loud."

Hannah bites back a smile. "Fine." She shakes the paper dramatically and clears her throat. "Dream girl," she says in an absurdly deep voice.

"That's not how I sound. If you're going to tease me, then you can read it silently." I lean over her shoulder so I can follow along.

Dream girl,

ME. I'm not saying I'm perfect. Hell, I'm miles from it. And I'm not saying that I'll always do everything right. We both know that isn't true. Half the time I can't speak properly because you're in the room. The mere thought of you has my stomach in knots. I'm not settling down, because lord knows being with you doesn't settle me. You've got me so wound up I have to work to be my impressive self.

But I will do all of that, every day, for the rest of my life, if you'll just say…YES.

Hannah straightens and turns, studying me. "What is this?"

"Put the letters together." I hand her the letters I've written over the last month.

Brow creased, she frowns down at them.

"Now look at the first word of each one," I instruct.

"Will."

With a thick swallow, she looks up at me.

I nod, signaling for her to move on to the next letter.

"You."

"Next."

She narrows her eyes and shakes her head, a little smile playing on her lips.

"Marry."

This time she stops herself, but I hold up a hand, telling her to go on.

"Me."

I press a kiss to her temple. "Now put them all together."

With an exaggerated sigh, she shuffles the papers so they're in order. "Will. You." Smiling, she peers up at me. "Marry." She picks up the last page, the final word barely more than a breath. "Me."

"I thought you'd never ask," I say with a smile.

"Daniel." Her lip quivers, her teary eyes locked on me as I drop down to my knees and grip her thighs. "You started writing these letters a month ago. Was this always your plan?"

"I had to write it down. If I didn't, I'd get it wrong." I blow out a breath as emotion clogs my throat. "I've done a lot of things wrong in my life, but I must have done something amazing in my past one to deserve you. Our life together—" Voice catching, I drop my head and just breathe, trying to collect myself.

When I look back up, tears flow freely down Hannah's cheeks. "I love you," she whispers.

It's just the thing I needed to keep going.

"Our life together is my dream come true. *You* are my dream come true. If I had to describe my perfect girl, I would say she's a little older, with a lot of sass."

Hannah laughs through her tears.

"She's got beautiful blue eyes I could get lost in, and these lips I think about at least once an hour. And her ass? It's incredible."

She shakes her head, her eyes dancing in amusement.

"But all of that is just the tip of the iceberg. It's your heart, Han, the way you love your friends, the way you love our son—" I choke on a sob. "And the way you love me."

She nods along with every word.

"So marry me. I'm not asking you because I won't risk the chance that you'll say no. I'm taking you. I'm making you ask me."

With a deep breath, she places a palm to my cheek and looks at me with enough love to knock me on my ass. "Will you marry me?"

"Why?"

Maybe it's ridiculous, but I need to know why she wants to do this. I need to be sure this life is what she wants.

"Because," she says, voice cracking, "if I had to describe my perfect person, I'd say he's six foot something, cocky, with the biggest heart

I've ever had the privilege of getting to know. He's the standard I'll use for every book boyfriend I create, though none will compare, and he was the first person to ever truly love me *just for me*."

"That's crazy." I tuck a lock of hair behind her ear, then stroke the sensitive spot just below it. "You are loved by so many."

She shakes her head. "No one has ever loved me the way you do."

I nod. "And no one ever will. I promise that for the rest of your life, you'll know that you and our children come first for me. You will always have my heart and everything else I have to give."

"So is that a yes?" she croaks.

I reach into the pocket of my sweats and pull out the ring, pinching it between my thumb and forefinger.

"Holy shit. I'm like Princess Diana," she screams.

Chuckling, I slide the sapphire ring onto her finger. "You're my princess. Forever."

She fists my shirt and pulls me to my feet, but she doesn't stop there. She lies back and pulls me down to the bed with her, kissing me like she'll never get enough.

"Can we do it tomorrow?" she asks between kisses.

"What?" I laugh, deliriously happy but also deliriously tired.

Hannah rolls to her side and props her head on her hand. "Marry me tomorrow, please. Just you, me, and Mav at city hall."

I stroke her hair. "Dream girl, I'll marry you whenever you want, but don't you want a wedding?"

"Nope. Just my boys." She bites her lip. "And maybe Ava. And I guess War can come and Noah and Ollie." Her eyes light up. "Oh, and Riggs and Ash…"

I smile as she rattles off the names of all the people she loves. She may not realize it, but she's always had a family. It may not have been conventional, and she may have yearned for more, but my girl has always been surrounded by love. Friends who would do just about anything for her and family forged through love rather than blood.

Now she has Maverick and me too. "Yeah, baby. We can invite all of them. But maybe let's wait until after your follow-up with the OB so we can really enjoy our wedding night."

Hannah sighs, and the prettiest smile lights up her gorgeous face.

"You know the rules," I remind her.

"Hmm?" she replies with a yawn.

"When the baby sleeps, we sleep." I pull her into my chest and press my lips to her crown.

"Sweet dreams," she whispers.

My body warms with affection. With comfort. How is this my life? Hannah is my dream girl, my fantasy, and now, she's my future wife. I close my eyes, content knowing that when I fall asleep, I'll see her in my dreams.

# EPILOGUE

A Year-ish Later
(March)

**Hannah**

"What about a clit piercing?" I say with a devious smile as I glance at my husband.

Noah sighs. "Why am I here again?"

Brooks shakes his head. "I have no idea why any of us are here. Me especially. I'd like to get home to my wife and baby, if you all don't mind."

Sara gave birth to a baby girl they named Taylor just last week. One by one the Bolts men are dropping like flies, getting married and making babies. I roll my eyes at his dramatics. "Your baby is fine. She's with my baby and Liv. And your wife was very clear. Tattoo her name on your balls like War did because she birthed a human for you."

War chuckles like the bastard he is and grins at his wife.

My bestie's mouth falls open. "You guys aren't supposed to tell people about that." She pinches my arm. "I told you that in private when I hated him."

He winks at her. "You never hated me, Vicious. But keep telling yourself those lies. You know I love it."

I wave a disgusted hand at them both. "Besides, it would be impossible to keep it a secret from the guys he plays with. They literally see each other's balls daily."

My husband squeezes my hip. "Not quite, dream girl."

I grin at him. "As I was saying, what about a clit piercing?"

"And as I was saying, why am I here?" Noah grumbles, his head falling between his shoulders.

"Team-building opportunity," I tell him. "You guys are all on fire this season and now that you have a new boss, it's time to celebrate." I may not work for Langfield Corp. anymore but Beckett had me consult on this most recent hire. It's not going to be a smooth transition and I'm happy to exercise some of those PR muscles again if it helps out my favorite people.

Noah's head whips up. "A new boss?"

Brooks grins. "It hasn't been announced yet, but Sienna is taking over. Beckett and Gavin appointed her as head of the hockey division yesterday."

Noah gulps, and I swear the expression that works itself across his face is dread. "Sienna, as in your sister?"

Brooks nods. "Yeah. Have the two of you met yet?"

Noah schools his expression and shrugs. "Not formally. Obviously she was at the wedding and some of the games."

That answer, or maybe the weird tone of his voice, has my spine tingling. Before I can work out why, though, the door to the tattoo shop jangles open and Lennox appears.

"Are you guys ever coming in here?"

Aiden is already inside, hands on his hips, staring at the wall. Probably looking at one of the many tattoo options since that's what we all actually agreed to come here for. I finally feel ready for my first one, and I've decided to go with something to honor my man, so we're getting matching ink.

*You keep me safe, I'll keep you wild.* His will be just above his ribs, and mine will be on my upper thigh.

I want another that represents Mav, but I haven't figured out quite what I want yet. Our little guy is already one and a complete handful. He loves spending time with his big cousins Ollie and Vivi, but his favorite thing in the world is to watch Daniel play hockey. We're at every single home game and travel with the team plenty too. It's one of the perks of our familial connection to the owner of the team, I suppose. Millie and I coordinate and usually travel together. We sit at the front of the plane with the kids, gabbing the entire flight. Then we take turns watching our little ones so we each have time to write— music for her, a new romance novel for me.

It's a beautiful life and far more than I ever dared to dream I could have.

And now Sienna Langfield will be joining us on those trips. I'm excited to get to know her better. She's lost a lot in the last year, and I think this will truly be her redemption story. It may be something she never even imagined, but with any luck, it'll be better than what she had before.

I certainly hope so. I believe everyone deserves to be as happy as I am. Everywhere I go, I'm surrounded by incredible friends and their devoted husbands and our growing families. I want everyone to have that. Especially Noah.

"Are we doing this?" I arch a brow in my husband's direction. "Or are you too nervous again, Baby Hall?"

He chuckles as he brushes a kiss against my shoulder. "Not nervous, Mrs. Hall. And of course I'm coming. I always do when I'm with you."

Noah gags. "Why the fuck am I here?"

I wrap my arm around my husband's waist and lead him inside. "I was thinking…"

"Yes?" my husband says in that amused tone of his. The tone that tells me he'll do whatever I ask. The man never says no.

"How do you feel about nipple piercings?"

Want to find out how Noah really feels about the Bolts new boss, Sienna Langfield? Preorder **Beauty** now.

*Our Wedding Day*

"If you were going to invite everyone, why not wait and have a big wedding?" War gives me a nudge.

I can't temper my smile as I survey the lobby of city hall. "What can I say? Hannah couldn't wait to make me her husband."

We had to wait the perfunctory three days for our marriage license, but like I promised, like my dream girl wants, we're getting married at city hall.

When I zero in on her, the same damn flutters I felt when she agreed to have dinner with me ten months ago come roaring back. She's a week postpartum and she's as gorgeous as ever. She's wearing a cream-colored sweater dress and a pair of bedazzled white boots—because she said *she* needed the glitter—and her hair is swept to the side in some fancy way that makes her look like she's about to walk the red carpet at the Oscar's. The prettiest thing she's wearing, though,

353

is a smile. She's holding Mav in her arms and talking quietly to the girls, oblivious to just how entranced she's got me.

Yes, we are having a simple ceremony at city hall, but every person on the list she rattled off the night I proposed is here. Ava and War will sign the marriage certificate as our witnesses, but all of our friends and family came to celebrate.

My father is chatting with Gavin and Lake just a few feet from me, and my guys stand in a loose circle with me. War, Brooks, Aiden, and Noah are here. And Camden even flew in.

Hannah insisted Beckett and his family be here as well.

It's a family affair. Noah's got Hannah's computer set up so all of her brothers and stepdads can be here virtually.

"You ready to become a husband?" my sister asks as she settles her head against my shoulder.

I wrap an arm around her and press a kiss to her forehead. "Never been more ready for something in my life."

"Not even your first hockey game in the NHL?" Millie teases, her dark, curly hair brushing my jaw.

"Not even that." Nothing, and I mean nothing, has ever mattered the way Hannah and our son do. Hannah is everything to me. Every dream I've ever had will start and end with her at the forefront.

"Aw, I'm happy for you, Danny." My sister pops up onto her toes and presses a kiss to my cheek.

The doors to the small room reserved for weddings opens, and an older man steps out. He searches the crowd and when he spots Hannah, he rightfully assumes she's the bride. "We're ready for you."

I make my way over to my bride and hold out my hands so I can take Mav from her. I want him in my arms during the ceremony because this moment is as much about him as it is about us. I still can't imagine that Hannah would have given me a chance if not for him. What I do know is that I wouldn't have stopped trying.

She sucks in an excited breath, all smiles and bright blue eyes. "Thank you for making this happen."

I press a kiss to her lips, gently cradling our son between us. "Are you kidding? It's probably obnoxious by now, but I'll say it again. You are my dream come true. This is everything I've ever wanted."

She cups my neck and kisses me again, deeper this time, being careful not to squish Mav.

"Come on, Playboy. Let's get married."

We get settled in front of the judge's bench, both smiling like loons.

Our friends hoot and holler. Can't take them anywhere. I love every second of it.

"It's come to my attention that a member of your group is ordained, and he's offered to make things a little more personal," the judge says with a smile.

"Well, if you insist." Beckett stands and tugs on the cuffs of his suit jacket.

"What are you doing?" Liv hisses up at him, trying to tug him back.

"Giving them a proper wedding." Beckett straightens his tie. "They're family, and I'm the one responsible for all of this." He holds out an open hand, gesturing to us.

Though our friends are either chuckling or groaning at Beckett's antics, Hannah's blue eyes are misty and her smile is wobbly. "Thank you, Beckett."

He strides over to her side and presses a kiss to her cheek. "You make a beautiful bride. Now, let's get you two kids married."

<Snapshot of Daniel dipping Hannah dramatically after Beckett pronounces them husband and wife. Beckett, standing behind them, beams.>

"Hey, I didn't hear him cry." Hannah walks into Mav's nursery, wiping sleep from her eyes. Her pajama bottoms are askew, the waistband dipping low enough to expose the soft curve of her hips and stomach.

I lick my lips, distracted by the sight. Holding out my arm, I beckon Hannah to join us as Mav and I rock by the window. It's become a routine for us. He loves to look out at the twinkling lights of the city, wide-eyed and awake, while the rest of Boston sleeps.

Hannah settles into the crook of my arm and kisses my bare chest. "I love when you hold him like this."

"Shirtless?"

She smiles. "Yes. I like you naked. What can I say?"

"Our baby's *right here*," I whisper-hiss in mock horror.

"You hungry, little guy?" She pulls him into her arms, unhooks the clasp on one side of her nursing bra, and helps our son latch on. I could watch them like this all night. Hannah was meant to be a mother. It's wild to think that she ever worried at all.

"You should go to bed. You've got to travel in the morning." She tucks her chin and smiles at our little guy. "You're only gone a couple of days, right?"

My chest tightens. I hate leaving her. Eventually, she and Mav can come with me sometimes, but traveling with a two-month-old would be hard. I'm already itching for summer break, even though we've still got a lot of juice left in this season.

But the team's chemistry is back, and we've got a real shot at the playoffs, so I'm doing my best to be content with the situation.

The only good news? Camden Snow is officially a Bolt again. We got him back just before the trade deadline. He'll meet us in Toronto for our away game. I can't wait to play with him and never have to look at freaking Smiles again. Miserable fucker that he is. Hope he enjoys New York. He'll fit in much better with all the assholes there.

"I'll be back on Friday. Then you and I have plans in Bristol." Lake and my father will keep Mav so I can take my wife on a proper date. Lake even offered to keep the little guy overnight so Hannah can actually get some rest.

Lennox has been spending a lot of time here when we're on the road. She's lonely without Aiden and she's been a great help to Hannah, snuggling with Maverick and insisting she take a nap in the afternoon or get some writing done without distraction.

"Can't wait." Hannah looks up and smiles.

God, she's gorgeous. I pull out my phone and snap a picture of her.

She giggles and dips her head. "You better not have gotten my boob in that."

"Of course I did." I snap another and smile. This image—the one of my wife gazing down at our son while she feeds him—might be my favorite picture in this album yet.

<collage of pictures of Hannah feeding Mav because Daniel couldn't pick just one>

"Do you think he's warm enough?"

I love seeing the two of them wearing matching Hall jerseys, but I worry that Mav will be cold in the arena.

Hannah rolls her eyes. "He has on a long-sleeve sleeper on under the jersey, Daniel. And he's wearing little gloves and booties. If we add another layer, he'll swelter."

"But his head." I run my hand over Maverick's dark silky hair. So far, it looks like he might have inherited his Aunt Millie's curls.

"Oh, I've got a hat for him." Hannah reaches into the diaper bag and produces a beanie.

I recognize the blue hat immediately. Eyes narrowed, I snatch it from her hand. "No way is my son wearing that?"

"Brooks's puck bunny," Aiden reads from over my shoulder. "Nice!" He gives Hannah a fist bump, then grasps Mav's wrist and bumps his hand too.

"Not nice," I grind out. It was one thing when my wife wore it. Yes, it's a joke between the girls, but my son is not wearing that. "Anybody have an extra toque?"

In a room full of hockey players, it's almost a guarantee. We're ten minutes from game time, so everyone is dressed, and Millie snuck Hannah into the locker room with Mav.

"He needed the full tour," she told her husband, who didn't look thrilled. He can't really complain because he used to wear Vivi on his chest during practice.

"Oh my god. You're ridiculous," Hannah says on a laugh.

"The hockey man jealousy is rearing its head, huh?" my sister jokes.

Brooks ruffles my hair roughly. "Aw, let the little guy live. He looks good in my hat."

"My hat!" Sara shouts as she appears out of nowhere. "Come on, I got one for you too, Daniel. Let's get a family picture."

With a sigh, I give in and let her slip it over my head. And when she insists on a picture of the three of us wearing our matching number 18 jerseys, with Brooks's Puck Bunny hats on our heads, I oblige.

And I even smile.

<Picture of the girls all wearing the hats, with Hannah and a smiling Mav in the middle>

"There's no way this is real" War eyes every person we walk by like they might recognize him. They won't. We may be a big deal in Boston, but here at this convention, we're nobodies.

"I think it's pretty cool," Sara says as she surveys the booth we're passing. "Oh my god, that's the girl who went viral for the way she says peanut butter." She points at a woman who's barely visible behind a long line of people.

"This is so weird," Brooks grumbles. "Why are we here?"

"Because you're all supportive friends." Hannah loops her fingers with mine. "These guys are important to Daniel, so we're going to support him and let him geek out over his weird daddy kink."

I pull my hand back. "I don't have a daddy kink. They're YouTubers who vlog about fatherhood." I was so excited when the guys announced that they'd be at Social Con in San Diego a couple of days before our game against the local team.. I made my friends fly in early with me so we could spend the day here.

"I have a daddy kink," Sara says.

"So does she." War thumbs over at his wife.

"Shut up," Ava hisses, cheeks flaming. She jabs him in the stomach, but it only makes him laugh.

He pulls her to his side and nuzzles into her neck. "Shh, Vicious. You're making me hard."

"Oh my god," she groans.

"You married him," Hannah says, wearing an evil grin.

"And you married the freak who dragged us here," War says.

"I hate you all. Why did I think it was a good idea to invite you?" My shoulder slump, but only for a second, because as I'm grumbling, I spot the guys.

A strange screeching noise escapes me, and my muscles lock up.

"What are you doing?" Hannah turns around, eyes narrowed on me, then follows my line of sight.

"That's them," I whisper, awestruck.

"Oh my god you weren't this excited when we got married."

"They're just so—"

"If you say hot, I'm divorcing you," she mutters.

I blink and shake my head. "Sorry, baby. It's just…they helped me become the man you needed me to be."

Hannah's blue eyes soften. "Aw, you're such a mush sometimes." She loops her arms around my waist. "Okay, Daniel, I promise not to make fun of you. Go geek out and get your daddy kink on."

<picture of Daniel cheesing hard surrounded by the dads from THE Vlog.>

"It's about time you two go on a honeymoon," Sara says as she snatches Maverick from his car seat.

Brooks cradles Taylor against his chest. Their daughter is a year younger than Mav but already a handful. She never stops babbling, and she loves Lake Paige music almost as much as her mother does.

"We've only been married for two years. I don't know why everyone makes such a big deal about it," I grumble.

Our wedding at city hall was perfect, but I was determined to have a proper wedding with all of our extended family and friends present.

I wanted to see my wife in a pretty dress and spin her around on the dance floor all night long. I wanted the wedding night, and until we had that, we weren't having a honeymoon.

"Daniel needed the wedding of his dreams before I could have a honeymoon," Hannah teases. She steps up beside me, carrying Maverick's bag. "Are you guys sure you don't mind keeping Maverick in your room?"

Brooks chuckles. "Taylor doesn't sleep. Believe me, we're fine with handling them both."

"Yes, and then you can *get it onnn*," Sara sings.

When Taylor mimics her, singing the same words, Brooks scowls. "Really crazy girl? We talked about this. No s-e-x talk in front of Blueberry."

Sara rolls her eyes while Taylor strings the letters together into a song. "S-e-xxx."

One of those sexy as fuck raspy laughs leaves my wife's throat. "Oh my god."

I point to Brooks, who's the shade of a tomato. "Don't use that language in front of Mav."

I try to affect a stern expression, but I quickly give in and laugh right along with Sara and Hannah. With promises to FaceTime before bed, we leave Maverick with our friends and head to the wedding venue. We're getting married at Daffodil Farms. The beautiful spot only an hour outside Massachusetts is famous for the gorgeous tulips and daffodils that bloom in the spring. The big white tent is set up, equipped with a chandelier that'll make it feel like we're dancing beneath the stars. We'll say I do—*again*—amongst a field of flowers.

"Still happy with the choice?" I ask Hannah as we stand outside the door of our room at the inn. Daffodil Farms is located in a small town without a large hotel, so I rented out the entire inn for our family and friends. The property abuts the harbor and the views of the mountains are incredible.

Hannah smiles. "You know none of this really matters to me. I'm just happy to spend time with you."

This woman. Fuck. She always knows just what to say. "I love you." I pull her against my chest and press my lips to hers.

"I love you too. Now open the door. But I'm warning you, if there are two beds in there, I'm going to lose my mind."

I chuckle. War and I have already been inside, setting things up, and there's more than one bed for sure. Sex with Hannah has always been incredible, but it only gets better with time. I've mastered the male orgasm, and now I can have multiple, just like my wife. But tonight I want to give her even more. On the other side of this door are toys, a bench, ropes, and whips I think she'll enjoy. Yes, Hannah and I are going to have one hell of a night before the wedding. With any luck, I'll wipe away the memory of the night of bad sex from her memory for good.

"I can't wait to marry you again tomorrow, Mrs. Hall," I murmur against her lips.

I push the door open, and as she steps inside, she gasps.

"Fuck me, Playboy."

"Oh, I intend to. All. Night. Long."

<Picture of Hannah and Daniel grinning in front of the Welcome to Daffodil Farms sign>

Want MORE of Daniel and Hannah? Make sure you keep an eye out next year for something *special* that takes place at Daffodil Farms.

# ACKNOWLEDGMENTS

I truly don't remember writing the majority of this book. It spilled out of me so quickly, the characters controlling each tap of my fingers against the computer keys. I had no idea how I'd follow up War because let's be honest, Tyler Warren destroyed us all, but Daniel definitely said I've got this. Are we surprised at all? The man has the confidence to take on Hannah and take her on he did.

While writing this I received a call I never even had the audacity to dream about and most of you should know as of the publication of this book that I signed a contract with Penguin Random House to write a cozy small town series called Hope Harbor which means you will be able to find a book written by me in STORES worldwide next year. So while editing this book, I dove into this whole other world but of course I had to throw in some of our favorite characters, including Daniel and Hannah. So make sure you stay up to date with that release because Darling Daffodil Farm will include a yet to be seen scene from Daniel and Hannah's second wedding.

None of this–seriously, not a single thing–would have been possible without the tremendous support of some very important people. Sara, this series only exists because I couldn't think what to buy you for your birthday two years ago. I guess we'll celebrate this year's birthday in London though. Love you! Jenni, my work wife and best friend, I adore you and the world we've created!

To my amazing beta readers, Glav, Sierra, Andi and Becca who offered insight and helped make this book better, I can't say thank you enough.

To my lovely editor Beth who literally never says no when I ask if she can squeeze in another word, another paragraph or another project. You are an integral part of my success and I can't thank you enough for always making my books better. I will never stop singing your praises.

To my Book Babes, Hockey Gals, and Swoon Squad, the incredible street team that you are, and the lovely ladies who help me promote my books day in and day out, Kylie, Kenzie, Glav, Courtney, Andi and Sara, every release gets better because of you!  I am always in awe of your friendship and support.

To my incredible family, your pride in what I do brings me to tears. Jack tells everyone his mom is an author and always wants to know the title of my next book and Mackenzie loves to help me 'design' the covers (as in come up with ideas and send them to the actual designers). And to my husband who's had to be dance dad quite a few times this year because Mommy can't be everywhere. I love you all.

Finally, none of this would be possible without you, my amazing readers. Thank you for all of your messages, your Tiktoks, your dms, your posts and your rants. There is nothing I love more than hearing from each of you how a character affected you, or a storyline made you laugh. I love your reviews, your anecdotes, and the notes you send to me.

I have so many more stories yet to be told. If you want to follow along on my writing journey and have sneak peeks into all the characters in Bristol and Boston (and Monhegan and Hope Harbor), follow me on Instagram, join my awesome Facebook group, sign-up for my newsletter and follow me on TikTok.

# ALSO BY BRITTANÉE NICOLE

**Bristol Bay Rom Coms**

She Likes Piña Coladas

Kisses Sweet Like Wine

Over the Rainbow

**Bristol Bay Romance**

Love and Tequila Make Her Crazy

A Very Merry Margarita Mix-Up

**Boston Billionaires**

Whiskey Lies

Loving Whiskey

Wishing for Champagne Kisses

Dirty Truths

Extra Dirty

**Mother Faker**

(Mother Faker is Book 1 of the Mom Com Series, but is also a lead in to the Revenge Games alongside Revenge Era. This book can be read as a Standalone, or after Revenge Era and before Pucking Revenge)

**Revenge Games**

Revenge Era

Pucking Revenge

A Major Puck Up

**Boston Bolts Hockey**

Hockey Boy

Trouble

War

**Standalone Romantic Suspense**

Deadly Gossip

Irish